Solaris Soars
Copyright © 2015 Janet McNulty
Cover Copyright © 2024 Janet McNulty

ISBN-13: 978-1-941488-02-7 (MMP Publishing)
ISBN-10: 1-941488-02-1

Library of Congress Control Number: 2015912523

Printed in the United States of America

At long last the final book in the Solaris Saga is finished. I want to thank all of you for joining Rynah on this adventure of hers. I hope you enjoy the ending and had as fun reading it as I had writing it.

Thank you.

Contents

Solaris Saga book 4

Janet McNulty

Chapter 1
TRE FOUND

General Delmar steered the ship towards the lone, abandoned-looking space station before him; the beacon grew stronger as they neared the floating pile of welded debris that resembled a crushed aluminum can more than a space station. Hylne sat in the seat next to him, watching the proceedings and keeping constant watch on the proximity gauges.

"It appears he has defensive measures in place," said Hylne. "You're sure this time that this is him? It looks deserted."

"Something tells me we are about to find out," replied General Delmar. He placed a thin metal band on his head, connecting himself telepathically to the ship. A laser cannon sent a blast at them; it exploded just off the hull, doing no damage, but jilting the ship to the left a bit.

Hylne placed the second metal band on his head. *I think he isn't happy to see us.*

General Delmar didn't respond. He directed the ship to veer to the left, but stay clear of the laser cannons. Another blast echoed around them, this time closer. As General Delmar studied the map, pinpointing the laser cannons in relationship to the space station, he realized that a small path lay in the middle, which would have been missed by most, but his skilled eyes noticed it.

Follow these coordinates. He pictured in his mind the path he wished the ship to go in.

Affirmative, replied the ship in a robotic tone.

More cannon blasts detonated around them as every cannon fired. Though they had been aimed so that any in the special path (the same one that Rynah had directed Tom to take when they were there weeks before) would not be harmed, the constant bombardment of the explosions' shockwave jostled the ship, forcing both Hylne and General Delmar to control their queasy stomachs.

I think he's on to us, Hylne said through the telepathic link.

General Delmar lined up the crosshairs of his weapon on one of the cannons. *Fire, but do not damage the station.*

The ship released an ionic missile at its directed target; the laser cannon burst into flames, broke away from its anchor, and floated out into space.

There's the docking bay, General Delmar said, finding a small port that looked more like a small conclave of deteriorated metal.

Reading General Delmar's thoughts, Hylne lined the ship with the docking arm, maneuvering the vessel into position until he heard the clamps snap into place, clacking and locking as they went, and the pressurized seal hissed as it locked in the breathable air. *We're locked.*

General Delmar threw off the metal band and popped open the hatch.

"Delmar!" Hylne tossed off his metal band and ran after his friend. "You don't know what's out there." He unhooked his laser pistol from its holster and held it up. "We should proceed with caution."

General Delmar grunted. He had had enough with being careful. Caution had gotten those he cared about killed. Caution has resulted in the deaths of billions of innocent lives. Caution is what killed Nula, a woman whose only crime was helping him and Hylne after their shuttle had crashed on an uncharted planet.

The hell with caution, he thought to himself as he pulled out his own laser pistol and peeked around the corner of the opened hatch into the musty darkness beyond. His boots left soft clomps on the metal grate floor as he crept through the dingy corridor, all the while remaining aware of his surroundings.

Drip! Drip!

General Delmar looked up at a leaky pipe above him that allowed pin-sized drops of water to fall to the floor, pooling in a rusted, tin bowl, its edges eaten away by rot. Only the sound of the life support system humming in the background could be heard. General Delmar motioned for Hylne to approach the right side of the end of the hallway. Hylne did so. Both peered around the edge, but saw no sign of an inhabitant, just a pile of torn boxes, moth-eaten blankets, mold-filled tarps, and rusted pipes forming a mound up to the ceiling, with screws and nails scattered about in front of it.

A second dilapidated pile of rusted and chipped pans tumbled downward; their clinking and clanking reverberated off the copper sheeting on the walls, forcing them to hunker low in case it drew the attention of the space station's lone inhabitant. Delmar pointed at the noise. Hylne nodded in affirmation and stepped out from behind a pile of scrap metal. Still no sign that anyone lived there.

Movement caught Hylne's eye. He burst from where he hid and chased the flurry of movement as it dashed behind a door with General Delmar right behind him. They chased the mysterious figure through the kitchens (filled with orange fruit that seemed to blink at them and have wavy arms, food encrusted pans, more rusted containers full of murky water, and some sort of netting that moved with each draft) and into a room full of holomonitors, screens, and holokeypads.

"Stop!" yelled General Delmar.

The figure continued to run down a long grime-coated hallway and around a bend. General Delmar and Hylne chased after the man, their feet pounding the metal grates with each long stride. As they rounded the corner, they stopped. The figure they had been chasing stood beneath a light, facing them and holding a weapon.

Panting, General Delmar studied the weapon in the man's arms and chuckled.

"A potato gun?"

"No, it's real," threatened the man, whom you know as Tre.

"What?" asked Hylne. "You seriously thought you could threaten us with a potato gun?"

"It's real!" shouted the agitated man, his baggy pants rustling with each frantic movement.

"Sure it is," scoffed Hylne.

General Delmar held up his hand, stopping Hylne.

"Tre?" he asked, his tone uncertain.

"Who wants to know?" demanded the strange man.

"Well, we do, obviously," snapped Hylne.

Tre's anxious face twitched. He hated sarcasm.

"Are you, or are you not, Tre?" General Delmar asked, his tone more serious.

"I want to know how you got here," said Tre.

"That's not important," replied General Delmar.

"I mean it,"—Tre raised his potato gun—"tell me how you got here, or I'll fire this at you."

"Careful, Delmar," laughed Hylne, "he's armed."

Not liking the man who had spoken, and the fact that he had always wanted to shoot someone with a potato from his modified, high powered potato gun (his own design, of course), Tre fired his weapon, sending a medium-sized brown potato right at Hylne and striking him in the lower abdomen. Surprised at how the wind had been knocked out of him, Hylne doubled over and crumpled to the floor, gripping the area where the potato had left a bruise the size of a softball. Tre tossed his potato gun aside.

"You're not going to test it on me as well?" asked General Delmar with a raised eyebrow.

"Nah," said Tre, "it only holds the one potato. And I forgot to grab a spare."

"Let me at him!" Having recovered from his initial shock at being struck by a root vegetable, Hylne lunged for Tre, but General Delmar stopped him. "He fired a potato at me!"

"You deserved it," said General Delmar, restraining his friend. He turned back to Tre, holding up his laser pistol. "Now, you never answered my question. Are you Tre?"

"Yes, yes!" said Tre, his tone sharp. "Why do you want to know? And why are you here?"

"We're looking for Rynah," said General Delmar.

Tre's eyes widened. He had never thought that someone would come searching for Rynah.

"Why?" he asked, wary of the intentions of these strangers that barged into his space station uninvited.

"She needs our help," replied General Delmar.

Tre did not answer for several minutes, until Hylne pushed him. "Do you know where she is, or not?"

"I don't know anyone by that name," lied Tre.

"*Brestyranan!*" shouted Hylne, using a word that, when translated for polite society, meant horse manure, not believing Tre's feigned ignorance as he glared into the man's eyes and the deception within them.

"I swear!" Tre yelled, stepping back.

Angered, and still sore from having been struck by a potato, Hylne snatched the potato gun from the floor and a nearby can and rammed it into the weapon, which was quite a feat, considering that a potato gun wasn't meant to hold tin cans. He aimed it at Tre, but before he could fire, General Delmar lunged for him, giving Tre the opportunity he needed to run away.

"What are you..." began Hylne, but stopped as he watched Tre disappear.

Both General Delmar and Hylne chased after him, but Tre darted to the side, pulling a lever, and jerked to the left, diving through an open hatch. A hoard of plastic wrapping, papers, empty cans, and nylon netting dropped from the ceiling as another hatch opened, covering them and forcing them to the floor. Hylne jumped up and dove through the hatch Tre had entered.

"I got him!" he shouted, grabbing hold of what he thought were Tre's feet and pulling hard, but it wasn't Tre he had in his grasp.

"A dummy?" said General Delmar.

"I'm going to kill him," growled Hylne, tossing the paper-stuffed dummy aside.

The stomping of heavy feet echoed above them. Both Hylne and General Delmar looked up. Above them, on a walkway, was Tre running for another open hatch.

"How did…" Hylne said before his voice trailed off.

"The hell with this." Pulling out his laser pistol, General Delmar aimed for the walkway supports and fired. The connected joints separated and the walkway lurched, flinging Tre forward, before breaking away and forcing him to tumble downward where he landed in a pile of trash.

Before he had a chance to scurry away, General Delmar and Hylne rushed the mound of garbage and seized him.

"All right! All right! You got me!" shouted Tre, flinging his arms.

"Where is Rynah?" demanded General Delmar.

"I don't…"

"Enough of this foolishness," said General Delmar.

"Bins and kribbits… she finds me and now everyone shows up," mumbled Tre.

"Where!" General Delmar shouted, his tone dark.

"I don't know her exact location," said Tre. "I haven't heard from her in over a week."

"Where did her last communication originate from?" asked General Delmar. "It is imperative that we find her."

Tre led them back to his computer room, lit with holoscreens and depicting images from space, mathematical algorithms, and lines of nonsensical text.

"The last communication I had from her came from these co-ordinates," Tre said as he brought up a star map and circled where Rynah had been when he had last spoken to her.

"That's the border of the Terra Sector," said Hylne. "What was she doing there?"

"She said that someone named Stein was heading to a planet called Earth, the same planet that those aliens were from, and that she intended to stop him."

"Aliens?" asked Hylne.

"Gangly creatures," said Tre, "except for one; strong as a *vilryr* he was, big and muscular, and unyielding. They had pale skin, but one, he had skin the color of the furthest reaches of space. Not from the Twelve Sectors, I can tell you that much."

"Obiah was telling the truth," said Hylne.

"It would seem so," said General Delmar. "Do you have the location for this... Earth?"

"According to my research, and in conjunctions with the location of her last communication, it should be here." Tre pulled up another star map, pointing at where he believed the planet was. "But, you will need more than the location of a planet to find her."

"What do you mean?" asked General Delmar.

"Planets are huge," replied Tre. "If she landed on it, you will need someone who can pinpoint her location from even the smallest of interstellar communications. Now unless you know someone..." Tre let his voice trail off as he leaned back in his chair, placing his hands behind his head.

"You're right," said General Delmar.

"Of course, I'm right," replied Tre.

"Which is why you're coming with us," General Delmar said.

"Exactly... what?" Tre bolted upright in his chair. "No-no-no-no, I'm not."

Tre waved his hands in front of him in an attempt to stop General Delmar from grabbing him, but it proved useless.

Both Hylne and General Delmar snatched Tre from his chair and dragged him back to their ship.

"Get off me!" yelled Tre. "I'm not leaving here! I'm not..."

"It's time you experienced the real universe," said General Delmar, his grip remaining firm, despite Tre's frantic struggles. They marched down the metal hallways to their ship and plopped Tre in one of the chairs once inside. Tre made a frantic dash for the exit, but Hylne had closed the hatch just as he reached it.

"This is kidnapping, you know," said Tre.

Both Hylne and General Delmar ignored his rants and settled in the pilot and co-pilot seats.

"Take us to the coordinates Rynah said she was headed," General Delmar ordered.

"I will not... whoa," said Tre, noticing the advanced technology of the ship. "This isn't your standard Lanyran vessel."

"Actually," said General Delmar, "we think it is Ancient Lanyran, or older."

"Ancient Lanyran?" Tre hopped around the shuttle, mimicking a squirrel with his movements, investigating each button, control, crevice, light, and window. "Extraordinary," he breathed.

"We need those coordinates," grumbled Hylne.

"Yes, yes, I'm coming." Tre hurried to the pilot's console and typed in the location for Earth. "This is where she said she was headed. I hope this ship is fast, though, because we might be too late." Tre crossed his arms, forgetting that he had not wanted to come aboard in the first place.

General Delmar started the engines, rechecked the coordinates, and separated the craft from the docking arm. After navigating away from the space station and its hazards, he jumped into hyperspeed, hoping they weren't too late.

Chapter 2
Small Acts

The escape pod bounced and shook from the force of re-entry; flames engulfed it, heating the outer hull to 2,966 degrees Fahrenheit. Sweat trickled down their faces as they plunged even further, punching through the upper layers of the atmosphere until they had reached the troposphere. Land came into view. Obiah steered the escape pod as best as he could; the force of re-entry had damaged the navigational controls. He punched in the coordinates that Klanor had given him, but the computer refused to recognize them; instead, it directed him to what it had mapped as the next closet location.

"I don't think that we are going to make it to our targeted destination," said Obiah.

"Do the best you can," Klanor replied. He glanced at Rynah, who still hadn't opened her eyes since receiving her wound.

The pod lurched as it dropped. They fell with increasing speed. Obiah steered them towards their destination, hoping that they would reach it, or at least get very close to it, before striking the ground. He set the controls as the ground neared.

1,000 feet.

Checking the navigation grid, Obiah frowned, as he knew that they would not even come close to the targeted coordinates.

800 feet.

The ground neared, growing closer and closer, filling the window.

400 feet.

"Strap in!" said Obiah, fastening the safety harness around himself while Klanor strapped Rynah in her seat, securing the harness before taking care of himself.

The pod smashed into the ground, creating a crater the size of a house; plumes of dirt filled the sky, raining rocks upon any below. The impact jostled them, grinding their teeth together. When all had stilled, Obiah unhooked his restraints and kicked open the hatch, releasing the pressurized air inside. Shaking himself back to his senses, Klanor undid his safety harness as well and rushed over to Rynah. She hadn't stirred. He lifted her out of the pod, stepping out into the morning sunlight. Warmth, with a hint of a chill, filled it, telling any who paid attention that the season was changing.

"How is she?" asked Obiah as he searched the landscape, seeing no buildings or signs of civilization.

"Not good," said Klanor. "The wound appears to be closed, but she is very weak."

Obiah looked at Rynah's face—her eyes fluttered before closing again—checking her pulse and feeling her forehead for a temperature.

"She needs medical attention."

He went back into the escape pod and tried its communicator, but only static greeted him when he turned it on. Throwing it against the dash, he cursed and stepped back out into the sunlight.

"We're on our own down here."

"Not completely," said Klanor. "We had discussed going to this New Mexico before getting separated. Rynah and the others believed that there is a Lanyran hiding on this planet."

"Impossible," scoffed Obiah.

"They didn't think so."

"Well, we need to know where we are."

Klanor spotted a silhouette in the sun's rays. "I think I might be able to help with that." Carrying Rynah, he and Obiah walked over to the sign, and as he read it, he realized that they were only six miles from the nearest city.

"Six miles," said Obiah.

"According to my conversions," Klanor replied, "one of their miles is two of our *hilyrs*."

"Can you..."

"I'm fine," said Klanor, interrupting Obiah as he strengthened his hold on the unconscious Rynah. "We should follow this sign. Where's there's a city, there is a medical facility."

"How are we to enter it?" asked Obiah. "I doubt that they will treat her."

"We'll figure that out when we get there," replied Klanor, determined to not lose Rynah.

They walked down the pavement, as bits of silt drifted across it in the wind, each hoping that Rynah would not get any worse.

* * *

"Get them back!" ordered Jifdar, pacing the floor of the bridge of his ship. Stein's interruption of his communication with Solaris and the others disturbed him, and he intended to see to it that it could not happen again.

How did he do it? Jifdar's thick-soled boots clomped hard on the metal grates that made up the floor of his ship, sending echoes of his frustration to every crevice. "Well?"

"I'm sorry, captain," said the pirate in charge of communications, "but I cannot raise them. Whomever intruded upon our communications has seen to it that we cannot contact anyone."

Jifdar cursed. He stalked back and forth, fuming and muttering to himself—his way of figuring out a problem—but no solution came to him. His fellow pirates watched his movements, taking care to stay out of his way.

"Captain," said Heller, his first mate.

"Yes, what is it?"

"You need to see this."

Heller turned on the holographic view screen; images of exploding ships filled it, as another pulled in a shuttlecraft with its tractor beam. Curious as to why Stein would eliminate his own ships, Jifdar watched as vessels of the same size and class were reduced to bits and pieces that burned in the Earth's atmosphere.

"What is all this?" he asked.

"We do not know why, but it appears that a rift has opened between Fredyr Monsooth and Stein, but that isn't what interests me."

Heller zoomed in on the holoscreen, bringing up the image of a small craft (the escape pod with Rynah, Klanor, and Obiah) as it fell to the planet below.

"Are..." Jifdar let his voice trail off.

"I don't know."

Jifdar studied the playback of the images. He hadn't heard from any of them, but did not wish to send a search party down since he did not know where to begin looking.

"Keep trying to raise them. Is there something else?" Jifdar asked his first mate when the man did not move.

"I keep thinking," said Heller, "perhaps the time has come for us to leave before we suffer the fate of those ships." He pointed at the floating debris and skeletal remains of Fredyr Monsooth's vessels.

"We are not going anywhere until I know what has happened to Rynah," said Jifdar.

Heller nodded and stalked off, leaving Jifdar to ponder his actions.

* * *

Nurse Betty walked out of the side exit to the hospital, cigarettes in hand. She knew she shouldn't smoke, but the stress of her job (20-hour shifts, changes in federal regulations, doctors who thought they knew everything and balked at her common sense, and patients who continued committing the same stupid acts that landed them in the hospital in the first place) made developing the habit easy. She tapped the pack of cigarettes upside down, popping one addictive slender, paper-wrapped tobacco and tar cancer-causing waste of money into her hands.

"I wish I could quit these," she whispered to herself as sirens blared around her, bringing another emergency victim to the hospital.

Nurse Betty ignored it. She was on her break, and needed it after working three back-to-back trauma cases. She stared at the cigarette in her fingers. She had tried everything to quit—patches, gum, even binging on hamburgers and ice cream, which made her gain 30 pounds—but none of it worked.

When she had finished nursing school and landed her first job at a hospital, Nurse Betty had thought she could touch people's lives and change the world, until reality hit. Most just looked upon her, if they looked at her at all, as another product of a troubled health care system. The politicians used her as an excuse to pass more laws, which helped them more than the people she tended on a daily basis, and others just cursed her for refusing to let them have their dose of whatever substance they were addicted to, which had put them in the hospital to begin with.

Once married, Nurse Betty had been happy, but a miscarriage and a husband who abandoned her for someone else ripped it away from her. Only her cigarettes provided any sense of consistency in her life. So that was when the habit started.

Nurse Betty—a name she received from a dying patient who had spent too many hours watching *Star Trek* reruns and referred to her as Nurse Chapel until she got him to change it to her real name— stuck the cigarette in her mouth and prepared to light it. The bushes next to her rustled. Wondering if some junkie was trying to break into the hospital for drugs, something that happened on a weekly basis, she investigated the noise. More rustling. Reaching into her pocket, Nurse Betty pulled out her pepper spray.

"I know you're there," she called. "If you need medical attention, you must go to the front desk."

Movement was the only response she received. Nurse Betty ripped the branches to the side, holding her bottle of pepper spray in front of her ready to fire and exposing three people with purple faces. She dropped her can of mace and the unlit cigarette fell from her open mouth. Two pairs of eyes stared at her, while the third—alien?—remained unconscious.

"Please," said one, "we need your help."

"You, you speak English," said Nurse Betty. She had no way of knowing that each of the strangers before her had been injected with nanobots that worked with the speech and language centers of the brain, translating different languages and helping them find the proper words to say.

"She's wounded and needs immediate medical attention," said one. "Will you help us?"

"But... the news says that you are dangerous." Nurse Betty bit her tongue for saying that last statement; it might provoke them.

"Please," said the other, holding the woman, his pleading and sad eyes locked with hers.

Her reasons for becoming a nurse 25 years ago, and her desire to help others, rushed back to her, pushing her fears aside. Nurse Betty held the branches of the bush back, allowing them to walk through it. She looked around (no one paid them any attention) and opened the staff door to the hospital building, thankful that the hallway was empty, though for how long, she didn't know. She ushered them inside. Taking the lead, Nurse Betty hurried down the corridor to a room she knew had been vacated an hour before. She wasn't worried about the security cameras, especially since the man who monitored them could be found sleeping during his shift.

"Stay here," she told them when they had entered the room. "I'll be back in a few minutes."

Putting themselves in her hands, they retreated into the darkened room and waited.

Nurse Betty ran to the supply closet, gathered what she could, and hurried back to where she had left her surprise visitors.

"Betty."

She stopped. Her supervisor had noticed her running around and came to confront her about it. She hid the vials of medicine and bandages behind her back, scrunching against the wall and hoping that her supervisor didn't notice.

"I need you in room 115," said her supervisor.

"I'm busy," replied Nurse Betty.

"Busy?" her supervisor gave her a piercing stare, her irritation at being rebuffed evident.

"Yeah, busy," Nurse Betty repeated in a more forceful tone.

She and her supervisor had never gotten along; her supervisor always ordered the nurses in her charge about, while keeping the easier, and more mundane, tasks for herself.

"I'm on my break right now and have 15 minutes left, where I intend to get a few winks after having been here all night. I'll be there when it's over."

"Break? I need you…"

"Why don't you get Charlene to do it? You'll find her in the closet with the janitor."

"We'll have words later," growled the supervisor as she walked off, disappearing down the hallway.

Nurse Betty hurried into the room where her uninvited guests waited for her to return, locking the door behind her. The two purple men stood up; the woman never moved.

"I got supplies."

She hurried over to the woman, admiring her heliotrope-colored skin, which formed a stark contrast to the darker purple shade of the other two. Nurse Betty decided that even on another world, different skin pigmentation would surface.

"How long has she been unconscious?" she asked.

"Several hours," said one.

Nurse Betty's gentle hands cut the material away from the wound, cleaned it, and stitched it closed where it had reopened.

"I know this is probably stating the obvious, but you all aren't from around here. Who are you, exactly, and why are you wanted by the FBI?"

The two men remained silent.

"No point in not talking," quipped Nurse Betty. "We're a little beyond that."

"My name is Obiah," said one, with caution, "this is Klanor, and she is Rynah. As for why we are wanted by your law enforcement, that's a long story."

"I need to do a blood transfusion," said Nurse Betty. "She's lost a lot, and if your physiology is anything like ours, she needs more."

"Our bodies typically have anywhere from eight to ten pints," said Obiah.

"Blood type?" asked Nurse Betty. "Here some people are O positive or negative, or AB..."

"Take mine," said Klanor, rolling up his sleeve.

"You two need to be an exact match, or..."

"Not for us," said Klanor. "On Lanyr, everyone has the same basic blood type. Now, do what you need to do."

Nurse Betty grabbed a blood bag, tearing it free of its plastic wrappings, and hooked it up, after inserting a needle into Klanor's vein, so that his blood filled it. Once done, she placed a needle in Rynah's arm and allowed the collected blood to enter her system. Nurse Betty hated doing it this way, since blood was usually separated into blood cells, platelets, and plasma, but she didn't have the time and Rynah needed it now, nor did she wish to get caught harboring fugitives. While she worked, Obiah and Klanor told her their story.

"So, this Stein guy means to destroy all of us?" she asked. "Why? What did we ever do to him?"

"You've done nothing, but that doesn't matter. He wants some sense of justice," said Obiah.

"It's my fault," Klanor spoke up. "I was the one who planted the idea of the crystals in his head. It was I who promised they could bring back his family. Oh, I was so naïve! And when he learned that it couldn't be done, he changed, and he is now taking his anger out on your world."

"How do I know I can trust the both of you?" Nurse Betty gave Rynah a shot of antibiotics.

"The question you should ask," answered Obiah, "is why did you?"

Nurse Betty thought for a moment. "I suppose, that if you were as dangerous as the news says you are, you would have left her out on the road to die, not risk bringing her here." She checked the transfusion and disconnected the bag from Rynah. "You will need to take it easy for a while," she said to Klanor. "As for her, I gave her something which should bring her fever down. The only thing you can do now is wait for her to wake up, but you can't stay here."

"We've nowhere to go," said Obiah, "nor do we have transportation."

"Here, take my keys." Nurse Betty handed Obiah her car keys. "Just press that button and the car that responds is mine. I'll have to report it stolen when my shift is over, but for now, take it. And here's some cash to buy food." She handed them the two $20 bills she kept in her pocket for meals when she worked double shifts.

"You've helped us enough. We can't…"

"Take it," Nurse Betty interrupted Obiah. "If this Stein guy is as bad as you say he is, then you all need to find a way to stop him."

Rynah moaned, shifting a little before going back to sleep, and Klanor lifted her into his arms, being careful not to wake her. After Nurse Betty made certain the hallway was clear and no one was just outside the exit, Klanor left with Obiah, while cradling Rynah.

"Thank you," he said.

"Don't mention it," replied Nurse Betty. She watched them hurry over the three-foot ledge and into the parking area where she kept her car. Though she had no way of knowing it, her small act would change the world.

Chapter 3
AFTERMATH

The fire crackled as it spit out embers into the night air. Joe and the others had driven through Denver, taking Interstate 25 south to New Mexico and only stopping when they were 20 miles from the border and could camp on the side of the road without attracting too much attention. Any cars that did drive past kept going, ignoring them, which is what they wanted. Alfric had built the fire, grumbling about the lack of good kindling, and cooked four rabbits in it; Joe refused to ask about the rabbits, deciding it to be in his best interest as he did not wish to argue with Alfric's sword.

Silence pierced the sullenness that followed them in the hours that had passed since the incident at the Wilmar Construction Site as no one had spoken. Solaris had confined herself to the back of the truck, refusing to speak or even acknowledge the others' presence. Her usual spunky demeanor had dwindled to a subdued manner, too subdued for the others. Concerned, each tried talking to her, but her response remained the same—silent and hollow-eyed.

Joe glanced at Solaris. Though he hadn't known her as long as the others, he knew that what had happened the previous night had changed her. Her snarkiness had disappeared, something he had come to admire and expect. He looked over at Alfric poking the fire he had built while glancing up into Solaris' violet eyes, the eyes of a haunted memory that the Viking could not tear himself free from. Joe snapped his head down when Brie, who had also been studying Alfric, looked in his direction.

"What is that?" asked Tom, breaking the quiet that surrounded them and pointing at the bits of stringy rabbit meat in the fire.

"Food," replied Alfric. "The hunt was meager, but we will still eat well tonight."

"They look a little scrawny," said Tom.

Alfric gave him a disapproving glare and Tom backed away.

"On second thought, it looks good," he said. "Yum."

Brie stepped over and turned the meat over to keep it from burning on one side.

"What bothers you?" she asked Alfric, trying to keep her voice low with the others around, but unable to ignore his constant stares at Solaris any longer.

"Nothing bothers me," grumbled Alfric, still jabbing the meager fire with a stick.

Brie placed her hand on Alfric's, its size dwarfing hers, and said, "Ever since Sunlil, you have not been able to stop staring at Solaris. What is it about her that troubles you?"

Sighing, Alfric glanced at Solaris, who stood away from the rest of them, with the faint edges of the shadows cast by the firelight wrestling at her feet. "Her eyes," he said, his voice stopping the conversation between Solon, Tom, and Fons.

"What about them?" said Brie, while fiddling with the pendant Alfric had given her, and which she had worn around her neck ever since.

"I've seen them before," replied the Viking.

The others leaned in, yearning to hear more about Alfric's past, knowing that there was more to him than the stoic face he showed the world, but he always refused to speak about his past.

"What?" said Brie, peering at Solaris, who remained in her place of solace, pretending to not be listening.

Alfric placed his stick in the grainy dirt around them, wishing that he had not said anything, as he had revealed too much about himself, but Brie watched him with those concerned and caring eyes of hers.

"About a year after Gróa died, I found myself climbing the cliffs near my home. They tower over my halls, casting their long and dark shadows in the late sun. I was hunting a wolf. It was alone, driven away by the other wolves, for there was something wrong with it. Night after night, it would break into the village and feast on the few chickens and goats we had.

"One morning, I had woken up to the sounds of a woman screaming and saw the wolf. Fresh blood—bright red and gleaming in the faint light—covered its mouth, while the woman lay dead. I snatched my father's spear and tracked the animal into those cliffs, following its crazed howls.

"A blizzard blew in that day. I found myself high in those cliffs and surrounded by the raging snow as it crowded in, blinding me and choking me. My foot slipped and I found myself falling. I had managed to grasp the ledge and cling to it. My fingers started turning blue from the cold, and I was unable to pull myself back up. I remember thinking that I was going to die that day, and what a dishonorable death it would have been.

"Then, a hand appeared—slender and white against the black rocks. I grasped it, and it pulled me up, away from the cliff's edge, and I found myself staring in the face of woman. Her face was fairer than a newborn babe and her hair was paler than the moon, but those eyes, gentle and warm, like roses against the snow—I'll never forget them and their violet color, just like the color of the flowers that bloom every spring."

"What happened to her?" asked Solon.

"I turned away for a second to grab my father's spear and she had gone. Vanished into the wind. Soon after, the storm ceased and I made my way home, where I told both my mother and my father about the mysterious woman who had rescued me that day. My father would hear none of it, but my mother told me to give thanks to Freyja, for it was her who spared my life.

"The wolf never bothered my people again, nor did I ever see those violet eyes again, with their raging fire calmed by a gentleness I had never witnessed, until Sunlil."

"Well," said Brie, "I'm glad someone was there that day, watching your back."

"Yeah," said Tom with a grin, "because, otherwise, who would catch all of these rabbits for us?"

Alfric glowered at him.

"What?" said Tom. "Humor. You know, this concept about laughing and joking around. Might want to look into someday, big guy."

Trying not to laugh herself, Brie took a piece of the cooked rabbit from the fire and ate it. "Needs salt, but not bad."

"Look at you, gone all Amazonian on us," joked Tom.

Solon's ears perked up, drawing him away from his usual pensive manner. "The Amazons? Are they here? I, very much, would like to meet one."

"Sorry, bud, but they're a myth," said Tom.

"Huh?" said Fons, waking from his nap. "What's a myth?"

"The warrior women of the Amazon jungle," replied Tom.

"No, they're not," said Fons. "They are real. Ten years ago, archeologists discovered buried bones that bore a remarkable resemblance to…" Fons continued talking about all the evidence he had uncovered about the existence of the Amazonians, and the others listened with mild interest, releasing a series of "Uh-huhs" at certain lulls in the conversation.

Solaris watched the others joke and laugh as they listened to Fons' stories. Not feeling like joining in, she walked away from the firelight and into the night, where her somber mood could not be seen, but Joe had seen her leave. He tapped Brie's elbow. Knowing what he wanted, she rose and ran after Solaris, unsure if she would be able to help her.

Solaris walked onward, unaware of Brie following her, past the shrubs and prairie dog holes, thoughts reeling through her mind; but most of all, Solaris dwelled upon the people she had failed to save. A rattlesnake slithered through the dirt away from the porous rock it had hidden under and towards her boot. Having never seen one, Solaris just watched it, ignoring the rattling sound it made as it reared up. It struck her boot. Startled by its reaction to her presence, she reached down and picked it up, holding the writhing snake close to her; since she was not flesh and blood, its repeated bites did not harm her.

"You should put that down," said Brie, appearing from the brush. "They are venomous, as in their bite is harmful to people and animals."

Solaris tossed the rattlesnake away and it slithered through the underbrush to safety, away from the strange person that was unphased by its fangs.

"I am neither," she said.

"I do not think so."

"That is your opinion."

"You may not bleed the way we do, but you are human in every sense of the word," said Brie.

Solaris stared at the night sky and the stars above her that belonged to constellations she did not know the names of. She remembered that once she had found Brie doing the same, a memory that seemed like it had happened so long ago that it was more myth than memory.

"I have failed."

"No worse than me," said Brie.

Solaris remained silent.

"Do you remember when I was first brought aboard your

ship?" asked Brie. "I was scared all of the time and I had allowed that fear to determine my actions. Because of it, I failed all of you, repeatedly. But you know, there was one person who believed in me, one, who told me to not be afraid, and to not let my fear guide me."

"Who was this person?" asked Solaris.

"You," said Brie as though the answer should have been obvious.

Solaris turned away. "I betrayed you. I had a choice between saving your sister, strangers, or Rynah, and I chose Rynah. I sacrificed your family to save someone I cared for more."

"I don't blame you," said Brie.

"You should," said Solaris.

"You did what any person would have done," said Brie. "Yes, I was angry at first, but the more I thought about it, the more I realized that I would not have done any different. If I had to choose between Rynah or my sister, I would have chosen my sister and others would have died because of it. Stein set that up so that no matter what you chose, people would die. It was a no-win scenario. You can't dwell on this, Solaris. You may have chosen your friend at first, but in the end, you still tried to save the others."

"Only after I realized it was a trick."

"But you still tried when others would have given up."

"But I failed."

"That is what makes us human. Sometimes we fail, yes, but what matters most is what we do afterward. You taught me that!"

"They died because of me."

"They died because of Stein. Joe told us how he had rigged the pit so that even if you had chosen to save them, it would still have blown up, burying them, and you, alive. It wouldn't have mattered what decision you made."

"There, you are wrong. It does matter. It always matters."

Solaris walked away.

"Solaris," said Brie.

"Brie, I know what it is you are trying to do, but it does not outweigh my guilt. I feel... I don't even know what I feel!"

"Solaris..."

"I'm supposed to guide you, to help all of you stop, first Klanor, and now Stein, and I've failed. Marlow trusted me. And it appears that his trust was misplaced."

"We need you, Solaris."

"No, you don't."

Brie watched as Solaris moved further from her.

"Solaris!" she called after her.

Solaris paused.

"If you leave, you will never stop running. If you leave, then you will have failed us."

Solaris never turned around; she disappeared from sight, becoming a faint shape in the darkness until she had vanished, leaving Brie alone among the shadows and the cold comfort of the rocks, wishing that she could help Solaris the way she had once guided her.

When the sun rose the next morning, Solaris had not returned. The others had asked about her, but Brie gave the same answer to each inquiry. "She left."

Brie never bothered to explain as no explanation was necessary. Solaris needed to work this out on her own, and in her current, depressed state, she had become useless to them.

"Solaris!" called Tom as he wandered the area in the golden glow of the morning sunlight. "Solaris!"

Tom charged over a hill, looking out at the vast desert before him, with Solon hurrying to catch up. Together, they searched the area, and two hours passed with no sign of Solaris, until Alfric had found a set of footprints. Their perfect shape told him that they were not animal, but those of someone wearing boots. Waving the others over, Alfric followed the tracks, leading them over an embankment. They stopped. Below them, was a swirling mass that appeared from thin air and grew until it had reached the size of a baby elephant, and in front of it stood Solaris.

"Solaris!" yelled Brie, but it was too late. Solaris had gone.

* * *

The sun hovered above the hills, rising higher into the pink and gold sky, watching the lone figure treading below it; the elongated shadow moved in time with the wanderer. By the person's posture, the sun knew that something bothered her. Doing what it always did, the sun rose higher in the sky, eradicating the pinkish-gold that had welcomed it that morning, and watched the figure beneath it, never learning that this lone person was Solaris.

If there was warmth in the sun's rays, Solaris felt none of it; her mind was too consumed by her mistake the previous night and her failures. She had made a choice and people had died because of it. Guilt filled her, so she ran away. If she could not trust her own judgment, how could she ask the others to?

The sharp ends of the naked brush (the buds had just formed) pricked her skin, but she did not register it. A bush rustled behind her as a rabbit sprang into it, hiding from what it perceived as imminent danger. She ignored it. For a brief moment, Solaris turned and looked behind her; the urge to go back tugged on her, but she disregarded it and continued on, treading through a world she did not know. She had failed them, and that was all that mattered to her. Marlow had once called her his guiding star, but how can she guide anyone when she felt lost and confused. No, Solaris thought to herself, *I am no one's guiding star.*

A lizard scurried across the sand before her feet. Solaris studied its movements a moment, once again faced with a creature she had never seen, before walking forward. She continued her trek. An ant-hill, with a line of ants spilling from it, attracted her attention for a moment as she thought about being one of them. Shrugging away the notion, she moved onward.

Faces loomed before her—panicked, frightened, and pleading, all reaching out to be saved, but she did not rescue them; she had allowed them to die. Rynah's face appeared in her mind. Her friend. Yet, how would Rynah feel when she learned that Solaris had abandoned their mission just to save her. *Rynah abandoned it for Brie,* a voice inside reminded her. Solaris stopped. She had heard others speak of intuition and gut feelings, or of small voices that guided them, but never thought it would happen to her.

Marlow. He would be furious with her; she had let him down and had broken her promise to him. What he must be thinking now, if he only knew. No, Solaris could not go back, her shame too great. The others were meant to save this world, not her, so she walked onward, turning her back on a promise, and those she had sworn to help.

Solaris stopped. A distorted, transparent shape lay just ahead, beckoning her to come to it, but should she? Taking cautious steps, she moved towards it, her eyes focused on the small swirls that lined the distorted mass until… she recognized it. It was a vortex, what some called a micro wormhole, much like the ones she had used to bring Tom, Solon, Brie, and Alfric to her and Rynah, but what was it doing there?

Her curiosity getting the better of her, Solaris approached it, her light footfalls crunching dried brush and unmelted patches of ice. The somewhat clear mass—warped rocks and bushes could be seen through it—remained, unchanging, as though it waited for her. The closer she went to it, the stronger the pull to step through became. With a final studious look, intuition—something Solaris thought she would never have—told her to go through and let it take her where it willed.

An Eastern Kingbird chirped as it flew overhead, forcing her to take one final look around at the world she had once thought she could save from the acts of a madman. Solaris lifted her right foot, and with dignified grace, started to step through the vortex, following her intuition, before rethinking her decision. She heard Brie call her name and tried to jerk away at the last second, but the swirling mass reached out and seized her, pulling her into it and disappeared with her in its grasp.

Back on the embankment, the others stood motionless as a part of them had been ripped away when Solaris disappeared through the anomaly.

"What are we supposed to do?" asked Tom as he stared at where Solaris had been.

"The only thing we can do," replied Alfric. "Continue."

"We can't just leave without her," said Tom.

"We can't just sit here either," Fons replied. "She just disappeared, and who knows if there is a way to bring her back."

"He's right," said Brie. "Solaris would be the first to tell us to go."

"But how are we to finish this without her? We've lost Rynah. Obiah is missing. We have not been able to contact Jifdar. And I can't believe I'm about to say this, but I would even settle for having Klanor here," Tom said as he looked at all of them, worry etched on his face.

"We have to trust that our friends are all right and will return to us," said Solon, trying to soothe Tom's agitated demeanor. "We still must complete what we set out to do."

"She's smart," said Brie. "Rynah may find a way out of Stein's clutches."

"We don't know that," Tom said. "Only they know the poem that we are supposed to be following."

"No they don't," Solon interrupted them.

All eyes turned towards the young scholar, whose once slim build had become quite muscular under Alfric's tutelage. "Solaris gave me access to her library of books and instructed me on how to use their holopads, as they call it."

"What are you saying?" asked Tom.

"Though she meant for me to read a particular book, I found the volume which contained the poem that Rynah has used to guide our steps. I memorized it."

"And you didn't tell us this before because…" began Tom.

"It was not necessary at the time," said Solon.

"You can lead us then," said Alfric.

"Hold on a minute," Joe stopped them. "You're talking about leaving one of your own out here in the middle of nowhere."

"We have little choice," said Alfric.

"Little choice?" Joe's brows scrunched together in agitation. "Listen to yourselves! What if she comes back?"

"Joe," said Solon, "there is no guarantee of that."

"It just doesn't seem right," Joe said.

"And think of what Stein will be doing to the people here if we spend precious hours waiting for something that might never happen," Alfric replied. "Solaris and Rynah are gone, but we are here."

"Wait a minute," said Tom. "We've always had one of them with us. How are we to do this without them?"

Alfric glanced at each of them before speaking. "The boy says he knows the ancient text. He can guide us. It is time for us to become the heroes that Rynah and Solaris think we are. It is time for us to do this on our own and prove that we are worthy of the songs sung of us."

"He's right," said Brie, though she loathed the idea of leaving Solaris behind. "We can't force Solaris to return."

Sadness filled Brie's voice, but what choice did they have? She knew that Solaris had chosen to leave them, and only Solaris could decide to return.

"Yeah, well, you're not going without me," said Joe.

"You don't need to come," said Alfric. "We never should have involved you in the first place."

"Yeah, well, according to your poem, I'm already involved, and at this point, there is no getting rid of me," Joe replied.

With Alfric's urging, they left, each knowing that they needed to stop Stein, and the only clue they had on how to achieve that end was locating a Lanyran in New Mexico. Brie felt torn between leaving Solaris to her fate and continuing their journey. Taking one last look in the distance, she searched for her friend, but only sand and brush answered her.

"Please, come back, Solaris," she whispered, before jumping into the cab of the truck.

Chapter 4
HOLE IN TIME

Six-year-old Charese bounced her yellow rubber ball, which was as big as her, down the driveway of her home, ignoring everything around her. Her tight black curls bounced with each exuberant movement she made, tapping her bistre-colored skin, as she ran to keep up with her rolling ball as it skipped towards the street. She snatched it.

Before she could roll it up the driveway and back to the house, a strange noise stopped her, compelling her to turn. An opaque, swirling mass appeared next to her with blue light spilling from it in little shocks and jolts, releasing loud sparks of electricity. The girl stared at the anomaly, unsure of what it was or how it had just appeared. She bounced her ball towards the swirling mass and it disappeared through it. Curious and unafraid, the girl walked toward the foggy mass as it spit out tiny bolts of electricity, wondering where her ball had gone and determined to get it back. Just as she stuck her foot out, the tip of a phalanx poked through the mass and out walked a Roman soldier.

The man looked around him, dazed and confused as to what had happened. He turned to flee back to where he had come from, but the anomaly had disappeared, trapping him in a different time.

Charese tapped the man's arm with her tiny fingers. "Have you seen my ball?" she asked.

Afraid, the man yelled at her in Latin, forcing the girl to scream and run inside. Minutes later, her parents charged into the yard, her father demanding to know why the man had accosted his daughter, but the confused Roman reacted the only way he knew how—he shoved the man to the ground and was about to jab him with his spear, when he stopped, staring at the crowd of people that had gathered around him.

The girl's mother yanked out her cell phone and called the police. Within moments, harsh sirens rang in the air as two police cars raced up the street and the man disappeared. He ran down the sidewalk, unsure of where to go, his wide eyes gawking at the scene around him and the moving cars, riding lawnmowers, the remote control plane that a group of children had, and the music that blared from someone's stereo.

"Drop your weapon and put your hands up!" yelled a police officer, jumping out of his car with two others, all of them aiming their handguns at the Roman soldier.

The Roman turned in circles, trying to decide if he should fight or run.

"I said drop your weapon!" yelled the same officer.

The Roman soldier raised his spear, screaming in his own language, and threw it in the air, striking the front right tire of one of the police vehicles. A loud hiss filled the silence around them as the air escaped. The Roman yanked out his sword, but before he could charge, a shot rang out, catching him in the hand and forcing him to drop his weapon where it clattered on the asphalt. Within seconds, the police had him on the ground and handcuffed him. Once he was contained, one officer got on his radio.

"Yeah, this is Sergeant Ramsey, I've got a suspect in custody who was disturbing the peace and wielding a deadly weapon. Another of the weird ones."

"Weird ones?" came a reply over the radio.

"Yeah, like the one found in the middle of downtown, except instead of looking like a knight from the round table, this guy looks like he belongs at the Coliseum, like he walked off a movie set."

"Geez, another one? There was a report of a third incident just a few minutes ago. Some nutcase just appeared in the middle of a shopping mall dressed like *The Last of the Mohicans*. Put a tomahawk through a mannequin."

"What do you want me to do with this one?" asked the officer.

"Bring him in. The captain has set up a place to keep them while we try to find some translators."

"Roger that," said the officer. He glanced at the Roman soldier in the backseat and shook his head, wondering what was happening to the world and where these people came from, and regretting that he had once wished for a more interesting job.

Chapter 5
A Trip to the Past

The micro wormhole spat Solaris out of its other end. She landed hard on the rocky ground next to spiral topiaries with ash-coated, pink flowers as razor-edged pebbles dug into her skin, and because Tom had fitted her with pain receptors, she held them up, cringing at the stinging pain. With care, she brushed the bits of rock off her hands and looked up. Solaris gaped at what she saw.

Fires burned, consuming stone buildings with their claw-like flames and turning them to ash. Thick, bulbous smoke filled the afternoon sky, blocking out the sun and turning day into night and mirroring what was to come if she and the others failed to stop Stein from spreading his madness. Terrified screams echoed around her, surrounding her, as people, with faces far paler than she had ever seen, darted about, desperate to escape the torment thrust upon them. A faint cough echoed behind her.

For the first time, Solaris noticed the man lying on the marbled floor of the building behind her. She ran through the towering archways to him and fell to her knees. With gentle hands, she lifted him up, spotting the open knife wound in his side.

"You'll be all right," she said, though she knew her statement was a lie.

"You cannot fool me," said the man. His blood soaked robes had once been a royal purple, with gold embroidery marking his station. Behind him was a thin, purple veil, which concealed a most prized treasure. "They said you would come."

Solaris looked at him in surprise. "Who?"

"The Java," replied the man, "said that you would come. A friendly face, the same as the one who stabbed me, so that I would see kindness and love before death, instead of the hatred in my murderer's eyes."

"I don't understand," Solaris replied.

"Don't you? You carry one of them with you, and it is a part of you now."

Solaris said nothing.

"They gave me a message for you," said the dying man. "What you see before you is what will become of your future if you continue your current course."

"How..." began Solaris.

"You must go back."

"How?"

"The same way you came here. Find a vortex and it will take you where you need to go. The thing you carry knows what you want." The man's words faded as his grip on her hand weakened before going slack. Staring into his vacant eyes, sorrow and anger filled Solaris. She closed his eyes; it seemed the right thing to do.

The ground shook as fire spewed from beneath it, consuming all in its path. The columns supporting the archways she had walked through split down the middle, slicing the eels carved into their sides and crushing them into tiny pieces, as the stone crumbled away. Solaris dove through the two archways just as they crashed onto the ground, cracking the tiled stones below it.

She stopped. Standing on the top of the temple steps, a lone figure framed by the orange glow of the fires, Solaris watched the melee below. Sides of buildings fell away, turning to dust. People ran in every direction; children cried and mothers screamed, while flying vehicles—more advanced than the hovercrafts of Lanyr and the automobiles of Earth—swerved to avoid collision, only to smash into rock barriers and explode.

Rockets fired above her as aircraft flew past her to the destruction below, dousing the flames with seawater, but to little avail. The earth split open, sending a firebomb into the air until it crashed into one of the flying vessels, knocking it out of the sky and sending it straight towards her. Realizing too late that she lay in its path, Solaris jumped out of the way. The blast from the fallen craft rammed into her just as the ground quaked again, sending her tumbling down the steps and to the base of the temple. Instinct forced her to check her body for damage, but the nanotechnology that Tom had fitted into her synthetic skin kept her from showing any signs of injury.

Boom!—Boom!—Boom!

A series of explosions rocked the area; inferno flames shot into the sky, torching pruned bushes, courtyards, gazebos, and any unfortunate enough to be in their way. Solaris spotted a swirling mass of air that refracted the light around it, distorting the background; others formed as well, ripping holes through the universe, adding to the destruction in front of her.

Rynah.

She had to get back to the moment when she had left the others. Cursing her own stupidity, Solaris ran for the vortex, hoping that it would take her where she wanted to go, all the while knowing that if she remained where she was, she would perish like those around her.

Another flying vessel rammed into the ground, sending rocks and paved stones reeling into the air, deadly missiles that sought a target. Violent quakes rocked the ground beneath her as she ran, causing her to stumble as it swayed; her faltering steps clomped on the pathways until she had regained her balance. Solaris ran faster.

A man crashed into her, knocking her off her feet. Landing on her rear, Solaris looked up, but the man who had run into her never stopped, and all she saw was his back as it disappeared behind the clouds of smoke. She jumped to her feet and bolted across what had once been beautiful green grass, cut to the height of three inches, but was now a charred ruin. A shriek stopped her.

Whirling around, Solaris watched as a woman tumbled over the side of a wall and faced a 100-foot drop to the ground below. A man reached over and grabbed her arm, but as the ground continued to shake, his grip slipped. The woman screamed again.

Just as Solaris was about to run to her, the roaring engines of a ship caught her attention. She looked up and watched as a vessel (Lanyran in design, though sleeker) rose from a landing pad, amidst the shooting flames and smoke tendrils that reached for it until it had faded from view. The woman screamed a third time just as the ground shook with such force that it forced Solaris to cling to a hanging rod, which had once been part of a support beam, to maintain her balance.

Her eyes focused on the woman clutching the wall and the hand of the man who tried to pull her up. Releasing her grip on the rod, she charged for the woman, refusing to let her die, in exchange for her life. Steam burst from a crack in the ground. Solaris dodged, avoiding its scalding heat, and continued her frantic charge for the woman.

The ground quaked again as jagged rocks burst from underneath; steam rose from their edges, as mounds of earth raced for the Lanyran man that held firm to the woman dangling in midair. A low rumble coursed beneath their feet. Still racing for them, Solaris watched, helpless, as a hole in the ground opened next to the man, releasing a pocket of steam that struck his entire body. Wailing in agony, he released his grip on the woman, while flailing his arms and running, aimless, until he stepped off a cliff and plunged to the raging waters below, mixed with molten lava.

Shrieking, the woman managed to grasp the protruding rocks, but the moisture coating them made her grip falter and her fingers slipped. Bracing herself for the inevitable, the woman prepared to release her grip when another hand snatched hers. She looked up into the eyes of the one responsible—though Solaris never noticed the exchange as she dashed across the uneven and swaying ground—and cursed her luck at him being the only one left to rescue her.

At the wall, the man held on to the slender hand in his grip; sweat made her slip with each passing second as the ground rumbled and rocked. A high pitched whistle sailed past them as another firebomb burst from the ground, arched, and crashed, its explosion consuming everything next to it. The ground reeled again, and the woman's hand fell free of his grip. Before he could react, and before she comprehended what had happened, a hand—Solaris' hand—reached out from the smoky veil and seized the woman's wrist.

They stared at one another, each surprised that the other had a Lanyran face; in her haste to help, Solaris never noticed that their skin was purple, like hers. She heaved the woman over the top of the wall and back onto solid ground.

"Thank you," said the woman. She turned to the man. "You wretch! You are the one responsible for all of this!"

"I… I'm sorry," pleaded the man. "I never thought…"

The roaring stopped, replaced by deafening silence. Solaris looked out at the shores and the sea beyond it, concerned by the sudden change. As she watched, the waters receded from the sand, replaced by dead fish, as the eerie quiet consumed them. A low rumbled sounded around them. In slow progression, it grew until it hurt their ears as a wall of water surged straight for them.

"Run!" yelled a voice.

The wall of water plowed into the tall buildings, snapping them in half. The crumbling of stone and brick drew Solaris' eyes upward, as the steeple above them broke free of its base and plunged to the ground, with them in its path. Solaris tackled the two before her, shoving them out of the steeple's path just as it struck the ground. Dust and rock billowed into the air, covering them, but something happened she did not expect—a vortex had formed nearby at the same moment, and the man she had saved fell face forward into the newly formed portal and vanished, while two strangers, a man and a woman, were expelled and swept away by the water.

Solaris lunged for the man, but another wave rammed into the buildings around her, drowning the fires that consumed them. Its impact sent her flying through the air until a solid wall stopped her. Before Solaris had time to react, another great quake, followed by a rush of water that covered the beaches and stopped halfway up the cliff, knocked her off her feet. Fire rained from the black sky, plowing into the scorched ground beneath her. A lava bomb soared through the air and arched for her. Solaris rolled out of its path just as it struck the dirt (rock and chunks of burnt grass flung in every direction), leaving a car-sized crater where she had been.

The woman Solaris had saved rushed for her, grabbing her arm and pulling her to her feet. "The transports!" she shouted, pointing to a series of square hovercrafts packed with people fleeing the destruction and attempting to escape over the water. Many of the crafts hung low, unable to achieve their full altitude of 1,000 feet in the air due to the excess weight they carried.

Solaris lunged to her feet and followed the woman to the docking bay with the transports. Another lava bomb crashed into the ground nearby, forcing them to cover their faces as they ran. Cracks split open the ground, spewing steam and fire. A split appeared before them, forming a sharp, eight-foot drop-off. The woman stopped, teetering on the edge. Solaris ran up behind her, seized her by the shoulders, and pulled her back away from the edge before she fell over. Thunder roared behind them as the immense, carved

structures that had once been the pinnacle of this civilization top-
pled over, buried by dust and smoldering ash.

Solaris looked over and watched as more transports disappeared. There was only one way to get to them. "Jump!"

She and the Lanyran woman leapt over the edge, landing hard
on the ground below, but they regained their feet, refusing to be
stopped, and charged for the docking area. A low rumble echoed
around them, starting soft before transforming into a tremendous
roar that deafened their ears. A tear ripped open the ground in the
bay, forming a deep hole that sucked in the water and any unfortunate enough to be nearby.

"Go now!" yelled one of those in charge of allowing people onto
the transports.

The ships took off. One failed to unhook from the dock properly and wavered in the air before plummeting to the water below,
disappearing into the black hole in the bay. The earth shook, reeling
back and forth in a seesaw motion, causing all who ran to lose their
balance. Solaris and the woman watched in horror as the recently
formed hole in the ground spit out the water it had just consumed,
ejecting it into the air, along with any ships that had fallen inside.

Solaris dove on top of the woman, forcing her to the sandy
ground, covering her, and taking the full impact of the rocks and
dirt that pelted them.

"Is there another way off this island?" she asked, realizing that
they could no longer depend on the transport ship to escape.

"There is a land bridge over there," replied the woman, "but I
don't know how long it will hold."

Realizing that it was their only chance, Solaris dragged the
woman towards the natural formation that served as a bridge connecting the island to the mainland. They hurried across the charred
grass that crunched beneath their boots, diving into the crowd of
panicked people that had decided to do the same. The worming,
squirming mass of bodies squished together, not caring whom they

trampled, as they squeezed their way through the archway that formed the gates to the land bridge.

A man slammed into the woman that Solaris had saved, knocking her to the ground. She screamed as feet stomped upon her, unaware that they trampled a living person. Determined to not lose the woman the way she had lost the people at the construction site, Solaris rammed her way through the crowd of people, despite their feeble attempts to push her backward, and shoved them aside. She reached the woman, hauled her to her feet, and clung to her as she pushed their way through.

One of the pillars supporting the archway cracked. Knowing they hadn't much time, Solaris quickened her pace while never releasing her grip on the woman, elbowing any who got too near out of her way. The stone pillar grinded together as the crack widened and bits of marbled rock crumpled away, allowing the top half to teeter to the side, its precarious balance warning all of its inevitability. More people scrunched together, choking Solaris and the woman, but Solaris refused to slow down and hurried to the open gate.

Rock fell from above as the top half of the pillars broke free. Terrified screams pierced the chaotic atmosphere as people were crushed by the chunks of marble that plowed into the earth. Solaris yanked the woman forward, and together, they ran for the gate, shoving their way through and onto the land bridge, before the stone pillars smashed into the ground, killing any who had gotten in their path and barricading their only salvation.

Solaris and the woman paused, looking back at the now blocked gate and those unfortunate enough to be trapped on the other side. Their sympathy went out to them, but both knew that there was nothing they could do, except turn back around and follow after the few survivors amidst the falling cloud of smoke and ash.

Chapter 6
AT THE CONSTRUCTION SITE

Red and blue lights flashed in circles as the ambulances and fire trucks sat idle in the oozing mud while emergency crews worked with diligence, pulling the charred bodies out of the pit. Black bags containing the unfortunate victims that had already been dug out lined the space between the emergency vehicles and the pit with tags on each one, identifying them as John or Jane Doe and a number. Others wearing jackets with FBI imprinted on them wandered about, ascertaining evidence that could be used in tracking down the ones responsible. Above it all stood Samuel.

A man shouting into his cell phone drew his attention. With a slight turn of the head, he looked at the owner of the site—no doubt on the phone with his lawyer to discuss how to avoid a lawsuit—stamping his feet as he screamed. Samuel watched the man, while anger boiled beneath his calm and collected exterior.

Who could have done this? he thought to himself. Only a person with a stone heart would have.

A low grinding and creaking filled the area.

"Watch out!" shouted an agent.

Samuel stepped out of the way just as the top half of a crane plowed into the ground where he had been standing, creating a crater the size of a compact car; its stripped, yellow paint bore signs of having been scorched, but not by any weapon he knew of.

"Are you all right, sir?" asked a fellow agent.

"Yes," replied Samuel. "See what you can get off that."

He looked over at the pit. More bodies had been dug out and bagged with a white tag stuck to the zipper. He did not envy the ones who would have the unpleasant task of putting names to the faces and contacting the family members to inform them of the unfortunate news about their loved ones. Samuel straightened his crooked tie, thinking of Joe and how he always kept his suit pressed, shoes shined, and never had a thread out of place, knowing that as the agent in charge, he must set an example. Funny how one thinks of such things while staring death in the face.

"Sir," said an agent, carrying a digital video player, "we have the feed from the security cameras. Most of them were knocked out, but one did manage to catch some of what happened here, though it's a bit garbled."

Samuel took the video player and played back the security camera feed. Despite the wavy lines, skipped scenes, and interference, he managed to make out some of what happened. It began with Solaris driving up and meeting with Stein—Samuel would never forget the face of the one who threatened the entire planet—before switching to Joe fighting with one of the aliens. The video cut out, replaced by an image of Brie running to a girl locked in a cage before… did the girl just vanish? Samuel rewound the video and replayed the scene. The girl did vanish. He continued watching the camera feed and the firefight that had taken place before the screen went blank.

"Is there any more?"

"Sorry, sir," replied the agent.

Samuel handed the digital player back to the woman. "See what else you can get."

The agent nodded, but before she could leave, Samuel stopped her.

"I want the security feed from the Smithsonian Natural History Museum during the heist that took place last week."

"The cameras were knocked out."

"There is always one that captures something," said Samuel, remembering what Joe had told him the day before.

The agent made a phone call and hung up two minutes later.

"That footage has been deemed classified."

"Then unclassify it," said Samuel as a hunch formed in his gut and he remembered Joe's words to him.

"I can't," said the agent.

Samuel clamped his mouth shut to prevent himself from speaking his mind. He knew someone who could help him gain access to that video. As he surveyed the Wilmar Construction Site, he thought about the last conversation he had with Joe, and how Joe had told him that more was happening to their world than he realized. Watching those purple-faced aliens attack another just like them, and his colleague, made Samuel question what Director Singuar had told him. His job was to bring in Joe and the others on charges of theft, conspiracy, attempted murder, resisting arrest, public endangerment, and breaking out of a secure FBI facility.

Could he have been mistaken this entire time? Samuel needed answers and he intended to get them.

"Sir?" said a female agent as a breeze picked up, whipping his tie in his face, followed by a swirling, gray mass that resembled thick fog. It grew in size, forming a circle the size of a man with streaks of electrical light escaping from its black center.

Like the others with him, Samuel watched, mesmerized by the scene and trying to make sense of it, but a minacious feeling filled the pit of his stomach, warning him of impeding danger.

"Get away from there!" Samuel yelled at the female agent, but it was too late.

The swirling mass created a vacuum, pulling loose pebbles, tools lying on the ground, and abandoned leaves of paper towards it. The suction grew in intensity, forcing Samuel to hang onto the dump truck he stood next to. He reached out for the female agent, his fingers brushing the tips of hers, but before he could grasp her hand, she had gone, disappearing behind the gray veil.

Samuel's feet rose into the air, being pulled towards the mass. He clung to the truck, gripping it so tight that the metal fenders cut his skin as he hung in the air. Just when he thought that he would suffer the same fate as the female agent, the vortex released its hold and he dropped to the ground; gravel tore at his jacket, coating it in a thin layer of silt. When he turned to face where the swirling mass and female agent had been, he found a man wearing a WWII-era Japanese uniform.

The Japanese soldier jumped to his feet, screaming in his native language and pointing his rifle at the FBI agents surrounding him. Having no time for this, nor did he have any love for the Japanese since his grandfather had been one of the those killed at Pearl Harbor, he kicked a rock, sending it skittering across the dirt. The Japanese soldier turned towards it, his arms shaking from fear and confusion. Samuel tackled the man, knocking the rifle out of the soldier's hands and punching him in the jaw, subduing him.

Within seconds, the other agents were upon them and handcuffed the Japanese soldier, placing him in the back of one of their vehicles.

"I need a translator now so we can interrogate him," said Samuel to one of his subordinates.

"Yes, sir," replied the man.

Rubbing his face, Samuel glanced at where the female agent had been before she disappeared into the swirling mass, and guilt at her loss struck him. She had graduated from Quantico two years earlier and just been assigned to assist him in investigating the Wilmar Construction Site because she was from there and knew the area, and now she was gone because of his failure.

"I'm sorry," he whispered to the spot where the vortex had been, wishing he had answers for when he informed the agent's family of her disappearance.

Jesus, Joe, he thought to himself, *what have you gotten yourself into?*

His cell phone rang.

"Agent Anders," said Samuel when he answered.

"Samuel," Director Singuar was on the other end, "I need you to get back here."

"Why?" asked Samuel.

"The President intends to host a press conference to discuss this alien problem of ours and I want you in D.C. now."

"Yes, sir," Samuel replied. Once he hung up, he used his phone to book the first available flight to Washington D.C., dreading what would happen once he arrived there.

Chapter 7
MERRICK AND STEIN

The constant hum of the ventilator provided the only comfort for Merrick as he sat, tied to a chair, in a solid, white walled room with no windows (not even a two-way mirror) and a single door, controlled by a coded, holographic keypad. His head lolled to the side; his stringy, sweat soaked hair covered his face, draping down his bare neck. Stripes from being lashed formed diagonal Xs on his exposed chest as the blood made his skin glisten, pooling on the floor next to his bare feet in the fluorescent light; in his wrath, Stein had resorted to more barbaric tortures from Lanyr's ancient past.

Since his capture by the tractor beam, Stein had subjected Merrick to hours of abuse out of spite, and as an attempt to get information. Angered by Rynah's (whom he vowed to make pay for Marlow's act at Brestef) and Klanor's escape, Stein took out his ire on Merrick, but Merrick remained silent.

A series of beeps forced Merrick's eyes to flutter open as the door unlatched, allowing Stein and his bodyguards to enter the interrogation room. He glared at the battered man before him, disgust etched on his face, and lifted Merrick's head up an inch, peering into the man's half-closed eyes, before letting go of his chin, allowing his head to flop to the side once again.

"Wake him up."

One of the men who had entered with Stein doused Merrick with a bucket of ice water. Merrick moaned.

"Nice to see you have wakened," mocked Stein.

Merrick spat bloody mucous onto Stein's shiny black boots in response. "You've changed, and not for the better."

"What would you know of my inclinations?" demanded Stein.

"More than you realize, brother."

Stein punched him. "We're not brothers!"

"Oh, but we are," said Merrick, "made so the day you married Ofylia—the day you married my sister."

"Ofylia is dead, or have you forgotten?"

"It's never forgotten."

"Of course not," said Stein, "because you never did let me forget that she had died, as though I didn't feel the absence of her presence every minute of every day. No, you always had to remind me that it was I who killed her and our child."

"I did you an injustice…"

"Injustice doesn't even begin to describe it! You badgered me for years, reminding me of my failure as a husband and a father, and now you want mercy."

"I never…"

"Do you wish to know who is truly at fault?" demanded Stein, his voice rising in volume as his temper flared. "You! You are the one who encouraged her to take that job in Brestef when we were content in the Trilin Province."

"You are not the only one to lose your family," whispered Merrick. "Mine died that day too, or have you forgotten that they were guests in your house at the time? You are not the only husband to lose a wife, nor are you the only father to lose a child. I was angry and took that anger out on you, and for that, I can never apologize enough, but this madness you have wrapped yourself in has got to end."

Merrick thought back the day he learned of his family's death, remembering how they had wanted to visit his sister and decided to meet with her in the center of Desmyr on the day of the horrific explosion that almost annihilated the Brestef Region.

"So now you are sorry," Stein spat, tearing Merrick away from his painful memory.

"I've always been sorry."

"You wish my forgiveness?"

"If you'll grant it."

"Then tell me where Rynah and her band of miscreants have gone."

"I cannot."

"Don't play games with me!" roared Stein. "Tell me where they have gone! Tell me, and I will grant you my forgiveness."

"So that they can die too?"

"Did you know that Rynah's grandfather was the one responsible for the destruction of Brestef?"

"Yes."

Stain's gloating ceased for a moment. He thought that he had something he could use to infuriate Merrick and convince him to betray Rynah, but it never occurred to him that Merrick might have already known the truth.

"And it doesn't bother you?"

"How many more innocents must die?" asked Merrick.

"There are no innocents," replied Stein.

"Stein, please," begged Merrick. "I've wronged you, I know, but this is not the answer. End this path you are on. As your wife's brother, I implore you to stop this madness, before it's too late—before you are no longer the man my sister married."

Stein glared at Merrick and his pathetic state. "It is too late."

Choking back a sob, Merrick looked up at his brother-in-law, saddened by his failure to get through to him and realizing that

Stein had changed long before the crystals, and long before he had met Obiah. The darkness within Stein's heart had always been there; it just never revealed itself until the one thing he loved was torn from him.

"Then I have failed you, and Ofylia."

Stein walked towards the exit.

"Why don't you just kill me?" asked Merrick.

"Oh, I will, but for now, I want you to witness the sprouting of the seeds you have sown."

"They are not my seeds, Stein. They're yours."

Stein huffed as he marched out of the interrogation room with his guards, leaving Merrick alone, once again, still tied to the chair with droplets of blood dripping from his chest.

Chapter 8
THRUST BACK TO THE PRESENT

Solaris walked among the few who had survived the destruction of the ancient island as they meandered along the path of the land bridge to the towering cliffs ahead of them. No one spoke. Five days had passed since the initial onslaught, and in that time, Solaris learned that the woman she had saved was named Isyr, but the earth still quaked and rumbled at intervals, letting them all know that the worse was far from over.

During the first day, many of the survivors wanted Isyr, and those she was with who had also managed to escape, to be punished for the loss of the crystals, blaming them for why their world had been ripped away. A riot almost ensued, but was squashed within minutes as the Java's apprentice stepped forward. With the Java, the guardian of the crystals, dead, he had become their leader.

"No harm shall come to them," the apprentice had said and the mob had dispersed. "This is not the way." He turned to Isyr and her companions. "You are welcome to come with us if you wish."

They had not seen any of the transports that had tried to flee with passengers, forcing them to wonder if any had escaped at all. Solaris glanced at Isyr, the woman she had rescued, and wondered why the name was all too familiar to her.

"I must admit," said Isyr, breathing hard, "that this land bridge looked smaller from the sky."

Solaris smiled. Most things did. She remembered a time when Tom had said something similar to her and her response had been to deal with it. All of that seemed so long ago. Thoughts of the others weighed on her mind. How could she have abandoned them? Guilt at running away when they needed her most plagued her and she wished she could return to them, but she didn't know how she had gotten here. The only possible explanation was the secret that she kept with her, the secret that Marlow had made her promise to keep.

"No one must know," he had told her when he gave her a tiny object wrapped in a cloth.

"You cannot expect me…" Solaris had tried to protest.

"I do!"

Marlow's harsh words had cut through her, and for the first time, Solaris had felt dejected and hurt.

"I'm sorry," Marlow had apologized when he noticed her silence. "Certainly, Rynah can…"

"It is best if she doesn't. Please, Solaris."

"I'll tell no one."

"Thank, you."

"A coin for your thoughts," said Isyr, bringing Solaris back from her memories. "You looked as though you were far away."

"It's nothing," said Solaris.

"You know, I don't remember you being a part of the expedition," said Isyr.

Solaris avoided her question, glancing at a few others who looked just like Isyr and must have been a part of the expedition she spoke of.

"And you don't even have a single scratch on you," continued Isyr, holding out her arm, which still bore a deep bruise from her harrowing escape and the scabs of cuts that tried to heal. "In fact, you are remarkably unscathed."

"Just lucky, I guess," said Solaris.

Isyr stopped her, taking her arms and studying them, her intense gaze missing nothing, not even the minutest ripples as the nano-skin reacted to her touch.

"Remarkable," breathed Isyr. "We have only just managed to create robotic lifeforms, but nothing as advanced as you."

"I am not a robotic lifeform," snapped Solaris.

"You're offended," said Isyr, surprised.

Solaris pulled her arms free of Isyr's grasp.

"I'm sorry," said Isyr, realizing that Solaris was no ordinary artificial intelligence. "Many of the artificial lifeforms we've created are not capable of emotion or have any sense of self-awareness. Who... never mind. It's not my place."

"His name was Marlow," said Solaris, knowing what Isyr had been about to ask. "He was my friend."

"What happened to him?"

"He died."

The sorrow in Solaris' voice did not go unnoticed, and Isyr wished she had been more tactful in her efforts at making conversation. "So, you are alone then?"

"He had a granddaughter."

"What happened to her?" asked Isyr.

"I abandoned her," said Solaris in a soft voice. "I abandoned all of them."

Thoughts of how she had left her friends—Brie, Alfric, Tom, Solon, Fons, and Joe—filled her mind and guilt accompanied it, showing in her somber face. She wished she hadn't left them. She wished she could get back to them.

"When are you from?" asked Isyr in a low voice.

Solaris stopped and looked at Isyr, wondering if she had heard the woman's question correctly, and judging by Isyr's expression, she had.

"What makes you..."

"The Java explained when we first arrived here that those crystals in their temple could control time, not in the sense that we think of it, but when one of those rifts appeared, I scanned it"— Isyr held out a scanning device the size of a container of lip balm— "and they all are holes through time and space. You never were on the ship with us when we came to this planet. So, that leaves only one other explanation."

"What happened?" asked Solaris.

Isyr's face fell. "Someone we all thought we could trust stole the crystals that these people revere. Herclai tried to get them back."

Solaris noticed a note of sorrow and loss in Isyr's voice.

"He was too late though. I hope he's safe. I never got..." She rubbed her belly a moment and sniffed, drying her tears. "How did you end up in one of those rifts?"

"By abandoning those who needed me," said Solaris. She wished she could go back. She needed to get back to them.

Isyr remained silent, reading the note of regret in Solaris' voice. "Perhaps you will see them again," she said.

The ground shook a bit underneath their feet, mimicking a gentle wave.

"I wish it would stop doing that," said Isyr.

A whistle stopped them. They had reached the cliffs. Palm fronds draped the charcoal cliffside, flapping in the wind and shielding a massive stairway that wove its way upward, carved into the rock.

They climbed the narrow stairs, stepping onto one stone step at a time and taking their time going upward. The higher they went, the fiercer the wind blew, drying the sweat that formed on their faces from the exertion of their ascent. A slight quake shifted the earth. Most paused, unsure of the safety of the stairs should another earthquake take place, but their leader urged them onward. If they stayed on the land bridge, they would drown the moment the tide

came in. The water had already risen some during their trek, drawing closer to the top of the bridge.

Higher, they all climbed, with Solaris and Isyr caught in the
middle, their breathing becoming more haggard as they pushed
themselves. Another quake shook them, more intense than the last.
Solaris glanced around, an ominous feeling filling her. She hurried
up the stairs, rounding a bend, and charging up another set of steps
to a second bend, with Isyr close behind.

The water slapped against the land bridge, forming white crests
and bubbles in its agitation before receding. The earth jerked, its
violence ripping the protruding stones from their place on the cliff.

"Go!" shouted Solaris.

Those on the stairs panicked, running up them in a desperate attempt to reach the top before another terrifying quake could take place.
The ground roared around them and shook with such force that the
stairwell cracked; the railing fell away, taking people with it and plummeting to the ground below just as a wave headed straight for them.
The wall of water smashed into the side of the cliff, crumbling stone
and breaking the rocky stairs away amidst a multitude of bloodcurdling
screams, as more people slipped and tumbled to the ground below.

Solaris and Isyr had just reached the top of the stairwell with
a few others when a terrified plea for help stopped her. She looked
down. A man clung to a piece of the steps that had broken away and
hung at a precarious angle, about to snap free at any moment. Memories of the terrified hostages in the pit at the construction site that
Stein had taunted her with, and murdered in an attempt to prove
how useless her efforts at saving them had been, flooded her mind.
She had failed them, but she could still save this man.

Solaris left Isyr and charged down the steps, past people who
clambered upward. She reached a gap in the stairwell. Solaris
jumped, clinging to the edge of a step and hauling herself upward.
The man's shouts echoed in her ears, propelling her onward.

Solaris dropped to her knees when she reached the dangling

man. Clutching what was left of the railing, she reached out with her other hand. She was too far. Scanning the surrounding area, Solaris realized that she would have to climb down to him if she wished to rescue the man.

She faced the cliffside. Bracing herself, Solaris hopped off the safety of the stairwell and eased downward, scaling the wall of rock. The ground shook again, forcing Solaris to grip the rock even tighter as she waited for it to pass. Once the earth had stilled again, she climbed downward until she had reached the man; his hands clutched the edge of the rock he hung from, his feet swaying in his efforts to hold on.

Solaris reached out to him. "Take my hand!"

The man stared at her, but made no effort to move.

"Take it!"

Regaining his senses, the man reached up and seized her hand, allowing Solaris to pull him upward to the sliver of a ledge she stood upon. His frightened eyes glanced at her as she helped him upward to the one set of steps that hadn't fallen away from the quaking earth. Clomping filled her ears. Solaris looked up just in time to see a mound of rock heading straight for her. She grasped hold of another ledge and tried to pull herself out of the way, but the rock slammed into her, knocking her away from the cliffside.

The world spun before her as she tumbled downward, and her mind raced to make sense of it, until she had plunged through another portal that had opened below her, leaving the chaos behind.

Chapter 9
GOING FORWARD

Rynah's foggy mind heard familiar voices grumbling and arguing with one another as they discussed what to do next. Still thinking she was asleep, she tried to focus on something else, but the persistent voices grew, until she could no longer ignore them. Her eyes opened. She lay on a bed—the lumpy mattress poked her back and the sheets smelled of spoiled mayonnaise—and stared at the plastered, gray ceiling above her. She turned her head as Klanor and Obiah continued to quarrel; they had not noticed her waking. She tried to move and grimaced when the pain in her side took hold until it subsided.

"Take it easy," said Klanor, placing a gentle hand on her shoulders and forcing her to lie back down, having noticed her movements.

"I'll go get us something to eat," Obiah said and left the room.

"Should he be going out there on his own?" asked Rynah, concerned that someone would see him and report him to the local authorities.

"Relax," said Klanor. "Obiah can take care of himself and it's nighttime. It's you we were worried about." He lifted up her shirt and removed the soiled bandage, replacing it with clean gauze that Nurse Betty had given them before they had left her. "It's seems to be healing nicely. That nurse knew what she was doing, and the antibiotics she gave you do not seem to have had an adverse effect."

"Nurse?"

"You were unconscious through most of it. You needed help, and Obiah and I decided to risk going to one of their medical facilities."

"That was a stupid idea," groaned Rynah. "What if you got caught?"

"It was a calculated risk," Klanor said. "You would have died otherwise."

Rynah looked around at the thin curtains and lopsided table in the single room. "Where are we?"

"In a motel," said Klanor, "the kind where they don't ask questions."

"How long was I out?"

"A day and a half."

Klanor took a plastic cup to the sink in the bathroom and filled it with water. As he returned with the full cup, Rynah watched him; concern filled his eyes, and she noticed a gentle air about him that she hadn't seen earlier.

"You've changed," she said, taking the water.

"Not so much."

"You have. On the ship, you could have left me there."

"No, I couldn't," replied Klanor, his voice soft.

"Why didn't you?"

"Where is Obiah? He should have come back by now."

"Klanor." Rynah's calm, yet stern, tone stopped him.

"I made that mistake once. I wasn't about to make it again."

"You've been different since Sunlil, less sure of yourself. I thought it was just an act, but now I see it in your eyes. You've changed. I should have seen it then, but my own convictions kept me from admitting it."

"You had good reason to doubt me," said Klanor. "When Stein left us all there to die, I saw what I had become and what I had turned him into. This whole mess is my fault, my doing. You tried to stop me, but I wouldn't listen, blinded as I was by my own desires."

"You offered me a chance to come with you on numerous occasions, but my own anger kept me from accepting."

"I'm glad you didn't," said Klanor.

The door opened and in walked Obiah with an armful of potato chips, cookies, and licorice.

"This, I suppose, is what passes for food around here."

He dumped it on the table. With Klanor's help, Rynah stood up, walked over to the table, and picked out a long piece of cherry flavored licorice. Her taste buds accepted the candy, but she would have preferred something more appetizing and wished she could have had her grandfather's *lafyrs*. Thoughts filled her mind of how she had made some once while still aboard Solaris, when Solaris was still a ship, and shared that bit of her home, her past, with four strangers who had become her friends.

"What were you two arguing about?" asked Rynah, as she fiddled with her grandfather's amber ring, which she wore around her neck and never took off, unaware of her actions.

"Nothing," answered Obiah.

"Don't lie to me." Rynah's austere voice and steel eyes forced Obiah to look at her.

"We need to find a ship and get off this planet," he said. "Klanor, however, wishes to remain."

"And what about the others?" said Klanor. "They will have gone in search of the next clue."

"The next clue! The next clue! That's all we've been doing is searching for whatever it is Stein is after, but the truth is he has been two steps ahead of us the entire time."

"And what about Solaris and the others?" countered Klanor.

"Since when have you cared?" demanded Obiah.

"Stop it!"

Both turned toward Rynah.

"Obiah is right. All we've done is lag behind Stein and he has managed to thwart us at every turn, but Klanor is right as well. We cannot abandon the others. Solaris will have taken them to this Albuquerque and that is where we are headed. I started this with them. I intend to see it through. We will finish eating and be on our way. In the meantime, we need to find a way to communicate with Jifdar."

"We should find the others first then," said Obiah, relenting. "Eat, the pair of you, and then we'll leave."

Obiah looked at Rynah, seeing an old friend that he hadn't laid eyes upon in a long time.

"You are like him in many ways."

"Who?"

"Marlow."

* * *

In the calm twilight of the New Mexican desert, a swirling mass bubbled, contorting the scenery behind it, as it increased in size with howling winds spewing from its mouth, blowing dust clouds into the air and creating what the local residents called a "freak sandstorm".

Out of it shot Solaris. She tumbled across the sand and sagebrush, rolling end over end for five yards until she stopped underneath a mesquite bush. She pushed herself up and stared back at where the vortex had been, but all that remained was the backdrop of the desert; the vortex had vanished as quickly as it had appeared.

The engine of a car hurried past behind her. Turning, she noticed the highway lay a few feet away, its pavement coated in the gritty particles of sand, turning its gray color brown. Her mind reeled from the journey she had just taken, still wanting to believe that it had been nothing more than a dream. Had she just witnessed the origin of the crystals' mythology? Another car sped past, oblivious to her lying in the dirt with bits of dead brush hanging from her emerald hair, scratching her face as it brushed her skin.

The others! Solaris jumped to her feet as her mind turned toward Brie, Alfric, Solon, Tom, and Rynah. Though she did not know how she would rescue Rynah, she knew that she needed the help of the others to achieve such a feat, though Solaris also remembered that Rynah was resourceful and adept at escaping dire situations.

She hurried to the road with its dotted yellow line marking the center. A pair of headlights peeked out at her in the distance, growing larger until they resembled white orbs that lit up the impending darkness. Waving her arms so that they would see her, she jumped up and down, shouting at them to stop. The Chevy did. Solaris ran past its rusted bumper to the rolled down window.

"Whoa! Look at you," said the man in the passenger seat.

To her horror, Solaris realized that in her haste to get the car to stop, she had forgotten to change her appearance to one acceptable among humans, but calmed when she noticed the garb that those in the car wore.

"You going to that comic con?" asked the man in the passenger seat.

"I need to get to Albuquerque," said Solaris.

"You forget to make a left turn there?"

Solaris cocked her head, not understanding the reference.

"That's where it is," said the passenger.

"Then, yes, I am going to this comic con."

"Then hop on in," said the guy in the passenger seat.

Solaris jumped into the backseat where two other passengers sat, dressed in the same costumes as the two in the front.

"So how long did it take you to do your costume?" asked one.

"Longer than you can imagine," said Solaris, still wondering what a comic con was, but not questioning the destination as it was where she wished to go. She hoped the others made it there with little difficulty, blaming herself for any trouble they may have suffered along the way.

"Yeah, well, see this?" said one, pointing to his attire (a cross between a mummy and a man made from steel) with pride evident in his voice. "Eight hours, baby!"

"That's nothing compared to the time I spent making this." One of the others held up what looked like a communication device, though clunky, and it seemed to be falling apart with each movement he made.

Solaris snatched it and flipped it open, tapping the buttons on it, but nothing happened.

"Hey," said the man, "it's not real. It's just plastic and cardboard."

Mortified, Solaris handed it back to him. "Sorry." Her communications device, which she had forgotten was in her pocket, chirped. Forgetting where she was and that she was to maintain a low profile, Solaris took it out and turned it on, allowing its holographic image to fill the car.

"Solaris?" Jifdar's face filled the small cab of the vehicle.

"Jifdar?"

"Solaris, can you hear me?"

"Jifdar!"

The hologram vanished. Solaris fiddled with the device, trying to get Jifdar back, but only static returned her efforts. Realizing that the others in the car had gone silent, she put her com unit away.

"What was that?" asked one.

Solaris' mind raced. Never before had she had to think up a story to calm those around her.

"It's a new global telecommunications device that a friend and I are developing. We plan to test it at the comic con, and if it works, it will revolutionize the way we communicate with one another." Solaris watched the faces around her as the questionable looks gave way to appeasement.

"Really? I want to try it," said one.

"No," Solaris replied, pulling her hand back. "It is only a prototype and has not been fully tested."

"Come on," pleaded the man.

"Leave her alone, man," said another. "She probably doesn't want anyone stealing her idea and filing a patent before she can. Now whose turn is it to pay for gas?"

"Mine," answered the passenger on Solaris' left as the driver pulled into a gas station.

"If you need the bathroom, now's the time to go," said the driver. "It will be at least three more hours until we get there."

"I'm fine, thank you," said Solaris. She watched as the others left the car and went into the convenient store. She pulled out her com unit again.

"Jifdar?"

Jifdar's face filled the car. "Solaris? Good. I thought I lost you. We've managed to reroute our communication signals through their satellites to make it more difficult for Stein to hijack them again, but time is limited. Where are you?"

"I am on my way to meet this Lanyran that has supposedly lived on this planet for the last several years."

"Where are the others?"

A pang of regret nudged Solaris as she thought about how she had left them, allowing her self-pity to dictate her actions.

"We were separated, but I am heading to the last set of coordinates we had discussed going to. Have you heard from Rynah?"

"No," said Jifdar. "We detected an escape pod leaving one of the ships that erupted and believe that it made it to the surface, but we are unable to determine who was aboard, much less if they survived. What should our next move be?"

Solaris thought for a moment. She longed to rescue Rynah, but doing so without any idea of what ship she was on was foolish and would result in others becoming Stein's captives. No, her best option was to find the mysterious Lanyran and follow the poem. It had never led them wrong.

Laughter spilled from the doors of the mini mart as the four occupants of the car returned.

"Stay put. I will contact you when I can and after I have found the others." She shut off her com unit, shoving it into her pocket just as the four returned.

"Ready?" asked the driver.

"Yes," answered the others.

"You know," said one of the passengers, "we never asked you who you were supposed to be."

"Or your name," said another.

"My name is Solaris and I am a Lanyran," replied Solaris as the car hurried down the highway at 70 mph.

Chapter 10
A Video and a Message

Samuel paced in the darkness of the backstage curtains, hopping from foot to foot as his nervousness took hold; his shaking hands tucked his unkempt shirt in for the fourth time as it had worked its way free again from his movements. He peeked out from behind the navy blue curtain at all the video cameras and flashing lights from pictures being taken, and the reporters in their pressed suits as they waited for the news conference to begin.

Director Singuar stood calm, ready to address the nation, having been summoned by the President who had called a press conference to address the recent incident caused by these alien invaders. The director had asked Samuel to fly back to Washington D.C. for the conference, wanting the agent in charge of apprehending the aliens to be there, so as to show the American people that the FBI was doing all it could to capture them.

Never in his life had he thought he would be here, standing behind the President of the United States during a press conference. This was not why he had joined the FBI. Where Joe's motives had been humble and honest, Samuel's lacked integrity. Action, that was what he wanted, and he thought the bureau could offer him that. He remembered watching the old cop shows on television as a child, laying on the couch and wallowing in his own fat, bemoaning the fact that he was the only third grader in his class that weighed over 100 pounds, and ridiculed every day for it by the other schoolchildren.

Excitement, thrills, a chance to capture bad guys, that was what he craved when he went to Quantico as a cadet, after having spent two years getting into physical shape. That was when he met Joe— dedicated, no-nonsense Joe. Samuel wished he had known the man better, maybe even have convinced him to leave the shooting range and join him for a beer, but he never did.

Samuel locked eyes with Director Singuar, who looked at his disheveled tie with a disapproving glare, forcing him to tug at it in an effort to straighten it. He detested being in the public spotlight, but could not refuse a direct order to be there. Samuel's phone buzzed. Taking a quick peek at the screen, a friend of his in the bureau, who also owed him a huge favor, had broken into the classified files and sent him the video feed of the Smithsonian when the crystal had been taken. Samuel stepped away from those crowding the entrance to the stage, awaiting the press conference to begin, and played the video. He watched, forgetting where he was, as Stein appeared in the museum, dragging a woman (Brie's mother) and yelling and waving a laser pistol, but that wasn't what wrenched his heart. As he watched Brie run for her mother, and Joe hold her back, dragging her away, despite her punching him in the face in response, Samuel wished he could have done something. Joe had warned him that Stein was a man who could not be appeased, and he held the proof in his hands.

"Samuel," Director Singuar said, waving him in the direction of the press conference.

He watched the video of Brie struggling to get to her mother again, his heart aching for her. What if it was his mother being held hostage? She hadn't asked for this, none of them had, and Samuel wondered, what if Rynah wasn't the villain in all this? He needed to talk to Joe, but how would he get a message to him?

"Samuel!" hissed Director Singuar.

Samuel put away his phone, thoughts roiling through his unsettled mind, and walked out onto the stage amidst the flashing lights and clicks from the cameras. His hands fumbled with a button that had worked its way loose on his suit jacket as he tried to maintain a stoic face, despite his desire to blink from all the lights. Hushed silence filled the room as the President walked in, and Samuel found himself turning in the President's direction, like the others in the room, watching as the man took his place at the podium in front of the microphones placed there.

"Good evening," said the President. "I want to thank all of you for coming. I have convened you all here to address the recent situation of the extraterrestrial being who calls himself Stein and the ones he claims to be searching for. We have already witnessed the demonstrations of his technological advances over ours, and the lengths that he is willing to go to, to get what he wants.

"I want to be very clear that this Rynah is not a friend to the people of the United States, or those of Earth. She is a fugitive, and those who are with her are also fugitives. Because of the devastation her being here has brought to our planet, Director Singuar and I have agreed that it is best to issue a shoot on sight order. She, and those who are assisting her, will be apprehended and handed over to this Stein."

"Mr. President," shouted one reporter, "some of those with her are American citizens. Doesn't arresting them without charge and handing them over to this alien violate their habeas corpus rights?"

"They are... uh... hardly being arrested without charge. These terrorists have shown no restraint for the law and have chosen to involve themselves in this intergalactic dispute, thus giving up their right to habeas corpus."

"But, Mr. President," continued the same reporter, but the President interrupted her.

"This Rynah is a terrorist, and she, and those with her, are responsible for much of the destruction that has occurred on the planet Earth. There is only one course of action and that is to give this Stein what he wants so that he will leave."

"Mr. President," said another reporter, "doesn't giving in to the demands of this Stein encourage others like him to come here and exploit us? We know now that we are not alone in this universe. Shouldn't we stand up to him?"

"And what of the people this Rynah is responsible for killing? Should she and her accomplices not be apprehended? Let me be clear, the United States has a zero tolerance policy towards terrorism."

"But, Mr. President," another reported chimed in, "there are reports that a member of the FBI is with them."

"It is unfortunate… uh… that one of our own has chosen to join this terrorist known as Rynah, but…"

"How do you know she is a terrorist?" challenged the reporter. "There are reports, eyewitness accounts, and videos on the internet showing that she and her companions have helped people. It looks more like they are being hunted by this Stein. Shouldn't we offer them sanctuary?"

"Let me be clear. They are terrorists. They… uh… uh… broke into an FBI facility and endangered the lives of innocent civilians. Uh… Uh…"

"How do you plan to apprehend them?" interrupted a different reporter. "So far, they have managed to evade law enforcement."

"I will allow the director of the Federal Bureau of Investigation to answer that," replied the President, giving the stage to Director Singuar.

The director of the FBI stepped forward, trying to tame the few strands of gray hair that did little to cover his balding head. "In a joint task force with the U.S. Marshall's service, the FBI has put measures in place to capture these terrorists and bring them to justice. We have…"

Samuel listened to Director Singuar continue speaking, describing how he planned to capture Rynah and her companions and hand them over to Stein. *Did they not watch the video?* he wondered to himself, unable to rid his mind of Brie's anguished face as she watched Stein threaten to murder her mother before her. A female reporter pulled him from his thoughts.

"There is a rumor that a 16-year-old girl is with them. Is she also subject to this new shoot on sight order?"

Samuel stepped forward, knowing that it was against protocol and he would be punished for it in the end, and interrupted Director Singuar.

"No," he said, his voice firm. "Though this Rynah and Stein may be locked in some sort of dispute, we know that the girl was kidnapped on her way home from school several months ago. It is our belief that these beings are the ones who kidnapped her. Though we are committed to ensuring the safety of the people of the United States, we are also committed to seeing to it that she is returned safely to her family. It is my belief that that is why the agent you spoke of earlier joined them, to ensure her safe return."

"So are you saying that the rumored FBI agent that is with them was sent there undercover?" asked a reporter.

"Yes," replied Samuel, "though he has not been in contact with us for several days and we fear that they may have discovered him."

Samuel glanced from the President and Director Singuar, knowing by their enraged expressions that he would pay for what he had just done, for rescinding their orders on national television.

"Of course," Director Singuar broke in, trying to save face, "we believe that the girl named Brie Reynolds is innocent in all of this and our goal has always been to return her home safely. She is merely a victim between the dispute that this Rynah and Stein have. Our committed Agent Samuel Anders is dedicated to finding her, as I was about to explain."

Samuel backed away, ignoring the reproachful glares of the other agents around him, while Director Singuar continued taking questions before returning the podium to the President. Once the conference had ended, Director Singuar motioned for Samuel to follow him to a somewhat secluded area.

"What was that?" he demanded.

"It didn't seem right to paint them all as terrorists," replied Samuel.

"You are not paid to determine what is right and what isn't. Your commander in chief made an announcement and you are expected to follow it."

"She is just a teenager," said Samuel, "and according to the one piece of video footage from the Smithsonian heist, it is obvious that she is acting under duress."

"That video was deemed classified," Director Singuar said. "How did you get access to it?"

Samuel kept his mouth shut. He did not wish to get his buddy within the bureau into trouble.

"Very well. I am assigning you a desk job and don't think that will be the end of it. The President doesn't appreciate being embarrassed on national TV," scolded Director Singuar. "There have been reports of unusual activity in the New Mexico area," he said more to himself than to Samuel. "I suppose…"

"Let me go," said Samuel, determined to do what he could to help Joe and Brie and detesting the new shoot on sight directive. Joe's words about things not being what they seemed ebbed at him, compelling him to disobey the director of the FBI if necessary. "After the stunt I just pulled, I know you want to be rid of me. Let me go down there."

"Fine," spat Director Singuar, "but keep me informed at every turn, and no more shenanigans. And don't think I won't be watching your every move."

"Yes, sir."

"Where will you look?" the director asked as an afterthought.

"There is a comic con convention in Albuquerque. I thought I would go there first."

"Albuquerque?"

"If there was ever a place where a being from another planet would try to hide, it's there."

"Are you certain?"

"It's where I would go," said Samuel. *And Joe*, he thought to himself.

Director Singuar eyed Samuel for a moment. "You leave on the next flight out," he said, before leaving. "And even if you do rescue the girl, don't bother returning here."

Samuel pulled out his phone with the security footage of the Smithsonian heist. He didn't trust Director Singuar—the man was ambitious to a fault, willing to do anything to move up—nor did he trust the President, who, like all politicians, just cared about the next election. Knowing that he would be arrested when they found out, Samuel uploaded the footage to the internet, spreading it across all of the social media platforms with the #alienwars before it, since that was what was trending on Twitter.

He shoved his phone back in his pants pocket and left, never knowing that within two hours, his video garnered over 30 million views and had the entire social media-verse talking about it. He just hoped that Joe received his message.

Chapter 11
A Lanyran on Earth

Obiah steered the car into the overflowing parking lot of never-be-fore-seen people, bearing marks and insignias that meant they belonged anywhere but on Earth. Glittering capes flickered in the breeze, reflecting the yellow sunlight and making their wearers appear almost godlike, a stark contrast to the mundane appearance of most humans he had seen. Their pointed and curve-toed shoes reminded others of the little elves in the story about the shoemaker.

Obiah slammed the brakes. Three people had stepped off the sidewalk, oblivious of the car approaching them, and crossed the street in front of him, desperate to make the first presentation, which was about how aliens had visited the earth before; their gray painted faces pointed straight ahead. As he eased the car through the mass of convention attendees, Obiah remarked at a mother and father, their skin painted blue with long braids that trailed behind, pushing a stroller that had been made to look like a flying saucer, with little planets bobbing up and down as they hung from the bottom.

Klanor yawned and stretched his arms and legs; he hadn't

looked outside the window, as he had just woken from his nap in the backseat.

"We should find a way to disguise ourselves."

"We might not need to," replied Obiah.

For the first time, Klanor noticed the gaudy costumes of those rushing to get inside the hotel. He glanced at Rynah, whose eyes remained fixed on the people who passed them by, some of whom had painted their faces purple and wore outfits similar to her security uniform. Obiah maneuvered the car to an empty space at the far end of the parking lot. They jumped out and left the keys on the driver's seat, since they planned to find a new means of transportation once they found the others.

"Where should we start looking?" asked Obiah.

"Inside," said Rynah, following the crowd.

Falling in line with the mass of shimmering outfits, armed with plastic weapons of a supposed futuristic era, they shuffled across the striped pavement to the open double doors of the hotel, unaware that their friends had already arrived.

* * *

In another part of the convention center, a beat-up vehicle pulled into a packed parking lot, overflowing with enthusiastic fans who were dressed as beings from other worlds. Solaris gawked at them, amazed at the imagination and creativity that went into their costumes and curious as to what made the people of Earth act this way. Nowhere on Lanyr, or any of the other Twelve Sectors, did people participate in such activities.

Her companions in the car jumped up and down with excitement, thrilled at being there among others like them. Solaris shook her head, not understanding their enthusiasm, but decided that it must be a cultural thing. She notice a set of doors where attendees filed through.

"Man, this is awesome!" said the man in the passenger seat, almost exploding from an overabundance of excitement. "Isn't this great?"

No answer.

The man turned around and dropped his mouth open at finding the backseat empty. Solaris had gone, changing her appearance as she disappeared among the crowd, determined to find her friends.

* * *

Joe and the others meandered through the overflowing lobby and banquet rooms of the hotel; every inch had been taken over for the science fiction convention. Overwhelmed hotel staff scurried to keep up with the demand for clean rooms, food, well- stocked re-strooms, securing amenities for the demanding guests. Every room had been checked out to extra-terrestrials, warring clans, explorers for some mythical organization—which mirrored those seen on popular television shows—and celestial beings, who were just nor-mal people that had painted their bodies in silver glitter.

"Are there monsters in this realm?" asked Alfric as both he and Solon turned circles while moseying through the crowded lobby.

"No," answered Brie, though she wondered if perhaps Alfric had been correct in referring to the people and their gaudy outfits as monsters.

"I challenge you to a duel!"

A man of Alfric's height stepped in front of them, holding out a bottle of hot sauce. Streamers swung from his orange painted hair, which formed spikes down the center of his head, matching the leather straps wrapped around his waxed chest, while flexing his muscles with pride, before melding into his shiny black pants.

Alfric started to pull out his sword, but Brie's hand stopped him.

"He means the bottle of hot sauce."

The man unscrewed the lid and held it out to Alfric; his orange lips formed a mischievous smile.

Solon took the bottle and sniffed it, his eyes watering the moment he had.

"My mother buys many spices from the market, but nothing as potent as this," he said, handing the bottle back to the man.

"Let's go," Joe urged them onward.

"Ha-ha! I told you he wouldn't do it," the man laughed with his friends. "The coward."

Alfric stopped in his tracks. He turned around. With long, quick strides, he crossed back to the man with the spiked orange hair, snatched the bottle of hot sauce from his hands, stuck it in his mouth, and drank it in three gulps. He held the empty bottle out to the man; his stoic face unnerved the man and his friends.

"Um," said the man, "you didn't have to, you know."

Alfric snatched another bottle of hot sauce from the table.

"Drink."

"Wha—wha—what?" stammered the man.

"A duel involves two people," said Alfric. "Drink."

The man stared at Alfric's unreadable face, unsure of how to respond, amazed that the Viking showed no adverse effects of having chugged the hot sauce, and unaware that Alfric's mouth burned from the liquid, but he had learned to control his reactions, making himself unreadable.

"Drink, or I shall sever your head from your body." Alfric pulled back the edges of his fur cloak, showing the man the hilt of his sword, his most prized possession.

With trepidation, the man took the bottle in Alfric's hands, his orange spikes quivering, unscrewed the lid, and took a mouthful. Alfric's unwavering eyes watched as the man tried to meet his steel gaze, but the spices of the hot sauce proved too much and he ran away to the water fountains, his friends close behind.

"He should drink milk," commented Fons as he pulled a jalapeno pepper from his pocket—and why he kept a jalapeno pepper in his pocket was anyone's guess—smothered it in the hot sauce that the man had abandoned, and shoved it in his mouth.

The others gaped at him, except Joe, who was used to Fons' eccentricities.

"What?" said Fons. "I'm hungry." He continued chewing on his snack, smacking his lips, much to the annoyance of the others, while licking the juices off his fingers.

"I see no signs of the others," said Joe.

Brie looked around for Rynah and the others, a part of her even hoped that Solaris would appear, but she found no sign of either of them, not that she had expected to.

"Halt!" said two men dressed in body armor and pointing what appeared to be advanced technology weaponry, but were really just spray-painted plastic tubes and cardboard held together with duct tape. "We said freeze, or you will witness the might of the Organgian Empire."

Having no patience for fools or games, Alfric ripped out his sword and sliced its blade through the two newcomers' weapons, leaving only the flimsy handles in their hands. The two young men's eyes widened in shock before hurrying away.

"Nice way to make friends there, big guy," said Tom, clapping Alfric on the back.

"What is this Organgian Empire?" asked Solon. "Have we insulted them?"

"I wouldn't worry about it," said Brie.

"I'm starting to think that we are the only ones here," said Joe.

No one said anything.

Joe shook his head in disappointment. "I guess we're still on our own?"

"Not completely," said a woman behind them as her blonde hair and golden-tanned skinned transformed into the familiar lilac-colored face and emerald hair of Solaris.

"Solaris!" Brie hugged her.

"I'm sorry," said Solaris. "I should never have left you all like that."

"What happened to you?" asked Brie.

"Later," said Solaris.

"We should find this Lanyran," said Alfric, "before others do."

Solaris held out a brochure with a list of the convention's events. "I think I have."

Tom took the brochure and flipped it open. "Hey! They got some guy in here discussing how reverse polarity of magnets can create frictional force, thus causing objects to move on their own. I remember him. I read his dissertation about the property of magnets and their relationship with the polarity of the earth. It's what I based my engine on. I need to meet with him."

Solon grabbed Tom's shoulder. "That might not be wise."

"The soothsayer is right," said Alfric.

Dejected, Tom hung his head, but conceded Solon's point, containing his desire to meet with the man who had inspired him to create his fuel-less engine.

Joe took the brochure and perused the list of events.

Abductees Anonymous. Share Your Experiences and Meet Others Who Have Been Visited by Aliens.

The Not-So-Happy-Cow. Mutilations and How Extraterrestrials Have Been Studying Us for Years.

Holo-that! The Future of Holographic Technology.

Otherworld Cooking. Learn the Art of Cuisine from Off-World Visitors.

Monuments of Origin. Famous Sites in the United States and their Extraterrestrial Origin, Including the Grand Canyon, the state of Montana, and Monument Valley.

"Oh, yeah, I can see that we are definitely in the right place," Joe said.

"The state of Montana?" scoffed Tom, his incredulous voice mirroring what the others thought. "Are these people serious?"

"Do you really need to ask that?" said Joe as he pointed at the extravagant attire of those ambling around the main floor of the hotel.

Solaris released an exasperated sigh and snatched the brochure from Joe's hands, ripped it open, and pointed out a particular presentation by a man named Achilles Satawer.

Joe took it. "Micro Wormhole Transportation. The Future of Space Travel. Presented by Doctor of Astrophysics Achilles Satawer." Joe studied the photographs included of the professor and noticed how his eyes and facial features resembled Rynah's and Klanor's and his skin seemed to have a purple undertone, despite cosmetic surgery to cover it up, something he only noticed because of the time he had spent with Rynah and the others.

"Are you sure he's the one?"

"I conducted a quick research about the man, using this building's internet connection, and there was an article about this man dated ten years ago. He tried to build a deep space vessel, having contracted with a private corporation. This all happened after he had submitted inquiry after inquiry to NASA, insisting that they quit, 'dilly-dallying around with childish experiments on the international space station and focus on exploring neighboring galaxies' and even offered to assist them, but they refused his services. Also, the information found on him matches what Fons looked up for us."

"What happened to the ship?" asked Brie.

"The corporation went under after the crash of 2008 and funding for the project dried up, thus forcing him to find a new line of work," replied Solaris.

"So he comes to nuthouse central?" said Joe.

A quizzical look crossed Solon's face as he said, "I do not see any food items resembling nuts of any kind. Just people in unusual attire."

"It's an expression," Tom whispered to the young philosopher, while Alfric huffed through his crooked nose, his knuckles whitening as he gripped his sword.

"If you wished to find someone who could help you get off this planet, where would you go?" Solaris challenged Joe.

"I would go to a place where people would be more accepting of the concept of deep space travel," replied Joe. "His presentation begins in a few minutes."

"Which is why we should go there now," said Solaris, "but we mustn't make a scene."

They hurried to the meeting room where the lecture on Micro Wormhole Transportation was to be held, unaware that Rynah, Klanor, and Obiah were already there.

"Achilles," Solon muttered to himself as he thought about the name of the man they wished to see, "a man whose anger almost destroyed his people."

* * *

The rapt attention of those within the lecture hall encouraged Achilles to continue talking as he explained the intricacies of wormholes and how they formed and created holes through space and time that allowed one to travel from one place to another in an instant, without aging, or fast-forwarding through time, as many prominent scientists had theorized.

His hands swept over the charts and graphs projected on the screen behind him, which was actually a holoscreen that he had created, making certain that it mimicked the technology of Earth, but kept to himself.

"Many think of wormholes as these massive, swirling whirlpools in space the size of stars or galaxies, but that is not always the case," he said.

Achilles stopped. Staring up at him, from among the crowd, was a purple face, framed by long strands of silky, emerald hair, but not one that looked to have been painted with makeup, but one whose skin was naturally that pigmentation, and those violet eyes that bore through him, as though they knew his secrets. He turned back to his graphs.

"Wormholes can be any size and are everywhere. All around us are micro-wormholes. They can range from the size of a nail to the size of a ball, but are so short-lived that we never notice them."

"But if that is the case, then how come no one has disappeared from them?" asked a boy in the crowd, wearing an *X-Files* t-shirt, faded from years of washing.

"Because they are not powerful enough to suck you through. These micro-wormholes dissipate at an exponential rate, meaning that they are gone before they ever had the chance to affect anything nearby them. They..."

Another purple face stared back at him, with an expression, saying that the individual already knew the science behind micro-wormholes and wondered why Achilles explained it in such a jejune manner.

"They are harmless," continued Achilles. "In fact, there are hundreds of them in this room."

He spotted a third purple face, similar to the previous two. Wondering if his mind played tricks on him, he looked back to where he had seen the other two, but they had gone.

"So?" said a woman in response to his last statement.

"Micro-wormholes are what make teleportation possible."

"Like *Star Trek*?"

"No," Achilles retorted, shaking his head. "It is physically impossible to dematerialize a living being, like a human, and then rematerialize them somewhere else without destroying their atomic and cellular makeup. But, with micro-wormholes, it is possible to tap into one and send an object or person through, possibly traveling hundreds of thousands of miles in a nanosecond. Think of the possibilities! By using a hole in space already in existence, we can go anywhere in the universe. Space travel, as we know it, will change."

"So is that how the aliens abduct people?" asked one in the crowd.

"Aliens do not go around abducting people," spat Achilles, annoyed that the attendees of his lecture seemed more interested in multiplications, abductions, and contests over who had the worst costume than learning factual science. He noticed another purple face staring up at him from the front row, similar to the others.

"How do you know?" challenged someone in the crowd.

"Because it's preposterous to think that you are so important to a civilization, which has thrived for thousands of years in another part of the universe, that they would take the time to do tests on you to learn more about your insignificant existence!" huffed Achilles, growing tired of the incessant questions that had nothing to do with what he tried to teach them.

"BOO!" yelled those within the crowd, while a few threw hard candy, popcorn, and open cans of soda at him.

Insulted, Achilles shut off his computer, slamming the monitor closed and stuffing it into its case, struggling to zip it close.

"If you all wish to know more about the nonexistent alien abductions, or how aliens have influenced human history, I suggest you go next door where Professor Xenius Darthford is delivering his presentation on Aliens and the Ancient World, or visit that Abductions Anonymous group, you ingrates!"

More angry shouts filled the room as wrappers, glow sticks, and half-eaten containers of fries sailed through the air, littering the stage and coating Achilles' clothes. He gathered his papers and laptop into his arms and hurried off the stage away from the jeering crowd, but paused near the exit when he noticed the same purple faces watching him. Shaking the saliva coated fries from his shirt, he fled from the room and bumped into a teenage girl with mousy brown hair.

"Pardon me," he quipped.

Achilles paused. He had seen her face before. *Wasn't she that missing girl?* he thought to himself, turning around and glancing back at where he had run into her. Ignoring the improbability of it, and wondering why she seemed to be tugging at her ear, he continued to race out of the room as loose leafs of paper trailed behind him, mimicking leaves in the wind.

"Excuse me," said a man with a deep voice, stopping him just as he exited the room.

"Yes, what is it?" snapped Achilles.

"Are you Achilles Satawer?" asked the man.

"Look," said Achilles, "if it's about those parking tickets, I paid them and the fine. Now if you'll excuse me…"

"I'm not here about parking tickets." the man held up an FBI badge. "I am agent Joseph Harkensen and I need to speak with you about an urgent matter. Is there someplace we can talk in private?"

Achilles looked behind Joe at one of the purple-faced people he had seen in the lecture room. Joe remained unaware of the stranger's presence, but his eyes did flicker in Alfric's direction as the Viking attempted to sneak up on Achilles from behind.

Sensing danger, Achilles threw his armful of papers in Joe's face, forcing him to step back, and darted off, his feet pounding the carpeted hallway as he headed for the lobby overflowing with people pretending to be from another place and time. He shoved his way through the crowd, with Joe and Alfric behind him. Achilles stopped. Up ahead was one of the purple-faced strangers. Turning, he ran to the left, delving deeper into the crowd. Another of the strangers blocked his path. Circling in place, he looked around, desperate for a place to escape to. His pursuers neared. Achilles dove to the right, landing on his hands and knees and crawled away, allowing the meandering feet of the convention attendees to conceal him, and snickering when shouts of surprise, as those who tried to catch him ran into each other, reached his ears.

"Joe!"

"Rynah! What are you doing here?"

"Same as you. Where is he?"

A whistle caught both of their attention as Tom waved them over, pointing at another hallway. Rynah and Joe pushed their way through the throng of people, garnering glares and insults as they did. Two security guards saw them. They jumped out at them, but Rynah ducked just as one yanked out his pepper spray, dodging its blast, and dropped to the floor, sweeping his feet out from under him. While the security guard tried to regain his senses, she wrenched the pepper spray from him and sprayed the other with its stinging mist.

"That way," said Tom, when Rynah and Joe reached him.

They followed where he pointed and ran into Obiah and Klanor. With no time for pleasantries, they all rushed down the hallway past rooms, and an irate maid who had to pick up the cleaning supply cart they had knocked over. Achilles puffed as he ran down the hall, turning another corner, and another, wishing that he was in better physical shape for this amount of running. He stopped. Alfric had somehow outmaneuvered him and blocked his path. Whirling around, he raced back the way he came, turning another corner and heading back into the crowd.

Arms wrapped around his waist as Solon tackled him. Rolling across the floor, Achilles kicked and flailed his arms in an attempt to break free of Solon's grasp, as people shrieked and hurried away from them to avoid getting involved. Solon wrestled Achilles' arms behind him with a strength he hadn't known he possessed, but had achieved due to Alfric's training.

Not willing to allow himself to be captured, Achilles head-butted Solon, stunning the young man, and scrambled free of his clutches, pulling a tendon as he did so.

Achilles jumped to his feet. Those after him closed in on all sides. Unwilling to find out who they were, or why they wanted him, Achilles bolted, ramming through the crowd and not caring who he shoved out of his way. Breaking free of the overcrowded lobby once again, he raced down a short corridor to where the lounge area was.

He spotted a security guard. Though he had little faith in security guards, as most people did, Achilles chanced it, knowing that the long-haired woman was his only hope for getting free of this chase.

"Excuse me," he said, out of breath, "there are some people chasing me. One even pretended to be an FBI agent."

"Show me," said the female security guard.

Achilles pointed to where he had just escaped from.

"Come with me." The female security guard grasped his upper arm and pulled him away.

Achilles allowed himself to be led away until he realized that something was wrong. He tried to pull away. The woman's iron grip remained firm, squeezing tighter with each tug.

"Hey, what are you—let me go!"

As Achilles yanked even more, the woman's appearance changed from that of a blonde to someone with lilac-purple skin, emerald-colored hair, and violet eyes, similar to one of the strangers he had spotted during his lecture. She dragged him to a secluded area, where the others waited.

Achilles stared at Solaris as though he had seen her before, though long ago, but she pretended not to notice his gaping look.

"Solaris!"

Solaris stopped, jerking Achilles to a halt.

"Rynah?"

Before anyone could rejoice in their reunion, Fons ran up to them. "Our little display has garnered some notice. We need to get somewhere private, and pronto."

"Do you have accommodations in this place?" demanded Alfric of Achilles.

"Who are you people and what do you want?" insisted Achilles.

"We need your help," said Rynah, "and we need it fast before more security shows up."

"I'm not helping anyone!" Achilles squirmed, but Solaris' grip tightened to the point where it bruised his skin.

"Please," Brie stepped forward, "I know you've seen the news and that man who has threatened us all. He has my mother and my sister. I just want to see them again, and right now, you are the only one who can help us."

Achilles ceased his struggling as he looked into Brie's tear-filled eyes, though she made a good attempt at holding them back, and the honesty within them.

He glanced back at Solaris and recognized the look within her face. "You're not here to lock me up in some facility for research?"

"No," said Brie.

"I have a room near the top floor, a suite. We can go there. And for goodness sake, let go of my arm!"

Solaris released him, but remained prepared to seize him again if he tried to escape.

"The elevators are over here."

They followed Achilles to the gold-plated doors of the elevator, which acted like mirrors, reflecting the people who moseyed around the hotel, oblivious to their movements. Once inside the elevator, Alfric and Solon looked all around, mesmerized by the doors that opened on their own as they rose upward to the floors above, and the glass walls that allowed them to watch the crowd of people.

"Extraordinary," breathed Solon.

"You've been to the edges of space and different planets and you think this is fantastic?" joked Tom.

"One should always appreciate the wonders of the universe, whether made by the gods or man," replied Solon.

Tom smiled at another one of Solon's bits of wisdom.

The doors dinged before opening, allowing them to step out into another hallway, with velvet carpet of a rich yellow, decorated with red and green geometrical patterns that draped across it. Achilles led them to a door with gold numbers on the top and opened it with his keycard, leading them to a room with floor-to-ceiling windows that looked out at the city below and a set of French doors which opened onto a terrace.

Each twirled around, awed by the holoscreens that filled the walls and the holokeyboards that popped up as he walked past, making them feel as though they had stepped into another world, and another time. Achilles had created his own portable holocomputers, as best he could with the material made available to him, and he set them up wherever he went.

"Welcome to my secret world," said Achilles, holding his arms out wide. "It took me many years to build this and some things are still outmoded. Your world is very lacking in technological achievement."

"I wouldn't say that," said Brie.

"Please," laughed Achilles, "when I first arrived here, you guys had just developed color graphics for computers and thought that the eight-track tape was amazing. And talk about clunky systems with zero memory! At least now you have discovered the terabyte, but you are still a long way off from any advanced systems."

A sudden crash surrounded them as one of Achilles' holomonitors smashed into the floral carpet, followed by books, notepads, computer hardware, and a forgotten bowl of tomato soup, creating a domino effect. In its center stood Tom, hunching his shoulders and doing his best to look innocent.

"What in the…" began Achilles. "That was months' worth of work you—what were you thinking?"

"Well," Tom shifted his feet as he braced himself for the others' ire. They glared at him with their arms crossed, except for Brie and Solon, who both covered their mouths in an attempt to not laugh. "There was this… um… glowing thing, and it had these weird symbols on it and… what's that?"

Tom had spotted a glowing, orange orb.

"Don't!" yelled Achilles.

Captivated by it, and what it might lead to, Tom reached out, but before he could press it, Rynah's seized his wrist and yanked him away, breaking the spell.

"What is that?" asked Tom as Achilles snatched the object Tom had been about to touch.

"Nothing," said Achilles, hugging the egg-shaped item.

"My preliminary scans indicate that you are holding a device that could help one fly," said Solaris, studying the object.

"What are you," said Achilles, "a walking computer?"

"Well, yes," said Solaris, as though he should have known what she was.

"Really?" Achilles set the item aside and approached Solaris, his fingertips touching his scruffy chin as he looked her up and down. "Remarkable construction. Who made you?"

"I did," said Tom. "I mean, I made her… vessel."

"No, seriously," said Achilles, "who made you?"

"Marlow created my consciousness, but Tom is the reason that I can walk and interact with all of you," replied Solaris in a dry tone, not liking the way Achilles dismissed Tom's achievement.

"The blacksmith did well in providing Solaris with a means of leaving her prison," said Alfric.

"Did you just give me a compliment?" said Tom. "See I knew we would become friends." He jabbed Alfric in the arm with his fist in a playful manner.

"You live here?" asked Klanor.

"Not in this hotel," said Achilles. "I'm only here for the convention."

"How long have you been here?" asked Tom. "On Earth, I mean."

"Too long," said Achilles. "I came here in your year of 1980 A.D. Such rudimentary technology. I was surprised that you had developed plastic surgery, but good thing you had. It took 10 surgeries to make my skin of the proper pigmentation so people would quit staring at me, though if you look closely, you can still make out a little of the original undertone. And thank goodness for hair dye. Thirty years, I have lived in this place. I don't think I'll ever get used to it."

"It is our home," said Brie.

"Yes," replied Achilles, "but I miss mine, and I shall never see it again, or the loved ones I left behind."

"Were you named for the great hero, Achilles?" asked Solon.

"My dear boy, I am him, or whom the legend is based on. You are from Ancient Greece?" Achilles eyed Solon, noting the olive-colored skin and manner of speech.

"Yes," replied Solon.

"Do your people not tell stories about a civilization that lived long before yours?"

"We do. There are tales of an ancient island that was swallowed by the sea. They had technologies far beyond our comprehension, the like of which we'd never see again. Their demise began when the gods descended from the heavens and visited them."

"Well, you have the gist of it, I suppose," said Achilles. "The first ancient myths, I guess you could call them that, come from what you call ancient civilizations, and they have been told and retold over millenia. Your myths refer to a civilization that has been forgotten by your modern one. I was Achilai then; through the various retellings and translations, my name got changed to Achilles, and the character had developed anger management issues and was present at the battle of Troy, which, by the way, did not exist when I first arrived to this planet."

"You have your own ancient myths?" asked Brie and Tom of Solon, amazed by such a thought.

"Yes," said Solon.

"Of course they did," interrupted Achilles, "but so much gets lost by time. Too much."

Growing impatient, Rynah cleared her throat. "Why don't you start your story at the beginning."

"Well, my dear, that was a very long time ago," said Achilles, pulling up a chair and taking a glance at Solaris, wondering why she looked familiar. "I was born in what you would consider the age before ages, roughly 300,000 years ago. Lanyr was quite advanced, more advanced than anything. We had achieved a way of telepathic communication and built our machines to accommodate that. But we also wished to explore. Me, most of all. I joined the research institute which funded space explorations. We had already mapped out the different systems and planets and had explored all of them, except one: 13.

"It was far away and the most mysterious. We knew of your planet's extreme weather conditions. Indeed, we had seen no other planet that housed deserts, frozen wastelands, jungles, great plains, or such vast oceans all in one sphere. One minute it can be pleasantly warm, and the next, bitterly cold. We believed that there could be no life here, but the council wished to be sure, wanting to make peace with all races of intelligence and technological advancement. So, a ship had been chartered to visit the Thirteenth Sector. Being a research scientist, I was asked to go and gladly accepted.

"When we arrived here, at what is now called Earth, we were amazed by what we found. We discovered a very advanced civilization, much like ourselves, except that they had only just begun space flight, centered near the equator in what you now call the Pacific Ocean. Well, I say just begun, but they had managed to reach your red planet. They called themselves Mulyra, which has since been shortened by your historians to Mu, or referred to as Lemuria. They flew on ships that reacted to their thoughts, much like us, and had power technology that did not rely on electricity, but was far more advanced and safer to use, powering their homes and vehicles. But besides their advancements, they were also very spiritual.

"We landed our ship and were welcomed. They were pleased to meet another race from the stars and eager to form a treaty and trade agreements.

"But they possessed something we had never imagined and would never fathom possible: six crystals of power, but not the sort of power you might be thinking of. These crystals were ancient, even to them, and their origin unknown. The Mulyrans referred to the crystals as the Javan, and their leader, trained since childhood and whom adopted the name Java upon accepting his station, thus abandoning his old self, was the crystals' protector. The Mulyrans and the crystals had a sort of symbiotic relationship, though more complicated than that. The Java explained that the crystals were alive. They speak to you—to your mind, or telepathically, if you will. What is in your heart, they reciprocate. It's as though they know who you are before you even know it yourself."

"So, what happened?" asked Tom.

"Matyr, the leader of the expedition, became enamored by the crystals, seeing only their potential as a military weapon, as a way to garner power. Sensing the darkness within his heart, Herclai devised a plan to prevent Matyr from stealing the crystals from the Mulyrans. We helped him—Isyr, Hermyra, Osyr, and I—but Matyr was not fooled by our acts of disloyalty and he tried us for sedition, sentencing us to exile. Matyr was confident that the extreme weather patterns on this planet would be the death of us.

"After his sentencing, the greed deep within his heart came out that day. While we were being escorted to the edge of the city, Matyr arranged a meeting with the Java—though Herclai managed to slip away—saying that he wished to learn more about their spiritual enlightenment, and before Herclai could intervene, murdered him. He then took the crystals, snatching them from their place of rest. Herclai tried to stop him. In the struggle, the crystals broke apart and two of them fragmented, turning six pieces into nine.

"Because of the telepathic link, the crystals fed off Matyr's greed and fueled it. Matyr became a madman and wanted to destroy the Mulyrans, slaughter them. But before he could wage his war against them, the cohesiveness of the planet fell apart, due to the breaking apart of the crystals."

"How?" asked Joe.

"It's difficult to explain," replied Achilles, "but at the time, the crystals had a direct effect on the planet, and their breaking apart started a chain reaction which destroyed the Mulyran civilization and almost the entire planet."

"I don't get how all of that is possible," said Tom.

"Think about it," said Achilles. "Many of your ancient myths speak of a great flood that almost destroyed all of humanity: the Sumerian myths, the Babylonian story of Gilgamesh, the Hebrew Bible, the Masai of East Africa, the Egyptian Book of the Dead, the Cree, the Chinese classic the Hihking, Plato's story of Atlantis, the Aztecs, the Ojibwe natives from what you now call Minnesota. There is even the Legend of the Nu'u from precolonial Hawaii. All of them refer to a cataclysmic event, a flood that almost wiped out humanity and all of creation to eradicate the evil that had taken hold in the world. It is all rooted here, in what happened at Mulyra, in what Matyr did."

"Can we get back to what happened to the crystals?" said Rynah, growing impatient.

Achilles sighed, annoyed at her querulousness, but continued his story.

"While distracted by his lust for the crystals, Herclai seized his chance and attacked Matyr, and wrenched the crystals from his grasp. During their struggle, one fell into the ocean and was lost, but the other eight remained with Herclai. He went back for the others, especially Isyr, who was his wife. Because of the chaos that surrounded us, those guarding us fled. Herclai found us, and together, we raced for our ship, desperate to get away, but Hermyra and Osyr were not as lucky. I'll always remember their faces as they died.

"The ground shook as it swallowed not only the buildings, but Matyr and his followers as well. Great waves sprang from the ocean and washed away the devastation that he had brought. We ran for a ship and had almost reached it when the ground split open and a wall of molten rock shot from it. Isyr and I were on one side, while Herclai was on the other. Isyr told him to go. And while the world fell away beneath us, a vortex opened and sucked me in. Soon after,

I found myself in a strange world. I later learned that I was still on the same planet, but that I had been catapulted forward by 300,000 years, roughly.

"I had to create an identity for myself and change my appearance so that I would blend in. For the last 35 years, I have wondered if the others lived or died that day. Since you are all here, I can only surmise that Herclai managed to escape with the remaining eight crystals. It's unfortunate that I shall never learn what happened to the others."

"I do not believe so," said Solaris. "The ancient tale speaks of four heroes with exiles' blood." Her eyes roamed over Brie, Alfric, Tom, and Solon.

"What are you implying?" asked Tom.

"That the others survived the destruction of the city," said Solaris.

"I don't see how," answered Achilles, "but, yes, it is possible. Evidently, someone survived it, because the legends about it still exist, even if they have changed over the millennia. So it's possible..." Achilles stopped speaking. "No! It can't be! She couldn't have been."

"What?" demanded Tom, his impatience showing.

Instead of replying, Achilles grabbed what looked like a pen and poked Tom with it, drawing a speck of his blood before sticking the pen in his holocomputer and tapping the screen.

"This is preposterous," he said as the results appeared in front of him.

"What is impossible?" Tom demanded again, rubbing the spot where Achilles had poked him.

Achilles turned and looked at him. "You have Lanyran blood in you. It's very minute, but it is there." He grabbed three more devices like the one he used on Tom. "May I?" he asked the others.

Brie, Solon, and Alfric allowed him to take a sample of their blood and put it in the computer for analysis.

"I can't believe it," said Achilles as the results popped up on the holoscreen. "You all have traces of Lanyran blood in you."

"How is that possible?" asked Rynah.

"I think I know," said Achilles. "Your people have theories as to how your race evolved. When we landed here, the Mulyra spoke of a primitive race that lived in remote regions of the planet, which they had set up as conservatories, in what is now the continent of Africa, and had become popular tourist attractions for the Mulyra, I might add. Those regions match up with where your scientists believe the human race evolved from."

"So human beings came from a zoo?" Tom said with sarcasm.

"If there were survivors," continued Achilles, ignoring Tom's mocking, "chances are, they would have gone to those conservatories, knowing that they could find food and shelter there. They might have intermixed with the very primitives they had looked down upon, thus giving rise to what you call the human race. If Isyr and the others survived, they may have done the same thing. After all this time, their genes would have been diluted, but you four have traces of it."

"Test Rynah," said Solaris.

"Well, obviously she has Lanyran blood in her," laughed Achilles.

"Does the Lanyran gene stem from the same source?" asked Solaris.

"What do you mean?" asked Achilles.

"Do their genes come from the same individual?" Solaris asked again.

Achilles rubbed the stubble that grew on his chin, wondering why she wished to know—as he had never thought about it—but soon became curious about the possibility.

"I'd have to run some tests and it might take a while."

"Test Rynah's blood as well," said Solaris.

"I fail to see the point in testing her blood," Achilles protested.

"So do I," quipped Rynah, not liking the way Solaris referred to her as though she wasn't there.

Solaris gave Achilles a pointed look. "I meant, test her blood to see if its genetic markers have any similarities with Alfric's, Tom's, Solon's, and Brie's."

A quizzical expression crossed Achilles' face as he looked into Solaris' eyes, curious about her motives for such a test; though not wanting to argue, he picked up a needle and a slide.

"May I?" he asked Rynah.

Just as intrigued about Solaris' actions as he was, and knowing that it was best she cooperated with her friend instead of arguing, Rynah held out her arm and allowed him to prick her skin, drawing a few drops of blood, and Achilles placed them on the glass slide. Achilles stuck the slide into the holocomputer, with the other four, and tapped in a series of logarithms before stepping back.

"It will take about ten, maybe 20 minutes for the program to complete the tests."

"I'm hungry," said Tom as his stomach gurgled, reminding him that it had been hours since he had last eaten.

Alfric approached him, his muscles bulging underneath his cloak. "You must learn to channel your hunger. Let it feed you until it drives you to vanquish your enemies and win this war."

"I will never understand you," Tom said.

"I think what he means," said Rynah, "is that no one cares about the state of your stomach."

"I will grab some food," said Joe, checking his pockets. "I have a few bucks."

"Here." Achilles handed him a wad of bills. "There's a McDonald's in the lobby. Bring back some chicken nuggets with honey mustard sauce."

Joe took the cash and nodded.

"I'll come with you," said Klanor.

Joe stopped. "But won't you…"

"With the way all of those people are dressed, who's going to notice me?"

Joe allowed Klanor to pass through the door. "Come on, Fons."

"I am not leaving this spot." Fons crossed his arms.

"All right," said Joe. "I guess a fish sandwich will…"

"Oh, no, you don't!" Fons jumped to his feet and rushed to the door. "You know I hate those and prefer a quarter pounder with cheese. You know that their fish always gives me indigestion. How can you possibly think…"

The door closed behind them.

"And the peppers don't bother him at all," mumbled Tom, to which Brie chuckled.

Rynah ran to Solaris, glad to see her again, and embraced Brie, Solon, Tom, and Alfric as well.

"What I don't understand," said Solon to Solaris, "is why you believe that we have the same ancestor."

Achilles' computer bleeped. He rushed to the monitor and read the results of the test; his jaw dropped.

"I don't believe it," he said.

"What?" asked Obiah.

"You all have the same genetic markers—minute at best, but still there—as Herclai."

"What?" said Solon, Rynah, Brie, Tom, and Alfric in unison. Though Solon and Alfric did not understand the words "genetic markers", they comprehended the fact that they shared familial blood with the others.

"I compared it to records I still had with me from before we were separated. The markers are a match. Despite the thousands of years that have passed, you all carry some of his genetics."

"How is that possible?" asked Rynah.

Achilles pushed his chair back. "Herclai and Isyr were husband and wife. He also had a brother, who elected to stay behind on Lanyr, instead of joining him on our mission. Herclai's brother had recently married and wished to spend that time with his wife. It is possible that Isyr was pregnant at the time we reached this planet and was unaware of it, or chose not to mention it. If she gave birth to them while trapped here, her children would have passed on his genes."

"And Rynah?" asked Solon.

"As I've said, Herclai's brother remained on Lanyr with his wife," said Achilles. "They must have had children, who passed on the same genetics to her."

"But that was hundreds of thousands of years ago," said Brie.

"Genes do not die from the passage of time. They may change slightly or evolve, even get diluted, but their basic structure will stay the same. Suffice it to say that you all are distantly related."

Solaris stepped back from the others; the jewel on her belt buckle had glowed and vibrated, causing her to lose her balance. She yanked the small opaque gem free of its hold and held it up before the others; Achilles' eyes widened as he recognized it and it's glow wafted over them.

"Solaris," said Rynah, "what is that?"

"My secret," replied Solaris.

"Care to explain?" demanded Tom.

Solaris shrank away, wishing that the others would quit giving her questioning glares, but knew that, this time, there was no evading their questions. The time had arrived for her to reveal the secret which Marlow had conferred with her.

"This is a crystal," she said. "Marlow found it during one of his many travels and entrusted it to me for safekeeping."

"Why didn't you say anything?" demanded Rynah, her voice hurt at being excluded from another of Marlow's secrets.

"Your grandfather had asked me not to," replied Solaris. "This is how I found each of you," she said to the others, "and brought you to the ship. It led me to you."

Curiosity taking its hold, Brie touched the thumb-sized crystal. A pale white and blue glow burst from it, filling the entire room and enveloping them all as it rose from Solaris' palm, hovering in the air and forcing them to take a step back as they circled it.

"What is happening?" breathed Tom.

"Long have I remained silent, but no more," said the crystal, telepathically to the others, speaking to each of them in a different voice.

Rynah and Solaris heard Marlow's voice; Brie heard her father's; Alfric heard what he had always thought would be Odin's voice, while Solon heard Athena's, the way he imagined it; Tom heard his grandmother's; Fons heard his mother's; Achilles heard Herclai's, while Obiah heard his father's.

"Who are you?" demanded Alfric with authority, afraid that a spirit played a trick with their minds.

"I am mercy, compassion, forgiveness. I am wisdom, knowledge, understanding. I am honor, courage, nobility. I am innovation, a seeker, curiosity. I am he who stands alone while others jeer. I am he who guides the lost until they are found.

"I know you, Achilles, and the hours you have spent alone in somber solitude, mourning the decision you made long ago, and the guilt that haunts your dreams. I know you, Rynah, and the regret you carry with you each day, mixed with anger. I know you, Brie, and the sorrow you still feel at the loss of your father, while you, Tom, strive each day to prove to others that you are worthy of their praise. I know you, Alfric, son of Erik, proud and courageous, but yet a possessor of a gentle heart. I know you, Solon, seeker of wisdom, while scorning those who do not appreciate the art of study as you do. I know you, Obiah, always mindful of how you failed to help a friend, and fearful that you will never be forgiven for it. I know Fons, and the pain that drives him to seclude himself. I know Klanor, a man who only wishes to help those he loves, but makes all the wrong decisions. I know Joe and his dedication to justice and truthfulness. And I know you, Solaris, whom Marlow rightfully named the guiding star.

"Isyr, indeed, was with child at the time of the Mulyrans' destruction, and with the help of a stranger, she escaped."

Solaris's head lowered as she remembered her temporary time in Mulyra and the woman she had saved. In the hours she had been back in our modern time, she wondered about the woman—a very human thing to do—and if she had survived.

"Do not fret, young one," the crystal said to Solaris. "She found refuge where your friends' ancestors emerged, giving birth to twins. Her boys grew into strong men, and each found a wife among the earthly race, fathering children of their own; and as time passed, their descendants separated—one line settling the far reaches of the north, braving the frozen land, while the other trekked to the savannahs of the south, where roamed beasts with ivory tusks.

"Long ago, I foresaw your existence and have watched you all your lives, lost and confused, but brought together for a common purpose. I am six made nine, but have always been one. You must find the remaining crystals and unite them to save not just the universe, but yourselves."

"I don't understand," said Rynah.

"I am he who made the crystals and gave them to the Mulyrans as a gift and a test. If the nine are not made whole, the greed of one will destroy all. So it has in the past, so it will in the future. Only star's light can destroy them.

"Only one pure of heart, pure of body, pure of thought, pure of desire, and pure of spirit can undo the damage wrought by darkened desire. As no one individual possesses all of these qualities, I have summoned you five, bearers of the blood of the one who tried to stop a misguided man. Redemption is his, if he chooses it. Separate you are, each pure in your way, who must now become one, to make whole what was broken."

"How?" asked Brie.

They each heard a part of the text.

> Seek the ancient people
> who dwell in desert sand
> where rocks form steeples;
> in barren scope as islands.

> Great monuments to those seeking refuge,
> tall and proud despite arid deluge,

reaching for the stars
and a people that have traveled far.

Seek these cliffs;
seek their gifts.

Find the path that dwells deep within,
fear not the dark, nor the echo,
but go forth companions of ten,
plus one more forced from his den.

Heed well the underground
constellations that surround
you with neon light.

Joe, Klanor, and Fons burst through the door and stopped when they noticed the crystal floating in the center of the room as it continued speaking.

Let starlit words guide you
to dragon's heart.
There the crystals must part,
Only then, will you stop foe's coup.

"Remember this," continued the crystal, "choices have been made, but forgiveness can be granted." Klanor paid great attention to this statement as the crystal's voice took the sound of Rynah's in his head.

"Without belief and faith, what is broken will remain." Rynah listened to this one.

"Sometimes, mercy is more valiant than the sword." (Alfric)

"And courage is letting go of not just your fears, but of the ones you love." (Brie)

"Value the mind, but do not let its chaos hinder you." (Tom)

"Value what each day can teach." (Solon)

"Do not dwell on your failings as they are a part of you; you must learn to rise above them." (Solaris)

The crystal ceased, turning dark, and dropped to the floor, where Solaris retrieved it.

"What in the name of…" began Tom. "What was that?"

No one answered.

"Seriously," said Tom, "I want to know. That thing talked… I mean… I heard a voice in my head, and it knew me!"

"Some things are beyond our realm of comprehension," said Solon, trying to make sense of it himself, but resigned to the fact that he might never understand.

"I don't want to hear…" protested Tom.

"Tom," said Rynah, "it doesn't matter. My grandfather once told me that this is just one universe that we live in. There might be others, other realities, and perhaps that is where this comes from. I am starting to understand what he did all those years ago. These crystals have a consciousness of their own, in a way, almost like an artificial intelligence, but instead of operating independently, they must tap into the mind of a flesh and blood being through telepathic means. That is how they operate. These crystals are advanced technology that seem to form a symbiotic relationship with the conscious minds around them. The crystal in the geo-lab maintained Lanyr's magnetic fields because the people who worked in close proximity all believed that that was its function."

"And then I came along and it absorbed my darkest desires," said Klanor, remembering how the crystals had turned blue for Brie when he had allowed her to handle one, while she was a prisoner on his ship, before Stein betrayed him.

"Yes, but it was no stranger to such a thing," said Rynah, glancing at Achilles.

"They feed off the minds of those around them," said Solaris, "because that is what powers them."

"So, let me get this straight," said Tom, "our minds power these things and they make our darkest wishes come true?"

"It's the best explanation I have," said Rynah.

"That was Marlow's conclusion," said Solaris. "Our minds activate them, and to ensure that they remain useful, they turn into what you need."

"Which explains why the Java in Mulyra had to be pure in his thoughts and desires and was the only one allowed to handle them," said Achilles. "The Java's goal had to always be the peace and prosperity of his people, and so it was, until I..."

"That is the past," said Rynah, not catching the last word of Achilles' statement before his voice trailed off. "What the crystals are, what we have done, it doesn't matter anymore. My mission hasn't changed. I need to stop Stein, and to do that, I need to destroy those crystals."

"We will stop him," said Brie.

"Yes," agreed Rynah, "we will."

While the room quieted, Joe remembered why he had burst in to begin with. "We have a problem," he said.

"What sort of problem?" asked Achilles.

At that moment, gunfire assaulted the door, forcing Joe to slam it shut, sealing all of them inside.

"That sort of problem," scoffed Obiah.

"Bar the door!" yelled Klanor. He and Obiah shoved a couch against it, piling a chair, table, entertainment stand, and sofa on top. "That won't hold for long."

Pop!—Pop!—Pop!

Gunfire besieged the door, undoing the lock, while those on the other side rammed against their barricade, attempting to get in. Rynah, Obiah, and Klanor hunkered behind side tables, their laser weapon pointed at the door. A hole appeared in the wood. They fired back.

"Who are they?" asked Brie.

"Federal agents," said Joe.

"But why didn't they tell us to surrender?"

"Because upon orders of the President and the director of the FBI, they are to shoot us on sight," replied Joe, having watched a replay of the broadcast, while waiting in line at the restaurant, of the President's news conference where he issued those orders. He rushed to the balcony, looking all around for a way down; the distance was too great. Above him was another balcony, and an idea formed in his mind, though on any other day, he would have preferred something less acrobatic.

"Alfric," he said.

Bang!

"Do you think you can climb this?" Joe asked the Viking.

Alfric sheathed his sword and shared a look with Joe before climbing on top of the white painted railing, balancing on it. He reached up, and with a huge jump, grabbed the edge of the balcony above him. His feet swung in the air as his muscles tensed from the effort of heaving himself over the other railing.

"Hey," said a man as Alfric set foot on the balcony, "what are you doing?"

The Viking pulled out his sword, allowing the sun to gleam off its steel blade. Without argument, the man dropped his crossword book and ran to the hallway, putting as much distance between him and Alfric as he could.

"The others," Alfric called down to Joe.

Joe grabbed Brie and helped her climb the railing as she reached up for Alfric's outstretched hand. Next, he shoved Fons to the edge—the man struggled and whimpered, begging to be let go, until Joe reminded him that he, too, would be killed on sight—placing his hands on his side to help him balance, as the man climbed up and lunged for Alfric. Fons gasped when his hand slipped and the Viking almost dropped him, but true to his nature, Alfric leaned further and gripped Fons' arm with both his meaty hands, refusing to lose anyone in his charge. Solon, Tom, Solaris, and Achilles—who snatched the egg-shaped item Tom had toyed with earlier—went next.

The gap in the door widened. Screeching filled the air as those on the other side shoved against the barricaded door, moving the piled furniture by an inch and sending an assault of bullets right at them.

"Come on!" yelled Joe.

"You next," Klanor said to Rynah.

Rynah ignored him, focused on disarming their attackers. Klanor looked at Obiah, and with a nod, Obiah seized Rynah's weapon hand and pushed her out the door to Joe, who helped her balance on the railing while Alfric hauled her to safety. Next he shoved Obiah up.

Gunfire shot off the latch to the minibar, allowing the door to swing open and revealing all of the tiny bottles of liquor. Klanor snatched one, and upon realizing what it was, threw the bottles at the door where they shattered, spraying their contents all over the frame.

"Go!" he yelled at Joe.

Joe obeyed.

With one last flicker of movement, Klanor fired his laser pistol at the alcohol-soaked furniture, lighting it up, before running to the balcony and leaping for Alfric's hand just as the agents on the other side broke through.

They all stood on the balcony above Achilles' hotel room, wondering where to go next, but before anyone could say anything, Joe leapt the four feet to the balcony next to them, clinging to the railing—his sweaty hands slipped, but before he fell, he tightened his grip and hauled himself over the metal bar. He turned and motioned for the others to follow. Brie balanced on the bar of the railing. No longer fearing heights, she ignored the wind and the shouts below, concentrating on reaching the other side. Joe held his hand out for her. She jumped, snatched it, and released the breath she had been holding as her feet hit a solid surface once again.

"Go," Brie told Joe. "I'll help the others."

Joe jumped to the terrace next to them, while Brie helped the others across, and they formed a line, jumping from veranda to veranda and crossing the side of the hotel building. With each movement, they attracted onlookers, who stared out their windows at them with perplexed expression, until they saw Alfric and recoiled in fear.

A bullet struck the exterior wall next to Fons' head.

"They have a sniper," Joe said to the others while they continued their precarious trek across the balustrades.

As they scaled the verandas, Brie found herself lagging behind until she ended up alone on a balcony with Klanor. Laser fire struck the terrace just as a lone hoverbike appeared from the shadows of the other towering buildings, ripping a portion of the balcony from the wall and shattering the glass door. The concrete beneath Brie's feet fell away and the veranda dipped, slanting at a precarious level. Shrieking, she dropped. Klanor dove for her, sliding on his stomach down the tipping balustrade, and seized her outstretched hand. He flung his other arm out, capturing a rung on the rail that was still intact and bringing them both to an abrupt halt, with Brie's feet dangling in the air as bits of concrete crashed into the ground below them, sending up swirling clouds of dust.

The hoverbike turned and headed straight for them. It lined up, with them in their sights. Brie and Klanor locked eyes, but Klanor shook his head, reading the thought within Brie's mind. The hoverbike neared, the high pitch of its engine piercing their ears.

A huge battle cry drowned the hoverbike's approach as Alfric jumped on the railing, gripping the uneven brick on the wall, and heaved a piece of broken glass at the pilot on the bike. It struck its target. The pilot reached up where the shard of glass pierced his neck and doubled over; the bike dropped, bursting into flames as it crashed into a neighboring hotel.

With the hoverbike gone, Klanor hauled Brie up until she could grasp the metal rungs. The terrace lurched. With slow, steady movements, both Klanor and Brie climbed to the other side of the balcony that faced the one their friends were on. It dipped again, sending their stomachs into their throats. Sweat coated their palms as they clung to the metal railing, each step causing the veranda to bob up and down.

Once they reached the other end, Klanor steadied Brie as she climbed over the rail and leapt to the outstretched arms that awaited her. The balcony dropped, forming a steep 60-degree angle. Klanor climbed the metal rail and jumped just as it fell away.

"Who was that?" demanded Achilles, still clinging to his treasured item.

"Probably a scout sent by Stein," said Rynah.

Gunfire urged them onward. Once on the last veranda, Joe leaned over; the fire escape lay just out of reach, a distance too far for them to jump.

Another bullet lodged itself into the hotel side just as Rynah leaped to the next balcony.

Brie tried the door on the final terrace that led into a room. Locked. An elderly woman stared at her, fear etched on her wrinkled face, frozen to the floor.

"Open the door!" said Brie.

The woman refused to move.

"Please!" Brie shouted.

No movement.

Without warning, Alfric shoved her aside and used the hilt of his sword to break the glass in the door, ushering her and the others inside, while Obiah helped the last ones over the railing. He looked over at Achilles and nodded. Achilles jumped, but his foot slipped and he plunged downward until Solaris seized his ankle, allowing him to dangle upside down.

"Pull me up!" yelled Achilles.

Solaris calculated the distance to the last terrace, where Obi-ah waited for them, a thought percolating in her mind. Somehow, Achilles knew what she was thinking.

"Don't you dare!" he screamed at her.

Using both her hands, Solaris swung Achilles upward, propelling him through the air and to Obiah's outstretched hand, where he clung to Achilles' wrist, and pulled him up. Solaris jumped, landing with a soft clomp on the last balcony.

"Where are you taking us?" demanded Achilles once they were all inside the connecting room.

"The fire escape," replied Joe. "It's our only way out."

"Won't they have those covered?" asked Fons.

"Yes," said Joe, "which is why…" His voice trailed off when he peeked out the door into the hallway and saw a cleaning lady's abandoned cart with bleach and ammonia containers on it. Joe snatched them and rushed back inside the room. "I need plastic bottles."

Tom and Brie rummaged through the room—Klanor, Solaris, Rynah, and Obiah took up stations near the door should any agents appear—picking up discarded bottles from its occupants. Brie discovered a 12-pack of bottled water in the small, complementary refrigerator. She handed them to the others.

"Dump out the water."

They snatched the bottles, dumping the clear liquid on the floor; even Solon joined them after observing how the bottles opened. As quick as they had emptied them, Joe snatched up the bottles, pouring in bleach and ammonia, while Fons and Achilles sealed the caps before the gas could escape.

"We'll need something to cover our mouths with," said Joe.

Brie jumped from the floor, hurrying to the bed—by this time, the elderly woman had hunkered in a dark corner, glad to have been forgotten by theses dangerous strangers—and ripped the sheets off.

"Alfric, I need your knife."

He handed it to her. Brie ripped the sheets into pieces with the sharpened blade, handing a piece to each of them.

"We have company!" shouted Rynah.

Gunfire filled the hallway as the agents had caught up with them. Bullets mixed with laser fire in a spectacular display of lights and minuscule explosions as both sides fought for the upper hand.

Joe tied the strip of cloth Brie had handed him around his nose and mouth.

"Now!"

The others secured their pieces of the bed sheet around their faces, covering their noses and mouths just as Joe threw one of the bleach and ammonia filled bottles—the cap loosened—down the hallway where FBI agents fired at them. The cap popped off, sending the contents everywhere and splattering on the wall, and the gas it created into the air. Coughing and gagging filled the corridor as the agents struggled to breathe from the noxious fumes, and they staggered away, their eyes watering.

All of them piled into the carpeted corridor, running for the door with the red-colored handle and the words "Emergency Exit" painted on it in white block letters. Alfric had been about to push it open when Joe stopped him. Bullets from the other end of the hall careened for them, missing them by inches. Rynah and Klanor fired back. With caution, Joe opened the emergency exit—knowing that more FBI agents waited for them on the other side—and chucked the bottles of bleach mixed with ammonia outside. They burst open, smothering the agents with their fumes.

Joe burst through the door, followed by the others. They shoved their way past the gagging agents, trying not to cough themselves for even though the pieces of cloth blocked some of the gas, it did not block it all. They stamped down the metallic stairs—Alfric threw one agent over the railing—and away from those who meant them harm. Shots fired from above. Covering themselves, they continued their race against the gunpowder-filled projectiles and towards the bottom of the fire escape.

Solaris paused when a bullet struck the metal railing in front of her. She snatched the laser pistol from Klanor as he rushed by, aimed, and fired at the sniper on the roof of the building next to them, before continuing on.

By the time they reached the end of the staircase, their commotion had summoned the attention of the convention attendees, who had gathered in the front and sides of the hotel, filling the sidewalks and parking lot, their phones out, filming everything. They threw those in their way aside as more bullets sailed towards them. Many within the crowd ducked, shrieked, and dove to the concrete in an effort to save themselves, forcing Rynah and the others to jump over hunched bodies, with the agents in close pursuit.

"Cease fire!" Samuel's voice rang out over the melee. "There are civilians!"

"We need horses!" shouted Alfric.

Achilles stopped, remembering that an RV, belonging to a rival scientist he loathed and wished to exact revenge on for when the man stole and published one of his theories about quantum physics, remained parked in the rear parking lot. "This way!" he called to the others.

They changed direction, vaulting over shrubbery, darting down a sideway, and rounding the corner of the hotel, which led straight to the rear lot. Sunlight glared off the swarm of windshields that greeted them, hurting their eyes as they ran past parked cars. Glass shattered beside them. Running faster, they raced through the rows of the lot, desperate to escape the agents chasing them.

"Where are you taking us?" demanded Rynah.

"There!" Achilles pointed at a brown and yellowed-white RV

that stood out among the Chevrolets, Ford sedans, and pickup trucks; its square shape looked like refuge to them.

"Is this yours?" asked Solon, staring at the massive vehicle in wonderment, unable to contain his awe, despite the fact that they were being chased.

"Uh, no," replied Achilles, "but I'm sure the owner won't mind us borrowing it." He forced the lock on the door and ushered them all inside, when Tom paused, watching the approaching agents and looked at the car next to them, thinking of a plan.

"What's the hold up?" demanded Achilles.

"I got an idea," said Tom, "but I need a stick and a knife."

Solaris yanked a steel rod from the top of another car and handed it to Tom, while Alfric, though with reluctance, gave him his knife.

"Meet me at the lot entrance over there," Tom said as he jimmied the car door.

Catching on to Tom's plan, Achilles jumped into the RV and hotwired the engine.

"Tom," said Brie, worried that he might get hurt.

"Go," Tom told her, trying to put her concern at ease. "I'll catch up."

While the others drove away, Tom started the car's engine, pulled it out of its space, pointing it at the enclosing agents. He shoved the vehicle into neutral, propped the rod on the accelerator, bracing it against the leather cushion of the driver's seat, and with quick movements, slammed the car into drive, jumping away before it took him with it. The small car careened down the lane—Tom hurried away while wondering why people drove such small vehicles—towards the agents. It crashed into a pickup truck, puncturing the gas tank and causing a tremendous explosion with a ball of fire shooting into the air.

Tom never looked back. He steadied his breathing as he bolted for the RV sitting idle in the parking lot entrance with Solon hanging in the doorway. Tom's firm grip clutched Solon's arm as the young philosopher yanked him inside and slammed the door shut.

Achilles hit the gas pedal. They sped off down the busy street, mingling with the traffic, before turning off and making their way to the interstate.

Back in the parking lot, Samuel watched them disappear, secretly glad that they had escaped, as he disliked the new policy regarding his friend and these otherworld visitors.

Chapter 12
A Desert Road

Samuel eyed the commotion around him as the agents under his command questioned the eyewitnesses at the comic con convention. He had half expected them to be frightened from all that had happened, but most were intrigued and watched his every move with wide-eyed anticipation, hoping for more excitement.

"There were two of them!" said one enthusiastic attendee. "Purple faces, just like on TV!"

"I thought I saw a third one," whispered another, "but her skin changed color."

"This is so cool!" said one 16-year-old dressed like Captain Kirk from *Star Trek*. "Wait until everyone back home hears about this and that I was here."

Samuel shook his head, having never liked these sorts of conventions. He always found them to be full of people who spent all their time locked in a fantasy instead of joining the real world.

"Sir," said another agent, handing him a cell phone.

Samuel groaned. He knew who was on the other end.

"Agent Anders."

"I want you back here immediately!" Director Singuar's irate voice erupted from the phone, forcing Samuel to hold it away from his ear.

"Sir?"

"There is a video all over the internet that shows exactly what happened at the Smithsonian!"

"As you are aware, sir, there were a lot of people gathered outside. I'm sure that they were all filming what happened with their cell phones."

"Don't play games with me. The video I'm talking about came from the museum's security feed."

"Intriguing," said Samuel, feigning interest.

"I know it was you," spat Director Singuar. "First, you pull that stunt at the press conference, and now this! Have you been letting them get away?"

"I can assure that…"

"You are to report back here now."

"I'm sorry, sir, you're breaking up."

"Don't…"

Samuel hung up and tossed the phone away. His time in charge of catching Joe and the others was limited. Samuel surveyed the multitude of shimmering costumes before him, wondering if Joe had the right idea in running off with Rynah and the others.

"Where are you all going?" he whispered to himself.

* * *

The RV bounced down the pothole-ridden highway as it sped through the desert, kicking up mounds of dust that intermixed with the bits of smog that escaped its tailpipe. Joe sat at the steering wheel, doing his best to keep the vehicle within the speed limit so as to avoid being pulled over.

"If we take this road, we should be able to avoid any major cities," said Achilles, using the GPS function on his smartphone.

"May I see that?" asked Joe.

Achilles handed his phone over to him and Joe tossed it out the open window.

"What do you think you're doing?" demanded Achilles as he hugged the egg-shaped, metal item he had insisted on taking with him when they fled the hotel.

"They can track that," said Joe, not taking his eyes off the road.

"And how are we supposed to navigate through this arid wasteland?"

"The old-fashioned way," said Rynah, dumping a pile of folded, and frayed, paper maps that had been marked up with a red marker in Achilles' lap. "It appears that whoever owned this vehicle loved to travel through these parts."

"Yeah," said Tom, holding up an *X Files* poster that he had found, "guess he was looking for aliens. Do you know that this poster would easily sell for $200,000 in 2099?"

"Seriously?" asked Brie.

"Yeah, it's kind of a cult classic," said Tom, folding up the poster and shoving it in his pocket, before Solon took it from him and placed it on the table.

"It is not yours," said Solon.

"I was just going to borrow it," Tom replied, "indefinitely."

"'Seek the ancient people,'" Alfric repeated the line of a poem to himself. "Who are these ancient people?"

"That is a very good question," said Achilles. "A lot of the local Indian tribes believe that they are ancient, brought here by the sky people. And then you get these ancient alien nuts who think that every major event in history was the result of aliens interfering with human history."

"Yeah," mumbled Tom, "because it's not like we have a real ancient alien sitting in the car with us."

Achilles glowered at him.

"It spoke of ancient monuments and great cliffs surrounded by sand," said Alfric. "There is plenty of sand in this place. Are there any monuments of cliffs?"

"The Grand Canyon," said Fons.

"But it is in the ground," said Joe. "This spoke of something that touched the sky, so it would have to be above ground."

"Monument Valley?" said Brie. "There are some very tall cliffs there. I once read somewhere that some believe that it has an other-worldly purpose."

"You're a genius!" Fons blurted out and kissed Brie, who shoved him away and rubbed her face with a corner of her shirt, while Alfric looked ready to run his sword through the man.

"Sorry," apologized Fons.

"You do that again," said Joe to Fons, having noticed that dark expression on Alfric's face, "and I'm going to let the Viking do what he wants with you."

Fons glanced at Alfric and scooted away from him, placing Obi-ah and Klanor between him and the Viking.

The RV lurched and sputtered as the engine shut off. Joe pulled to the side of the road just as they passed a small café that stood alone in the southwestern desert that also had a souvenir shop.

"What's wrong?" asked Rynah.

"We're out of gas," said Joe. "Wait here." He jumped out of the RV and walked across the street to the café, where he talked with the owner, before coming back.

"There is a gas station some two miles from here. I can walk it, but we need cash," said Joe when they got back.

"Here," said Achilles, handing him some bills. "It's all I've got."

"What are you," said Tom, staring at the wad of cash, "a walking ATM?"

"I don't like credit cards," said Achilles.

"I'll go to the station," said Joe. "You all stay here and stay out of sight."

Chapter 13
DARK HOLDINGS

A holomonitor flickered as it displayed the two video feeds: one of Merrick, crumpled on the copper floor, the other of Fredyr, pacing his cell. Stein's rancorous eyes fixated on the images; the line of his lips curved into a tiny smirk, but there was no pleasure in it. Stein chuckled to himself as he remarked at how Fredyr's grandiloquent attitude had disappeared, turning the man into the wretches he had forced to serve him. He watched as Fredyr continued his incessant pacing, turning on his heels, only to stroll to the other end of the room and repeat the process again, head hung low. He thought Fredyr's current circumstances fitting.

A small bit of movement on the other side of the screen made him turn his head. Merrick had tried to stand up, but his legs gave out and he collapsed onto the floor, gasping as the air was knocked out of him. Fury clouded Stein's face as he glared at the screen and the man he had once called family, all the while thoughts of what he wished to do to him filled his mind, each replaced with a more sinister and sickening plan. Memories flooded his head. Despite his attempts to be rid of them, the memories prevailed, forcing him to focus on one in particular.

Stein remembered the day well. A month had passed since the death of his wife and child because of Marlow's recklessness at the Brestef region. Stein had spent his days in a stupor, unable to move or speak. He just stared out a window. Merrick had been the one to force his hand.

"Look at you," Merrick had chided him. "Look at what you've become."

Stein never moved, but had continued staring out the opal window, watching a robin hop from branch to branch in the nearby acorn tree.

"Where were you?" Merrick had continued. "You didn't even come to your own wife and child's funeral."

Still no response.

"Where were you when it happened?"

Nothing.

"It should have been you that had died in the blast. Why is it you were saved and my sister died? Why you and not her and my wife? And you just sit there. Is this how you honor them?"

Infuriated, Merrick stormed over to a bookshelf and snatched a framed image of Stein's wife, holding their son, and waved it in front of his face.

"Look at them! You worthless piece of—I said look!"

"Leave me," Stein had whispered, and he remembered how hollow and hoarse his voice had sounded from weeks of not speaking to anyone.

"You were supposed to protect them! To keep them safe, but you let them die. Why were you not with them?"

"Leave," Stein had said, his voice a bit louder.

"I swear to you that I will not rest until…"

"I said leave me!" Stein had snatched the image from Merrick's hand, shoving him into the bookshelves, knocking off a small, misshaped ornament that his son had made in school, and smashed it on the floor where the ornament had shattered.

Infuriated, Merrick had glared at Stein.

"It should have been you that died that day," he had said before leaving.

Stein looked at his crooked fingers as he remembered picking up the delicate pieces of the broken ornament and the picture, his anger from that day rushing back to him. He remembered Merrick, how he had treated him, and how Merrick's taunts had grown worse with each passing day, becoming more abusive, becoming darker. Merrick had wanted him to suffer because of his failure, but now he lay in Stein's clutches.

As Stein watched Merrick's pathetic form continue to moan in pain on the floor, his twisted mind thought of ways to punish him. Merrick would understand the meaning of pain when he was finished with him, starting with forcing him to make a most difficult choice, much like what he did to Solaris.

Chapter 14
NEXT

"**Y**ou have some strange creatures on this planet," said Obiah as he held a tarantula in his hand, while they all waited for Joe to return with some gasoline. The tarantula reared back, stretching its front legs out towards him, displaying its fangs in a defensive posture.

"You might want to put that down," said Brie.

"What is this sort of creature?" asked Obiah.

Alfric and Solon both approached the tarantula, curious about it as they had never seen one before.

"A tarantula," replied Brie. "Normally, they're harmless, but they will bite you if frightened or threatened. It's usually best to leave them be."

"I dare you to touch it," said Tom to Solon.

Solon glared at him in response.

"You're not scared, are you?" Tom teased.

Alfric scooped the hairy tarantula into his meaty hands, holding it close to his face for a better look.

"An ugly creature," he said before Solon took it from him.

Solon held it up, studying it and admiring the gangly thing.

"Here," he said, offering it to Tom, "take it."

"Heck no, I'm not taking that nasty thing," Tom replied, recoiling from Solon.

"One day, my friend, you will learn not to urge others to do something, unless you are willing to do it yourself."

Tom looked at the unsympathetic faces staring back at him. "Brie, help me out," he pleaded.

"You did question their honor," Brie replied with a grin, entertained by Tom's bit of embarrassment, which he had brought upon himself.

Tom's hesitant and shaky fingers reached out for the tarantula and grabbed it around the middle. A disgusted look crossed his face as he held it out at arm's length, looking into its eight eyes and curled fangs.

"Me and my big mouth," he muttered to himself.

Laughing and enjoying Tom's reaction, Brie took the tarantula from him and placed it back on the dusty ground, shooing it into the sagebrush.

"I thought you did not like arachnids," said Solaris, "and according to the data I accessed from your internet, a tarantula is one."

"I still don't," replied Brie, "but I no longer fear them. I don't fear a lot of things anymore, as we have more important things to worry about." Her eyes fell upon Klanor when she said that, but he glanced away, knowing full well what she meant.

A yellow jacket buzzed around his head and Klanor had been about to touch it, out of curiosity since such things did not exist on Lanyr, but Brie snatched his hand before he could.

"Don't do that!"

He looked at her in surprise, not because of her forcefulness, but because she had saved him from committing a mistake—a most painful one that he would have regretted, as did anyone dumb enough to touch a yellow jacket.

"It's a yellow jacket," said Brie. "They sting."

"Sting?" said Rynah.

"Yeah," replied Brie. "They have a large stinger that they stick you with if you get too close. It not only is very painful, but can make you swell up if you are allergic to its venom. There are lots of insects that either bite or sting, but yellow jackets are some of the worst. They are the tarantula's natural predator, immobilizing it with its venom, laying its eggs inside, and leaving. As the eggs hatch, the larvae survive by eating the tarantula from the inside out."

"Not exactly dinner conversation," muttered Tom to himself.

"Though you can pet bumblebees," continued Brie, having not heard his remark. "They have stingers, but are very mild in temperament, so if you are gentle, you can pet them."

Everyone stared at her.

"Sorry," said Brie, "a bit more info than you wanted."

"You have a most interesting planet," said Obiah.

Rynah walked up to Brie, her face calm and full of respect and newfound admiration for one she had once derided and looked down upon. "I never knew that you were so knowledgeable about such things."

"No reason for you to," replied Brie.

"Solaris was right," Rynah said, glancing at Solaris, who busied herself with the yellow jacket, enthralled by how it flew from place to place in a pattern and unaffected by its constant stings. "I should have made a more conscious effort to get to know you all."

Joe's heavy footsteps crunched the gravel as he walked up with the canister of gasoline and a bag containing scarves, two hats, and sunglasses, which he had stolen from the convenient store at the gas station.

"Here," he handed the gas can to Tom, "fill her up."

Tom glanced at Solon and the two of them ran off to pour the liquid fuel into the gas tank of the RV, as Solon was thrilled to learn more about this world he found himself in.

"Well, I got some good news and some bad news," said Joe. "Which do you want first?"

"The good news," said Rynah.

"Well, I think I know where the caves are. It's Monument Valley."

"And the bad news?" asked Alfric.

"The FBI, the U.S. Marshall's service, and the local police are all looking for us, and there are a lot of them between us and where we want to go."

Achilles snorted. "Somehow, I don't think we are getting in there."

The roar of a bus, with a sign that read "Desert Gardens Tours", rumbled as the behemoth of a vehicle pulled into the small café on the side of the highway across from them, releasing a high-pitched squeal as the brakes were applied. The doors opened. Out walked a mob of people (of various ages) dressed in the typical garb of t-shirts, shorts, hats, and sunglasses of tourists, gabbing in loud voices so that all within the vicinity heard them.

"I think I know how we can," said Brie, as she remembered flyers that had hung in her school announcing the Desert Gardens, which would be opening all over the New Mexico and Arizona area in the spring.

"A tour bus?" laughed Achilles. "You've got to be joking!"

Ignoring him, Brie ran over to the tour bus driver. "Excuse me!"

The driver turned towards her, while wiping the sweat off his brow before putting his navy blue cap back on. "Sorry, girl, but this bus is all filled up."

"That wasn't what I wanted to ask," said Brie. "I just wanted to know which gardens this tour goes to."

"Heck, everywhere." the bus driver softened his tone when he realized that he spoke to a teenager. "Sorry, girl, I meant to say that this bus goes to all of the most well-known regions of the New Mexico and Arizona area. We started in Albuquerque, went through Santa Fe, and will be heading up to Monument Valley before stopping at the Grand Canyon and ending in Phoenix."

"Monument Valley?"

"Yeah, but I don't have any room for more passengers."

"That's fine," said Brie. "I was just curious. My mom was thinking of doing the tour later this month." Brie's eyes darted to the small LCD TV screen hanging from the front of the bus and the press conference that took place.

"Yeah, well, tell her to go to desertgardens.com for a list of tour dates. This tour isn't ending anytime soon; we'll be doing it throughout the summer and well into the fall."

"Thanks!" Brie hurried back to the others.

"What was that all about?" asked Joe.

"I've seen this tour advertised before. They are traveling up and down the southwest, touring sites and monuments famous to this region, including Monument Valley. That means that there should be other tour buses up there right now; we can blend in."

"Good thinking," said Joe. "We should go."

"Wait," said Solaris, "we need to contact Jifdar. I told him that I would after finding all of you."

"I can rig your communications device so that Stein is unable to hijack it," said Fons, wanting to be helpful and quite enjoying this adventure he found himself involved in.

"You're volunteering to help?" asked Joe.

"I might as well since you dragged me into this mess," Fons replied, but Joe detected the false agitation in his voice.

Solaris handed him her communications device, but as Fons tried to grab it, it slipped and fell to the ground, breaking into four pieces.

"Sorry," he mumbled.

Though irritated, Rynah held her temper. "Don't worry about it," she said. "We'll find another way to contact him."

Obiah pulled her aside. "We cannot all just go tramping off together. We need a plan."

"We cannot go off alone either," replied Rynah. "For now, we should stay together."

Obiah's curled eyebrows betrayed his thoughts, but he nodded at Rynah, accepting her decision.

"I need a phone, or something," said Brie.

"Why?" asked Achilles.

"I saw something playing on the television on the bus," replied Brie, "and it looked important."

"Phones are too traceable," said Joe.

No one noticed Solaris walk a couple of feet away, staring at the bus as she concentrated on the signal that the television received, until she turned back towards them, cupping her hands together and relaying the broadcast. The others faced her, amazed at her capability to play a television broadcast on her hands with the image as crisp and clear as it would be on an actual television screen.

Images of a press conference, the same one that Samuel had taken part in, danced across her cupped hands. They watched as Samuel stepped up to the microphones, interrupting Director Singuar and the President, something that Joe marveled at, since not only did it go against proper etiquette and decorum when in the same room as the President, it was just never done.

"Though this Rynah may be the cause of all of this, we know that the girl was kidnapped on her way home from school several months ago. It is our belief that these beings are the ones who kidnapped her. Though we are committed to ensuring the safety of the people of the United States, we are also committed to seeing to that she is returned safely to her family," they heard Samuel say.

They watched as the remainder of the press conference unfolded, before the roar of an engine interrupted them, and the video that Solaris played for them faded as the tour bus drove away.

"I'm sorry," said Solaris. "I have lost the signal."

"It's okay, Solaris," said Rynah. "Joe, are you okay?"

"Fine," replied Joe, doing his best to pretend that everything was all right, but Samuel's actions puzzled him, and a part of him couldn't help but think that Samuel was trying to send him a message. He smiled at Rynah's doubtful expression, knowing that she would question him about it later.

"She's all filled up," said Tom, running up with the empty gas can and Solon. "What next?"

"Monument Valley, to see what trouble we can get into there," said Rynah, hoping she had pronounced the name properly, "and whatever awaits us there."

"Yes!" Tom jumped into the RV.

"His excitement worries me," Solaris said as the rest of them piled into the vehicle and left.

Chapter 15
STARLIT WORDS

Joe steered the RV into one of the crowded parking lots of Monument Valley National Park; two tour buses had parked closest to the newly built information center—which contained restrooms, a gift shop, a theater explaining the history of Monument Valley, and local residents serving as tour guides—and taken up four spaces each. A sign with a black arrow pointed them to the outdoor garden, containing a multitude of desert plants, and had been built within the last nine months as a way to attract more visitors.

Joe pulled into a space far away from the building. "We cannot all go in there together."

"We will split up," said Rynah. "Brie, you and Solon will go first. Tom, you're with Achilles and Fons. Joe, you're on your own. Alfric, you and Klanor will go together, and try to stay out of sight if you can; I'm sure that most will not appreciate your outward appearance. Obiah, you and I will go next, and again, we will have to stay out of sight. The sunglasses and hats that we have will cover us some, but not completely. Solaris…"

Solaris stared out the window, distracted by internal thoughts of the past—she still regretted her actions at the Wilmar Construction Site—while wondering why Monument Valley looked familiar.

"Solaris?" said Rynah.

Solaris faced her friend.

"Are you all right?" Rynah asked.

"Yes."

Rynah cocked her head to one side, unsure if she believed Solaris' curt answer, but ignored her intuition.

"Do you know where the cave is?"

"My scans indicate that there is an unusual energy source due west of here. It is not Earth, in origin."

"What?" said Fons and Tom together, but everyone ignored them.

"You will also go alone," Rynah said to Solaris. "We will meet on the..."

"We should take this trail," said Fons, who had pulled up a map of the park on a tablet that was left by the owner of the RV, "but it is only accessible if you are accompanied by a Navajo guide."

Solaris glanced at the tour guides waiting for their groups and changed her appearance, matching their hair color and darkened skin until she looked like a young Navajo woman.

"Let's go," said Rynah, "and remember, meet at the rendezvous in 30 minutes. And try to act casual."

She wrapped a scarf around her face; Klanor and Obiah did the same, covering her head with a straw hat before putting on a pair of sunglasses.

They went their separate ways, with Obiah, Klanor, Rynah, and Alfric taking extra care to stay out of sight. Brie and Solon feigned interest in the garden area; Joe went to the lobby of the building, while Tom, Achilles, and Fons visited one of the outlooks facing the valley itself. Solaris decided to converse with the tour guides, picking up their language with ease, to learn more about the history of the area; all the while unable to shake the feeling that she had seen this place before. She spotted a vendor selling bottled water and moseyed over there, snitching enough for her companions and slipping away before anyone noticed her. Time passed quicker than expected, forcing them to meander to the hiking trail where they had agreed to meet.

"No one is allowed beyond this point without a guide," said one tour guide, who had noticed them congregating on the trail.

"We..." began Brie.

"They know," said Solaris, approaching the group, still disguised as a young Navajo woman. "I am their guide."

The man eyed her in disbelief.

"You can take it up with the front office if you wish," Solaris said.

The man noticed Klanor's purple skin; though concealed by his low hanging hat, a bit of it poked out. Peering closer, the man's eyes opened wide.

"Your..."

Alfric hit him on the head, rendering him unconscious. "He was about to warn the others," said the Viking, when Brie gave him a piercing glare.

"We need to hide him," Joe said.

He and Alfric moved the man into the shade of a boulder and placed Klanor's hat on his head. For a bit of fun, Tom took the flower from Brie—which she had received from the guide in the outdoor garden area as a gift—and placed it in the man's hands.

"That's not funny," Brie chuckled as they all left.

"I do not understand the reference," said Solon.

"It's a joke," said Tom. "Usually, when a person dies, he is buried with flowers, and sometimes they are placed in the person's hands."

"Drachmas would be of more use," said Solon. "How else will one pay for passage into the underworld?"

A sharp hiss from Rynah stopped their bantering and they hurried after her.

They all walked down the empty and dusty trail, relishing the warmth of the bright sun. While much of the northern regions of the country experienced cold temperatures, the southwestern region was much milder, allowing them to hike in relative comfort. Each carried a bottle of water, hoping that it would last until they reached their destination. Bumps appeared on their exposed arms as the balmy wind wrapped itself around them; a hint of briskness was mixed in, winter's way of telling them that it intended to battle summer for its hold over the land.

After three hours of hiking over rocks and uneven ground, their sluggish legs yearned for rest and refused to move another step, and poor Fons weaved side to side from exhaustion. Not wanting to stop just yet, Solaris pushed them onward and led them off the path and into the heart of the desert towards one of the monuments that stretched high into the sky.

Evening approached and the sun lowered, allowing a few stars to poke through the purple veil that crossed the sky, warning them of impending darkness. They hiked as far as they could, but when it became too difficult to see, Rynah had them stop for the night.

"Keep the fire small," she said, when Achilles attempted to add more kindling to the tiny flames that Alfric had started. "We don't want to attract attention."

Achilles threw the sticks into the dirt—one cracked from the force—and stalked off, mumbling about the need for warmth as it would get cold. He wandered away from the others and found Solaris standing alone, her back to the others, staring out at the desert valley. She had no difficulty seeing in the dark, but realizing the limitation of her companions, had agreed to stop for the night.

"You spend much of your time alone," said Achilles, having noticed Solaris' fondness for solitude.

"I have much on my mind," she replied.

"Want to talk about it?" asked Achilles, taking a keen interest in this artificial intelligence that seemed more human than many of the people he had met in his life, who seemed to care more about their handheld devices, taking no interest in the world or people around them; but Solaris marveled at, and appreciated, everything she saw.

"You lied," said Solaris.

Her statement caught Achilles off guard.

"I beg your pardon."

"About Mulyra"—Solaris faced him—"you lied about who stole the crystals from the people there. It was never Matyr who tried to take them, but you."

The color drained from Achilles' face as the memory of where he had seen Solaris before slammed into him, bombarding his mind with thoughts he longed to leave buried in the past. After 35 years, he had almost forgotten the mysterious woman who had appeared from nowhere and saved Isyr from falling to her death.

"I knew I had seen you before," he breathed, "but you haven't aged a day. How is that possible?"

Solaris held out the crystal in answer.

"So it is the reason you were there." Achilles stared at the small object, remembering the time when he had tried to steal it and the others, and how Herclai had stopped him. "Why is it you never said anything?"

"Why is it you lied?"

"Fear," said Achilles. "I was afraid that if all of you knew what I had done, you would not listen to me."

"And should we listen to you now?"

"No," Achilles said, his voice a whisper as he shrank under Solaris' harsh tone. "I should not be here."

The crystal glowed in Solaris' hand and she remembered a bit of the ancient poem and its words stung her, reminding her of her iniquity, before it went out.

> But remember this:
> all have committed vice;
> forgiveness is my advice,

do not dwell on his remiss.

"How do we know that you have changed?" asked Solaris, testing him.

Achilles closed the gap between them, not wanting the others to overhear. "I have lived each day, wishing that I could change the past. Because of me, a man I once called a friend is dead. Because of me, his wife was left stranded on a world she did not know. I will never be able to atone for that. Many a night, I have longed to change what I have done."

"You can never change the past, but you can decide what you will do now," said Solaris, wincing at the asperity of her own words, and how she should listen to them as well. "I'm sorry. I should not be so harsh."

"You have every right to be," replied Achilles. "This is all my fault. If I hadn't..."

Solaris remained silent, reading the sadness and pain of his words, knowing what thoughts tortured his mind, as the same had filled her thoughts each day.

"This Stein," said Achilles, controlling the tone of his voice, "he wishes to possess the power of the crystals?"

"Not in the way you may think," said Solaris. "It's different. Klanor seized them for personal gain and the delusion that he could be a god among men, but he never fully understood the crystals. With Stein, it isn't about power or glory, it's darker than that. His heart has turned black, consumed by his grief and hatred of the one who gave that grief to him. He will not rest until everyone understands and experiences his pain, even if it means destroying countless lives."

"Can you and your friends stop him?" asked Achilles.

"I do not know," said Solaris. "I once thought that if we acquired all of the crystals, then it would be enough, but now, I am no longer certain. Rynah still believes that that is enough, and for now, it will have to suffice, but after that, I don't know what to do."

Solaris faced Achilles, and if she could have cried, she would have, as the guilt she still carried within rushed back to the surface.

"How can I guide them, when I can't even lead myself?"

Achilles' concerned face studied this created being, both amazed at her ability to feel and plagued by the shame she carried as he realized that something troubled Solaris. For the first time in his life, he felt pity and empathy, and he thought it poetic that it was not another human he felt it for, but an artificial intelligence.

"It appears that I am not the only one to have hurt the ones I love."

"Those people are dead because of me."

"Who?" asked Achilles, confused, hearing the despairing note in Solaris' voice.

"Stein had taken Rynah hostage," said Solaris, "and he proposed a trade: her for the crystals. She is my only friend, so I decided to make the trade, but Stein had something else in mind. He forced me to choose between Rynah, Brie's sister, or a group of strangers that I had never met. I failed to save them, to save Brie's sister, and to save Rynah. I failed them all, and now a group of innocent people are dead because I tried to make a deal with a man who cannot be reasoned with."

"But Rynah is here now."

"Only because Klanor helped her escape."

"You say Stein has Brie's sister."

"Stein kidnapped her sister and mother as a way to control her," replied Solaris, "and yet she has managed to stay focused on the mission. She has..." Solaris glanced back at the others and noticed that Brie sat a few feet away, her despondent face turned toward the stars and she knew, right then, that the same thoughts filled the girl's mind that also consumed hers. "She has succeeded where I have failed."

"I think I am beginning to understand this Stein," said Achilles. Solaris remained silent.

"Have you looked at the stars lately?" asked Achilles.

"What?"

"Specks of light in the night sky they are, guiding many a weary traveler. Oh, I've read tales about seafarers who used the stars to guide them at night, or those who have gotten lost and used them to find their way home, but have you noticed that once in a while a cloud covers them? Even a star dims in the night, but it always returns brighter than before.

"Solaris, the great star of Lanyr. Even my people used it as a guide when traveling the farthest reaches of space. I think you were named well."

Solaris looked into Achilles' gentle eyes, amazed that of all the people to provide her comfort, it was the very man who destroyed an entire civilization because of his own selfish desires.

"I will help you, all of you," said Achilles. "Maybe then the nightmares will go away."

"And you aren't helping us just because you happen to be stuck with us?"

"Well, maybe it's a little of that."

Solaris looked up at Achilles, seeing Marlow's troubled face within his, remembering the nights he lay awake, tortured by the carnage he had caused in the Brestef region, yet he never had the courage to admit his guilt. On such nights, she had recited old tales to him in an effort to help him find peace. "Marlow once said that everyone stumbles; the key is to pick yourself back up."

Achilles' face fell when he saw the pain within Solaris'.

"Though," continued Solaris, "I could use a helping hand."

"Then we will help each other and, perhaps, you will take your place among the stars, as your namesake suggests."

"I cannot fly anymore," said Solaris; a part of her ached for the ship that had held her consciousness for so long, giving her the ability to swoop in and rescue her friends when needed. She had once thought that she would never miss it, but now wished to have it back.

In a rare moment, Achilles smiled at her, as though he could read her mind, taking her words to be a metaphor, instead of the literal way she had meant them. As he watched her, his inventive mind filled with ideas of what he could create for her, to help her, and he remembered the egg-shaped metal object that he had insisted on bringing with him and struggled to keep Tom's curiosity away from.

"Then I shall make you wings, so that you will soar."

Solaris eyed Achilles, trying to read him, unsure of what he meant. Unable to decide, she inclined her head in appreciation of his consoling, and together, they returned to the others with a spirit of camaraderie, each understanding the other.

She glanced at Brie, who still sat away from the others and noticed that Klanor had approached her. She took a step towards them, but a grip, stronger than she would have thought possible from the one who possessed it, clutched her arm, pulling her back. Turning to the side, Solaris' eyes met Solon's—she hadn't seen him sitting in the shadows—as he shook his head, warning her to leave them alone, before ambling away to sit with the others.

Solaris glanced at Brie and Klanor one last time, before taking a seat next to Rynah, who listened to Alfric tell stories about his home.

Solaris needn't have worried about Klanor's intentions. Since the day he was betrayed by Stein, he had wrestled with what he had done to Rynah and to Brie; such guilt was sealed when he watched helplessly as Stein waved Brie's mother in front of her at the museum, threatening to kill her.

"May I sit here?" he asked Brie, his tone gentle as a part of him wished to comfort her and remove the despondent look from her face.

"No one's stopping you," replied Brie, not bothering to look at him.

Klanor sat on the grainy dirt, crossing his legs as he settled in, his mind wrestling with words that yearned to burst free from his mouth.

"I'm sorry," he said, "for what I did to you."

Brie pulled her focus away from the stars and turned towards him.

"I'm not saying this because I think that it is what you or the others want me to do."

"Why are you saying it?" asked Brie.

"Do you remember the day that I had tried to bribe you to get you to turn against Rynah and join me?"

"You let me hold one of the crystals."

"Yes," said Klanor, "and it turned a whitish-blue. Such a color on my world means purity, compassion, loyalty, but most importantly, it mean merciful. I have thought about that instance since, and when the pirates rescued us all from Sunlil, you had a chance to exact your revenge and put me out an airlock, just like the others wanted, but you didn't. Of all the people in the universe, you were my only advocate."

Brie leaned forward, her gentle eyes taking in the sadness that plagued Klanor's face.

"I don't deserve your forgiveness, nor shall I earn it, but I hope you will accept my apology."

"Before my father died," said Brie, "I decided to teach my sister how to swim. Our neighbor had a pool, so I snuck in there with her and placed her in the water, confident that I could teach her. She almost drowned. My father had watched us leave the yard from his bedroom window, so he followed. Good thing too, because if he hadn't, he would not have been there to pull Sara out of the pool and give her CPR."

Brie's voice choked at the memory. "He was angry, but that anger left him when he saw how frightened I was. I thought I had killed her and she would have died that day because of my stupidity."

Klanor listened in silence, realizing why Brie had such a strong sense of protectiveness towards her sister.

"I didn't speak to anyone for the rest of the day, not until my dad came into my room to coax me into eating supper. I remember crying in his shoulder, begging for his forgiveness, and do you know what he said?"

Klanor shook his head.

"He said, 'Forgiveness is never earned; it is given.' You can never earn a person's forgiveness, but I choose to give you mine."

"Now I know why they risked everything to save you. You are more than just a friend to them, you're their humanity."

A few seconds of silence passed before Brie spoke again.

"Thank you," she whispered, "for saving my life."

"No," said Klanor, "you saved mine."

"All right, everyone!" Tom's voice drowned the private conversations that took place, its echoes continuing throughout the desert. "Alfric here, scourge of the northern lands that are always covered in snow and ice, and so cold that only those with no real sense would stay there, has agreed to my challenge of arm wrestling!"

"And what is the wager?" asked Solon, with a smirk.

"Wager?" said Tom. "Um, the wager is, if he wins, I'll stop teasing him so much."

"I could just cut out your tongue and be done with the matter," muttered Alfric as he chewed on a piece of cooked lizard.

"I'd rather you didn't," replied Tom, garnering a few bits of laughter. "Of course, I can always forgo this little challenge, if you think you are in too weakened of a state to accept," he added, knowing how to goad the Viking into doing something.

Alfric chucked his half-eaten piece of roasted lizard in the fire, rising to his full height and causing Tom's knees to buckle a little as he tried to meet the Viking's intimidating stance.

They found a rock big enough to be used as a table, with each of them taking their position at opposite ends.

"All right, boys," said Rynah, playing referee; she never noticed Solaris' grin upon seeing her have a little bit of fun, "one round of arm wrestling. If Alfric wins, then Tom will quit teasing him, as futile of a prospect that might be. If Tom wins then, Alfric will be his personal bodyguard."

Alfric and Tom interlocked hands, each awaiting Rynah's command.

"One, two… three!" said Rynah.

Before Tom had a chance to react, Alfric slammed his arm on the rock, causing him to flip through the air and land a foot away amidst a gale of laughter.

"Uh, best out of three?" said Tom, shaking sand from his clothes.

"I think you best stop now while your limbs are still intact," chuckled Solon.

Rynah looked up at the sky, trying to stifle a yawn. "I think we should all get some sleep."

Agreeing with her suggestion, they all found a place to settle in for the night, knowing that morning would come soon.

As the sun peeked over the horizon, a small line of black shapes could be found trekking across the flimsy sand of the desert, surrounded by rock spires that stretched to the sky. Determined to reach their destination, they started their hike before sunrise and kept walking, not even bothering to rest when tired or stop for water at the creek.

Solaris stopped.

"What's wrong?" asked Rynah.

"I sense a signal, and it does not originate from this planet."

"Sense?" said Tom.

Much like what had happened when they had found the ancient ruins while they had stopped for supplies, Solaris had detected a transmission that did not match any of Earth's communication signals. She changed course, heading straight for one of the mesas in the valley. After two hours of walking, they reached the edge of its shadow—each welcomed the relief from the sun—and climbed its base.

"It's here," said Solaris. "Look for a cave, anything that goes underground."

They searched for an underground opening, but found nothing. The sun moved to its highest point in the sky before starting its slow descent to the horizon, and still they found no entrance. As the water they had brought ran out, tempers swelled; each snapped at another, frustrated that their long walk in the desert had proven fruitless. All the while, Solaris insisted that they had reached the place, but even she began to doubt herself.

"I'm just saying," said Tom, his frustration evident, "that we would have found it by now."

"I know it's here," replied Solaris, her voice curt.

"Then where is the entrance?" demanded Klanor.

Having grown tired of their bickering, Solon interrupted them in his usual calm and pensive manner. "Perhaps instead of trying to find what wishes to remain hidden, we should wait for it to come to us."

Klanor threw up his hands, tired of Solon's habit of speaking proverbial bits of wisdom.

"So, what?" said Tom, losing his temper, "we should just wait for an invitation? Maybe we should knock and it will open the door for us."

"It would not harm you to learn patience, my friend," said Solon.

Tom stalked off in a huff, his mood matching the others'.

While the others moved off, too irritated to consider Solon's suggestion, the young scholar roamed the ground once more in the afternoon light, his studious nature dictating his movements. His eyes searched every rock, every crevice, for anything that did not belong, and just when he was about to give up, the winds shifted, blowing the sand off a granite stone near his foot. Solon knelt down, the grainy silt molding around his knees, and brushed his hand over it, revealing a Lanyran symbol; he recognized it as Lanyran because it possessed the same characteristic as the hieroglyphs on Rynah's ship.

Another rock caught his attention. It wasn't the rock itself that intrigued him, but the way it seemed to have been carved and casted into a rectangular shape that was even on all sides. Solon hurried to it, rubbing the sand off and revealing another symbol. He rushed from rock to rock, in a straight line, brushing them off, as more Lanyran symbols were unearthed, until he reached the tower of rock before him with a matching insignia. He leaned in close and blew the grit off it, clearing it away until the hieroglyph shone in the fading sunlight, his heart pumping with excitement at such an archeological find.

"Over here!"

The others rushed over.

"What?" said Tom.

Solon pointed at the symbols.

Achilles and Fons stepped closer.

"Well, I'll be damned," said Achilles. "These are Lanyran symbols."

"Ancient Lanyran," said Rynah, taking a closer look.

"See!" Fons waved his finger at the symbols. "I told you! I told all of you! And you didn't believe me—Joe laughed at me even—but they've been here before."

"Okay," said Joe, tired of Fons' badgering, "you were right. Extraterrestrials are real. They've been here before. We're with a bunch of them right now. Now can you let it go?"

"Maybe," said Fons, "if you say you're sorry."

Joe glared at his friend, hating being in this position, especially with others around watching their exchange.

"I'm sorry," he said through gritted teeth.

"What?" said Fons, placing his hand on the edge of his ear. "I didn't quite hear you."

"I'm sorry," Joe repeated in a loud voice amidst a few giggles from the others.

"I don't understand this symbol," said Achilles, ignoring Fons' and Joe's exchange. "Why this one, the same one over and over again?"

"Explain," said Alfric.

"This symbol means hope," replied Achilles. "Who would put the symbol for hope on all of these rocks? Though that isn't what is most puzzling? This is the language of my people, my time, what you now call a dead language. So who could have put it here, and why?"

"Another puzzle," said Brie.

"Well, this is all well and good," said Tom, "but we are no nearer to getting in there."

"Maybe you should knock," said Joe, half-joking, remembering Tom's sarcastic suggestion from before.

To prove how asinine a suggestion that was, Tom knocked on the rock with the carving on it.

"Hello! Any one in there? You going to let us in now?" He walked away. "See? Won't work."

A soft grinding rumbled around them.

"What was that?" asked Brie.

"Just the wind," said Klanor, his mind focused on the ancient hieroglyphs before him as he pondered how and why they were there.

"Maybe we should check one of these other piles of rock," said Tom, not paying attention to the noise that had intrigued Brie, "because I think we're in the wrong place."

"I'm not so sure anymore," mumble Obiah as the noise grew louder.

"Come on, guys…" began Tom.

"SHH!" Rynah hissed at him.

"It's not like the ground is going to fall out from under our feet," Tom continued.

At that moment, the ground did fall out from under his feet, opening wide and swallowing Tom as he crashed to the floor below, amidst a pile of rock and rubble.

"TOM!" yelled Solon.

"I'm all right," Tom coughed, brushing dust off his arms and shirt. "Me and my big mouth," he mumbled to himself. He looked up at the hole above him and the particles of dust that danced within the sun's red-orange rays, noticing a slender stairwell, carved into the rock, and laughed to himself at how he had spotted them after he had already fallen through the ground.

What the others didn't know was that the rock Tom had touched was no rock at all, but a scanning pad disguised as a part of the cliff. It had waited hundreds of thousands of years for someone with a certain DNA code to touch it, thus opening the doors—which Tom had unwittingly stood upon, thus giving credence to the phrase "famous last words"—and allowing them entrance.

The others walked down the silky smooth stairs, marveling at how they showed no sign of aging. The smoothness of the steps matched the walls surrounding them; they were not the natural formation of rock, but had been built by design.

"One day," said Solon, helping his friend up, "you will not let your impatience get the better of you."

"Or your sarcasm," said Solaris as she strolled past.

Brie stepped through a low archway, its edges lined with a thin sheet of charcoal-gray metal that gave off a rainbow of colors in the faint sunlight. Lights flickered on, forming pale white lines down the length of the stone walls—with no nicks, chips, marks, or discoloring—and illuminating their path. Brie touched the thin strip of light with the tips of her fingers. Its cool touch surprised her, but its smoothness matched the walls around all of them, having been built into the stone with a transparent, marble covering, instead of plastic or glass. Her wide eyes marveled at the tunnel they stood in, and for a brief moment, she had forgotten about Stein, her mother, and sister, as she stroked the side of the wall and how it squeaked from having no dust on it.

"Solaris' ship," she whispered to herself, remembering when she had first boarded Solaris and at how clean the antiquated ship was.

"Where are they getting the power from?" asked Tom, bending low to examine the lights and lack of wiring that connected them.

"Power crystals," said Klanor, pointing one out. "But how could anyone from our time have known to come here?"

"You make the mistake of thinking you are the only ones to have used them," said Achilles. "We used power crystals—though we didn't call them that—to power everything, including our ships."

"Sorry," muttered Klanor.

Brie marched down the tunnel.

"Brie, where are you going?" asked Tom.

"To see where this goes," replied Brie. "I'm tired of waiting for something to happen. I want to know why this is here, and it better not be more riddles."

"She's right," said Alfric, gripping his sword. "We should follow this path and see where it leads, for time is against us."

"You know," Tom said to Alfric, "I'm going to have to teach you some modern slang. This archaic way of speaking—"

Alfric glowered at Tom, his muscles bulging.

"—is wonderful. Very educational. Keep it up, big guy," finished Tom, changing his tone and patting Alfric on the back before following Brie, who was several feet away. "That guy seriously needs anger management," Tom muttered to himself.

With caution, they trekked through the corridor and its eerie silence. Unlike tunnels of the earth, this cavern had no moisture on the walls, no dripping of water, no moss, no critters—not even the multi-legged, crawling kind—no unevenness, not even a breeze. It ascended up the rock tower in a soft incline that spiraled in a circle, making their climb an easy one; not one of them panted when they reached the end of the path.

A metal door opened the moment they reached it, closing behind them once they had passed through. More lights turned on. They stood upon a circular pad, 15 paces in diameter, with a matching pad on the ceiling above them; gray circles dotted the strange pad, but that isn't what caught Tom's attention. While the others wandered about the room, and the circular pad covered in more circles, Tom crept over to a metal box with a red button in its center, as though waiting for someone to push it. Most would have left it alone, but Tom allowed his curiosity to rule him, like he did on most occasions, and reached out, forefinger extended, pushing the red button.

ZAP!

"What was that?" demanded Obiah, spiraling on his feet. As he and those with him glanced around, he noticed that their number had decreased—Tom, Brie, Solon, Alfric, and Rynah had disappeared.

* * *

On a faraway planet, once colonized by the Lanyrans of Achilles' time and called *Dongya* (meaning 14), and a beacon of civilization, Rynah, Tom, Alfric, Brie, and Solon materialized under 2½ rose-colored moons. Chest-high blades of grass, which had cushioned their rough landing, waved in the crisp breeze that caressed their cheeks, bringing with it the fresh scent of lemons and orange blossoms.

"When will you ever learn," stormed Rynah at Tom. "WHEN WILL YOU LEARN THAT NOT EVERYTHING THAT CATCHES YOUR FANCY MUST BE TOYED WITH?"

"I'm not sorry," said Tom, folding his ebony-colored arms. "That button begged to be pushed."

"What?" Rynah said.

"That button wasn't put there by accident," replied Tom.

"And I suppose it spoke to you," Rynah scoffed.

"In a manner of speaking," said Tom, "it did. It said, 'I've been here forever, locked in this dark cave. Please, someone, push me.' So I did. Deal with it."

Rynah held her hands before her mimicking a choke hold. "I could strangle you sometimes."

"And I'm sure big man over there will be happy to help you," Tom said.

They all looked at Alfric, who had said nothing, but stared at the night sky and the constellations within it with a pondering look on his face.

"What's wrong?" asked Brie.

"These stars are not our own," replied Alfric.

The others looked up, mouths gaping.

"Where are we?" asked Brie, circling in place and surveying the area they now found themselves in.

"I don't know," replied Rynah, "but that pad we were standing on in those tunnels must have been a teleportation device." She brushed the grass away from the ground, pulling it out by the roots and uncovering another white pad with gray circles across the surface. "This matches the other back on earth."

"Why did only we get transported here?" asked Brie. "Why not the others?"

"I cannot say," replied Rynah. "We need to figure out where we are."

"The real question," said Solon, "is not where we are, but why we are here."

"You know where we are," said Tom.

"No, but I know where we should go," replied Solon.

He beckoned them to follow him through the grass—for while the others argued about their current whereabouts, Solon had explored the surrounding area to find the answer—leading them to the edge of a hill that looked down upon what had once been a great city.

"Whoa," said Tom, when he saw it.

Buildings taller than the Eiffel Tower loomed over them, their shadows crisscrossing in the moons' rosy glow. Vines snaked up the sides of the structures, twisting into gnarled knots and covering the stained-glass windows, overhangs, balconies, and metallic sides so that they looked more like manmade trees than city dwellings.

They trekked down the hill and passed through an archway made of amber; each looked all around, necks craned upward, as they strolled through the black streets and under elevated rails. Lights flared up, activated by their movements, bringing signs and holographic displays to life, each advertising a product or service.

"How is there is still power?" asked Brie.

"Crystals," replied Rynah, finding one such crystal and showing it to the others. "Achilles had said that they used them in his time."

"But how is it still standing?" asked Alfric. "If this place is as old as he, should it not be in ruin?"

Rynah paused, looking around at the spiraling buildings and the images (though pixelated and not clear) that scrolled across them, noting at how nature had tried to take them back, but they showed no signs of crumbling. She spotted Tom, who had knelt down, examining a wall that had once served as a planter and was attached to a dome-shaped structure, and walked over to him, placing her hand on it and jerking it back as ripples stretched the length of the wall and floated up the sides of the building. Rynah poked it with her fingers again, thinking she had just stuck her hand in a pan of water, yet it remained dry, marveling at the ripples that appeared again.

"Remarkable," breathed Rynah. "It's nanotechnology embedded in the building's structure."

"Can you elaborate?' asked Solon, trying to understand what she had just said.

"It's something we were experimenting with back home," said Rynah, her voice choked at the memory of Lanyr, "but was still in the pretrial stages. It's what has kept this place from disappearing. The nanites absorb any damage done to the exterior and conduct repairs. Scientists on my planet theorized that such a thing could make it where our cities would stand for thousands of years and look as though they had just been built.

"It appears these... nanites," Alfric said, pronouncing each syllable, "have a finite existence." The Viking pointed at another building that had crumbled away, buried by mounds of brown grass and yellow vines that intertwined, forming a braided carpet over what had once been an eatery.

A firefly buzzed around Rynah's nose. She swatted at the glowing speck as it flittered about in circles around her head. In fact, this was no firefly at all, but a mechanical robot disguised as a firefly and programed to activate when they had arrived. Rynah swatted it again, but missed. In an effort to avoid being squished—it had a mission to complete, after all—the tiny mechanical insect settled on Rynah's elongated nose.

"I think it likes you," joked Tom. "Aw, look, it's giving you kisses!"

Annoyed, Rynah scowled at Tom and raised her hand to smack the firefly, but Brie stopped her.

"No, don't!"

She crept over to Rynah and with care, cupped her hands over Rynah's nose, scooping the firefly into them. "It's harmless," said Brie, studying the insect; she had always wanted to see a firefly in person.

"It still tickles," snorted Rynah, wrinkling her nose.

"Tom," Brie held the winged insect out to him, "I don't think this is a real firefly. It seems... mechanical."

Tom peered at the insect in Brie's hands, watching as its wings flapped in rhythmic motion, too perfect for a real firefly, and noted the ridged markings on its lit rear.

"It is mechanical—an insect-sized robot."

The robotic firefly flew off, darting around them before disappearing into the distance. They didn't move. Within seconds, it appeared again, whizzing around their heads—frustrated at their inability to get its message—and disappeared again.

"I think it wants us to follow it," said Solon.

"How can you tell?" asked Tom.

In answer to his question, the firefly robot appeared for a third time, even more aggravated at their lack of response, and buzzed around each of their heads, before hovering before them.

Alfric walked towards the hovering insect. "The soothsayer is right; we should follow this omen."

Relieved that they had finally understood its wishes, the robotic firefly flew off, its glowing rear a beacon in the night. They chased after the mechanical insect, jumping over rubble, protruding roots from trees that intruded on the city, and fallen rails in an effort to keep up.

The firefly stopped. Skidding to a halt, they stared at the glowing orb, wondering why it had stopped underneath an arced overhang, big enough to cover a plaza. As they stepped beneath it, silver lights danced up and down its edges as glass icicles hung from it, twirling in the cool breeze. The firefly flew up to the overhang and disappeared; it had gone to where the controls were, as it had been programed to do, and pressed the switch.

"Where did it go?" asked Brie.

The dancing lights ceased; in its place appeared symbols, written in yellow lights, that none of them, except Rynah, had ever seen. The characters filled the underside of the overhang from edge to edge, lighting the astonished faces below them.

"What is this?" demanded Alfric.

"I think they're words," replied Brie.

"They are," said Rynah, as she read the text above her. "It's Ancient Lanyran, or a more archaic form of it, but I think I can make out the message." She read it.

In the beginning was the word
and the word was with the dragon.
Its treasure makes clear what time has blurred
and will brighten what has been blackened.

Seek dragon's secret lair;
act without fear.
One, now three, must be one again.
Only legend's blood can enter its glen.

But be warned, for not all are worthy;
sacrifice must be endured
to prove honor and earn mercy.

Search deep within darkened waters
whose depths remain unknown.
Not sea, nor river,
but on land it was sown.
As tall as the highest peak,
a border most unique,
near fiery ring that mires the meek.

Search night's white orb.
Sun's light it absorbs.
Mysterious cavern you must tread
before its shadow spreads.

Search red star, for a star it's not.
Many men follow what it has taught.

Warfare, is its legacy.
Peace, it considers heresy.

"Oh my gosh," gasped Rynah. "This is the missing text!"

"What?" asked Solon.

"There is a portion of missing text in the poem, well, so faded, and it looked like someone had tried to purposefully erase it, that you couldn't read it—this is it! But why would it be here?"

"We should go back and discuss it with the others to find out what places on Earth this text refers to," said Brie.

"How can you be certain that it refers to our planet and not this one?" asked Tom.

"For one," said Brie, "the text talks about one moon; this planet has two and a half. For another, it also talks about a red star and there isn't one here."

Having spent much of her time with Solon during their training sessions with Alfric, she had learned how to read the metaphorical references in poetry.

"She's right," said Rynah.

"Ares," said Solon, interrupting them.

"What?" asked Tom.

"These lines refer to the god of war, Ares," said Solon.

"The Romans referred to the god of war as... Mars," Brie said, her face lighting up. "We have to go to Mars! It is often referred to as the red planet, and sometimes appears as a red star in the night sky."

"Do you mean that desolate planet we passed on the way to yours?" asked Rynah.

"Yes," replied Brie.

Rynah couldn't believe it. When she first laid eyes on the planet Mars, she referred to it as a spot of caked blood amidst the black, poison to any vestige of life.

"There are two other vessels," said Alfric. "This verse refers to three in total; you have only discovered the location of one."

"One might be on the moon," said Tom. "Brie said that the poem referred to it. Many astronomers have noted the caverns on the moon; their depths are unknown. So it is possible that something might be hidden within them."

Alfric scrutinized Tom, surprised that he had deduced a line of poetry and read through its metaphors, despite his tendency to follow his unfocused mind. "Not bad," he said, which was as much of a congratulations Tom was going to get from the Viking.

"But what about the third verse?" asked Solon. He repeated the stanza once more.

> Search deep within darkened waters
> whose depths remain unknown.
> Not sea, nor river,
> but on land it was sown.
> As tall as the highest peak,
> a border most unique
> near fiery ring that mires the meek.

Rynah looked from one to the other as the silence loomed, growing stronger as the seconds ticked past.

"Do none of you know?"

Solon shook his head. "There is no fiery ring where I live, except for the sun."

"No way anything could be hidden there," said Tom.

Rynah glanced at Alfric.

"My home world is frozen most of the year and the sea is our water."

Both Tom and Brie shuffled their feet, doing their best to think of what the poem referred to.

"The only thing I can think of is the ring of fire," Brie said.

Tom's face lit up. "Oh!—I'm such and idiot!"

Alfric clenched his mouth shut, grinding his teeth and resisting the urge to make a sarcastic remark, despite the open opportunity Tom had provided.

"Ring of fire?" asked Rynah.

"It literally is a ring of volcanoes that circles the perimeter of the Pacific Ocean," said Tom. "One of the most famous bodies of water near there is Lake Tahoe. It's a great place to visit. I once went there with a friend of mine and we…"

"That's right," Brie cut Tom off. "It is in the Sierra Nevada Mountains and not attached to any other body of water. It is, in a way, on the highest peak, and part of it is in California while the other half is in Nevada."

"'A border most unique,'" Solon quoted.

"Two years ago," said Tom, "a group of marine geologists tried to measure the depth of Lake Tahoe's center. They said there was this spot where they reached 3,000 feet before running out of rope—so to speak—and still had not located the bottom."

"I thought they measured its depth at around 1,600 feet," said Brie.

"That's what they want you to think," said Tom, thinking of some of the conspiracy theories one of his academy friends had told him regarding Lake Tahoe. "Someone I know said he went diving there and found an area that was deeper than 1,600 feet and seemed to go on forever."

"And he's the one that gave you that 3,000 feet measurement?" said Brie.

"Well, yeah," answered Tom.

Brie started laughing. "He was pulling your leg!"

"I'll have you know," Tome replied, "that we have some very sophisticated ways to measure underwater depth. And…"

"You got played," said Brie.

Insulted, though realizing that Brie was probably right, Tom folded his arms in a defensive stance.

"There are unexplored caverns under the water."

"I guess it is possible that a spaceship might be hidden under there," conceded Brie. "And considering everything that we have witnessed in the last several months, it's worth a look."

"It's settled then," said Rynah, bemused by Tom's and Brie's little exchange. "We'll have to explore those three areas. For now, we should return to the others before they wonder what has happened to us."

Though still confused as to how the lines of ancient Lanyran text came to be written on the overhang of an even more ancient set of ruins, they started to walk back to where they had arrived.

"Rynah."

Rynah froze upon hearing the all too familiar voice. She turned around and almost gasped when she saw the man standing before her. It was Marlow, but not the old, decrepit man whose body had been consumed by illness; he looked as she remembered him from her childhood, more youthful and stronger.

"Grandfather?" she whispered, her lips parted in disbelief as the word hung in the air.

The others watched her with a mixture of confusion and sorrow as they saw the mixture of sadness, disbelief, and joy on her face.

"My darling girl."

"How…" began Rynah. Her hand reached up and touched the amber ring that she wore around her neck—Marlow's ring. She remembered the day he had begged her to keep it safe, and how she had turned her back on him. As she stared into the familiar gray eyes, those memories rushed back, slamming into her and she wished that she had paid more attention to his request.

"You died."

The man who stood before them lowered his head.

"I know. I am not really your grandfather, but a holographic projection of him, with a portion of his consciousness, giving me his memories."

Tom regretted having pushed the button that brought them there, as he watched a somber and tortured expression cloud Rynah's face.

Marlow's holographic form took Rynah's hand and turned it so that the wristband she had always worn glinted in the pale light, showing its engravings to everyone.

"I remember when I gave this to you. Well, when the real Marlow did."

Rynah twisted her wrist, admiring the small bracelet and remembering when she had entered her 14th year and Marlow had given it to her.

"Keep it with you always," he had told her after placing it on her arm. And so Rynah did, having never taken it off.

"I'm sorry," she said. "I never should have..."

"It's was never your fault, Rynah, but mine," said the holographic Marlow. "I should have been home, with my family, with you, not trapesing through the Twelve Sectors looking for myths and legends."

"I'm sorry to interrupt," said Brie, but a question begged to be asked and she knew that the others back on Earth would be worried about them, "but why are you here?"

The holoimage of Marlow chuckled. "It's no interruption at all. Marlow knew that you would all come here in your quest to finish what he had started. The warrior, the philosopher, the inventor, and the lover."

Brie cringed when he said the word lover.

"Oh, I don't think it was ever meant like that, my dear," laughed the holoimage of Marlow. "More like a mother's love, and the capacity to forgive."

"Know?" said Rynah. "How?"

In answer to her question, the holoimage of Marlow bent down and drew a symbol in the dirt, the same as the watermark on the missing page of the book. The others did not understand the gesture, but Rynah did.

Marlow's holoimage straightened up. "I was to be activated when those words on the overhang appeared. I was put here to give you a message."

"What message?" asked Rynah.

"You have all that you need with you. You have carried it with you always. And, remember the power of three."

"That doesn't make any sense," said Rynah.

"I am sorry," said the holoimage of Marlow, "but that was it."

Rynah bit her lip, trying to maintain control of her voice and composure, not wanting to show weakness in front of the others, in front of those she had learned to call friends.

"Can you come back with us?"

"I'm sorry," replied the holographic Marlow. "But once you leave, I will be deactivated and my program will be erased."

"Maybe I can..." began Tom, but Marlow's hologram cut him off.

"No. This is how it must be."

"I miss you, so much," said Rynah, losing control.

"I know, my dear," said Marlow's holoimage as he reached up and wiped a tear that left a glistening trail on his cheek. "But it is time for you to leave."

The holographic image vanished. Rynah choked back the tears that wanted to burst free, regaining her usual self-contained and disciplined manner.

"Let's go."

Tom had wanted to say something, but Solon shook his head, knowing that now was not the time, as there were no words to be said that would comfort Rynah. He clamped his mouth shut and followed after his friends as they walked back to the transporter pad.

Unknown to them, the robotic firefly saw them depart and buzzed over to Rynah, following its programing, and hid in her pocket.

"How do we get this thing working again?" Tom asked when they neared the teleportation pad.

In answer to his question, the moment that they all stood upon the pad, it activated, transporting them back to where they had come from.

"Oh," said Tom as they vanished, "that's how."

Chapter 16
ACHILAI

The pad back in the underground bunker lit up and with a—Pop!—Rynah, Brie, Tom, Alfric, and Solon appeared. They looked around at the gaping faces of their friends—Solaris looked dejected more than curious—knowing that they would have to explain where they had gone, though they remained unsure of how it had happened.

"How long?" Rynah asked.

"Nearly a day," replied Obiah. "What happened?"

"That is what I want to know," said Joe. "You drag me all the way here, disappear, and then show back up as though nothing happened. I want an explanation."

"I'm not sure I fully understand myself," said Rynah.

"We thought Stein might have taken you," Obiah said, "but Klanor disagreed."

"There was no reason to think he had," Klanor stepped forward.

"There is every reason," Obiah argued. "He's..."

"I never knew about this place, or had any inclination of it,"

Klanor interrupted. "How could Stein, who has had the same information I had."

"It is clear to me," said Obiah, with a dangerous undertone, "that you never knew him very well to begin with."

"DNA scanners," Solaris said, breaking up their argument. She had wandered over to the transporter pad, investigating why only five of them were allowed through; she had examined it earlier, but needed at least two readings to make a proper conclusion.

"DNA filtering," she said again when the others stared at her in confusion. "This transporter pad was designed to be used by someone with certain DNA properties—one in particular. Achilles, you might recognize it."

Achilles bent over and studied the scanners. He did indeed recognize the patterns as the same he had seen when testing Rynah's, Brie's, Tom's, Alfric's, and Solon's blood.

"Herclai," he whispered. "He must have built this entire compound."

"How is that possible?" asked Brie. "Wouldn't it take him years to do it on his own?"

"Not necessarily," replied Achilles. "We had tools that allowed an individual to build an entire home, even a complex, in less than a day, all on their own. It is quite possible that he did build this compound, but when, and why, I cannot say."

Achilles looked around the underground compound as though seeing it for the first time, remembering a period when he and Herclai were allies, not enemies, wishing that he could undo the past.

"Achilles is right," said Solaris, remembering why Monument Valley looked familiar to her; she had seen a tattered and faded painting with the same structures depicted in Marlow's workshop once, long before her consciousness had been put in the ship that bore her name. *Was it possible that he had found this place?* she thought to herself. "This transporter pad was designed to work only for those with his genetic markers; the same markers that each of you carry."

A note of dispiritedness filled Solaris' voice. She had wished to have gone with them, after having accompanied them on their other adventures, and Solaris wished to be a part of this as well, detesting the feeling of being left out.

Rynah noted the somber tone in Solaris' voice. "Solaris," she whispered to her friend, "is that disappointment I hear?"

Solaris hung her head in a guilty fashion. "I just thought…"

Rynah placed her hand on Solaris' shoulder and gave her a reassuring smile.

"So, where did you go?" asked Fons, voicing what the others wished to know.

"Not sure, exactly," replied Rynah. "I had never seen that planet before, but I know that it was not in this sector—the stars were wrong—but we found this ancient ruin of a city, not like the ruins of stone we have seen before, but more…"

"Futuristic," Brie finished for Rynah.

"That is one way of putting it," said Rynah.

"The lights and material of the buildings were very much like what you have here," said Alfric, "and similar to that of your vessels, but they had been deteriorated from time, as though not a soul had lived there for nearly an age."

"But its lights and signs still worked," said Tom.

"And the buildings had nanotechnology built into them," Rynah added.

"That could be any place from my time," said Achilles. "Was there no distinguishing characteristic?"

"Two moons," said Solon, "and another, half gone, devoured by the night."

Achilles rubbed the stubble on his face as he thought back, remembering the places he had visited in his day that might—he remembered it!

"*Dongya*," he said. "It was in the Fourteenth Sector and was the only habitable planet there. Herclai had a winter home there—we all had homes all over, never staying in one spot—but *Dongya* was an unusual planet. It had two moons that stayed full year round and one that always looked to have been half-eaten, never changing, despite the season."

Rynah, Klanor, Obiah, and Solaris listened with rapt attention to Achilles' description of *Dongya* and the days when it was a central place of economic activity, still not believing that there could ever have been more than 13 sectors. Traders came and went from *Dongya*, selling the items they had acquired from the outlying systems. It made modern metropolitan areas looked like rural communities in need of life.

"I miss that place," Achilles finished, reminiscing about the past.

"We found the missing text there," said Rynah.

"Missing text?" Klanor asked.

"You read the book," Rynah replied. "Do you not remember that there is a page in which the words had faded so much they're unreadable?"

Her mind jumped from the smudged words of the text to the last page of the book—the page that had been ripped out, but bore the mysterious watermark, a mark she knew well.

"Yes, but..."

"The words from that page were there," said Rynah, "in the ruins of that city, as though waiting for us." She repeated the lines of verse.

"Waiting for you?" said Joe. "How could they have been waiting for you? How could this man, who died long before either of us existed, have known that you would be there, at that precise moment, to read the words, not to mention the fact that this ancient text you are using was written long after he died."

No one answered. They all wondered the same.

"Because he did not put them there," said Solon from across the room.

While the others conversed about the strange trip to the planet *Dongya*, Solon explored the rest of the bunker, stumbling upon a series of holographic journals. Having spent countless hours poring over the book that led them through the maze of Sunlil, he had learned enough of the language to be able to decipher some words on his own.

The others gathered around him. Solon took a thin, penny-sized disk and placed it in the playback device, something he had learned to do from watching Tom and Brie do the same on numerous occasions. A holographic image of Herclai fizzled to life, zapping and sizzling before solidifying.

Achilles watched the Herclai hologram, his eyes wide as a longing expression covered his face; his mind remembered the echoes of the past. Memories flooded his mind as he recalled the day Mulyra sunk beneath the sea in a crust of lava and steam, buried for eternity.

"I don't have much time," said a panicked Herclai; explosions echoed in the background. "They found me and I must seal this place before they take it. The heads of the council wish to have the crystals for themselves, possessed by the same darkness that overtook Achilai. I made the unfortunate mistake of telling them about these rare gems that... seem... to possess a will of their own, upon my return."

More explosions rattled the background as bits of dust fell from the ceiling, coating the holographic Herclai.

"These crystals cannot fall into the hands of those who wish only to use them for their own gain. I built this base as a safe haven as I searched for you, but now I must abandon you once again and look for places to hide the pieces of the crystals, though one was lost the day Mulyra's fate was changed. I've long since wondered what happened to them, and you, my wife.

"The Java once told me that together, the crystals draw their strength, but apart, they grow weak. As there seems to be no other way of destroying them, I hope that by separating them, they will lie dormant, and perhaps, will pass into the vestiges of myth and legend and be forgotten.

"I am sorry, Isyr, that I must leave you like this, in a place more foreign and inhospitable than any we have ever encountered before. I put security measures into place to prevent any, except you or me, from entering this place; but should those fail, the transporter pad is your best defense. Isyr, if you did get my messages that I have left scattered across this planet, and if you do trace them here, use the transporter pad. It is set to your, and mine, genetic code. Only you or I can use it."

They watched as Herclai had been knocked from his feet from another explosion that rocked the underground compound.

"They expect me to fly out of here, but I will not lead them to the Mulyran ship, which I have hidden with great care. I have one more crystal to hide. I shall use the transport to leave this place, and find another ship. Once I have hidden this last crystal, I shall return my search for you. Until then..."

The recording ceased. All eyes turned to Achilles, who tried to melt into the dim background.

"You," spat Alfric. "You have lied to us!"

"Now, now—look here," said Achilles, holding his hands up in a defensive posture, "I didn't really lie; I just... omitted a few things. My real name is Achilai Matyr-ka-san. I took the name of Achilles when I ended up in this time and learned that an entire myth had been written, though exaggerated, about me."

"Omission by design is still a falsehood," said Solon.

"You destroyed those people," said Klanor, with a note of disbelief, forgetting about the damage he had caused to other civilizations.

"You are no better than him," said Obiah. "How many have you killed in your quest for the crystals? And what about Lanyr?"

"This isn't about me," hissed Klanor.

"Of course it is!" Obiah's voice thundered off the stone walls and ceiling of the chamber. "You two are quite a pair, both giving into your greed."

"And what of you," retorted Klanor, "abandoning your friend when he needed you most."

"How dare you…"

"Klanor…" began Rynah, but he cut her off.

"No, this must be said," Klanor screamed. "You all are quick to accuse me and look in my direction whenever something terrible happens, but you should be looking at yourselves!"

"I never meant…" Achilles tried to speak, but was cut off.

"Meant what? To cause harm?" said Joe. "I've seen a lot of terrible things caused by people who never meant to harm anyone."

"I should have your head put on a spike," Alfric growled at Achilles.

"Let's not do anything drastic," mumbled Fons, while Brie looked horrified by the hostile look on the Viking's face.

"She knew!" Achilles pointed at Solaris, but regretted it the moment the words were out of his mouth.

"What?" breathed Rynah with disbelief. "You knew and never said anything?"

"It wasn't my place," said Solaris. "It was for him to decide."

"So you've allowed us to seek the help of the very man who started this whole mess?" Rynah said.

"Technically," said Solon, with unusual calm, "the person who wrote your myth provided the very framework for someone to begin searching for the crystals."

"Now might not be the time," said Tom.

"I want to know," said Obiah to Achilles, "were you planning on betraying us after you acquired the crystals again?"

"Now, wait a minute," said Achilles, "I never once considered it."

"So you say," Obiah spat.

The rage of the others continued; their shouts and yells reverberated off the walls, echoing around them and fueling their outrage. The others, except Brie, had crowded around Achilles, backing him into a corner and screaming at him, and at one another. Soon, a brawl broke out, as they each gave in to their frustrations, anger, and flying fists. Joe tried to calm them, but it proved useless.

Alfric yanked out his sword, pointing it at Achilles. Within moments, Joe was upon him, trying to pull the weapon out of the Viking's grasp, but Alfric shook him off. The fighting raged around them as everyone gave into the chaos. As the shouts and screams increased, no one noticed Brie—or the robotic firefly as it left Rynah's pocket and flew over to the computer console—pushing and shoving her way into the melee. Once again, Alfric charged Achilles.

Brie jumped between them. "Alfric, no!"

She reached for the blade, but Alfric, in his frenetic state, threw her off before he had become aware of her presence. Brie flew across the ground, ramming into the wall and dropping to the concrete floor. In a rage, Alfric screamed, forcing the others to back off, which they did the moment they noticed Brie lying motionless.

Alfric ran to her, guilt written on his face.

"Is she…" began Rynah.

Alfric shook his head. "Only unconscious. Brie." He shook her with a gentleness none would have thought possible coming from him.

"Brie?" said Rynah.

Brie sat up, rubbing her head, still groggy from having struck the wall. "I'm all right."

The others watched her, their apprehensive faces betrayed their guilt over bickering with one another.

"I am sick and tired of all of this," she said as she rose to her feet, with Alfric's help. "Once again, we are all fighting amongst ourselves while Stein is out there doing who knows what! When are we going to stop distrusting one another and start listening?"

"How can you forgive him when he is responsible for the crystals being torn from their home in the first place?" demanded Klanor, referring to Achilles.

Brie stared him in the eyes, her face stern. "I forgave you."

Klanor clamped his mouth shut and backed away, shamed by Brie's answer as the memory of what he had done to her, and the fact that he was responsible for Lanyr's demise, filled his mind, yet she had harbored no ill will towards him.

"Solaris," said Brie, "you said you knew. How?"

"His face looked familiar," replied Solaris, explaining about the man she had seen when she had been transported through time to when Mulyra had fallen, and telling them the story of what had happened when she had left them. "I confronted him, privately, wanting to be sure and he confessed. He regrets that day."

"Do you trust him?" asked Brie.

"Yes," replied Solaris.

"Then, so will I," Brie said as she walked over to Achilles, who still cowered in a corner, afraid of what the others might do to him. "Look me in the eye and tell me," Brie said to him, her authoritative and stern voice surprising even her, "are you the same man?"

"No," Achilles replied, ashamed to look into her calm and forgiving eyes.

Brie held her hand out to him. Achilles took it and she helped him to his feet.

"I don't know about the rest of you," she said, "but I am tired of always being two steps behind Stein. We should find the parts of this dragon ship, figure out how it fits into all of this, destroy the crystals, and stop Stein once and for all. And as for you two, this is your chance to make things right."

Both Klanor and Achilles glanced at their feet before looking at Brie.

"I'm sorry," Klanor said to Achilles before shuffling off.

"You would give me that?" asked Achilles. "Why?"

Brie looked him square in the eye, concentrating on making her voice firm. "Because it is the right thing to do."

Solaris watched from the sidelines, a small smile upon her lips, pleased at Brie's stance and the firmness with which she spoke, captivating all of them. A memory of Marlow flashed through her mind, disappearing within seconds. She remembered how Marlow had informed her of his illness.

"You'll have to guide them without me," he had told her, his pallid face wincing from the pain he experienced when doing even the simplest of movements.

"How can I?" Solaris had asked.

"The same way I guided you," Marlow had replied.

"But I haven't your knowledge, or experience."

"The knowledge I have passed to you. Study it. Experience, well, that comes from living."

"Rynah needs you," Solaris had pleaded. "They all will need your guidance."

"That you will have to provide it. Remember what I taught you."

"I can't."

"You must." Marlow looked in Solaris' direction; he would have peered into her eyes if she had possessed bodily form.

"Rynah will not listen."

"You will have to make her."

"Don't leave me," Solaris had pleaded. "You are my only friend."

"In truth, I do not wish to," Marlow had replied, out of breath, "but there are some choices that are taken from us. Just remember that even the one who appears most weak can be the strongest link."

Solaris pulled herself back to the present and watched as the others calmed themselves, having been shamed by Brie.

"You were right," she whispered to Marlow's memory.

"Hey, guys," Tom called from across the way. He had wandered off and found another tantalizing button that was flat against the wall and begged for his attention. The robotic firefly had flown over to it, thus attracting Tom's attention to it, before going back to Rynah's pocket.

"DON'T TOUCH IT!" everyone screamed at him, forgetting their little spat the moment they had seen him standing next to another button.

Tom pulled back. "Okay. Okay. I wasn't going to anyway. Sheesh!"

Solaris rushed over to him and inspected the thumb-sized pad, making certain that it wasn't attached to another transporter pad. She pushed it. A doorway appeared in what had been a solid wall, opening before them and allowing an opal-blue light to drape over the floor as it stretched for them.

Stepping through, their eyes widened as a single ship—sleek in design with nobs for wings—waited for its owner to return; its coal-colored hull blended in with the shadows and rocky backdrop. Rays of yellow sunlight dropped down from above as a hangar door opened and a launch ramp appeared, lifting the ship up at a 45-degree angle.

Experiencing a bout of curiosity, and giving in to the desire to touch something new and extraordinary, Solon crept up to the ship and placed his palm on the cool exterior, remarking at how smooth it was. A soft whir filled his ears as a hatch materialized and opened.

"The oracle was right," Solon whispered.

"Oracle?" asked Tom.

Solon faced his friend. "Two years ago, my father took my brother and me to the oracle of Delphi. It told my brother that he would be a great warrior, to which my father was pleased, but when I stood before it, the oracle said that I would touch shadows and a door would open before me, taking me to the heavens, and I would fly like the gods. Have I not flown through the skies like the gods?" Solon glanced at the sleek ship before them. "This looks like a shadow, does it not?"

Tom stepped closer and studied the ship from a new angle before agreeing with Solon.

"Fons," said Rynah, "do you think you can use this to contact Jifdar?" She pointed at a computer console.

"Yes."

"Do it, please," said Rynah, "and make sure you encrypt it."

Chapter 17
DESTINATION REACHED

Jifdar paced the command center of his ship, ignoring the way the soles of his boots stuck to the floor. His ingrained movements guided him as he stepped around the worn through hole in the floor, which had been there for months.

Why hadn't she contacted me, yet? he thought to himself, his mind filled with scenarios, each more dismal than the last, as he grappled with going in search of her or staying where he was, an act uncommon to his pirate nature.

"Anything?"

"No, cap'n," one of his pirates answered.

Frustrated, Jifdar continued his pacing, but stopped when he noticed a portion of the metal railing that circled the room, its gleam a stark contrast against the black substance that coated most of his ship; Solaris had wiped it clean with her sleeve her first day aboard, unable to take the mess any longer.

Intrigued, as he hadn't seen any part of his vessel so clean in such a long while that he had forgotten what it had looked like,

Jifdar stroked the smooth rail, amazed that it did not discolor his scaly fingers. He wondered who would have bothered before his mind settled on Rynah and the others. His attention snapped back to his unease as he waited for a message from those on the planet. Solaris had said that she would contact him, but no transmission ever arrived. Something had gone wrong; he knew it.

"Anything, yet?" demanded Jifdar.

"Sorry, cap'n," replied the same pirate.

"Captain," said Heller, his first mate, in a hushed whisper, "a word?"

Jifdar led his first mate to another room where they could seal the doors and talk in private

"Speak your piece."

"What are we doing here?"

"Waiting for Rynah to contact us."

"Why?" challenged the first mate. "Why are we here at all?"

Jifdar had no answer. In truth, he had wondered the same. Why had he stayed? He had kept his initial end of the bargain that he had made with Rynah and her band of misfits, so why did he feel the need to remain?

"We came here to find the man responsible for killing our kin— good pirates—and we have," continued Heller. "Yet, instead of having his head, we allow him to live while sitting here like a bunch of *Brasur*. We should kill him and be done with it. Leastways, we should leave. This isn't our fight."

Jifdar listened to his first mate, as the man voiced the exact concerns he had. He had asked himself the same questions many times in the last few days, but never liked the answer—he wasn't always a pirate.

"Captain?" his first mate pressed.

"I have given my orders."

"But why…"

"We will wait here until Rynah contacts us," Jifdar's stern voice silenced his first mate. "Until then, you will do as I say, understood? Now get back to work."

The first mate headed for the door, but Jifdar's voice stopped him.

"I know," he said in a gentler tone, "that my actions have been irregular. We should at least keep our bargain with Rynah and await her communication. After that, we will decide whether to stay or go."

"Fair enough," said Heller, before leaving.

"Cap'n!" In rushed the man at the con. "A ship approaches."

Jifdar ran into the command center, his misgivings put on hold as he focused on this new threat.

"Show it!"

A holoscreen filled the room as a strange vessel flew from the front to the rear, its luminescent and sleek design foreign to all who watched.

"What sort of vessel is that?" asked Heller, mesmerized by the strange new vessel that had appeared.

Jifdar had no answer. He stared at the pyramid-shaped craft with a stubby tail on the rear and wings that arced backwards, like a hawk's did when flying, as it glided through space, heading straight for them.

"Destination?"

"It appears to be heading for the planet," said one of his pirates.

Jifdar's mind raced with the possibilities of what this new ship meant, or who commanded it. Fearing that it might be a new threat, he decided that the best course of action was to destroy it.

"Fire!"

A plasma blast erupted from his ship's cannons. Jifdar watched the holographic image as it sailed for the new vessel, striking its target, but the ship's hull absorbed the energy of the plasma blast.

"What?" breathed Jifdar. "How is this possible?"

None of his pirates had an answer.

"Switch to the ionic cannons," ordered Jifdar.

The pirate at the helm made the switch, awaiting the order to fire.

"Fire!"

The ionic cannon sent out its blast, striking the strange vessel in its center, rocking it, and forcing the pilot to dive. Jifdar watched as the ship veered to the left before tilting upward—a few smoldering flames poked from its sides.

Now knowing if the ionic cannon damaged the ship, Jifdar gave the order.

"Fire again!"

Two more blasts from the cannon burst from his ship, flying straight for the strange vessel. Jifdar eyes stayed fixated on the holographic image as the ship jerked to the side—one blast erupted in the new void—and pointed at him in a head-on collision. The second ionic blast exploded just off the port bow of the sleek ship, jerking it to the side before the pilot steadied its course. In horror, Jifdar watched as the vessel headed straight for him.

"Hard to starboard!" he yelled.

Though his pilot cranked the controls, the largeness of his vessel caused it to be slow to respond, while the smaller ship that charged speeded through space, with him in its sights.

"Full reverse!" yelled Jifdar.

The ship closed in. Jifdar could only watch, waiting for the inevitable, as this new quarry closed the distance until... it jerked upward, speeding past his ship, missing it by a foot. Releasing the breath he held, Jifdar turned to his gunman.

"Whatever we got, I want to—"

"Sir," said the pilot, "they are hailing us."

Confused, Jifdar looked back at the holographic image of the strange ship; it hovered in front of him, a viper poised to strike.

"On speaker," said Jifdar.

"Stop firing," came a voice over the com unit.

"Identify yourself," Jifdar demanded.

"My name is General Delmar. We mean you no harm."

"Why are you here?" asked Jifdar, doubting the man's claims.

"Don't waste your time talking with him," came Tre's voice in the background. "They're pirates!"

"Our business is best not discussed over an open com," replied General Delmar.

"Oh, I wish you had never forced me from my station," whined Tre.

General Delmar hushed him. "Please," he turned back to Jifdar, "cease your fire and let us leave in peace. I swear to you that we mean you no harm."

Jifdar pondered over the man's request. "How do I know I can trust your word?"

"I bet he's working for Stein," Tre's accusatory voice came through the com unit. "He might even hold Rynah prisoner."

"Silence!" General Delmar hissed at him.

Rynah? Jifdar's eyes narrowed as he remembered the name of General Delmar. "You are friends of Rynah?"

General Delmar's head shot up when he heard the question.

"Yes," came his tentative answer. "Do you know her?"

"We are allies," replied Jifdar.

"It could be a trap," said Hylne's voice from the side.

"No tricks," Jifdar reassured him.

"Let me speak to her," said General Delmar.

"She isn't aboard."

From the prolonged silence, Jifdar knew that General Delmar thought he had lied about being allied with Rynah.

"I vow not to fire upon you. If you park your ship in my hangar bay, we can discuss matters more securely that way," said Jifdar.

"Agreed," said General Delmar, before cutting the transmission.

"Heller, I'll meet you in my meeting room," said Jifdar as he left the command center through the sliding door, his thick-soled boots, with a steel rim lining the edges, clomped as he schlepped down the metal stairs, sending a series of bangs as he hurried to the docking area. He raced through the musty corridors of his ship, ignoring the tendrils of spongy worms that wriggled and waved as he passed by, his grease-stained coat flapping behind him.

The whine of a ship filled his ears as he neared the hangar bay, pausing before the sealed doors and waiting for the red light to flash green. It changed. Stentorian clangs echoed around him as the locks released, allowing him entrance. Jifdar squeezed through the doors, his coat catching on a protruding scrap of steel and putting another tear in it, as he forced his way into the room.

Controlling his heavy breathing from the exertion of rushing down to the hangar bay, Jifdar stood, hands clasped behind his back, as he took on a stoic pose, not wanting to give these newcomers anything to use against him. The ship—its sleek design and luminescent hull enthralled Jifdar as his pirate mind calculated the total sum he'd receive for the parts—lowered its ramp, revealing three figures. He watched as they stepped down, two in regal stances, while the third tripped over his own feet, fell, and rolled the rest of the way down the ramp. Jifdar maintained the thin line he had forced his lips into.

"The captain of this vessel, I presume," said one of the men as he walked up to Jifdar, hand extended. "I am General Delmar. This is Councilman Hylne and Tre." He pointed at the two men with him; Hylne had paused to help Tre get back to his feet.

"I never should have left my space station," moaned Tre as his tattered trench coat knotted around his legs while he flapped his arms in an effort to untangle himself.

"You may call me Jifdar," replied the pirate captain, his voice even. "Follow me."

Jifdar swept through the hangar doors, leading them into the dim hallway, immune to the sludge that covered the corners where the wall met the floor, and doing his best not to comment at Tre's hopping around in an effort to avoid what Jifdar called, "His ship's character."

Hylne did it for him. "Will you stop," he hissed at Tre, doing his best to keep his voice low.

Tre crossed his arms, hugging them close to his torso as he skipped around.

"Look at this filth! My place was much cleaner."

Unable to contain themselves, and remembering the rusty rails, piles of garbage, and tin pots that were strewn through his space in an effort to catch the drips from leaky pipes, both Hylne and General Delmar faced Tre.

"Well, cleaner than this place," mumbled Tre.

Jifdar's tapping foot broke up their grumblings and spurred them onward. They followed him up a stairwell, with Tre still hopping about, afraid of the sludge that blinked at him, and entered a room with its warped table that wobbled at the slightest touch, illuminated by the annular lamps and their musty glow. Heller waited for them.

"Have a seat, gentleman," said Jifdar, doing his best to display some civility.

General Delmar, Hylne, and Tre each pulled out a chair, the nickel coating stuck to their palms, and seated themselves, while Jifdar took the chair next to his first mate.

"Why are you here?" demanded Jifdar.

"You tell us," replied Hylne. "Why are you here in a sector that none go to?"

"I'll be asking the questions," said Jifdar. "You said you are looking for Rynah. How do you know her?"

Hylne opened his mouth to speak, but clamped it shut when General Delmar lifted his hand.

"I knew her grandfather well," said General Delmar, "and I was once her commanding officer in the Lanyran fleet. How is it that she got involved with pirates?"

Jifdar grimaced, preferring to be the one asking the questions, but knew that this one would come up.

"I stole her ship and left her on Iklor. Later, I rescued her and her band of misfits from Sunlil."

"You stole her ship and then rescued her with it?" said General Delmar.

"No, I saved her in this ship," replied Jifdar.

"I'm confused," said Hylne.

"Let's just say that a lot happened in between," replied Jifdar, not wanting to get into details.

"Indeed," muttered General Delmar. "Why are you here?"

"Let's just say that our interests are aligned," said Jifdar.

"It's not like a pirate to help someone, not without compensation," General Delmar said.

"Is it like a Lanyran general to abandon his fleet?"

"Enough of this nonsense," spat Heller. "They should get back on their ship and leave."

Jifdar sliced the air with his hand, telling Heller to mind his tongue.

"I'm here, and here for one reason only—Klanor."

"And yet he still lives," said Heller.

"Quiet," Jifdar hissed at his first mate.

"Lives?" said Hylne. "Where is he?"

"On the blue planet here," said Jifdar, "with Rynah."

"What?" Tre, who had been leaning back in his chair, balancing it on two of its legs, blurted out. His chair fell over and him with it. "What do you mean, with Rynah?" he continued, unphased as he hauled himself to his feet, clinging to the table.

"Just that," Jifdar replied. "Rynah chose to go to the planet with him. She never gave her reasons and I didn't question them."

Heller snorted.

Jifdar glowered at him. He knew that his first mate had not agreed with his decision to follow Rynah's orders, his discontent growing each day they remained parked behind the moon.

"What are your interests in this matter?"

"Not long ago a man named Obiah, a friend to Rynah, had come to us asking for our help. The Lanyran council turned him down. I—we chose to leave and to find her. She shouldn't have to do this on her own," replied General Delmar, saying that last part to himself.

"She isn't here, and neither should you all be," said Heller. "She chose to go off while we sit here—"

"That's enough."

"—and await her orders as though we're *trusarn*."

"Heller!" Jifdar's voice silenced his first mate. "I think you should go check on the helmsman."

The two locked eyes a moment; the tension between them filled the room, swallowing all within it. Heller knocked his chair back and stormed out of the room.

"Now, where were we?" said Jifdar, as though nothing had happened.

"Is it true?" asked Hylne. "Did Stein turn on Klanor?"

"Yes," said Jifdar.

"Honestly, do you guys ever clean this place?" mumbled Tre, his wandering mind had focused on a dung beetle that trekked across the table, and he flicked it with his yellowed fingernail.

"Where is Rynah?" asked General Delmar.

"Gentlemen, I would like to help you, but I think it is best that you get back in your ship and…"

"Where is Rynah?" General Delmar demanded again.

"Not here," replied Jifdar.

"If you have done— "

"I've done nothing except what's she asked. It's time for you to leave."

The doors swooshed open and the pirate monitoring the com units rushed in.

"Captain! There is an incoming transmission from the planet. I think it's Rynah."

Each of the men jumped from their positions and rushed out of the room, anxious to hear from her.

Chapter 18
PLANS

"Do you have them?" Rynah asked, watching over Fons' shoulder as he deciphered the ancient alien technology in front of him—his fingers tapping holographic bubbles that floated before him—and twirling the amber ring she wore on the chain around her neck.

Fons had spent the last hour poring over the computerized system—though it resembled something more from the future than a modern-day computer—still not sure how to bring up the communications unit. Rynah's incessant foot tapping and breathing down his neck did little to help matters. While the others moseyed around in small circles, their impatience growing, Fons had managed to find the stored data on the ancient computer, and he had an idea of how to encrypt further communications, since the more he fiddled with the it, the more he learned; binary codes were universal.

"Anything?" Rynah asked again.

"For the last time, no," Fons said, his annoyance at her hovering growing, "and if you insist on breathing down my neck, we won't get anywhere."

A clatter forced her to jerk her head. Achilles sat in a corner fiddling with the device he had insisted on bringing with him when they were forced to flee the hotel he stayed at. A small chuckle spilled from her lips as she watched Tom approach Achilles, snatch a pair of pliers, and try to fiddle with the strange device.

"Get your hands off that!" Achilles slapped Tom's hands away, clutching his prized possession even tighter.

"You know, I can help you," said Tom.

Achilles grunted in response.

"For starters," said Tom, "you might want to separate that connection into two different wires. It will help take the strain off…"

"I don't need to…" began Achilles, before rethinking Tom's suggestion. "That's not a bad idea. Get me those clamps over there and make yourself useful."

Grinning with excitement at being able to help build something new, Tom snatched a box of tools and sat down next to Achilles.

Rynah stopped eavesdropping and turned back to Fons. "You have anything?" she asked again, tapping her fingers on the back of his chair.

"Not yet," snapped Fons. "I can't work with you constantly breathing down my neck!"

"Rynah," said Brie, pulling her away, "perhaps we should sit over here and leave Fons alone."

As Brie led Rynah to a chair, Rynah glanced at Solaris; an idea hit her, and she wondered why she hadn't thought of it earlier.

"Solaris, can you figure this thing out?"

Solaris' eyes narrowed. "I think I might know what makes it tick."

"Why didn't you say anything before?" demanded Rynah.

"You never asked," came Solaris' quip reply.

Rynah glowered at her. "You could have offered."

"Stop, please," said Brie, breaking them up. "Solaris, if you can help him, please do it."

Solaris went over to Fons, who still toyed with the holographic bubbles, which in turn, opened up file after file. In truth, she wasn't certain at first how to use the ancient technology, as it not only pre-dated her, but was much more advanced. After observing Fons for the last hour, she began to understand the computerized systems.

"Got it!" cried Fons in triumph. "I told you I would figure it out." He tapped two more holographic bubbles, and up popped a holographic room around them, with Jifdar in the center, talking to a group of strangers.

Solaris placed her hand on the computer panel. "I've encrypted this as best I can," she said, "but if Stein is watching communications, it will only be a matter of time until he finds it, and us."

"Complete transmission," ordered Rynah.

Fons did.

"Jifdar?" Rynah said to Jifdar's holoimage, which looked very lifelike.

"Rynah!" Jifdar whirled around, pleased and surprised to see her. "How did you—where have you been?"

"We've run into complications, but have discovered something of acute interest." Rynah stepped back, allowing Jifdar to look around, noticing the compound for the first time.

"Rynah!" A curt voice called from behind. "Rynah!" Tre pushed his way past Jifdar and stared at Rynah, anger etched on his face. "You led them to me. After everything I had done—after all of the help I had given you—you go and lead them to me."

Tre stopped speaking. He looked at Alfric, Tom, and Solon, having met them before, but then his eyes turned to Brie, Joe, and Fons. As his eyes locked with Fons'—and in quite a comical moment that could never be repeated even if planned—they both jumped up, screaming, "Aliens! More aliens! It's an infestation!"

Joe grabbed Fons by the shoulder, forcing him back into his seat, while Jifdar punched Tre just to shut him up.

"You're near an alien planet, you imbecile," shouted Jifdar.

"Sorry," said Tre. "It's a reflex, you know."

"Rynah."

A man Rynah had not seen since the day Klanor had stolen the crystal stepped away from the crowd. His broad shoulders stood straight back, like she remembered, and his facial features, though aged, remained stern, yet a resolution possessed his eyes that she had never seen before.

"General Delmar?" whispered Rynah. "It's been…"

"Too long," the general finished for her. "Obiah," he nodded his head in Obiah's direction, "I am pleased that you are here." He noticed Klanor and his eyes flashed with rage. "What is he doing here?"

"Perhaps," said Rynah, stepping between General Delmar's holographic image and Klanor, "we should start with explanations."

The next hour passed with Rynah telling Jifdar, General Delmar, Tre, and Hylne what had happened since her last communication with Jifdar. She described hers and Klanor's capture by Stein and how, without Klanor's help, they never would have escaped, explaining that since Brie trusted him, then so did she. General Delmar had glanced at Brie during this part of the conversation, and decided that if Rynah chose to trust this being from another planet, then he would as well, believing that he had trained Rynah well and knowing there was little he could do about her decision.

The talks continued with General Delmar telling how he and Hylne searched for Tre in an effort to find her. He apologized for not accompanying Obiah when he first had the chance. And so the hour passed until Rynah finish telling about the planet and the lines of verse that told of three ships.

"And you think that they are located in this sector?" asked General Delmar.

"Yes," replied Rynah. "It wouldn't make sense for us to be brought back here if the ships were elsewhere. We need to find them before Stein does. It is essential if we are to destroy these crystals once and for all."

"Where are they?" asked Hylne.

"One is on this planet," said Rynah. "Another we believe is on their moon, and the third would be on a planet in this sector known as… Mars," Rynah let the name roll off her tongue, unsure of how to pronounce it.

"Are you certain?" asked General Delmar.

"Certainty is a luxury," said Rynah, repeating a phrase General Delmar had once used when she had reported for duty on his ship as a newly commissioned officer of the Lanyran fleet.

"We will break up into groups," continued Rynah. "Alfric, you will go with Klanor and Fons to Jifdar's ship."

Fons choked on his own spit. "I'll what?"

"You"—Rynah faced Fons—"are going to explore your moon with Klanor and Alfric, and maybe a few pirates."

"Pirates?" whimpered Fons.

"Time for you to expand your horizons," Joe whispered to his friend.

"Tom, Solon, Joe, and Obiah," said Rynah, "you four will go to the planet Mars. Brie, Solaris, Achilles, you three and I will look for the ship that is here. General and Councilman Hylne, I need you two to keep tabs on Stein's movements. He's been quiet, too quiet."

"I understand," said General Delmar.

"With your permission," said Joe, "I'd like to contact someone I know from the bureau. I think he can help, if Obiah and the others are willing to make a quick stop."

"I don't think…" began Rynah.

"I have trusted you since the day you walked into my interrogation room," said Joe. "Now, I am asking you to trust me."

"Very well," said Rynah. "Obiah?"

Obiah nodded his agreement.

"It's settled," said Rynah to Joe, "but don't take too long."

She turned back to the holograms before her. "Jifdar, Tom and the others will meet up with you shortly, after Joe runs his quick errand. From there, you will break off into your respective groups. You will have to help Alfric and Klanor scour the surface of the Earth's moon."

"What are we looking for?" asked Jifdar, who had remained silent through most of the meeting.

"Any sign of a ship," replied Rynah, "an ancient ship. Solaris."

Solaris rose to her feet and pinched her wrist, causing her eyes to project a holographic map of the moon's surface for all to see.

"My preliminary scans indicate that there are caverns, the depths of which remain unknown."

Lights flared up on the map, indicating where the underground caves were.

"It is possible that one of these caverns holds a vessel from a civilization that is long gone. I am sending you a signal, a sort of homing beacon that drew me to the ruins that turned out to be Herclai's home; it should guide you to this mysterious ship. I will give the same signal to the others as well."

Jifdar paced the room, his brow furrowed as he processed what Rynah had told him over the past hour, not liking any of it.

"Let me get this straight," he said to her, "you want me to help you search the surface of this rock for some ship that is millennia old, while you send a number of your group to examine another desolate planet, and you stay where you are, looking for a third vessel, all because the lyrics of a poem told you to?"

"Yes," replied Rynah, as everyone focused their attention on them.

"And then what?" demanded Jifdar.

Rynah glanced at Brie, Tom, Alfric, Solon, and Solaris, knowing the answer.

"We face Stein, and bring him hell."

"What are you planning?" asked Jifdar.

"I'd rather not discuss this at the present moment," said Rynah. "It's best if we secure the ships first. Can I count on you?"

"I'll leave the door open," said Jifdar.

"It's settled then," said Rynah. "We'll—"

"Rynah," Jifdar stopped her, "may I have a word with you in private?"

Rynah eyed Jifdar, wondering what had soured his mood and why he questioned her.

"Give us a moment," she said to the others.

The room emptied as the others departed to an adjoining chamber, while on his ship, Jifdar's pirates and guests did the same.

"Something on your mind?" Rynah asked.

"What are you doing?"

"I should think it would be obvious," replied Rynah.

"You misunderstand me," said Jifdar. "You have the man responsible for Lanyr's demise. When I agreed to help Obiah find you, it was so I could find the one responsible for the death of many of my pirates. Now I understand that you have had a previous relationship with him and are unwilling to…"

"To what?" demanded Rynah.

"Your man, Alfric, as you call him, defeated one of my best men; you managed to escape from Ikor, and you managed to steal your ship back from under my nose. You have earned my respect, and because of that, I will respect your decision where Klanor is concerned."

"Why don't you speak what is on your mind."

"What are you doing here, Rynah? You've lost the crystals and Stein has focused his attention here, on this planet. He is no longer interested in the Twelve Sectors. You could leave. We could all leave—go someplace far away and live the rest of our days in peace. This is no longer our fight."

"What are you saying?"

"They are not your people, Rynah," said Jifdar.

Rynah's ears burned from the anger that welled within her upon hearing Jifdar's words.

"I can't just leave them!"

"Why not?"

"Because—because I can't!"

"Why do you care about them?" demanded Jifdar. "Why are you willing to die for them? Their leaders have issued orders for your capture and execution! You are a woman without a home. Some of your people survived the decimation of Lanyr. Join up with them; help them find a new home."

"You cannot ask this of me!"

"I'm begging you to consider what will become of you if you stay here. The people here will kill you, make no mistake of that. I'll take you wherever you wish to go."

"And what of Brie, Tom, Solon, or Alfric? Will you abandon them to their fate as well?"

"They can come with you," said Jifdar.

"You know they won't," replied Rynah. "And I won't abandon them."

"This is not our fight," said Jifdar.

"That is the pirate way, isn't it? While the universe burns, you stand by and watch. If you want to leave, then go; no one will stop you. I made the mistake of standing by once—I'll not do it again. Do you think that Stein will stop at this planet? You've seen men like him. He must be stopped, and we are in a position to do it!"

Jifdar lowered his head. "I am not like you, Rynah."

"Stay with us," urged Rynah. "We need you."

"I'm sorry," said Jifdar. "I'll help with this last part, help you locate the ships, but I must think of my men." Jifdar moved over to click the button, thus ending the holotransmission.

"I guess Brie was wrong about you," said Rynah, stopping him and remembering something Brie had once said to him. "She said that you deserved our trust, that you were more than just a pirate, that you would do the right thing in the end."

Jifdar clicked off the transmission, his mind and heart awash in old desires and sentiments from the days before he had turned to piracy.

Chapter 19
A Ride

Samuel's phone rang. He picked it up and stared at the screen with the words "Unknown Number" on it. He wandered away from the other agents around him.

"Agent Anders," he answered.

"Samuel."

Samuel almost dropped his phone when he heard the voice on the other end.

"Joe!"

"I got your message."

"Look, you need to turn yourself in, or something. The President is serious about ending this whole aliens on Earth business and Director Singuar is more than willing to go along."

"I can't."

"Joe, I can't keep…"

"Listen to me," said Joe. "There is more going on here…"

"You've said that before."

"Stein is not planning to leave this planet," said Joe. "He wants

Rynah and her companions, but he also wants this planet. By the time he is finished, there will be nothing left."

Samuel's slumped his shoulders; he had suspected that Joe's claims were correct, but had wished he was wrong.

"What do you need me to do?"

"Samuel, there is no going back from this. You'll be charged with insubordination, conspiracy, maybe even treason."

"Joe, I've never cared about much in my life you know that. But right now, all that matters is ending this and ensuring that no more people get hurt. Now tell me what you need."

"I need you to go to my place and ditch your phone."

"Your place is 3,000 miles away. How am I supposed to get there?"

"Your ride will pick you up in about 30 seconds."

"What?"

A high-pitched hum tickled his ears as his tie and coat flapped in the downdraft created by an incoming shuttle that lowered itself to the ground. The surrounding agents hurried away, aiming their weapons at it. Samuel backed up, his mouth opened wide, as he watched the shuttle hover just above the ground amidst clouds of airborne sand. The rear hatch lowered, forming a ramp that hung inches from the ground.

"Come on!" yelled Joe, crouching on the ramp, his hand stretched out.

Taking a quick glance at the agents that stared at the spectacle, Samuel pulled out his badge and tossed it away with his phone. He jumped, grasping Joe's hand, and disappeared into the shuttle.

"Welcome aboard!" said Obiah as Joe led Samuel, who jumped back in surprise, away from the closing hatch and the ship ascended high into the atmosphere.

"I can't believe you pulled that stunt," chastised Fons, with three harnesses holding him in his seat; his way of making certain that he wouldn't perish if the shuttle crashed.

"Don't mind him," Joe said to Samuel.

Samuel remained silent, having never made such a defining choice before, and unsure of what to say to the strange faces that surrounded him.

"I need to know that you are on board with all this," said Joe.

Samuel looked around at Klanor, Obiah, Tom, Fons, Alfric—his overbearing stature unnerving him—and Joe.

"As I've said, what do you need me to do?"

"We're going to drop you off near my home in Philadelphia. I need you to go inside, the alarm code is 9658, and go into the basement. Uncover the shelves and bring me the stuff on them. I have a truck in the garage. The keys are under the seat. Load up the truck and head west."

"To this… Nebraska," said Solon.

Joe looked at him, wondering why he had insisted on that location, but Solon's unwavering expression stopped him from arguing.

"You heard him. I'll contact you in a day or two."

"How?" said Samuel. "I threw out my phone."

"There is a desk near those shelves. Look in the top drawer."

"What exactly am I bringing you?" demanded Samuel.

"A little something I prepared in case of an emergency." Joe winked in Fons' direction.

"We're here," said Obiah.

The shuttle lowered on the darkened streets of an urban Philadelphia neighborhood; the ramp on the rear hatch lowered as the craft hovered two feet above the asphalt ground.

"I'm trusting you on this, Joe," said Samuel.

"Have I ever lied to you?"

Samuel shook his head and jumped off the dangling ramp, landing on the cool asphalt of the street below. He took one last look at Joe's silhouette as the ramp raised and the hatch sealed shut before darting off into the night, heading straight for Joe's house. His heavy feet clomped as he hurried down the street, staying within the shadows of the few trees and avoiding the street lamps. Once he had reached Joe's small bungalow home, with a shaped lilac bush underneath the front bay window, he jimmied the lock with a credit card and slipped through the steel enforced door. Silence consumed him, broken by the slow beep of the alarm as it counted down the seconds before summoning the police. Samuel typed in the code Joe had given him.

A screech filled the air, followed by a few choice words, when Samuel smashed into a small side table, banging his knee on the pointed corner. With his knee throbbing, he searched for a light switch, feeling the smooth wall until his fingers crossed a small bump. Samuel flipped it. Soft, white light filled the narrow hallway that led from the front door to the living room, complete with an oversized reclining chair and an HD flat screen television screen that took up an entire wall that rested above a credenza overflowing with DVDs.

A doorknob stuck out of the wall in the hallway. Samuel gripped its cool surface and turned it, revealing a stairwell that descended downward into a black hole. He found a switch and flipped it up, turning on three bulbs at the bottom of the stairs. His heart throbbing in his ears, Samuel crept down the steps, his minds awash with images of what Joe kept in his basement, each scenario as unlikely as the last.

He stopped. Shelves covered in camouflage green, canvass tarps lined the walls, each with their own layer of gray dust. Tut-tutting—Samuel had never known Joe to be untidy, even his desk at the office lacked dust—he stepped over to one set of metal shelves and ripped the tarp off, releasing a raging storm of choking dust. Samuel took two steps back, his legs wobbling beneath him as his mouth hung open, not believing what he saw: rocket launchers, jumpsuits, AR-15s, an M134 General Electric Minigun, whip chains, a display case of knives (each blade curved and serrated), crossbow, brass knuckles, rifles, and… a flamethrower?

"Jesus, Joe," breathed Samuel, wondering if Joe had somehow

known all along that a group of aliens would show up. In actuality, Fons' paranoia about extraterrestrials invading Earth and the rise of terrorism and instability in the Middle East, had persuaded Joe, a man who loved to be prepared for the worst, to build his own arsenal.

A lone desk caught Samuel's attention. Remembering what Joe had told him about it, he pulled open the top drawer, finding a burner phone in it. Samuel snatched it, shoving it in his pocket.

Over the next half hour, Samuel packed what he could in Joe's truck and left, hoping that whatever Joe and his friends planned would work.

Chapter 20
LUNAR OUTING

The ship lurched as it drew closer to the pirate vessel for docking. Fons sat next to Joe, tapping his foot on the floor while drumming his fingers on his bobbing knee. Joe reached his hand out, stopping him.

"Sorry," muttered Fons. "I get a bit nervous when flying."

"You've never been on a plane," said Joe.

"I've never been in space either," said Fons.

Obiah steadied the ship as he eased it into the docking bay, with Klanor in the co-pilot's seat. Though they had all been forced to accept Klanor's help, none of them fully trusted him, but they accepted Brie's judgment, realizing that, for the moment, they had little choice but to trust the man.

"You're coming in too fast," said Klanor.

"I was flying ships long before you were in diapers," Obiah replied.

His eyes darted from the readings on the dash to the ship in front of him as the bay doors opened, allowing him entrance. With adroit skill, he guided the shuttle into the docking bay, setting it down with a soft thump as clamps seized the landing gear, locking the small vessel into place.

"We've landed," said Joe to Fons, who still clung to his seat as sweat streamed down his face, dripping onto his shirt.

"No," said Fons, "we've haven't landed. We're on a spaceship with extraterrestrials."

Shaking his head, Joe threw off his harness and disembarked the shuttle with the others.

"You know," said Tom, "after everything that has happened, you'd think he would be used to the idea of an alien invasion."

Fons' face turned white upon hearing Tom's statement, to which both Joe and Alfric shoved Tom out of the shuttle with an annoyed grunt.

"I get the feeling they don't like me," joked Tom to Solon.

"I think it is your lack of diplomacy they do not care for," Solon replied.

"Listen up!" Jifdar pushed his way towards them, putting an end to their jibing, hands clasped behind his back. "Those of you who will be exploring the planet's moon, over here, the rest of you, I suggest you get back aboard the shuttle and be on your way."

"So much for pleasantries," muttered Tom to Solon.

"I do apologize if my actions seem abrupt," Jifdar said to him, "but we do not have time to waste."

Obiah, Joe, Tom, and Solon stepped back onto the shuttle without another word. As he stepped through the hatch, Joe gave Fons—who jumped when he saw Jifdar's scaled face and roughhewn clothes covered in oil stains and what looked like dried blood—an encouraging squeeze of the shoulder. Jifdar led the others away from the docking bay as Obiah lifted off and left, the ship humming as it passed through the bay doors.

"All right," said Jifdar, leading Klanor, Alfric, and Fons to another room where General Delmar, Hylne, and Tre were. "I guess introductions are in order."

Upon seeing him, both General Delmar and Hylne lunged for

Klanor, knocking him into the far wall. With lightning quick movements, Alfric seized them both, flinging them away from Klanor.

"Enough!" he roared, his overbearing demeanor stopping them
as he held his sword out, ready to strike if necessary.

"Why do you defend that monster?" demanded Hylne.

"Because we have more important matters to attend," replied
Alfric, "and I gave Rynah my word to abide by her wishes where he
is concerned."

Both General Delmar and Hylne backed away, feeling threatened by Alfric's impending size and defensive posture.

"It seems you already know each other," said Jifdar. "The man is
right, we have more important matters. Rynah thinks there is a ship
hidden on the surface of this rock. Alfric and Klanor, you both will
be going to the surface with me."

"And me," said Hylne and General Delmar together.

"No," Jifdar said.

"I'll not let him go down there without one of us," General
Delmar screamed, pointing an accusatory finger at Klanor.

"I need you…" began Jifdar.

"I'm not letting that monster out of my sight," Hylne said, his
resolute manner garnering him a small amount of respect from
Alfric, who watched the exchange with an unreadable face.

"Very well," Jifdar relented, "Hylne, you may come. General, I
want you to stay here."

"Now wait a minu—"

"This is my ship," Jifdar interrupted General Delmar, "and you
will do as I command. Understood?"

"Rynah would prefer your skills to remain here," said Alfric,
his calm, but firm voice quieting all within the room. He wished
to end this discussion and had heard Rynah speak of this man,
whom she regarded as a great commander, and every ship needed
its commander.

General Delmar acquiesced. "Understood," he said.

"As for you two"—Jifdar turned to Fons and Tre—"I want you both to…"

"Solaris gave us this locator beacon to help find the ship," interrupted Fons.

"Let me see that." Tre took the beacon from him, turning it over in his open-gloved hands, enthralled by its design. "Amazing. If we were to mask this with an algorithmic map, which I can use to scan the surface of this moon, we could—"

"—pinpoint where this ship is supposed to be with more accuracy," finished Fons, excitement filling his voice.

"Exactly! Then we wouldn't waste time scouring the entire surface," said Tre.

Both Fons and Tre rambled off a series of computer equations, which confused the others in the room, oblivious to the perplexed faces staring at them.

"You two will stay here," said Jifdar, breaking up their conversation, though Fons and Tre did not hear him, as they were too involved in their own conversation, "and do your… map. Alfric, Klanor, Hylne, to the shuttle bay."

Jifdar walked off with Alfric, Klanor, and Hylne trailing after him, leaving Fons and Tre to continue their ramblings. They hiked through a door that led to an adjoining hangar bay; Hylne scrunched his face at the moving bits of sludge, which he swore watched him and wondered how the others managed to ignore it.

"In," ordered Jifdar when they reached a shuttle with its hatch standing wide open for them. They all entered without a word, wanting to get this next assignment over with, and each wondering what secrets the moon held, their hands gripping the sides of their seat as the shuttle vibrated from departure while they careened downward to the moon's desolate offering.

The cramped shuttle bounced as Jifdar flew it over the lunar surface. Klanor huffed in the back, not liking the way the others ignored him, though he knew why they treated him with such distaste. Alfric and Hylne sat statuesque in their rusty seats, with the Viking ignoring the black mass that oozed down the walls behind them, while Hylne's eyes kept darting back to it. Not even the shuttle's odor of decayed food bothered Alfric.

The craft jostled again as Jifdar zoomed over the surface, flying at a dangerous altitude as it skimmed the rocks.

Klanor opened his mouth to voice his concerns, but shut it after rethinking his actions. Jifdar was a pirate and would do as he pleased. White powder pelted the window as he dove even lower to the surface.

"See anything?" asked Fons over the com unit.

"A lot of rocks," replied Jifdar with sarcasm.

A snort echoed over the com unit.

"I don't see anything that resembles a ship," said Jifdar.

Static remained until… "There should be something. Tre and I calculated and recalculated, and according to our figures, and this beacon, you are in the vicinity of the ship."

Jifdar groaned. He never cared for academic types and people who lived behind their holomonitors instead of going out and experiencing the real world.

"I'm telling you that there is nothing but white powder and rock."

Klanor stood up and walked to the front window, despite receiving a piercing glare from Jifdar. He looked out at the moon's surface, studying the formations and the craters as an incessant beeping blared through the com unit. Jifdar turned it off.

"Turn it back on," said Klanor.

"That annoyance won't get us anywhere," Jifdar replied.

"Solaris said that it would beep as you got closer to the ship," Klanor said.

Jifdar scoffed at him.

"Turn it back on," said Alfric; his stanch demeanor commanded obedience, causing the pirate captain to recoil.

Jifdar reached over and flipped the switch to the com unit, allowing the annoying beeping to continue.

They all listened as the beeping faded before picking up in intensity.

"There is something down there in that crater," said Klanor.

"How do you know?" demanded Hylne.

"Intuition," Klanor replied.

"Take us down," commanded Alfric, not caring if Jifdar was the captain—he was a king.

Though annoyed at being ordered about on his own shuttle, Jifdar refused to argue, having grown curious about the crater himself. He banked to the left and steered them lower, nestling the small craft in the elongated shadows of the crater, away from prying eyes.

"Now what?" asked Hylne.

"We walk," said Klanor.

Not liking the situation, Hylne did not argue, knowing that he was outnumbered and the small craft might not be able to take them where they needed to go. Each of the four men secured themselves in spacesuits and exited the shuttle. They walked with ease in the soft silt of the moon, except for Alfric; though he had worn a spacesuit while underwater, and one while aboard Rynah's ship, he had never trekked across the surface of another planet before, even if it was the moon. He clutched the hilt of his sword even tighter; the others had found a way to strap it to him as the Viking never went anywhere without his most trusted weapon.

With slow and steady steps, they hiked across the base of the crater, the soft dust transforming into ragged rocks that scraped against the bottom of their boots as the crater's shadow stretched over them. Both Jifdar and Klanor took the lead; Klanor because he had an idea of where to go, but Jifdar did not want him getting too far ahead. Onward they went, four blue-suited beings walking in a line across the moon, leaving unsteady footprints that would never fade. Its sereneness gave the impression of tranquility, but all knew—even Alfric, despite his unfamiliarity with space walking— how deceiving such appearances could be.

"What's going on out there?" asked Fons over their helmets' radios.

"Nothing," replied Jifdar. "We have decided to go out for a stroll."

"Stroll? On this moon?" said Tre.

"I think he's being sarcastic," commented Fons.

"I knew that," Tre quipped.

The beeping continued, its pace quickening.

Klanor stopped, listening to the beeping and studying the side of the crater. He circled around, his eyes roaming along the walls of the basin, his brows scrunched together. He approached the caldera wall, placing his hand upon a darkened spot that didn't seem to belong, yet he found nothing unusual.

"What is it?" demanded Hylne, growing impatient.

"Does this seem right to you?" said Klanor, pointing at the darkened spot.

"It's just a spot on the rock," said Hylne.

Klanor listened to the beeping as its intensity grew each time he neared the darkened spot.

"I'm telling you that there is something odd here."

"What do you mean?" asked Jifdar.

"It..."

"Ah, come on," scoffed Hylne, "he's just buying time for when his people come to save him. Let's go. There's nothing here."

"Now wait a minute," said Klanor.

"Don't think that I'll be fooled by your newfound piety," said Hylne. "You murdered our people and you deserve to die for it."

"And you deserve to answer for the pirates, whose lives you took," added Jifdar.

"We are not here for that," Klanor said. "Rynah..."

"Rynah isn't here," said Hylne, "and seems to believe in the existence of some ship that we have yet to find."

Amidst their arguing, Alfric remembered a tale his father had once told him about how things are not always as they appear. "Trust your eyes, but trust your instincts more," his father had told him once.

Alfric stared at the darkened spot and agreed that its placement seemed strange, even in this unfamiliar place, almost purposeful. He unsheathed his sword; if sound could be heard in space, the others would have listened to its ringing steel as he freed it, but they ceased their fighting regardless, seeing the gleam of its polished blade. Alfric stepped over to the brown marking, rubbing his suited hand along its edges as he observed every detail.

Hylne, Klanor, and Jifdar watched as Alfric picked at the spot with the tip of his blade, dust particles floated around him before disappearing into the black canvass above them. As he worked with diligence, an edging appeared that was small at first, before becoming more pronounced.

"There seems to be an opening here," said Alfric, his deep voice stopping any arguments the others had.

Leaning closer, the others held their breaths as they watched the Viking clear away more of the crumbling rock, revealing a rectangular door with a space just wide enough for a man in a spacesuit to squeeze through. He went inside. Not to be outdone, and brimming with curiosity, Jifdar, Hylne, and Klanor followed, stepping through the darkness and into a cavern.

Steps that looked like stone, but had a metallic twang to them, led downward, sinking a little under their weight. They turned on their suits' lights, illuminating the underground tunnel as it delved deep within the moon. Hylne bent low and ran his fingers along one of the steps, leaving lines in the white, powdery dust that had pooled there, and stretched up and shined his light on the ceiling. Though it dimpled and had the appearance of natural rock formation, it seemed too perfect.

"Look at this," said Hylne. "I think lasers did this."

"It is rock," said Alfric.

"Rock is never this symmetrical," said Hylne. "It is metal made to look like rock, and the entrance was disguised well, as the natural formation of a crater. Only on closer inspection would one see its displacement."

Hylne glanced at Klanor, locking eyes for a moment and knowing he owed the man an apology, but turned and headed down the stairs, unable to humble himself.

As he passed Alfric, the Viking held his sword up, blocking Hylne's path.

"Do not speak ill of Rynah again," he said.

Hylne said nothing. He stared into Alfric's unyielding eyes, remarking at how blue they were, mirroring ice, and continued on down into the mysterious tunnel.

Their boots thudded as they stomped down the strange stairwell, their pale lights dancing in every direction. Rusted, copper-tone lines stretched across the walls in perpendicular fashion, stretching in every direction, but none of them could figure out where they led. They just followed the steps. No one spoke, not even to Fons or Tre, as their radios had cut out the moment they had entered the underground cavern.

The steps ended. One by one, they gathered at the bottom; dismay filled them when they noticed that the singular tunnel diverged, granting them two paths. They shined their lights down both, unsure of what to do.

"Which way?" asked Jifdar.

Klanor looked down one, before turning and staring down the other. He backed against the wall, his mind awash with indecision; without the help of Tre and Fons, and the beacon that had ceased its incessant beeping, he had no idea where to go.

"I don't know."

"You studied the text that led us here," said Jifdar.

"It's not like it gives you specific directions," said Klanor. "It only spoke of a vessel that's supposed to be in this place. It never said what to do if the road forked."

> For when thy darkened path diverges,
> go forward, until in light thee emerge.

The others cocked their heads in Alfric's direction when he had finished reciting a line of verse from the book that Solon had found, which had guided them through the labyrinth of Sunlil, their unspoken question clear. He had lain awake one night, listening to Solon recite the verses in his sleep, and those lines stuck to his mind, though he could not explain why. Perhaps Odin was guiding him.

"We will split up," said Alfric, refusing them an answer.

"Wha—no! Bad idea," said Jifdar.

"I'm afraid I must agree," said Klanor. "We have no idea where either one of these tunnels lead. What if one goes to the ship and the other does not?"

"Which is why we must split up," replied Alfric, "so that one of us might find this ship."

"And what of the others?" asked Hylne.

Alfric said nothing; he didn't need to. Hylne had guessed the answer.

"Very well," said Jifdar. "Kla—"

"Klanor and I will go this way," interrupted Alfric, pointing to the right, still refusing to let Klanor out of his sight.

Jifdar opened his mouth to protest, but closed it upon seeing Alfric's unwavering manner and the way his gloved hand gripped his sword. The Viking was best obeyed, not questioned.

Jifdar and Hylne walked down the left tunnel, while Afrin pushed Klanor through the other.

Silence ensued as Hylne and Jifdar trekked through the cavern, its dimpled walls indicating that water had once passed through, yet no bodies of water existed on the moon. The cleanliness of the floor surprised them; not even a speck of dust marked it, a welcomed relief to Hylne after spending hours among walls that secreted their own slime. They shifted from side to side, half-walking, half-bouncing, as they trudged through the tunnel in the confines of their suits; the snowflake-shaped spots on the wall (of their lights) swayed from side to side, bringing little life to the drabness of the dark cavern.

If they hadn't been wearing their suits, they would have heard the slow drip of water as it fell from the ceiling to the ground in a slow, rhythmic succession. They continued onward, shining their flashlights into every crevice and marveling at how ridges spiraled downward, mimicking the swirls of silky ice cream from an unseen dispenser.

Something glittered in the furthest reaches of the beam. Hylne swung it back, peering closer. Was it water? He moved his flashlight from to side to side. There it was again: a small glam that sparkled.

Hylne motioned for Jifdar to follow him, but warned him to be careful as he touched the moisture, wondering how it could have gotten there. He brushed his gloved hand across it, focusing so much on it that he failed to realize he had just hit a concealed switch. The ground rumbled beneath their feet as penny-sized pebbles clacked against the ground, skipping across the surface. Both Hylne and Jifdar stepped back, wary of the shaking walls and dust that swirled around them.

"What did you do?" asked Jifdar as cracks appeared in the cavern walls.

Hylne said nothing.

The ground crumbled away beneath their feet, plunging them downward into a dark pit of rock, dust, and… metal pipes? Even while falling, both wondered about the gleam of copper piping that surrounded them. They slammed into a hard surface, rolling and spinning as rubble crashed around them, caking them in silt. Looking up, they noticed a slab of the ceiling heading straight for them. Both Hylne and Jifdar scrambled out of the way just as another rock plowed into the ledge beside them, forcing them to jump out of the way and land on another level ten feet below.

When the dust had cleared, Hylne looked up, finding no sign of Jifdar. Worried that something had happened to the pirate, and afraid of being alone in this foreboding place, he rummaged around the area, searching for Jifdar. A speck of blue met his eyes, Hylne tore across the chamber, turning the still form over. When he saw the cracked helmet, he feared the worst and expected to find a corpse, but to his surprise, a hand gripped his arm just as Jifdar inhaled sharply.

"You're… you're breathing," stammered Hylne.

Jifdar jerked to his feet, amazed that he was not dead. "There is air here."

The pirate removed the remains of his helmet and stopped when he turned around. Industrial lights flared to life, allowing them to see where they were: a cavern the size of a hanger. Jifdar and Hylne stood upon a walkway and below them was a ship, a dragon's claw that gripped the ground, ready to tear through any adversary. The untarnished hull glistened unlike any metal they had ever seen before, forming a perfect mirror. Both Jifdar and Hylne stepped towards it and stared at the unrecognizable faces that glared back at them.

"I wonder how Alfric is faring with Klanor?" mumbled Jifdar as he studied the area, noting the tubes that hung from the ceiling.

While Hylne and Jifdar explored one tunnel, Alfric and Klanor trekked through the other, in terse silence, as the Viking kept Klanor four paces ahead of him; his hand never left his sword. Klanor stopped.

"Why have you stopped?" demanded Alfric.

"There is something here that doesn't belong," replied Klanor, studying the wall. "Give me your knife."

Alfric refused.

Annoyed, though understanding why the Viking remained still, Klanor scraped his gloved knuckles across the soft rock of the tunnel wall, clearing away chunks of it and revealing a copper pipe. Curious, Alfric stepped forward and helped Klanor remove more of the rock wall. They stepped back when they had finished, awed by the maze of piping that stretched before them in a haphazard fashion.

"We should follow it," suggested Klanor.

Alfric nodded his head, clamping his mouth closed before Klanor noticed his astonishment, motioning for him to go first.

"You don't trust me; I get that," Klanor said as they walked, never taking his eyes off the piping.

"You understand nothing," grumbled Alfric, keeping him in the beam of his flashlight.

"Yet, you have refused to strike me down," continued Klanor. "I know you want to. I see it in your eyes. So why don't you?"

Alfric grunted in response.

"Brie," whisper Klanor. He had watched the way Alfric interacted with her, his protectiveness, and his willingness to put himself in harm's way if it kept her safe. He remembered the museum where they had stolen a crystal and how Alfric had shoved her away from the laser fire when they had gotten pinned down, something he had done for Rynah.

"I know that you would do anything for Brie," Klanor continued, "but it isn't love, it's almost like fatherly affection… no… a brother."

Alfric stopped cold.

"Yes, I see it, now, in your eyes. You lost a sibling. Brother? Sister?"

"You do not know me," Alfric said, a scowl filled his face.

"Then, don't make the mistake of thinking you know me," Klanor replied. "I've done terrible things, I know that, but much like you have sworn an oath to Rynah, I have given her my word as well."

"The word of a murderer and a thief."

"Are we really so different, you and I? I saw it that day we found the ruins of that outpost. You've committed atrocities—I saw it in your eyes—and yet you judge me."

"I am not like you," Alfric pointed his sword in Klanor's face as a warning for him to remain silent.

"You're exactly like me," Klanor said. "You justified to yourself, I'm sure, as to why you did what you did, but in the end, all that happened was pain and suffering. Now, you hope to make it right, by helping Rynah save a planet that isn't even hers. Wipe your slate clean."

Alfric and Klanor looked at one another in the shadows of the tunnel.

"I wonder if they know," Klanor said, breaking their silence. "Oh, don't worry, I won't tell them. It wouldn't do any good, and they have about as much faith in me as you do."

Alfric pushed Klanor onward. He wondered how Klanor knew. Was it because he had done the same once that the man had been able to read his innermost thoughts? He remembered the day his sister had died because of his cowardice, the day his father ceased speaking to him, the day he vowed to prove his worth.

The first chance he got, Alfric joined a Viking party and sailed with them to a distant land to prove his valor, where he joined in the murder and looting of a small and unprotected village. While those around him reveled in the glory of their spoils, Alfric shrank from it, feeling empty, but he continued anyway. Their vacant, frightened eyes and mangled bodies haunted his nights, but his father praised him for the glory he had showered upon their clan. Soon, Alfric led the raiding parties, garnering more wealth for his father's kingdom than any thought possible. After five years, he had his own ship and sailed up and down the coasts, marauding as he went; his men were always well-paid.

Then, he met her, a woman of Saxon heritage, and with a beauty none could surpass, but she also had a gentleness about her. She calmed the storm within him, showing him a different way of living. When word reached Alfric that his father had died, he took her with him back to his home and made her his queen, but he never learned mercy, despite her efforts to teach him.

Fate must indeed be calculating, thought Alfric as he thought about how he had ended up on Rynah's ship with a girl frightened of every passing shadow who possessed Gróa's eyes, his sister's eyes.

"Do you believe in forgiveness?"

Klanor's question jerked Alfric from his reverie.

"Brie does," said Klanor, unsure of why the girl's kind nature affected him so. "That is why she trusts us, I think. She forgives those who harm her and gives second chances to them."

"Not to everyone," said Alfric, remembering the way Brie fought with Fredyr, her manner as unyielding as his own.

"No, you're right. Maybe only to those who deserve it." Klanor thought back to the times he had been telepathically linked to her in his failed efforts to glean information from her.

"I have too much blood on my hands," Alfric whispered to himself, but it carried over the com unit to Klanor's helmet.

"As do I," Klanor replied.

A low rumbled echoed beneath their feet, forcing them to stop and glance around as the ominous feeling that something was wrong struck them. The walls shook; dust rained down upon them and bits of rock dropped from the ceiling. Unsure of where to go, Klanor and Alfric backed into a corner, waiting for the small quake to cease. Everything stopped. Silence rang in their ears as they looked around, wondering what had caused the cavern to tremble. As Alfric opened his mouth to speak, the ceiling collapsed.

Klanor gasped as both a boulder and Alfric shoved him away from the mass of rock that crashed around them.

"Alfric!" Klanor yelled as he watched the Viking struggle to break free of the chaos, only to succumb to it.

More rubble headed for him. Klanor jumped clear of it, covering his head as best he could as more rock and clumps of dirt fell around him. When the last pebbles skittered into the depths of the tunnel, he looked up, shining his light to where Alfric had been. Glittery particles of dust formed a wall before him, blocking his path. Wary of disturbing the loose dirt and causing another cave in, Klanor crept over it.

"Alfric!"

A grunt in his earpiece answered him.

"Where are you?"

A blue hand appeared, wriggling in the swirling light. Klanor knelt down, clearing away the rock and dust that covered Alfric before grabbing his arm and tugging—a pained scream answered his efforts.

Shining his light even further up, Klanor noticed that a beam had landed atop Alfric, pinning him to the ground. As he studied it, he decided that a lever would work in freeing the Viking; he just hoped that no ribs were broken or the suit was damaged.

His foot bumped something. Alfric's sword lay next to him, untouched by the collapse. Klanor picked up the blade, remarking at its quality, and held it before him as he rose to his feet, locking eyes with Alfric.

"Do it," said the Viking.

Klanor heaved the sword above his head and jabbed it downward, plunging it beneath the beam that pinned Alfric. Vaporous breaths fogged his visor as he struggled to lift it. It budged. Klanor strained against the weight of the beam, but managed to move it just enough for Alfric to wriggle free.

"Why didn't you just kill me?" asked Alfric as he caught his breath.

In answer, Klanor held the Viking's sword out to him.

Alfric took it.

Just then, the floor beneath them tipped upward, flinging both of them onto a slide. Klanor and Alfric bumped into one another as they slid on their backs down a metal ramp that twisted and turned until they had become dizzy and unable to focus. The slide fell away from them. Weightless ness took hold for a second before the two men plunged even further downward, landing on a solid, jagged surface.

"I'm really starting to not like this trip," said Klanor; his head ached from the commotion.

"Join the club."

Jerking their heads, both Klanor and Alfric saw Jifdar and Hylne standing behind them, their helmets off.

"You're not..." began Klanor, staring at Hylne and his broken helmet.

"There is air here," said Hylne. "We can't explain it, but this entire place is sealed and oxygenated."

Hylne and Jifdar helped the other two to their feet as they took off their helmets. Both took long, deep breaths, relishing the fresher atmosphere of the underground cavern to the recycled air of their suits.

Alfric turned and stopped. "By Odin's might."

The others joined him in staring at the ship below—tubing and rubber hoses stretched from it to the chamber's ceiling—its sleek, angular design stunning them. Depending on where one stood to gaze upon it, their position determined whether the vessel appeared green, red, or bronze. Its massive size dwarfed a castle, and none argued when Alfric described it as the talons of a mighty beast.

A set of stairs to their left led down to the ship. Each circled the vessel, searching for a hatch, or any sign of a way in, but found nothing. Undaunted, but growing impatient, Alfric shouted his name out to the ship.

"I am Alfric, Viking king and Saber-slayer, and I demand entrance." Nothing.

"Maybe you should beat it with your fists," joked Jifdar, earning him a scowl from the Viking.

"Maybe you should touch it," Klanor said, remembering how they had entered the underground chamber back on Earth.

Seeing the merit in Klanor's suggestion, Alfric took off his suit's glove and placed a sweaty palm on the unblemished hull, whispering, so that none, but him, heard, "Please."

A hum reverberated around them as the ship glowed and a doorway materialized in the seamless side of the hull, allowing a gangplank to stretch out, beckoning them to enter. Taking the lead, Alfric walked up the plank. Once inside, a transparent tube appeared around him, trapping him, while the others watched in horror as the small prison filled with noxious fumes. Choking, Alfric struck the sides with his sword, but the sharp blade made no mark.

Hylne, Klanor, and Jifdar rushed the tube, pulling on it, beating their fists against it, and searching for a way to release Alfric as he choked to death.

A man materialized before them, wearing colorful, silk robes and a white beard that swayed, even though there was no wind.

"Intruders!"

"Release him," demanded Hylne.

"You do not belong here," said the man.

"You're killing him!" Hylne shouted.

The man looked at him without sympathy, his holographic form flickered, and said, "Only the worthy are allowed passage. He bears the same blood, but you all do not. You must prove your worth, or your friend dies."

"This is madness!" Jifdar pulled out his laser weapon and fired at the tube holding Alfric. It ricocheted off the walls before being stopped by the mysterious man.

"You all have darkened hearts," said the man, "driven by treasure, lust for power and self-gratification, or the delusion of grandeur. If you wish to save your friend, if he is your friend, then do so."

Jifdar seized a bar from the ground, and before he could strike the glass tube, the man stopped him.

"Strength is not your ally here, only what lies in the depth of your soul matters."

Confused, they glanced from one to the other as Alfric dropped to his knees, his face turning blue, until Klanor had a thought. He remembered the time he had spent sifting through Brie's memories and one in particular caught his attention—the memory of her choosing to die in order to save Rynah and the others. The moment he had experienced it, it gnawed at him: her willingness to sacrifice herself to save those she cared about and the lack of doubt in her actions. Klanor knew what he had to do.

"Take me instead," he said, receiving surprised stares from both Hylne and Jifdar. "He does not deserve to die like this, but I... I do."

"What?" said Hylne. In the past, he would not have questioned being rid of Klanor, but here, watching Alfric struggle for breath, it just did not seem right. Nula popped into his mind and how she helped him and General Delmar, at the expense of her own life, shaming him.

Jifdar, too, struggled with the parlousness of the situation as he remembered the day Alfric had been willing to die to spare Brie from his lust and the ignominy he would have brought her.

"We all do," he said.

"He's right," said Hylne.

"Spare him," Klanor pleaded. "If it's blood you want, then takes ours, but leave him be. Our friends need him most."

"Is this your choice?" demanded the man.

"Yes," said Hylne, Klanor, and Jifdar together.

The tube disappeared, while vents turned on, sucking the gas into them and away from the others. A compartment opened.

"Take the mask and put it on his face," said the mysterious man.

Klanor snatched the clear oxygen mask and strapped it to Alfric's face.

"Breathe slow," he said to him.

The holographic man vanished, leaving them alone on the ancient ship.

"What in the hell was that about?" demanded Hylne.

"We had to prove that we still had a bit of a soul left," replied Jifdar, his voice hollow as he struggled with his promise to his first mate of leaving the Terra Sector, and the urge to stay and help Rynah defeat Stein.

Chapter 21
CRIMSON SANDS

Tom watched as Obiah steered the ship—which they had found in the underground bunker in Utah—closer to the red planet, not happy about being shoved aside into the co-pilot's seat. Ever since Rynah had taught him the basics of piloting a spaceship, and he had managed to escape a fleet of pirates, he had grown to love it and was quick to jump at a chance of flying, but Obiah had insisted on piloting the vessel himself, being unfamiliar with Tom and his skills. Tom grunted. Obiah had asked him to keep a steady watch on the controls, but Tom knew that it was just a way of making him feel useful, as Obiah was capable of doing it all himself.

Tom glanced at Joe staring out the window, marveling at the stars around them and the looming red planet that most only saw from Earth's surface. He remembered when he had first been brought to outer space and how he examined everything. A fleeting thought about the professors at the academy, and what they would think of him now if they knew he had waged space battles in a distant solar system, flew through his mind, and a satisfied smile crept across his lips. Tom pushed it aside.

He turned to Joe again, who still stared out the window, except this time, Solon stood next to him, discussing the planets and the gods of his time. Tom turned back to the windshield. He gasped. Mars loomed before them, a red, desolate place, with small striations from where solar winds had disturbed the feather-light silt.

"How did we get here so fast?" he asked.

"I know a few things about flying that you don't," said Obiah.

Tom crossed his arms, hating being reduced to the role of student. Joe leaned over Tom's shoulder, staring out the window, his mouth hanging open in wonderment.

"I used to think only astronauts got to see such things."

"A dismal place," quipped Obiah, having seen many planets similar to Mars during his lifetime.

"But it's still beautiful," replied Joe. He leaned further as he watched plumes of red sand rise far into the atmosphere of the planet, forming a wall as solar winds carried it across the frigid, red desert. "Like its own version of the Sahara."

"Makes you glad you aren't down there," commented Obiah.

"Sahara?" asked Solon.

"A massive desert," replied Tom, "in northern Africa. Egypt is a part of it."

Understanding dawned on Solon's face. "I have heard stories about the great sand plains of Egypt and the wealth that dwells beneath them."

"Start the beacon," said Obiah.

Tom flipped a switch, turning on the locator beacon that Solaris had given them to aid them in finding the mysterious ship. It beeped slow and steady, with purpose. Obiah brought them into a high orbit above the planet.

Beep... Beep... Beep...

The steady sound continued growing—neither stronger nor more insistent—and maintaining its slow pulse as they orbited the red planet. Tom stared at the screen before him, but nothing appeared to indicate that they had found anything.

"Could we be searching in the wrong spot?"

"Probably on the wrong planet," said Obiah.

"No," said Solon as he watched the ground below, "it is here. This is truly where Ares resides."

"How do you know?" asked Joe.

"The sand gleams red, like blood," replied Solon. "Where else would you expect to find the god of war?"

Obiah ran two more passes over the planet, his impatience growing.

"Well, I think we came a long way for nothing."

Though disappointed, Tom did not wish to give up. Rynah was so certain, and so was Solon. He glanced out the window and saw the mysterious face that he had read about in several books. Scientists had disproved it as being anything remarkable, saying that it was just a mountain that when viewed from a distance, looked like a face because the mind always looks for patterns, or things it would recognize.

"Maybe we should try down there," he said, pointing at the face.

"Down where?" asked Obiah.

"There," replied Tom.

Obiah frowned, doubting that anything would be found there, but saw no harm in humoring the lad. He veered the ship lower.

Beep… Beep… Beep!—Beep! Beep…

"What was that?" demanded Joe.

Unsure himself, Obiah took another pass over the face, receiving the same double beep from the beacon.

"I think we got some…" began Tom, but his words were cut off as a laser blast ricocheted off the stern of the ship.

Obiah banked to the right just as a moon-shaped vessel sped past, almost clipping them.

"Who's that?" demanded Joe.

"Who do you think," said Obiah as he jerked back on the controls and shot upward into the upper atmosphere of Mars.

The strange ship turned and headed straight for them again, firing laser blasts at them, each exploding just outside the hull and leaving scorch marks on the smooth exterior. Obiah headed straight for their new adversary, breaking away just before impact. He jammed the controls downward.

"Tom, the controls—now!"

Tom fastened himself into the co-pilot's seat, grasping the controls in his sweaty palms. When Obiah jerked left, Tom followed; when he veered to the right, Tom followed.

When they had left Jifdar's ship, one of Stein's patrols had spotted them and pursued them, waiting for the perfect moment to attack.

More laser blasts pummeled the vessel. Obiah and Tom flung the ship to the side, making its belly face their opponent as the two ships streaked past one another. Obiah jerked the spacecraft downward, causing Joe and Solon to lose their footing and fall forward. Their ship sped straight down towards the surface of Mars with alarming speed. Joe watched, his eyes widening by the second as the ground neared.

"Obiah," said Tom.

"Keep the ship steady," Obiah said.

Tom watched as the ground neared and more laser blasts streaked by, turning into flaming balls of smoke and fire and missing them by just a few feet.

"Obiah," he said again, worry in his voice. His grip on the controls tightened, prepared to take over if Obiah maintained this suicidal course.

"Obiah," Tom said again.

Still no response.

Tom's hands shifted.

"No!" Obiah stopped him. "Trust me."

Tom stared into Obiah's eyes, his hands relaxed, while behind him, Joe and Solon gripped the edges of their seats, their eyes glued to the rocky surface of the planet as it neared.

More laser fire pounded outside the ship as red filled the windshield.

"Now!" yelled Obiah.

Tom yanked back on the controls, mirroring Obiah's movements and jerking the ship upward. It wobbled from side to side before leveling out, as the ship that pursued them crashed into the ground, bits of shrapnel and fire flying in every direction.

"All right!" cheered Joe, but he was too quick in his praise.

Another moon-shaped ship appeared from above, falling in behind them and firing an incessant amount of laser fire that rocked the ship. They zoomed over the surface of the planet, kicking up plumes of red sand. The ship remained behind them.

Obiah thought about the sandstorm. He checked his sensor screens, confirming that it still raged, and wasn't far from them. They needed to gain altitude, and they need to do it without the other ship on their tail.

"Tom," said Obiah, "when I say, cut the left engines."

"Are you crazy?" demanded Tom.

"Just do it!"

Trusting in Obiah's experience, Tom nodded his head, waiting for the command. Just then, laser fire struck the ship, causing the port side to catch fire. Within moments, Joe sprung from his seat, snatched the fire extinguisher, and sprayed foamy liquid over the flames, quelling them. He tossed the extinguisher aside when the flames dissipated.

"Now!" yelled Obiah.

Tom cut the port engines. The moment he did, the ship dropped to the left, flinging Joe to the side and causing him to slam into the wall. Obiah strained against the controls, holding them to the right and forcing the ship into a sharp U-turn before leveling.

"Restart the engines."

Tom did. Fire burst from the port engines as they restarted, kicking up more sand and rock as the ship behind them struggled to make the same sharp turn. Obiah steered the ship through canyons and across dried river beds that were billions of years old, zipping across the surface of the planet, while dodging protruding rocks and cliff faces.

More laser fire rained down upon them, striking the rocky over-hangs and dumping boulders that clipped the ship, sending loud bangs throughout the hull. Obiah and Tom swerved to the right and the left, avoiding the blows as best they could.

The sandstorm lay just ahead. Tom glanced at Obiah, whose eyes remained locked on the storm that raged in front of them. They burst through the semi-solid wall of red sand—the grit pelted the window, chipping it—holding the ship steady. The spacecraft be-hind them followed. Winds ripped around them, while rocks and sand pounded the outer hull; their roar echoed around them, filling them with dread.

A laser blast struck the right wing, tearing off its tip. The ship lurched. Hands turning white, Tom clung to the controls, holding the ship steady, while Obiah navigated the storm. The vessel vibrat-ed and bounced as it was tossed by the raging winds that tried to rip them apart. More laser fire struck the outer hull.

"Doesn't this ship have any weapons?" shouted Joe, growing tired of the constant barrage of laser fire.

Obiah cringed. The ship they had found in Herclai's secret bun-ker was just a transport ship, meaning no weapons. His silent re-sponse told Joe what he needed to know.

Tom jumped from his seat, his harness clinking against the met-al supports of his chair, and yelled, "I got an idea!"

He rushed to the rear of the ship, flinging the door to a storage locker open. Items dropped to the floor as he rummaged through the locker, searching for something that could be of use to his plans. He snatched and grabbed anything that he thought might help, dump-ing them on the floor, and paused when a thin metal band, similar to the ones he wore when connecting to Solaris' consciousness when she was just a ship, and picked it up, holding it in the light.

"Hold this," Tom said, handing a ball of wadded tape to Joe when he approached to ask what was going on.

Tom worked fast, connecting tubes, a power crystal, and bits of plastic in a makeshift explosive device. The ship lurched. Maintaining his balance, Tom concentrated on the task at hand, his mind blocking out all distractions. Once finished, he gave the device to Joe to hold.

"What are you doing?" shouted Obiah.

"You'll see," said Tom. "Just keep the ship steady."

Tom took the thin, metal band, studying it. He spotted something that looked like a connector. Hoping that the band was what he thought it was, Tom hooked it up to the connector and placed it on his head.

Scanning for DNA match, said a computerized voice in Tom's head. *Match verified. Awaiting command.*

"Place it there, by the hatch," Tom said to Joe, pointing at the device.

Joe did as ordered, stepping well away from it.

Erect a force field around the stern hatch, Tom ordered the ship. Lights flickered as a shield popped up, surrounding the device and the hatch. "Everyone hang onto something," said Tom to the others. *Open hatch,* he directed the ship.

Opening the hatch at this velocity is not...

Open the hatch! Tom reiterated.

The rear hatch opened, ripping the makeshift explosive device out of the ship. It tore through the thin atmosphere of Mars until it struck the craft behind them, clinging to the hull.

Close hatch! Tom told the ship just as his device detonated, releasing a spectacular display of fiery, rainbow lights that disintegrated the vessel that chased them through the sandstorm.

The force of the explosion flung their ship forward, causing the tail end to rear up before leveling out. Tom went flying to the bow of the ship, banging his head on the armrest of a chair. Dazed, he rolled down the aisle, while Solon and Joe threw themselves at him, each seizing one of Tom's arms and pulling him to a halt.

In the pilot's seat, Obiah struggled with the ship to keep it steady, while the winds of the sandstorms pivoted and bucked the vessel in conjunction with the explosion.

"What was that?" he demanded.

Tom crawled back into the co-pilot's chair. "I used one of the power crystals to make a bomb," he replied.

"How'd you know it would work?" asked Obiah.

"I didn't."

Obiah held the ship steady, hoping that they would push through the sandstorm soon. He didn't know how much longer the engines could take the bombardment of rock and silt.

"Look out!" yelled Joe.

A cliff jumped out in front of them, blocked by the veil of red sand swirling around them. Obiah and Tom jerked the ship upwards, avoiding the cliff, the bottom hull scraping the sharp rocks and tearing holes. Another cliff appeared. Veering to the right, they avoided it, before banking to the left to miss another. A fourth cliff appeared. They pushed the ship upward, flying high into the sky before stalling. The engines shut down.

Obiah fiddled with the ignition, but the engines refused to re-start, having become clogged by red sand. The sleek vessel hovered in the air for a moment, giving them all the sensation of weightlessness before plunging to the red ground below. Obiah and Tom leveled the ship as best they could, extending the flaps to slow their descent.

"I think we are going down too fast," said Solon.

"It's called crashing!" shouted Obiah.

The ship vibrated with violent force, pivoting from side to side as they plummeted to the ground. Metal clinked as they all snapped their harnesses into place. The red ground filled the window.

"Brace for impact!" shouted Obiah just as the ship plowed into the planet's surface; clouds of dust shot into the atmosphere, creating a red fog as the they skidded across the ground before coming to a sudden halt.

Tom raised his head; blood trickled down the side of his face from a small cut. He glanced around at the others before recent events rushed back to his mind.

"Is everyone okay?"

Joe slumped out of his seat, his feet unsteady as his mind still reeled from the impact.

"How are we still breathing?"

"Shields," said Obiah. "They must have kicked in after we crashed, but they won't hold for long. We need to get into suits before the air leaks out."

Beep... Beep... Beep...

Obiah snatched the locator device, amazed that it still worked. He turned on the ship's computers, scanning the area for the face of Mars, as Tom had referred to it.

"Well, gentlemen," said Obiah, charting their course, "from here on out, we walk."

They scrambled into spacesuits and opened the rear hatch, each stomping down the gangplank to the solid surface of Mars. Solon paused when he reached the bottom of the plank, marveling at the red landscape that surrounded him, convinced that he had just entered Ares' home.

"Come on," said Obiah, holding the locator beacon and taking the lead. "We only have a few hours of air in these suits, so there is not time to waste."

Fierce winds, unlike anything they had experienced in their travels, howled around them, inundating them with mounds of sand and ice. They trekked across the barren landscape, their anvil-like boots weighing them down so that they would not float away and leaving rectangular, ridge prints in the crimson gravel. Sand swirled around them, growing thicker until it encompassed them in a dust devil the size of a small house. They each turned and spun around in confusion until the storm had passed.

Obiah urged them onward. Taking the lead, he held the beacon that Solaris had constructed for them, following its signal and hoping that he had made the right decision. They trudged through the inhospitable wasteland over razor-edged rocks that threatened to slice their suits, marveling at the sand snakes that slithered through the red dust floating across the ground, mocking their efforts.

Something gleamed next to Tom. He turned and noticed the land rover 3—sent to the red planet a month before Brie had been summoned to help Rynah—complete with its NASA logo on the side, though it had chipped some from the brutal weather. Tom stared at the robot in curiosity. Not knowing what else to do, he lifted his hand and waved, wondering if anyone watched back on Earth. Indeed, someone had been watching—a man with speckled skin and black-rimmed glasses, who had been given the boring job of monitoring the rover's data, had just settled down to eat his lunch when he saw Tom on his monitor waving at him; his cup of lo mein dropped to the floor.

More winds whipped around Tom, reminding him of the imperative need to keep moving. He glanced at Joe, who stood still, staring up into the sky at the crisp stars that dotted the inky blackness, amazed at how clear they appeared.

"Hey," Tom said.

"Look at them," Joe said, pointing at the stars. "Somehow, they seem closer here than they do back home."

"That's because there is hardly any atmosphere here," said Tom. "We should keep going."

They walked forward, following Obiah as he navigated using the beacon, in a single line of white specks moving across a red surface. Low hills, resembling spiked towers, which looked more like something from Bruegel's *The Triumph of Death* than an unexplored region of an even more mysterious planet, blocked their path. Despite the difficulty, they climbed upward, their gloved hands slipping every few inches as they planted the heels of their boots into the ground for support. Fog developed on their visors from each strained breath they took as they trudged upward. Pebbles clacked as they bounced down the side of the hill, disturbed from their peace by the newcomers.

Tom reached up, grasping the ridge, and heaved himself over it. He turned and helped Solon, who had managed the climb with little difficulty, thanks to Alfric's training in physical exercise. Once they had all crested the hill, they stopped.

Their eyes roamed over the surface of the planet, taking in the dust devils in the distance that mirrored reddened smoke, burned by the sun that rested on the horizon. Rock spires twisted around themselves as they rose into the air, casting long shadows that interconnected and formed shapes of monsters and beasts from legend on the cracked lakebed below. The cracks in the soil snaked across the ground in jagged zigzags, jabbing one another until they formed irregular shapes that coated the surface.

"There," said Obiah, pointing to a small mountain. "The beacon is leading us there."

Tom and Joe both stared at the small, rounded mountain before them, each thinking the same—this was what the face of Mars looked like from the ground. Joe stepped downward just as an invisible force slammed into him, almost knocking him over. They all turned. Behind them charged a wall of red sand, speeding across the planet's surface and crushing everything in its path.

"Go!" yelled Obiah over the radio.

They all jumped down the hill; rocks slid out from under them as they landed and rolled downward until they were able to stop themselves. Tom's grip slipped. He felt himself float for a moment before plummeting to the ground.

A hand seized his, gripping it with a strength he wouldn't have thought possible from a bookworm and heaved Tom to the ledge. Tom patted Solon on the back, thanking him, when a gust of wind rose around them with swirling sand and dust that blinded them before pounding the side of the hill with a thunderous roar and lifted Solon into the air.

"Solon!" yelled Tom as he watched his friend being carried by the raging storm, before disappearing into the wall of sand that had overtaken them.

Tom let go of the ledge. He skidded down to the bottom, with Joe and Obiah close behind, and watched in horror as Solon crashed into a boulder and slumped to the ground, unmoving. Tom half-ran, half-hopped to his friend, fearing the worst. Once he reached Solon, he turned him over. Solon's face had turned purple as he struggled to breathe—his oxygen tank had been damaged in the storm.

With little time to lose, Tom took his tank, ignoring the cries of both Obiah and Joe, and plugged Solon's suit into it, making one tank serve them both. As the air flowed into Solon's suit, his gasps ceased, becoming steady breaths.

Obiah and Joe reached them.

"What…" began Obiah, but stopped when he saw Solon's broken tank and how he and Tom were connected to the same one. "How much air do you have left?"

"Enough to get us to where we're going," replied Tom.

Obiah frowned, knowing that with two suits hooked up to a single tank that had already been half used, they would be lucky if they lasted an hour.

"Let's go. The beacon is getting stronger. I think we're almost there."

Joe helped Solon to his feet as Tom rose to his. Once again, they followed Obiah as he led them across what had once been a lake (eons ago) to the hills ahead. They staggered forward amidst the blinding sand that pelted them, driving them back and warning them to stay away. The closer they got to the face, the more the sandstorm raged.

Each agonizing step winded both Tom and Solon as the single tank feeding their suits drained at rapid speed. Winded, their breathing shallowed, and water vapor filled the inside of their visors, cutting them off from the world around them. Their legs turned to rubber with each step, flopping onto the flaming red dirt and causing dust to puff into the air before being carted away by the wind. Tom sank to his knees.

Within moments, Solon lifted him by the shoulders.

"We cannot stop now. Our destination is close," he gasped.

Tom summoned the strength to stand just as Joe reached them, placing a hand beneath both their shoulders.

"How much farther?" he asked Obiah.

Obiah studied the beacon, its incessant beeps quickened with each passing second.

"Not far."

The sun lowered even more on the Martian horizon, casting burnt rays of fiery sunlight upon them and transforming their white suits into the shade of blood. They reached the base. Once there, both Solon and Tom collapsed, their knees sinking into the gritty sand as clouds of it enveloped them, knowing their time had ended.

Obiah raced around the base, searching for a way inside as the beacon beeped in rapid succession. If this was a hangar, he saw no door.

"Anything?" asked Joe?

In response, Obiah continued searching the base of the low mountain, its varied striations of red, pink, orange, and white circling around it like a shirt collar.

Solon fell face first into the sand; Tom followed. Joe rushed to them, his hurried steps causing him to float through the weaker gravity of Mars. Once there, he checked the oxygen levels of their tank. It had been depleted—Tom and Solon now breathed carbon monoxide. Glancing back at Obiah as he continued his frantic search for a door to what they had come to Mars for, Joe knew that there was only one solution. Remembering what Rynah and Solaris said about how Herclai's blood (whomever he was) was needed to fly the ship, he did the only thing he could do—he unhooked his own oxygen tank from his suit and plugged it into Solon's and Tom's.

Sweat poured down his temples as he struggled to breathe, inhaling the tainted air that remained in the confines of his suit. He watched as Tom and Solon's eyes opened again, their faces brightening. Joe had bought them time, but how much, he could not say. He glanced over at Obiah one last time as the man pressed what

appeared to be an ordinary, rounded edge of the rock, but unbeknownst to Joe, it bore the crest of Herclai and the locator beacon
vibrated in Obiah's hand when he neared it.

"Joe," said Tom, but his voice sounded far away.

Just as Joe's eyes closed, a yellow light surrounded them and
they disappeared.

"Joe! Joe!"

Tom tore off Joe's helmet, allowing him to breathe the air inside—he wasn't sure where they were. A metal railing surrounded
them, its burnished silver adding to the gloom of the area, but a
welcomed relief to the whirling red sand outside.

Joe inhaled sharply, filling his lungs with the stale air of what
looked to be another bunker, glad that he could breathe again.

"Where are we?"

"Not sure," replied Tom.

"How long was I out?" asked Joe.

"Ten minutes. You didn't have to give us your tank. You could
have died."

"Goes with the job," said Joe. He heard Tom's appreciation in his
voice, even if the young man refused to admit it.

"How are you feeling?" asked Solon.

"I'll live," said Joe, sitting up.

Without warning, lights flashed around them, scanning them,
as weapons the size of cannons, and looking a lot like machine guns,
rose from the floor and popped out of the walls with them in their
sights. They froze.

"Identify," said a computerized voice.

"Uh," said Tom.

As though to make its point, the weapons fired a laser pulse at
them, blackening the floor where the blast struck just in front of
their feet.

"Hey!" yelled Tom, incensed at such an act.

"Unauthorized access has been detected," repeated the computer.

Remembering something the oracle had told him about giving his name when faced with imminent death, Solon stepped forward; the weapons followed his movements.

"I am Solon, son of Deon, and brother to Halius. I seek the dragon's heart."

"Two of you bear Herclai's blood, but two of you do not," said the computerized voice.

"They are friends," said Solon. "Allies."

More lights passed over them before the computerized voice spoke again.

"To find the dragon's heart, you must make whole what is broken."

The weapons disarmed and sealed themselves behind metal panels as though they had never existed. The lights turned off, plunging them into darkness, before flicking on again, illuminating the whole interior of where they were; it was not a bunker they were in, but a ship. What had been colored in gloom brightened, transforming to the purest gold that sparkled and gleamed with each turn.

They all leaned over the rails as stairs appeared to their right, leading down to the deck below, where lounge chairs and a kitchen was, poised before a gigantic window that showed the fury of blowing red sand outside. Tom gasped as he realized where they were—the face of Mars was not some formation of rock and stone, but a ship! His excitement from that realization boiled over as he skipped down the metal stairs to the deck below, followed by the others. As they walked, holographic books and shelves appeared. If they looked at one for ten seconds, it opened before them, displaying lines of text and images of an era that most thought was a myth.

Solon read the text that appeared before him, amazed that he understood it. Though he could not have known, the ancient Greek language was a variation of the Mulyran alphabet, which allowed Solon, who had always had a knack for the written word and different languages, to decipher its content. He absorbed every bit of the text, taking in as much as he could about this ancient civilization that existed before his own.

Solon's elbow bumped a box the size of a large book—its rounded corners decorated with geometrical designs that spiraled down the sides—and it thumped as the lid flopped open. A clatter resonated around him, its sharp ring bouncing off the interior wall of the ship in a jubilant melody of its own. He bent down, picking up a thin, slate-colored, metal band that lay on its side on the mosaic floor, twirling it in his fingers as he studied it.

"What do you have there?" asked Tom.

Solon held the band out to him.

Tom's face scrunched in concentration as he took it, mesmerized by another piece of technology. As he flipped it over to examine its inside, the band turned green, casting faint shadows on his ebony-colored face as it blinked. His fingers slipped across the lustrous band and it flashed red.

"Obiah!" he called.

Obiah and Joe rushed over to him, taking the slim band. His eyes narrowed as they focused on the blinking band as it shifted colors, going from slate to green to red, before returning to its original coloring. He spotted the box. Opening it, Obiah's softball-sized hands scooped up more of the bands from their neat position in the velvet interior coffer.

"I think these are tracking bands," he said.

"Tracking bands?" asked Joe. "You mean, a form of GPS."

"To put it in your terms," said Obiah. He rubbed his forefinger along the side and symbols flashed across it. Obiah smiled.

"Homing beacons."

"Homing beacons?" asked Solon, confused.

"Basically, it's like a target that the ship can hone in on," said Tom. "Think of it this way: if you wear this, you become a target, and the ship is the arrow coming straight for you."

"So, like Solaris, this vessel can navigate itself," said Solon.

"I think it's safe to say," replied Obiah, "that this ship has an autopilot."

Solon took another band, cradling it in his bony hand, an idea forming in his mind.

"We need to find the command center," said Obiah, interrupting Solon's musing and placing the band back into their snug coffer. "It should have a communications portal. We've wasted enough time here."

Solon tore himself away from the holographic books and the wooden box of armbands, vowing to come back when he had more time, but for now, they needed to contact Rynah. He seized Tom's shoulder—who had found an interesting piece of equipment and was about to turn it on when Solon stopped him—and followed Obiah and Joe to the most logical location for the command center: the uppermost deck.

Chapter 22
A Test for Merrick

Stein paced before the line of handcuffed men and women before him, each with their eyes cast at their feet, not daring to look at him. His steel-toed boots clomped against the smooth, metal floor, echoing off the high walls around him as he circled those who dared to turn against him. The black doors of the cargo bay, the only barrier between them and the inhospitality of space, towered over them, giant monsters waiting to devour each of them. Stein's slow and steady steps instigated fear into all who watched. He had summoned the entire crew for a demonstration of what happens when one dared to question his authority. They had gathered outside the cargo bay, watching through its transparent walls.

A dark look filled his hollow eyes, the same eyes that once knew joy and love before embarking on the slow transformation from sadness to insanity. His stern face and pinched mouth conveyed only anger—at losing Klanor and Rynah more than loathing for a few rebellious crewmembers—and mercilessness. If they wished to leave the ship, then he would grant that desire.

"It has come to my attention," he said in a low voice that carried, piercing the hearts of any who listened with fear, "that some of you are not pleased with the new direction of this armada, that some of you are displeased with my leadership."

Stein stopped in front of a man whose quivering body amused him and a smirk crept to his lips before he continued.

"Many of you once swore to serve Klanor, but he abandoned all of you when he chose to join forces with Rynah and her small band of misfits. He promised you power and well-being, much like he promised me, but he broke such promises. Now he seeks to destroy what he once swore to give you."

What he once swore to give me, Stein thought to himself.

"I have attempted to fulfill this promise, but some of you refused to accept my authority, calling my takeover a coup. I never betrayed Klanor; he betrayed us. I only sought to deliver on what he failed to achieve, but those of you who stand here refused to accept that. Instead, you sought to supplant me, to get rid of me, and take this ship for yourselves. Traitors, all of you, can now stand before your peers—people who once trusted you—and be judged."

Two security guards rushed into the cargo bay with Merrick in tow and threw him to the floor. His bloodied feet left tracks in the white linoleum, sullying it with Stein's legacy. He slumped forward, hands tied behind his back, chin to the floor as he caught his breath. Each exertion pained him, and Merrick breathed in sharp gasps as he tried to sit up to look Stein in the eyes.

"Ah, Merrick," said Stein in a honeyed-lemon voice, "how nice of you to join us."

A guard seized Merrick by the collar and hauled him to his feet.

"You see before you people who, like yourself, have lost faith in me."

"Why am I here?" demanded Merrick, his voice harsh from having not spoken in days.

"Redemption," answered Stein. He placed a hand around Merrick's blackened shoulder, ignoring him as he winced from the pain,

and dragged him forward. "I offer you this choice. From among the
people you see here, one shall have a chance at forgiveness; you get
to choose who that individual will be."

Merrick craned his neck so that he could face Stein and looked
at him through his swollen eyes.

"What?"

"You wished to save me—to spare me from the error of my
ways," said Stein. "Well, I offer you this chance to spare one of them
from their punishment."

Not believing Stein's actions, Merrick stared at him with a blank
expression mixed with horror.

"You cannot ask me to do this!"

"I just did," came Stein's icy reply.

Merrick looked at the line of sullen faces before him. His stomach reeled at the sickening choice that Stein placed before him.

"Stein, stop this."

"The clock is ticking, Merrick. You best choose before I choose
for you."

"I cannot," said Merrick.

"Then, they will all die," Stein whispered in Merrick's ear. "Come
now. You have the chance to save one life; are you going to waste it?"

Merrick glanced at the downcast faces before him. Some shook
and others wrung their hands, while the rest stood still, resigned to
their fate. He wished to choose, to save one, but whom, and how would
he live with the knowledge that he condemned the others to death?

"Time's up," said Stein. "Who will it be?"

Merrick faced Stein, and for the first time, he saw the monster
that had replaced the man who had married his sister.

"I'll not play a part in your games."

"Very well, then." Stein snapped his fingers and the two guards
snatched Merrick, dragging him through the doors and to the adjoining room with Stein close behind.

Once through, Stein turned, looking through the transparent

walls at the condemned members of his ship. He glanced at the man with the lever that controlled the outer doors of the cargo bay and nodded. The doors burst open, thrusting the line of people out into the cold, harshness of space, before sealing shut once again. Stein watched with an impassive face, neither enjoying nor loathing the moment, as his eyes roamed the faces—some frightened, some as cold as his—around him who witnessed the proceedings.

"This," he said to them, "is what happens if you fail to abide by the rules on this ship. There is no room for error. There are no second chances."

Stein glanced at Merrick, whose shocked face forced him to laugh.

"Don't look so surprised."

"How could you?" demanded Merrick.

"I am not an unreasonable man," replied Stein. "They wished to leave the ship and I allowed them to. You could have saved one of them."

"We both know that you would have killed them all anyway," spat Merrick.

"Perhaps," said Stein.

The guards took hold of Merrick's arms and hauled him away to his cell, leaving Stein alone as he looked out at his ship the way a callous nobleman, who valued nothing, observed his manor.

Chapter 23
MYSTERIOUS DEEP

Solaris rowed the small boat into the center of the lake. Tiny waves crested beneath the soft wind that brushed the top of the crystal blue water, which mirrored the sky and its white, fluffy clouds above. Solaris glanced at the sky. Like Rynah—who had spent the last 30 minutes staring at it—she had never seen a sky that was such a deep blue, a feat that amazed her. Achilles sat at the bow of the boat, looking out at the water and the occasional jet ski that zipped past, while Brie remained in the center, checking the diving equipment.

Solaris returned to her rowing. Since she never fatigued, she volunteered to row the small boat to the very center of the massive lake.

"Breathe deeply," Brie reminded Rynah when she appeared to be a bit faint.

Rynah smiled. She had never spent so much time at high altitude, not unless she was in a pressurized ship that orbited other planets. She gazed at the snowcapped peaks surrounding them.

"It's beautiful here."

"Eh, not much to look at," quipped Achilles.

Brie glowered at him. "It is wonderful out here."

Solaris stopped the boat. "We've arrived."

"How do you know?" asked Achilles.

"I've calculated the circumference of the lake based on the number of miles it takes to circle it and calcu—"

"Forget I asked," mumbled Achilles, to which both Rynah and Brie chuckled.

"Aren't you coming?" asked Brie when she noticed that Achilles had not put on his diving gear.

"I… uh… I thought I would look after the boat."

"I don't think anyone is going to steal it," said Brie.

"You can never tell about some people," Achilles said. "I think it would be best if I stayed here."

"You're not afraid of the water, are you?" asked Brie.

"No," began Achilles, "I just don't fancy being so far under the water with nothing between me and certain death, but a single tank of oxygen."

"You once traveled the galaxy," said Rynah, "and you're afraid of diving?"

"Afraid is a rather strong word," said Achilles.

"I agree," said Solaris, "he should stay."

Achilles shot her a look, surprised at her sudden response. "You don't have to be so quick to agree."

"Maybe you should stay here," Rynah said, cinching up her wetsuit, "there is no guarantee that we'll find anything down there. If we're not back in an hour, leave without us."

She jumped over the side of the boat.

Brie squeezed Achilles' shoulder before leaning back, splashing in the dark blue water, with Solaris right behind her, leaving Achilles alone to entertain himself.

Remembering her time in a spacesuit, Brie breathed slow and steady as she swam after Rynah and the trail of bubbles she left that danced in the pale bluish-yellow rays of the sun. Downward they swam, deeper into the dark depths below them, as the sunlight thinned before plowing through a black veil and plunging into com-plete darkness. They pulled out their waterproof flashlights that they had tied to their wrists, shining the beams before them. Green-ish-white bubbles floated upward in small swirls, looking more like tiny dots.

Rynah waved her hand, pointing down and jerking it back as a sharp sting stabbed her hand. She looked at the small, red welt that formed and ignored the burning sensation that encompassed it, despite the icy water surrounding her. Shaking her hand, Rynah pointed again at what she had spotted. Both Brie and Solaris shined their flashlights where she directed, but found nothing. Shaking her head in frustration, Rynah swam off, kicking her finned feet hard in disappointment, while Solaris and Brie chased after her. They drift-ed along the bottom over reefs and soft silt that burst into clouds around them from the slightest touch.

Brie checked her tank levels. They had been down there for 30 minutes already. Amazed at how quickly time passed when they need to find something pressed them, she swam harder. Doing her best to remember the lines of the poem, Brie searched for any clues to a ship under the water, but found nothing, only rock, sand, and algae.

A speck of light caught her attention. Brie paused, floating in the water while Solaris and Rynah swan onward. Only darkness greeted her. Confused, Brie kicked her feet, stopping when the faint light blinked again. Peering into the dark waters, Brie watched as the flashing light appeared to be far away, yet close by at the same time.

Mesmerized, she reached for it when—Ouch! Something pierced the skin on her forefinger. Reeling back, Brie focused the beam of her flashlight on it, revealing a small spot of red where she had been poked; her finger burned and throbbed, the pain increas-ing with each passing second. Wincing, Brie did her best to ignore the searing pain as it worked its way up her arm, never noticing the caterpillar-sized water worm, with a stinger on its end, slither away, melting into the darkness around her.

Solaris waved at her. Brie shined her light on her and saw what looked like a cave entrance, with an overhang that drooped, covered in slimy, red algae, and… blue seaweed? Curious, Brie swam over to the drifting tendrils of the seaweed, certain that they could not be what she thought they were, but it looked like sea weed—blue like the water, but with twisted, lavender lines that wrapped around them.

Rynah paused by Brie's side, enchanted by the waving plants as well. Together, both reached and touched the slick arm of blue seaweed, enthralled by its underwater waltz and marveling at how it wrapped around their arms, almost as though it caressed them; but it did not feel like a plant, more like thin bits of rubber, yet softer, and smooth.

Solaris motioned for them to enter the cave. Brie and Rynah obeyed after checking their oxygen tank levels again. Fifteen minutes left. They entered the tunnel, its blackness fading into a turquoise glow that emanated from glow worms that crawled across the rippled, porous walls, creating tiny weaving lights. Rynah stopped swimming, hunching over in the water and clutching her stomach. Brie and Solaris both swam to her, but she shooed them away, swimming faster to prove that she felt fine.

As Brie watched Rynah swim off, her head spun and her vision blurred a bit before clearing again. Shaking her head, she looked into Solaris' concerned eyes before copying Rynah's movements and speeding away, not wanting to cause her friends to feel concerned. They swam single file through the circular tunnel as the walls closed in around them, growing narrower; the worms glowed brighter. Soon, their exposed skin turned blue from the light of the glow worms as the cavern walls narrowed even more, the smooth protruding edges brushing against their arms.

The walls tickled Brie's skin as she swam onward, slowing her pace to squeeze through the tunnel—it was now shoulder width apart. She stopped. Rynah drifted by a small opening, her head swaying in the current. As Brie approached her, her sense of balance disappeared, causing her to float to the side unable to swim in a straight line. She checked their tank levels—empty.

Brie reached what appeared to be a hole, but her hand slammed into solid metal. Shining her flashlight upon it, she realized that it was a door, but a door to what? She pushed on it, glancing at Rynah's floating form and noticing a spot of red on her hand. Curious, Brie snatched Rynah's hand and compared it to where she had been stung on her forefinger; they had the same prick mark.

Solaris appeared. With no time to think about the mysterious mark on their hands, Brie pointed at the door, hoping Solaris understood. She did. Solaris swam off, her flashlight forming a fan on the walls of the underwater cavern as she searched for a lever or control pad that might open the metal door that blocked their path. Nothing.

Growing more dizzy, Brie snatched Rynah's arms to prevent her from drifting away in the current. In doing so, they bumped into the door, and in an effort to catch herself, Brie's palm rested flat against the metal. A green line stretched from the top of the copper door to the bottom before disappearing. With a loud click, muffled by the water, the metallic door opened. Water pressed in on them as it rushed through the new opening, shoving them forward until they crashed onto a solid surface, drenched and spitting out foamy liquid. The door closed, sealing them inside.

Brie ripped off her tank and ran to Rynah. Her legs buckled beneath her, causing her to collapse to the floor, gasping. Her chest felt as though a pile of bricks lay upon it, crushing her as she struggled to breathe. She looked up. Rynah wheezed as well, her heliotrope face turning blue. Brie glanced at her hand, realizing that what had stung her was not a fish or underwater creature, or some innocuous plant, but something with poison in it.

Hands, softer than she would have imagined, seized her, turning her over and forcing her eyes to focus on a worried Solaris. Brie pointed at Rynah. Solaris rushed to her friend with the same troubled look, unsure of what to do.

Lights popped out of the ceiling above them, scanning them, before vanishing.

"Identify yourselves," said a harsh voice as a man walked up to them, wearing long robes made of a material they had never seen before.

"Help them," cried Solaris, unsure of what ailed her friends.

"Identify yourself," repeated the man.

"My name is Solaris"—Solaris rose to her feet, infuriated by the stranger's lack of concern—"and these are my friends, Rynah and Brie. Now help them."

A neon orange light emanated from the man's hand as he scanned both Rynah and Brie.

"DNA match."

"What's wrong with them?" demanded Solaris.

"They have been poisoned," said the man, emotionless.

Brie looked up at the man, thinking he looked a bit strange as her breaths came in shorter gasps.

"Poisoned? How?" Solaris' voice echoed throughout the hollow chamber, her worry growing by the second. "Where's the antidote?"

"You are the antidote," said the man.

Solaris glared at him, her eyes wide with fear—an emotion both Rynah and Brie didn't think was possible for her—as she looked at her friends.

"This vessel is protected. Only those who are worthy may pass. They are of Herclai's line, but you are neither living, nor dead, and cannot pass."

"Help them you *Gryswea!*" shouted Solaris, cursing for the first time since Rynah had met her.

"Sacrifices must be made," said the man. "What would you give for their lives?"

Solaris' eyes darted from Brie's face to Rynah's as her mind flashed back to the sickening choice Stein had put before her only a week before. She had chosen Rynah then. She had chosen to sacrifice one for the other, but not today; she would not make the same mistake twice.

"Take mine."

"You are not alive," said the man.

"Take me," repeated Solaris, "and spare them both."

"You must choose," said the man.

"I will not choose one over the other. My life for both of theirs." Solaris' voice hardened as she was determined to not repeat her mistakes.

"But you are not among the living."

"If you shut me down and take me apart, it is as good as dying, for I will cease to exist. Take my existence, in exchange for their lives."

The man smiled and disappeared. Only then did Solaris realize that he was just a hologram. A hiss filled the air around them as two panels dropped from the ceiling, breaking apart and turning into syringes that pricked Rynah's and Brie's shoulders. Within seconds, both took deep, sharp breaths as their lungs opened and their heads cleared. Solaris knelt by each of them, checking their pulses, relief washing over her face as she realized that they would live.

"You have proven yourself worthy," said the man's voice as lights flared up, illuminating the entire room and the chambers beyond. As Solaris helped both Rynah and Brie to their feet, they all realized that they stood in a ship. They had found what they were looking for.

The floor lowered beneath them, carrying them to the level below, as more lights turned on, showcasing the gold plating on the walls, covered in intricate designs and woven together to form delicate patterns that sparkled. Only on closer inspection did they notice that the patterns consisted of individual characters from a language long since extinct. Indigo lights flared up on the floor, forming a path that they were meant to follow and stretching down a gangplank to another level below.

"What was all of that?" asked Brie, referring to the man and his insistence on Solaris making a sacrifice.

Rynah unzipped her wetsuit, taking it off.

"We had to prove that we were worthy."

"Worthy?" questioned Brie.

"Think about it," said Rynah, remembering the stories Marlow used to tell her when she was a child sitting on his lap with apt attention, "in every story you have ever listened to, ever loved, the hero must prove himself worthy. What better way to do it than by making the ultimate sacrifice?"

"I'm no hero," said Solaris, thinking back to the construction site.

Rynah placed a gentle hand on her shoulder, giving her a warm smile. "I disagree," she said as she thought about all of the times that Solaris had saved her life, and those of the others.

Brie wandered down the gangplank, following the small, dotted lights to the lower level of the ship. The moment she crossed the threshold—its square edges aloft in carved, floral designs—more lights flickered to life, bestowing upon her their soft, light-orange glow. Holographic shelves filled with books and scrolls appeared with each step she took.

"Over here!" called Brie.

Solaris and Rynah ran to her, their heavy boots echoing on the metallic floor. They stopped. Amazed by the amount of books, if one could call them that, they stared at the rows and rows of what looked like scrolls and bound parchment. Rynah touched one with the tips of her long fingers, afraid of damaging its delicate nature, but being holographic, she needn't have worried. She unrolled it with care, still not believing that it was just a hologram (and a solid looking one at that), and watched as characters and lettering appeared, though she could not decipher them.

"Do you think you can read this?" she asked Solaris.

Solaris took the holographic scroll, studying the ancient writing as she accessed her memory banks. Rynah and Brie watched her as she thought back to when she had first seen such writing; Marlow had been studying bits of holed paper, its edges burnt, with the same markings.

"What is that?" she had asked him, her scanners storing images of the pages and its calligraphic writing.

"An ancient language," Marlow had replied.

"It is not ancient Lanyran," Solaris had said.

"No," Marlow had replied, "it's not. It is far older than that and not from this world."

Solaris remembered being confused by that statement, though as she studied the same writing on the ship under Lake Tahoe, she made the connection.

"I want you to study this," Marlow had told her. "I managed to decipher what some of the letters mean, but not all, though you might be able to. Study it. Memorize it, Solaris, you may have need of it in the future."

At the time, Solaris did not think much of Marlow's statement, passing it off as the musings of an eccentric old man, her creator. Now, she realized how wrong she had been.

"I know these markings," Solaris whispered.

Rynah and Brie stepped closer, intrigued and curious about how she knew them.

"Marlow showed me similar writing once," said Solaris.

Rynah's face fell upon the mention of her grandfather, and once again, she wished she had paid more attention to his rants, instead of abandoning him when he needed her most.

"It was a few months before he died," continued Solaris, "and he acquired these crumbling pieces of paper. They fell apart, disintegrating into dust as he unfolded them, so he had me scan them and store them in my memory banks. As I did, he taught me what some of the symbols meant."

"Can you translate them?" asked Rynah.

"I might be able to," replied Solaris, "but it will take some time."

"Time is not a luxury that we have," said Rynah.

"I'm sorry," Solaris said, "but these things cannot be rushed."

"See what you can do," Rynah said. She grabbed Brie, and together, they explored the rest of the ship, going in different directions.

Once away from the others, Rynah's arm brush something and a panel opened, revealing a dusty, archaic book. Rynah took it, almost dropping it when she realized that it looked just like the book of the ancient poem that her grandfather had given her upon his death, which she had been thinking about at the time. A perfect replica in every way, except one—the last page was still there and there was no watermark. Rynah put the book aside and closed the panel. Testing it, she brushed the holopad again while thinking of a glow light. The panel opened, and within its confines was a yellow glow light.

An idea struck Rynah. She closed the panel again and thought of the fake crystal, which they had found on the desert planet, and had born a particular mark on it, her mark, and at the last second, though of how she used to have a recording device. The panel slid open. Amazed, Rynah reached in and pulled out a perfect replica of the crystal, but it blinked, waiting for her to record a message, for the replicating device had created both a crystal and a recording device, making one item, which bore an insignia, her signature. Her mind raced as she put together the pieces of the puzzle. Rynah knew just what she wanted to record and where she wanted to put the crystal she held in her hand, though how she would get it there was a matter to be solved later, so she recorded her message, shoved the crystal in her pocket, and continued exploring the ship.

While Rynah and Brie meandered among the ruby colored, metal-plated floor (with geometric-patterned tiles), Brie noticed a strange, octagonal box surrounded by transparent walls with a slender opening. She moved closer to it. Sea blue lights flared to life the moment she stepped upon the pad to its doorway. Startled, Brie jumped back.

Rynah had noticed the lights and hurried over, intrigued, and with an idea of what it might be. She touched one of the sheer panels of the wall. Words and symbols sparked to life, covering the panel and zipping past at a rate that proved too difficult for Rynah to read. She placed the tips of her fingers on the panel again. The symbols stopped.

Following Rynah's example, Brie brushed her hand against the sheer panel encasing the strange room. It, too, came to life as strange symbols darted across it.

"It's a computer," she whispered to herself as she watched the strange symbols fill the section of the transparent wall.

"Rynah?" said Brie, "do you know what this is?"

"It might be a transporter," said Rynah, recognizing its design from the one on Sunlil that Tom had used to transport her and Usef away from Klanor. She pressed a few symbols on the panel that looked similar to the mathematical characters she had studied while at the university.

The octagonal-shaped box hummed to life as burnt orange lights sprang up. Rynah punched in the coordinates for where they had left Achilles.

"What are you doing?" asked Brie.

"Bringing in a translator," Rynah replied.

She finished typing in the coordinates. The transporter lights brightened, shedding light on the entire area and casting away the dark shadows as it whirred and hummed so loud that Brie covered her ears. Rynah had guessed correctly about the usage of the transporter and, on the surface of the lake, Achilles talked to another couple on a boat about the best place to go bass fishing—a favorite pastime of his—when the yellow and orange lights swirled around him, ripping him away from his conversation, for which he was less than pleased about.

His irate face appeared on the transporter while his hair stood on end from being transported.

"Wh—what—do you know what you've done?" spluttered Achilles.

Rynah glared at him. "Brought you to the ship," she replied in a curt manner.

"I was in the middle of a conversation!"

"And we are in the middle of a crisis that could mean the end of this planet!" Rynah rounded on him.

Achilles backed away, remembering why they were there. "I

apologize. I just don't like being ripped away from somewhere without any notice."

"We need your help," said Rynah. "Solaris found these texts, but they are in a language far more ancient than anything we've ever encountered. I was hoping you might be able to translate them."

For the first time, Achilles realized where he stood. He looked up to the dimpled ceiling with copper tubing and neon wires running through it in a mesh, each sparking to life as white lights, with a green tinge, hurried down them, similar to the way neurons fire in the brain.

"You found it!"

He twirled around, looking at the gold-plated walls, with ripples running down the sides in a rainbow of colors that twinkled with each ray of light that passed over them. As though remembering the past, Achilles lifted his left foot, remarking at the ruby colored tiles—that looked like actual rubies, but were made from a metal, yet to be discovered—that joined together in a puzzle, forming a maze of violet lines.

"Solaris," Rynah called, "Achilles is here to help you."

Achilles followed her to the lower floor where the holographic library was, touching each volume and scroll that appeared as he walked past, text he hadn't seen in 35 years. He tapped one scroll. The moment he did so, it floated away from the others and unrolled before him, allowing him to read the symbols and calligraphic writing that only he was familiar with, since he helped write them.

"I have deciphered some of this, but most of it is tricky," said Solaris. "I do not know how Marlow managed it."

"Perhaps I can help," said Achilles, taking the holographic book from Solaris and flipping through the pages.

Memories flooded his brain as he scanned the text, reminded of the people he had helped write the scrolls. When he had landed in Mulyra with Herclai and the others, he had been charged with familiarizing himself with their trove of knowledge. Months Achilles spent learning the Mulyran language and written word. Months he had spent penning the scrolls in his efforts to learn their language. That was when he discovered the nature of the crystals.

Words and drawings describing the Mulyrans' encounter with an alien race pained him. Achilles bit his lip in an attempt to not focus on his misdeeds, but instead, to concentrate on the task at hand. Book after book he flipped through, searching for what Rynah and the others wished to know, how to destroy the crystals. Though he knew a little about their origin, even he did not know how to render them inert.

Something caught his attention. Peering closer, with a pensive look on his face, Achilles read the lines on a holographic scroll. Could he have found what they searched for? As he read further, his heart leapt with excitement, overjoyed that he had found something that could save a people, and perhaps undo the wrongs he had committed. He showed the books to Solaris and she snatched it, amazed that he had already discovered something of value.

"I think we've found it," said Solaris.

Rynah and Brie hurried over to her, excitement coursing through their veins at the possibility of being able to rid the universe of the crystals, and return home.

"What is it?" asked Rynah.

Solaris showed her a holographic scroll with the drawing of the sun on it. Rynah took it, unsure of what she was looking at.

"It says here that," continued Solaris, who had translated the text with Achilles' help, "a gift from life's source they are and to their origin they must return."

Rynah looked puzzled.

"What does that mean?" asked Brie.

"The Mulyrans," said Achilles, "believed that the sun was the source of all life. To an extent, it's true, because without it, there would be no life on this planet."

Brie thought that sounded reasonable, since even some cosmologists believed that life stemmed from the stars.

"The Java explained that the crystals themselves were a gift from the sun, their point of origin," said Achilles.

Rynah repeated a bit of text from the ancient poem she had spent so many nights studying since this venture had begun.

> See you now dragon's treasure,
> vast and rich beyond measure.
>
> Take thee now to the belly of the beast
> where time stills and worries cease.
> Study well the dragon's heart
> where the end must now take part.
>
> Its gleaming scales reflecting the sun,
> and watch as it returns to where it's come
> from, back to its noble home,
> back to its mighty hoard.

Achilles' brows furrowed as he scoured through another volume, one that stood out among the others and did not belong, as the written word within it was not as neat as that of the others, and the binding crude. As Achilles studied it, he realized that the handwriting belonged to Herclai, and once again, a pang of guilt struck him. Achilles read from it.

"I have separated the crystals and hope that they remain hidden, but some within my government do not agree with my actions. I am now a criminal to them and will never be allowed to return, but I write my last exploits in these pages, hoping that if they are found, it is by someone worthy of such a find. The Java told me that they came from the sun as a gift and that they read a person's heart and innermost thoughts, compounding it and feeding off it, until consumed. Perhaps that explains why Achilai tried to steal them. Maybe he did not know of the darkness that dwelled within him. I just hope…"

Achilles stopped reading.

"Hope what?" asked Solaris.

"It ends there," said Achilles, "but it appears that Herclai was once on this ship, but why, or how he gained permission to be here, I cannot say. This is a Mulyran vessel and they did not allow just anyone aboard."

"I wish someone could give us some straight answers," said Rynah in frustration.

"Perhaps I can," said a voice, the same voice that greeted them when they had first boarded the ship and forced Solaris to choose between saving herself or rescuing Brie and Rynah.

They all whirled around, startled.

"Who are you?" demanded Rynah.

"The artificial intelligence that guards this vessel. You should be familiar with such a thing, as your companion is one herself," replied the holographic man.

"Why have you shown up now?" asked Rynah.

"You demanded answers and I am programmed to obey the commands of those bearing the blood of Herclai."

"Why?" Solaris asked, but the holographic man refused to answer her, remaining silent.

"Why?' Brie repeated Solaris' question.

"Before Mulyra was destroyed, this vessel was used to house the crystals. When they were stolen, two touched them, the man who now accompanies you and Herclai himself. Upon doing so, an imprint was left upon the crystals, a DNA fingerprint, if you will, and only those bearing the same can return them to their rightful place."

"Meaning that only Achilles and Herclai can touch them," said Solaris.

"Or their children, but there is a catch. One snatched the crystals for greed, while the other grabbed them in an effort to stop the theft and the destruction of Mulyra. If the one who stole the crystals were to touch them, they would turn dark and destroy all within their reach."

"So then Herclai must be the one to return them," said Solaris.

"Or those bearing his blood, the only reason you were granted entrance aboard this ship, so long as their hearts are pure. But be warned. They have been split apart for so long, and fragmented into nine pieces, that to put them together is not without its dangers. They will be instable, and the closer they are in proximity, the more unstable the universe becomes."

"How do we stop all of this?" asked Brie.

"From life's source they came, and to their origin, they must return," replied the holographic man. "Incoming transmission."

He disappeared, and before any of them could say a word, lights flashed, flowing down the length of the walls, as a buzzing sound alerted them to an inbound communication. Rynah rushed to a console and tapped the holographic screen.

"Rynah?" Obiah's face filled the screen.

"Obiah, it's me," replied Rynah. "Did you find it?"

"Yes," answered Obiah.

Another buzzer blared as the lights flashed again before Hylne's face filled a second monitor.

"Hello?"

Rynah clicked the screen. "Yes?"

"Rynah," said Hylne, "we found your ship."

"Do you know what to do next?" asked Obiah of Rynah.

"We found a library of sorts here," Rynah replied, "but all we have discovered is a line of text saying that the crystals came from life's source and to their origin they must be returned."

"What does that mean?" asked Tom.

"The Mulyrans believed that the sun was the source of all life," Achilles said.

"Then we must return them to the sun," Solon said.

"What?" Tom asked.

"If the Mulyrans believed that these crystals came from the sun, then that is where they must be returned."

"But will it work?" asked Hylne.

"Why not?" said Brie. "The sun is hot enough to melt asteroids and planets; it should be able to destroy the crystals."

"If that was all that was needed, then why didn't this Herclai guy do it himself?" asked Tom.

"Perhaps he, too, was tempted by their power, in the end," said Solon.

"It's possible," said Achilles, "but it is equally possible that he did not know how to be rid of them. Much of what I have read in these scrolls and books I read when I helped write them, but their words made no sense until today."

"There is one other thing," said Obiah, "Solon here claims to have found something of interest."

"I found a library, if you can call it that, and a transparent scroll with writing on it. Some of the symbols I recognize, but others I do not. But if my translations are correct, I believe there is a shield that has been placed around our world to protect us from the war of the gods."

"A shield?" said Brie.

"Can you show this scroll to us?" asked Rynah.

Solon held up the holographic scroll, while Rynah stepped back, allowing both Solaris and Achilles to study the ancient writing. Achilles' eyebrows scrunched together as he rubbed the stubble on his chin, studying the scrolls.

"It does speak of a shield. One created by beings from the... oh, wayfaring stars... It can't be!"

"What?" demanded Rynah.

"Fool that I am, how could I have forgotten!" Achilles slapped his forehead in frustration and anger towards himself. "There is a shield built around the Earth. I remember the Java speaking of it and how the crystals had warned him that it would be needed one day. After all this time, I had forgotten. The Mulyrans built these triangular towers all over the planet—many of the local primitives treated them like temples—almost like broadcasting towers. I just don't remember how they work or where to find them."

Joe, who had been silent the entire time, noticed something on the holographic scroll that Obiah held up for all to see. He took it from him.

"These markings look like a map. Is there a way to bring this up on all three ships?"

In answer to his question, Solaris placed her hand on one of the computer consoles, communicating with it, and up popped a holographic sphere on all three ships, depicting the map that Joe had seen.

"Well, I'll be damned," said Achilles. "It is a map."

"This point here looks to be the closest," said Joe, peering closer at the dots. "In fact, it is the closest. It's right here near Monument Valley."

"Really?" Tom studied the map, and a broad smile crossed his face as he jumped up and down in exuberance. "Oh my gosh! It's Shiprock! This is so awesome! I had a friend who believed that Shiprock was really just the remains of some ancient civilization and used for ferrying ships to and from space."

"This ancient alien stuff has been debunked by a lot of scientists," said Joe, receiving a reproachful glare from Fons.

"We're kind of debunking the debunkers," said Tom.

"Solaris," said Rynah, "could this be part of the shield generators Achilles mentioned?"

Solaris remained silent for a moment as she accessed the information she had downloaded from the internet and correlated it to the map sitting before her.

"This Shiprock that Tom has referred to does match up with this point here. I believe it is worth looking at."

"But what are they looking for?" demanded Obiah.

In answer to his question, Solaris recited lines from the ancient poem.

Salvation lies beneath arid sand,
below a cliff's lofty tower.
Search for hunter's belt made of rock,

and enter the temple below
by undoing the lock.

Be wary of the hunter's darkened spear.
Touch it not, until you see shimmering sphere.

"That doesn't make a lot of sense," said Tom.

"Like most of this poem, I'm sure it will once we're there," said Rynah. "Someone should go."

"But who will volunteer?" asked Joe. "And who knows enough about advanced technology, or ancient, as the case may be."

Rynah had a thought; though she knew that those involved would detest her for it, she punched in the coordinates for teleportation and transported Fons and Tre from Jifdar's ship to the one she was on. "You two will check this out."

"Wha—what do you think you're doing?" stormed Tre, incensed at being ripped away from someplace once again.

"You and Fons will check this out," said Rynah.

"On a planet full of aliens!" said Tre.

"Uh, Tre," Tom said, "here, you're the alien."

Growing irritated, Rynah cut everyone off. "I need you both to look for the thing on this map. If there is a way to erect a protective barrier around this planet, then we must try, and you two are the only ones who can."

What Rynah did not tell them was that if there was a way to protect the planet from any further destruction Stein would wrought, she'd take it, but her main goal was to get them out of harm's way as best she could.

Tre squeezed Rynah's shoulder in agreement. She punched in the coordinates for the dot on the map, sending Fons and Tre to investigate this underground temple, and never noticing that the robotic firefly, which had hidden in her pocket when she left the planet with the ancient city, left her and hid in Fons' shirt pocket.

"This is crazy," muttered Achilles, but no one heard him.

"But," said Tom, "Stein still has the crystals."

"Then we need to devise a plan to get them back, unite these ships, and bring the crystals here so that we can be rid of them," said Brie.

"Sounds simple enough," joked Tom.

"No," said Rynah, her voice cutting all of them off.

"Rynah…" began Solaris.

"We rescue Brie's mother and sister first," Rynah said.

"But…" Hylne started to say before Rynah cut him off.

"I promised you that we would save your family"—Rynah looked at Brie—"and that is what we will do."

"What?" demanded Achilles. "Are you insane?"

"Rynah," said Hylne, "we don't have time."

"I made a promise," said Rynah, "and I intend to keep it. We are going to rescue Brie's family. The crystals can wait a bit longer."

"You don't…" began Brie.

"But we do," both Rynah and Alfric, who had been thinking the same as Rynah, said together.

"How?" demanded Hylne.

"There is a way to do both," said Solon, silencing everyone.

"What?" Hylne said. "How?"

"Achilles," said Solon, holding up the metal bands he had found, "can you tell me what these are?"

Achilles' brows bunched together as he studied them, and a look of recognition crossed his face.

"Where did you get those?"

"Here," replied Solon.

"Those are miniature transportation devices, but they also serve as homing beacons. Most of the pilots in my day wore those, and if they crashed or became lost, the band would lead a rescue team to them. Then, they could transport directly to the rescue ship. Why?"

"And do these ships have a way of…" Solon paused, trying to find the right set of words, but Tom finished for him.

"Do they have an autopilot?"

"Yes," said Achilles. "I can show you how to set it."

"Is there a way for us to communicate with one another?" asked Solon.

"I think I can find something," said Obiah.

"And these ships' transporters, as you call them, do they work? Can they send us back to—"

"—Earth," finished Tom.

"Yes," said Obiah, as he watched Solon's calculating mind work.

"Good," Solon replied. "Joe, I noticed a summons soon after we found you, hanging in the public square. It had the word Nebraska on it and showed what looked like an army. Is there a battalion there?"

"There's an Air Force base in Omaha," replied Joe, realizing why Solon had told Samuel to head to Nebraska.

"It will serve us well then," said Solon.

"That still doesn't answer my question," said Hylne. "How are you planning to get the crystals from Stein and save the girl's family?"

"We will lure Stein in, the way he ensnared us," Solon said, to which Solaris smiled, understanding the young scholar's plan. "Though we will need a way to get his attention."

"I know just the thing," said Klanor, who had been listening from a distance, but caught onto Solon's plan as well.

"It's perfect." said Solaris.

"It's perfect," scoffed Achilles. "You don't even know what it is he is planning!"

"But I do," said Solaris. "The question is, are you coming?"

"Am I coming? Am I coming? On a damn fool mission such as this, and you want to know if I'm coming? Well, of course I'm coming with you!"

* * *

Samuel yawned as he drove down the dark interstate, heading west as Joe's strange friend had told him to after leaving him near his home. He stretched as best he could to wake himself up, not wanting to get pulled over by a state trooper, considering that he had a trunkful of firearms.

The phone he had picked up from Joe's house buzzed. Samuel flipped it open and snorted when he read the text and the set of coordinates given. He put the phone away and increased his speed, determined to not be late for whatever Joe and his gang of unusual friends had planned.

Chapter 24
MERRICK'S LAST ACT

Stein stood erect, hands clasped behind his stiff back, lording over those who worked the consoles below. Their frightened fingers hurried over the holomonitors, aware of Stein's most ardent followers watching them with their weapons raised. Satisfied at the effect he had on them, Stein smiled that victorious smirk of his as his cold and hollow eyes observed those below him.

"Bring up the screens," he said.

A frightened attendant at a computer console tapped a button, allowing the command center to be filled with holographic images from five of the most major cities of the planet below: New York City, Sydney, Tokyo, Moscow, and Mexico City. The cities' residents scurried about, unaware of the people from above spying on them and the one man plotting their destruction.

"Ready the pulse cannons," said Stein.

The attendant hesitated.

"Sir," he said, his voice shaking, "I don't think…"

Strong hands ripped him from his seat as Stein's followers seized the wary attendant, shoving him to the far side of the room and executing him. Another of Stein's followers sat in the now vacant seat and reached for the command button with his gloved hand; he pressed it. Circular, maroon bursts of light, that resembled jagged stars, stretched from the main armada vessel down to the serene, blue planet below.

"Stop this!" yelled Merrick, pulling against his restraints.

Stein ignored him, his eyes focused on the holographic images as his gift, as he called it, reached its target. Fires erupted on the ground, creating craters the size of football fields, as shapes and shadows disappeared behind spike-shaped walls of dirt and buildings exploded into shards of missiles, seeking prey. In all five cities, panicked screams filled the air as a motherless child cried for the comfort of his parent's arms, or a father looked for his missing girl.

Merrick stared at the images in horror; his eyes rested upon a pink ballet slipper—the bow on the tip had been stained gray from ash—standing alone among the rubble. He looked up at Stein's callous face and the rigid jaw line that pulled tight as the man locked away all emotion and forbade himself to feel. Turning away from the slaughter, Merrick forced back the tears and blocked out the wails of those dying, unable to believe that this was once a man he had embraced as a brother before circumstances forced them apart.

The icy point of a laser rifle poked the tender flesh under his chin and forced his head upward so that he faced the holoimages. Stein did not wish him to miss anything. Merrick's eyes widened with each passing image—a man with a missing arm before being struck by another pulse from the cannon, people darting about in a frenzied panic, and a woman looking helpless as a nearby blast whipped her black hair away from her angular face—and he wished he could make it stop.

"Stein…"

Now you know what real suffering is," said Stein, his hardened voice echoing around them, causing some within the command center to tremble.

He turned back to the holoimages.

"Broadcast my message. If kidnapping that girl's family didn't work, then perhaps a public execution of them will."

The girl! thought Merrick. His mind raced as he remembered Rynah speaking of it during one of her communications with Obiah. Though he had failed in everything else, perhaps he could help the girl's family.

Stein's guards grasped Merrick beneath the elbows and dragged him away through the double doors and into the hallway beyond. Merrick studied the movements of the two who led him to his cell, searching for a weakness. He found one. One of the men limped just a little, covering it well, but faltering on occasion, thus allowing Merrick to catch it.

Once they were halfway down the corridor, he rammed the heel of his foot into the sore leg of the one guard, while plowing his entire body into the other. Stunned, the guard with the limp reached for his weapon. With lightning movements, Merrick elbowed the guard on the ground in the neck and lunged for the other, knocking his weapon from his hands. They wrestled for it until he snatched it and jabbed the guard with the point of the barrel.

The second guard regained his senses. They glared at one another for a moment before Merrick dove to the side, missing a well-aimed blast from the guard's laser weapon. He rolled on the floor, came up behind the man, and wrapped his restrained wrists around the man's neck. Once certain that both guards were subdued, Merrick pressed the thumb of one of the guards on the restraints' holopad and undid them.

Footsteps sounded behind him. He whirled around just in time to deflect a shot from another approaching guard. Merrick raised his laser weapon and dispatched the man. Looking around, he made certain that there would be no more surprises as he bolted down the hallway. A computer console blinked at him. Taking extra caution, Merrick ran for it and tapped the screen, scrolling through duty rosters and patrol lists until he came to the files pertaining to the detention area. Once he had their cell number, Merrick raced down the corridor, dodging patrolling guards and a few who had strayed from their stations.

He reached the elevators. The doors binged as they opened. Merrick dodged behind a corner and watched as more of Stein's followers stepped off, disappearing down another hallway. Before the elevator doors could close, Merrick dashed out from behind his corner and slipped inside just as they sealed. He tapped the holographic button for the detention center. Once there, he peeked out and ran for the doors, using the guard's keycard that he had swiped to gain entrance.

Silence followed. Merrick studied the area, taking careful note that no guard stood present. Empty. Though thinking it was odd, he chose not to dwell on it as he hoped to save Brie's family—his last heroic act. He hurried past the cell doors, searching for cell C57. He found it. Merrick swiped the keycard, bringing up a holopad, and typed in the code that undid the lock. With a hiss and a click, the lock released, allowing the white, steel door to open.

Merrick forced his way in and stopped. Hunkered on the floor was a woman, holding her child in a protective stance. She glared at him with hate-filled eyes, but her hair and cheekbones matched Brie's, telling Merrick that he had found the right cell.

"Come with me," said Merrick.

The woman's eyes flickered to his weapon.

Understanding her hesitance, Merrick shouldered the laser rifle and ignored the sharp pain as it weighed against his bruised and damaged shoulder.

"I am here to help," he coaxed her, his voice soothing and calm. "I'm here to take you to Brie."

"You know her?" asked the woman as she clung to her whimpering child and studied the marks on Merrick's face.

"Yes."

Allowing the smallest bit of hope to fill her, Rebecca Reynolds stood up, holding her daughter, and followed Merrick into the hallway. They ran for the exit, made certain there were no patrolling guards, and raced down the empty corridor to the shuttle bay as Merrick led them through the ship, pausing when he saw someone and only moving when the person passed. They reached a set of stairs. Merrick waved Brie's mother and sister up them, taking up the rear. Voices sounded in the distance. Afraid of being discovered, he urged them to hurry, picking up the child and carrying her over the last step, just as two women in uniform appeared, lost in their conversation. They turned a corner and...

A fist with sharp knuckles punched Merrick in the face. He staggered backward, dazed, his laser weapon dropping from his grasp. The man that had attacked him, and who had snuck up on him while he had been distracted, stepped forward and a grin spread across his face as he watched the weak Merrick stumble and struggle to get back up. He kicked Merrick in the stomach.

Though dizzy from the impact, Merrick summoned his strength and tackled the man, wrapping his arms around his attacker's waist and ramming him into the far wall. A grunt told him that he had succeeded. Merrick stepped back and punched his attacker, but not before the man had landed a few good hits of his own. Another well-aimed strike rattled Merrick's jaw, causing his vision to blur for a second. As he struggled to regain his senses, his attacker leaned in for the kill when...

A laser blast plowed into him, knocking him off his feet. Merrick turned around and found Rebecca Reynolds holding the laser rifle he had dropped, a determined look filled her face. He took the weapon from her, and she picked up Sara as they darted down the hallway.

Laser fire pelted the wall next to then when they reached another corner. Merrick yanked them back. Looking around, he saw the door that led to the shuttle bay.

"Run!" he yelled at Rebecca as he stepped out into the line of fire, releasing a hailstorm of his own.

They bolted through the door to the shuttle bay and stopped. Standing in front of them was Stein, with a handful of his most loyal servants, and Gaden. Merrick's heart dropped, but he worried most about Brie's family.

"Did you honestly think," said Stein, "that you would succeed?"

Merrick said nothing.

"I had a feeling you would try to save the girl's family, as she has shown no inclination to do it herself." Stein brushed a cracked and dry hand across Sara's face; she recoiled in fright. "I had hoped that they would provide some usefulness, but I guess I was wrong."

Merrick said nothing as a sickening feeling filled the pit of his stomach.

"Kill them," Stein ordered.

"Including the girl?" asked Gaden, his voice aghast at such a notion.

"Do you have a problem?" demanded Stein.

Gaden's eyes darted back and forth between Brie's family and Stein. "She is just a child."

"Indeed." Stein whipped his hand back and backhanded Gaden, sending him back a couple of steps. "The next time I tell you to do something," Stein hissed into Gaden's ear, "you do it."

"Let them go," pleaded Merrick.

"I intend to," replied Stein.

"Stein..." began Merrick.

Stein pulled out his laser pistol and pointed it at Sara. As his finger squeezed the trigger, Merrick dove in front of the girl, taking the full impact of the blast and dropping to the ground. Stein stared at his brother-in-law's still form and the sorrowful eyes that looked back at him before closing; no guilt, no remorse filled him. He pointed his weapon at Brie's sister.

"Sir!" said a man, running up to him.

"What!" demanded Stein, angered at being interrupted.

"I have a message," said the man, "from Rynah. She wishes to make a trade for the girl's family."

Stein looked at Rebecca and Sara, a plan formulating in his dark mind. "I guess there might be some use for you after all."

He waved his hand, and his men seized Brie's mother and sister and dragged them away, leaving Merrick's body on the cold floor in the shuttle bay.

Chapter 25
DECISIONS

Back on his ship, Jifdar stared out the giant window of his cabin, unsure of what to do. Heller, his first mate, wished to leave, to go back to the Twelve Sectors, forget about the blue planet, and let the people of Earth and Stein settle their differences, but Rynah had begged him to remain. Torn between two worlds, Rynah's words about Brie repeated in his mind: *Brie was wrong about you.* What was it about that girl that made him reconsider the choices put before him? This business with Stein and Brie all brought back sentiments he had abandoned long ago, emotions he had never felt since he had first been captured by pirates himself.

A hurricane of thoughts about the incidents on the lunar surface, the ancient and mysterious ship hidden beneath it, and the sacrifice asked of him rolled through his tormented mind. He had hesitated. The very remembrance of it gnawed at him, at his very core. Jifdar sighed, releasing the storm of pent up emotion and frustration within.

Long years had passed since he had been a young man, fresh-faced, full of ideals, and on his first deep space mission of the

Cataran fleet. That was when he had been taken captive by space pirates. That was when he had questioned his principles. Now, he was faced with the same questions again.

Brie. Why did she always factor into the equation? From the moment he had first seen her, shivering from fear and unsure of herself, Jifdar knew she was different, and not because she refused his offer of taking her aboard his ship. There was something in her eyes. *Brie was wrong about you;* Rynah's words repeated in his mind, again.

"You wished to see me?" Klanor walked up behind him, his stern voice disturbing is internal wrestling as he struggled to know what he should do..

"Yes," said Jifdar, "I haven't had a chance to have a heart to heart, if you will, about your recent activities."

"You mean that you still doubt my loyalties," Klanor said.

"Perhaps, but I am starting to see why the girl has faith in you."

"You mean Brie."

"What I want to know is, why she believes in you, yet you tortured her with that mind interrogation."

"Perhaps you should ask her," replied Klanor.

"I did," Jifdar said, "but she said to talk to you."

Klanor glanced away from the pirate captain, unsure of how to respond.

"You had many chances to run away. First, on that planet, when we lied to you about needing an energy crystal; then again, when you and Rynah had both been imprisoned by Stein. Why didn't you?"

"Why the sudden interest?" demanded Klanor. "Not that long ago, you wanted to jettison me from an airlock."

Jifdar looked back out the window in response at the gray craters beneath him.

"What made you change?"

Klanor thought about it; he wasn't sure himself. When he betrayed Rynah, the feelings of abandonment and loneliness from when he had been a child, and a waif, came back to him. Those times spent in Brie's memories brought all of those emotions back. Then, the guilt came.

"I don't know," he said. "One day, I saw myself as Rynah did, but I also saw what Brie had seen. And when Stein turned on me, that's when I realized what I had become, what I had turned him into."

"Was the girl wrong about you as well?"

"I believe that she was right."

"Do you believe that people can change?" asked Jifdar, his brooding voice soft and hollow.

"Yes," whispered Klanor after several moments of silence passed between them. "It's the decision I made while on their moon that bothers you, isn't it?"

Jifdar did not wish to admit it, but Klanor had struck the truth of the matter; out of all of them, he was the first to volunteer to give his life to save the Viking's.

"In case you are wondering, I would make the same decision again, without hesitation," said Klanor.

"I would not," Jifdar whispered, referring to his lack of willingness to help Alfric. If given the chance again, he would be the first to volunteer so as to be rid of the shame he felt.

"There isn't much time left," said Klanor, referring to the inevitable confrontation with Stein. "I hope you have found the answers that you seek, because it's time to execute the boy's plan."

"The bookworm," chuckled Jifdar, referring to Solon.

"I would not dismiss him," Klanor said, remembering the training sessions he had watched Solon participate in with Alfric and Brie. "He may not be as useless as you think."

A knock sounded on the door and in walked Heller.

"Captain, everything is prepared. We can make the jump for the Twelve Sectors upon your orders."

Jifdar released a slow, steady sigh. The time had come for a choice—his choice.

"Change of plans," replied Jifdar, leaving his cabin and heading for the command deck of the ship, followed by Klanor and Heller.

"Attention, please," said Jifdar when he reached the control room on the command deck, ignoring the rippling sludge that seemed to have a will of its own. "I have decided to remain and do what I can for the people of this planet. You all are ordered to the escape pods. They have enough fuel to get you to the outlying posts of the Twelve Sectors. From there, you can make your way back home."

"Captain," Heller hissed at Jifdar, out of earshot of the others, "what are you doing? This isn't..."

"Do what you must," Jifdar said to him, "but I know what I must do."

A single pirate rose from his seat, silencing the murmuring that had filled the room.

"Request permission to join you, captain."

With a slight nod of his head, Jifdar gave the pirate approval, surprised that the young man, who had only been a part of his crew for nine months, would decide to remain, even if it meant certain death.

Others followed his example with cries of "Aye!" echoing around them. Jifdar turned to Heller, who grimaced and stalked out of the room, followed by the few who believed as he did, that the Earth and Stein were not their concern.

"Captain Jifdar," came General Delmar's voice over the com unit, "everything is ready."

Jifdar shared a look with Klanor. He knew that the man wished to be on a ship with Hylne and General Delmar, but the pirate had insisted that he remain with him, as a part of him still wished to keep an eye on him.

"Acknowledged," said Jifdar. "Now it is up to them," he finished, referring to Rynah and the others and hoping that their faith in Solon was not misplaced.

* * *

"I am standing here in Omaha, Nebraska where another alien attack has taken place," yelled a reporter into her microphone as explosions erupted behind her and smoke wafted past, hiding her from the camera. "As you can see, the downtown area is in ruins as survivors wander about, hoping to find their loved ones. The one who calls himself Stein has issued another warning to the people of Earth, saying that if we do not give up those he is searching for, he will destroy the entire planet. The President has issued orders for the one called Rynah, and any who are with her, to be found, and delivered, dead or alive, to this Stein."

She paused as she listened to her earpiece when the anchorman back in the studio asked her a question.

"Emergency personnel are working overtime to rescue any caught in the rubble. They…"

Orange and yellow lights appeared near the reporter, forcing her to stop speaking, as Rynah materialized. Stunned, the reporter let go of her microphone, while the cameraman dropped his camera, frightened away by her intimidating presence. The camera clacked on the asphalt, but continued filming as Rynah strolled up to it, holding her laser pistol in her right hand and the crystal in her other.

"I have a message for Stein," she said, her voice clear and determined. "You hold Brie Reynolds' family hostage. I propose a trade."

She held up the crystal and waved it in front of the camera, ignoring the gathering crowd around her.

"I have what you seek. Come and find me."

Rynah aimed her laser pistol at the camera, and fired.

Chapter 26
AMONG RUINS

Rynah and Solaris stood erect among the wispy, gray smoke that drifted around them amidst the smoldering fires of the cars and buildings that still burned from Stein's latest attack, watching the triangular shuttlecraft hover in the sky above them and descend to the ground. It's engines roared with furious fervor as they blasted the charred pavement beneath it, sending plumes of air that whipped both Rynah's and Solaris' long tresses in raging circles that smacked their flushed cheeks. Both bore stoic expressions as they waited for the hatch to open once the shuttle had landed. A slow hiss told them to prepare for the inevitable—the time had now come—as the gangplank from the spacecraft stretched out, touching the silt-covered road.

Stein marched out of the shuttlecraft—his arms rigid as they hung by his side—with two others, Gaden and a man they did not know.

Taking her cue, Rynah walked up to Stein, a grim line on her face. "Where is it?" demanded Stein.

"In a moment," said Rynah.

"I'm not a patient man," Stein warned her.

"Where is Brie's mother and sister?" demanded Rynah, her voice firm and her hand near her laser pistol.

Stein smirked.

"We had an agreement, the crystal for the release of Brie's family." Solaris held up a bag, allowing them all to see it.

"The crystal first," said Stein.

Upon a nod from Rynah's head, Solaris tossed the bag to Stein, who caught it with his left hand, his glove creaking as he clenched it.

"The girl's family," repeated Rynah.

Stein's grin widened as he stared into Rynah's narrowed eyes, pleased that he had won.

"Yes, about that," he said, "I thought that you might prefer to have one of your friends back."

With a jerk of his hand, the second man that had accompanied him stormed into the shuttle and came back, dragging a limp body, which he flung down the gangplank, allowing it to roll to the bottom, before stopping by Rynah's feet. She looked down at the still form and bit her tongue to keep from showing the seething rage that boiled within her as Merrick's frozen face stared back at her.

"I thank you for the trade," said Stein. He turned and headed back to the shuttle.

"What happened the last time you tried fitting a fake crystal into that weapon of yours?" Rynah's cold voice stopped him.

Stein whirled around, eyeing her, unsure of what game she played. He yanked the bag open, pulled out an opaque, with a yellow tinge, crystal—a plastic one that Achilles had bought from a souvenir shop—and held it up in the red-tinted sunlight. His face hardened. Furious, Stein chucked the plastic crystal at Rynah, who dodged the projectile with ease.

"Where is it!" screamed Stein.

The second man with him aimed his laser rifle at Rynah's head as a warning.

"Per—"

"Now!" screamed Stein, interrupting Gaden when he tried to speak.

While holding up one hand in surrender, Rynah used her other to pull out a pair of binoculars from around her belt and held them out. Stein snatched them from her hand.

"There." Rynah pointed in the distance.

Stein peered through the binoculars, his brow furrowed in anger, as he spied a dark shape, silhouetted by the morning sun, on a rooftop several blocks away, with her hand outstretched and an object within them. Stein tapped a button on the binoculars, zooming in before dropping them and glaring at Rynah, as the shape on the rooftop disappeared.

Brie had the crystal.

"Kill them!" Stein ordered.

Before the man with the laser rifle could pull the trigger, Solaris detonated a flash bomb, just as Rynah knocked the weapon out of his hands and ducked. While Stein, his loyal follower, and Gaden recuperated from the effects of the flash grenade, Rynah and Solaris ran away, disappearing among the rubble.

"Kill them!" thundered Stein. "Level the entire city and bring me that girl and the crystal!"

"But the people here," said Gaden, "they will…"

Stein backhanded Gaden, his fist like the force of a hammer, sending him flying backward. His enraged face glared at Gaden, who cowered beneath his overbearing stature with a streak of blood dripping from the corner of his lower lip.

"There are no innocents! Now, do as I ask, or you can join him," Stein said, pointing at Merrick's dead form.

Shaking, Gaden rose to his feet and issued the order for the invasion to begin and the girl with the crystal to be found.

Brie raced across the rubble encrusted rooftop to the other end, where she stood upon the edge, teetering and looking down at the alley below. The signal had been given. Rynah had told her to wait until she saw the glint from the binoculars before running off. She glanced at the building next to her, but it was too far to jump. A soft whine filled her ears, growing louder until it turned into a deafening roar. Looking up, Brie watched as the rose-blue sky filed with dark, triangular shapes that zipped about, firing laser blasts at nearby buildings and heading straight for her.

She glanced back at the other rooftop. Desperate, Brie searched the area for anything that would allow her to escape her open prison. A hook, suspended in the air by the crane it was attached to, hung just to her right. Brie raced for it. She leaned over the concrete edge of the roof, studying the crane and inspecting it. It seemed stable enough.

Something whizzed above her, forcing her to duck low and cover her head with her arms. As Brie watched the hoverbike—which looked like a jet ski with triangular wings—fly off, she jumped to her feet and ran to the middle of the roof. Taking a deep breath, and reminding herself that jumping rooftops is nothing compared to space diving, she ran. Her heart throbbed in her ears as she focused on the crane's hook and the roof beyond. She reached the ledge. Brie used all of the power within her legs to jump as far as she could, hands outstretched, and clung to the hook the moment her fingers touched its warm surface, while the thin band around her wrist glowed red in the sun. Her stomach lurched as she swung in midair. Timing herself, Brie let go, not even daring to look, and tucked and rolled when her feet slammed into solid concrete.

Brie looked back at the crane, relieved that she had survived one more ordeal. She checked to make certain she still possessed the crystal—it was tucked away in her backpack. Her hair lifted, floating around her as though she swam in water. She looked up. Above her was a swirling mass of fog, turning counterclockwise and growing by the second as the center formed a black hole. She ducked, covering her head, just as a flock of birds—the likes of which she had never seen before—burst from the swirling fog, soaring upward in a graceful arc. Craning her neck, Brie watched in awe as the sun's glow gleamed off their orange feathers, giving them the appearance of gold waves. The flock of birds swarmed upward, crashing into the hoverbikes that soared above her and forming round balls of fire, tiny fireworks that ripped into the serene dawn.

Another hoverbike headed straight for her. Brie leapt to her feet and ran for the fire exit at the other end of the roof as laser fire pelted the surface around her. Bits of chipped concrete tore through her jeans and pricked the skin around her legs. She reached the fire escape just as the hoverbike almost plowed into her, forcing her to stumble and sending her tumbling down five steps before she caught herself.

Unphased, Brie was back on her feet, charging down the rickety steps two at a time and turning the corners with ease. Each movement shook the staircase as its bolts worked their way loose, made so by a previous attack from Stein. The hoverbike returned. Brie watched, unsure of what to do. She had nowhere to go, but down. Her pace quickened. The hoverbike neared. Brie found herself locked in a race to reach the end of the fire escape before the hoverbike reached her. The pilot lined her up in its sights. Her hands slipping on the railing, Brie jumped down the steps three and four at a time, not even pausing when her ankle burned from landing wrong, just hoping to escape.

"Tom? Solon?" said Brie in her earpiece. "I need some help."

When she was still one flight above the street, the hoverbike released a hailstorm of red and blue laser fire, severing the fire escape from its hold on the building. It jerked. Brie clung to the rail as it dropped a foot and tilted to the side, forcing her off balance. Her brown eyes opened wide as the hoverbike veered off and returned for another pass.

Her foot slipped. With the fire escape leaning so far to one side, Brie could no longer run down the staircase. As she hung from the railing, she looked around for any sort of salvation, but there was nothing she could use as a rope, and the fall would—she spotted a piece of piping attached to the outer wall of the building. It was just big enough for her climb down. Brie stretched for it, but it lay just out of reach.

The whine of the hoverbike returned. Focusing all of her attention on reaching the pipe, Brie looked up just in time to see the hoverbike swerve to the right, do a tailspin, and crash on the ground below her.

"Take that, you earth annihilating scum!" shouted Tom as he tossed another water balloon at the hoverbike from atop an overturned truck, with Solon by his side.

Brie hopped up and squeezed her feet against the sides of the narrow pipe while grasping it with her sweaty hands. She slid down the rest of the way to the asphalt below her, landing on her rear.

"Thanks!" she yelled back at Tom.

"Anytime," replied Tom. "Who says water balloons aren't handy?"

He and Solon both chucked a water balloon at two more approaching hoverbikes, catching their riders in the neck and forcing them to crash.

"Remember the plan!" Solon shouted at her.

Brie jumped to her feet again, making sure the crystal remained safe in her bag, and ran off. *Remember the plan: keep them chasing you for as long as possible.*

As Brie ran off down the street, dodging between overturned cars and a pile of rubble, Tom and Solon continued throwing water balloons—which they had stumbled upon while waiting for Rynah's signal, left there by a birthday clown on his way to a gig before Stein's attack—at any hoverbikes that strayed too near. When they had noticed Brie's plight and heard her plea for help, they abandoned their station and ran to help her, dragging the bag of water balloons with them. Another hoverbike zipped past Tom. He chucked a balloon at it, striking the pilot in the head.

"Score!" he yelled, earning him a quizzical look from Solon. "It's an expression."

"I think she is safe for the moment," said Solon. "We should return to our allotted position."

"Right."

Tom and Solon jumped off the overturned truck and ran away from the street, down an alley, and to another street that looked much like the one they had just left. A low rumble made them stop. Both Tom and Solon looked up to find a football field-sized ship moving over the city. Its doors opened up, releasing a slew of hoverbikes that swarmed the city of Omaha and barraged the buildings and streets with laser fire.

Solon snatched Tom's arm and yanked him out of the way of the onslaught, pulling him behind an old Volkswagen, just as a hoverbike flew over them.

"Kind of wish we had some more of those water balloons," said Tom.

"Actually," said Solon, "I was thinking we might want one of those."

Tom's eyes followed Solon's gaze to the hoverbikes. As his mind thought about how he might acquire one, he noticed a long-range acoustic device, left there by the riot police—who had been trying to stop those who used the upheaval as an opportunity to loot local businesses—when Stein began his attack, and a big grin spread across his face.

"I've got an idea."

Tom ran out from behind the Volkswagen, scooping up the top of a metal trash can and using it as a shield, and raced down the littered street. Solon followed after him. They jumped over a fallen streetlamp, stumbling a bit, and continued their race to the acoustic device. A hoverbike swooped low, buzzing the tops of their heads and forcing them to crouch to the ground. It turned back around, heading straight for them again.

"Do what you need to," said Solon as he ran away from Tom and toward the approaching hoverbike.

"Solon!" yelled Tom.

"Go!"

Obeying Solon's orders, Tom scrambled to his feet and ran for the long-range acoustic device, hoping that his friend succeeded in whatever plan he had concocted.

While Tom ran for the device, Solon dove to the pavement, snatched the side mirror of a car, which had detached itself and lay on the ground, and raised it in front of him, catching the light of the sun and reflecting it into the eyes of the man on the hoverbike. Blinded, the pilot jerked the controls and crashed into the ground, skittering across the asphalt past Solon. The young philosopher hurried over to the man on the ground and kicked him in the head, before snatching the laser pistol from his belt.

The tinkle of broken glass caught his attention. Turning, Solon watched as armed men in masks, wearing the same uniform as those under Stein's command, approached. He raised the laser pistol and fired, catching two in the chest, before ducking behind cover. He glanced over at Tom, who had just reached the acoustic device. A part of him chuckled as he watched Tom clamber around on the device, pulling wires, entangling himself, and tying them together.

Solon turned back to the armed men walking towards him, filling the street. He fired two more blasts. Something moved from behind. Solon turned just in time to see a laser rifle aimed at his head. With lightening reflexes, and using the maneuvers taught to him by Alfric, Solon yanked the laser rifle out of his attacker's arms and rammed it into the man's stomach. The man staggered back, but regained his composure, lunging for Solon and knocking the weapon out of his hands. Solon flopped on his back. The laser rifle clattered across the ground.

A sharp pain in Solon's jaw dazed him, as he reached for the weapon. A blur swiped past his eyes as his attacker's fist headed for him again. Solon reached up, blocking the attack, and rammed his knee into the man's back. While his attacker remained confused,

Solon pivoted, rolled onto his side, and flung his opponent off, before spinning on his back and kicking the man in the face. He leapt to his feet and dove for the weapon. Before he reached it, strong hands seized his ankle, pulling him back to the ground. Solon rolled onto his back and kicked the man in the face again, while scrambling to break free of his grasp. The fingers around his ankle slipped. Seizing his chance, Solon crawled on all fours to the laser rifle, snatching it, and fired at the masked man that had attacked him.

A bolt of laser fire whizzed past Solon's head. He jerked his head up and saw Tom standing by the acoustic device with a laser rifle in his arms and one of Stein's men at his feet. One look behind him told him that Tom had just saved his life from a man that had snuck up from behind.

"Come on!" yelled Tom.

Solon hurried over to Tom; both hunkered behind the acoustic device, watching as more armed men approached. The whine of a hoverbike caught their attention.

"What's your plan?" asked Solon.

Tom reworked some wires, while one hung in his mouth.

"I'm going to get us one of those flying bikes."

"How?" Solon fired at those who approached.

"Sound," replied Tom. "Sound can be used to move objects, as well as set a trap."

"Are you sure?"

"Remember that planet with the man-eating plants?"

Solon smiled. He did remember that place, and hoped to never visit it again. He fired at a masked man that had gotten too close.

"Whatever you are going to do, do it quickly!"

Tom finished rearranging the wires' connection on the device and handed Solon a pair of ear protectors.

"Just cover me."

"What do I do with these?" asked Solon, holding up the ear protectors.

"Put them on," replied Tom, demonstrating how.

He climbed to the top of the device, where the controls were. Laser fire sailed past him from every angle as Stein's men tried to stop him. Once at the controls, Tom hunkered behind the plastic shield, rammed the ear protectors over his ears, and waited.

"Tom!"

Tom ignored Solon's urging. He watched as the hoverbike arced towards them, waiting for the precise moment. A scorch mark appeared on the edge of the transparent aluminum shield as laser fire struck it.

Solon remained at the bottom, firing back, but there were too many.

"Tom!"

"Just a little bit longer," whispered Tom to himself, his attention focused on the ever-nearing hoverbike.

Solon released more laser fire, but he could not keep up with the encroaching hoard of men.

"Tom! Do it now!"

Tom turned on the long-range acoustic device, sending a pounding, sound pulse at a decibel that damaged the eardrums of any in its path and focusing the sound wave on the hoverbike, stopping it midair. The pilot fell to the ground, landing among the swarm of Stein's men who stumbled around with their hands over their ears, while Tom used the generated sound wave to direct the bike to the ground. Once it had landed, Tom shut off the device, threw off his ear protectors, and jumped to the ground.

"Come on," he said, tapping Solon on the shoulder, who followed him.

They both jumped on the hoverbike.

"Do you know how to operate one of these?" asked Solon.

"We'll find out."

Tom started its engine, grasping the handlebars in a tight grip as the craft floated into the air. Hoping that it was similar to a real motorbike, and remembering how he had flown Solaris, Tom pressed the pedal that his foot had found on the rung. They shot forward, zipping through the air; wind whipped their hair as it smacked their faces, making their eyes sting and water. Tom shifted the handlebars just a bit. They dove to the ground, spiraling, before he managed to pull them back up, noting that the slightest movement caused them to turn.

Solon tapped Tom's shoulder and pointed at the giant spaceship above them that hovered over the city. Getting the message, Tom banked to the right, twisted around, and made his way to the ship, flying above it.

Laser fire whipped past them. They had one on their tail. Tom swerved out of the way, zigzagging in his attempt to evade their pursuer. Despite his moves, the hoverbike behind them remained locked on their position, following every movement he made and firing laser blasts at him and Solon; one such blast struck too close to his foot. Tom dove, heading straight for the ground.

Wide eyed, Solon clung to Tom's waist, praying that they would not crash, and just when he thought they would, Tom yanked back on the controls, pulling them upward. Their pursuer mimicked his moves. Frustrated, Tom looked around for any way of ridding himself of the bike behind him and Solon. A cannon blast exploded just to their right, forcing Tom to jerk the controls and send them into a barrel roll as they flew above the city.

Once he straightened the hoverbike, Tom glanced back and cursed. The man was still behind them. Solon tapped his shoulder again and pointed at a low hanging crane. Understanding what to do, Tom veered toward it, punching the accelerator. They raced across the sky, ignoring the laser fire that headed for them as they raced for the crane. Solon tightened his grip. Tom's eyes focused on the crane, and the plan. He kept the craft steady, not allowing it to swerve in the slightest until, at the last second, he dropped in altitude and the one that chased them crashed into the crane, creating a fiery explosion.

Pleased, Tom headed back to the ship. He flew around it, below it, and above it, searching for a way to destroy it until he spotted something that looked promising. In the center of the ship was a mass of swirling, electric blue light with what looked like lightening shooting out from it at various intervals. Guessing that it was the engine's core, he steered their way to it, lining the swirling mass of electric light in his sights. Tom steeled his nerves, remembering how he flew Solaris when evading space pirates. He drew closer, the target centered in his sights, and fired. Laser blasts shot from his hoverbike and sped to the swirling light.

The blue light turned orange, red, and black, as fire erupted from within it; Tom's aim had been true. He banked to the right, taking them away from the ship, as flames swept through its interior, bursting from its sides, swallowing any hoverbike that strayed too near, and dipped low before plowing into a four-story parking garage.

"Yes! Yes!" screamed Tom, ecstatic that his plan had worked.

"Good job, my friend," said Solon, "but though we have had this small victory, we still have a war to win."

Tom smiled at Solon's propensity of giving bits of wisdom, even during life-threatening situations.

"We should find Achilles," said Solon.

Tom agreed and headed for where the crazy, old Lanyran was supposed to be, hoping he had finished his assigned task.

Joe had crouched behind an overturned dumpster and watched as Stein's shuttle landed and he and Rynah exchanged words, waiting for the signal. The moment Solaris released her flash bomb, he fired upon Stein and his men with the laser weapon she had given him, catching two. Joe watched as Rynah and Solaris ran away. Laser fire struck the dumpster near him. He rolled out of the way, bringing up his own weapon, and hit the man in the chest.

Two more stood away from him, guarding the shuttle. Joe whistled at them.

"Hey!" he yelled and ran.

The two guards chased after him, firing their laser weapons as Joe led them away from the spacecraft, hoping that Obiah and Alfric would succeed in their part of the plan, and watched as two shapes ran from the rubble and to the shuttle, disappearing beneath it.

"Rynah," he said in his earpiece, "It's done."

Stein's words still echoed in Rynah's ears as she and Solaris hurried away from him and his shuttle, their long shadows soon becoming enjoined as the sky filled with black dots and massive round shapes that blocked the sun. Rynah's boots stomped in tune with Solaris' lighter steps as they raced for cover, while laser fire pummeled the asphalt beneath their feet.

She jumped over fallen power lines and stopped when she noticed that Solaris was no longer beside her: Solaris' foot had become entangled in a power line.

Rynah raced for her friend, hoping she reached her in time as she watched the electricity jolt through Solaris, turning her nanobot infused skin different colors with differing shades, and dodged hoverbikes that raced past as she ran for Solaris. Rynah reached her. The power lines zapped, releasing deadly sparks of electricity.

"Run!" yelled Solaris at her. "Leave me!"

Rynah refused to listen. She studied how Solaris' foot had become caught, and knowing she would die if she touched the wires, she pulled out her laser pistol, aimed, and fired, disconnecting Solaris from the main line. Using the heel of her boot, for it had a thick, rubber sole, Rynah pried the wire away from Solaris, who used her hands to finish freeing herself.

A hoverbike flew by, almost clipping Rynah, but Solaris had snatched Rynah's arm—the thin, metal bands on their wrists made a stark contrast against the gray backdrop with their red glow—and yanked her to the ground. She grabbed Rynah's pistol and fired, hitting the engine of the small craft and causing it to burst into flames. Together, the two jumped to their feet and ran further into the center of the city where the tallest buildings were, racing past cars blown in half, fallen street lamps and traffic lights, and smashed signs that had been severed from their base.

Laser fire surrounded them as they ran for cover. A hoverbike headed straight for them.

"Help me with this," said Solaris as she reached for a fallen piece of a street lamp.

Rynah dove for the other end; her muscles strained when she lifted it up, while Solaris carried her end with ease, and maneuvered it where directed. They held it up as high as they could. The hoverbike neared. By the time the pilot realized their trap, it was too late; he rammed into the pole and was knocked off his bike, which skidded across the ground several yards away. They dropped the rod. Both glanced up as a city-sized ship moved over the metropolis, before hovering over its center. Doors opened underneath the spaceship as an orange glow filled the vacant areas. Knowing what came next, Rynah ran.

"Let's move!"

She and Solaris hurried toward a hollowed out area where the street had opened up (similar to the way earthquakes split them), burrowing into the darkened area and shielding their heads and eyes as an intense, and bright, light plowed into the buildings around them. Chunks of concrete and shards of glass bombarded the earth around them, striking any unfortunate enough to be in their way.

Silence fell.

Rynah looked up. The ship had used what energy it had in its weapons and prepared for another strike. The cry of a child filled her ears. Shocked, Rynah turned towards it and saw a little boy hunkered amidst the devastation, holding his dead mother's hand, while a man, near where she was, called to him.

Before Rynah had time to react, Solaris bolted from their place of safety, racing for the child. She dodged falling debris and laser fire, focused only on her goal. A hoverbike dove for her. Solaris somersaulted across the ground, avoiding the blow, and continued her race for the boy in fluid movements. She reached him. Solaris scooped him into her arms, forcing him to let go of his mother, and ran back to where Rynah waited for her.

Rynah watched as Solaris hurried back to the hole under the split pavement they had hidden in. The whine of a hoverbike prickled her ears. Glancing up, she noticed the same bike returning for another chance to stop Solaris. Whipping her head around, she saw a chain with a weight attached to the end. She sprang for it. Rynah wrapped her fingers around the chain and swung it high above her head in circular motions, releasing it just as the hoverbike reached her. The weight struck the pilot on the top of his helmet, while the chain wrapped around his neck, choking him. Stunned, he released the controls of his hovercraft and plowed into the pavement.

The frantic screams of the man and the increasing roar of the ship above her caught her attention. With a quick look at Solaris, who was halfway across the street, clutching the wailing boy in her arms, Rynah jumped at the man, snatched his arms, and forced him back into the protected hollow under the upturned street. They all reached it just as the massive craft above them released a burst of fire—which vaporized any organic matter it touched—and struck the ground, pounding their ears with its deafening thunder and drowning the child's screams.

When it ended, they all looked up. The ship recharged its weapons. Rynah turned to the man and said, "Is there a place you can go that is underground?"

"My… my wife…" stammered the man.

"I'm sorry," said Rynah, "but you have to protect him now." She pointed to the boy, who had calmed down in Solaris' gentle and protective arms.

Swallowing, and resigning himself to what he must do, the man said, "There is a place we can go."

"Get there"—Rynah handed him her laser pistol—"and shoot anyone dressed in those helmets that try to harm you."

The man took the weapon.

"Just point and pull the trigger," said Rynah.

She and Solaris helped the man and his boy out of the hollow before running off.

Rynah paused by the pilot she had killed and snatched his laser pistol before joining Solaris by his bike. She righted the hoverbike and jumped on, with Solaris seated behind her, and started the engine. Nothing. She tried again. Still, nothing happened.

A low roar echoed around them as the ship above them recharged it weapons and prepared for another attack; the orange glow filled the empty hollows within its belly. Desperate to get away before the next strike, Rynah kicked the starter, her incessant movements becoming more frantic with sweat pouring down the sides of her face, as the roar grew louder. The engine started and the hoverbike hovered inches above the ground. With one last look at the man and his child as they disappeared around the corner—she hoped they would be safe—Rynah punched the controls and flew off just as the ship released its third attack, speeding away from the flames that reached for her and Solaris.

They rose into the air, high above the oval-shaped ship. Rynah frowned when she noticed more coming. She knew that Klanor had amassed a huge armada, which now lay in Stein's hands since his coup, but she never realized until then just how massive it was. From her place high above the buildings, Rynah watched as fire engulfed where she and Solaris had just escaped from.

"We need to take out their weapons!" she yelled to Solaris over the roar of the air as they flew.

Solaris snatched the laser pistol from Rynah.

"Drop me on top of the ship."

"What!"

"Drop me on the ship," repeated Solaris, "while you go through the airflow tube that stretches its length."

"Are you saying what I think you're saying?"

"Just like a story here on Earth, you're going into the whale's mouth."

Knowing she would never win this argument with Solaris, Rynah arced over the massive spaceship and hovered just above, allowing Solaris to jump on top of it. Rynah sped off, flying to the other end of the ship where the airflow tube was. While in space, the tube remained sealed, but whenever the ship entered a planet's atmosphere, it would open the tube, which ran the length of the vessel, in order to maintain stability within its gravitational pull.

Grimacing, Rynah stared at the hole, which was just large enough for a hoverbike to pass through, as she charged for it. She leaned over the handlebars of the hoverbike as she approached. Sunlight disappeared, plunging her into near total darkness; only stark blue lights, spaced at intervals of 50 yards, allowed her to see anything. The hoverbike bumped against the sides of the metallic tube, creating yellow and burnt orange sparks that sprayed the area behind her.

Sweat filled Rynah's enclosed hands as she gripped the handles, her muscles straining from her efforts to maintain control of the hover vehicle. The bike jostled and vibrated from the close quarters. A spot of red caught her attention—it was an emergency valve. Rynah lined it in her sights and fired. It exploded, releasing pressurized air and gas just as she zipped past it. She found another. Setting the charge of her weapons to repeated fire, Rynah aimed at various points within the tube and released a hailstorm of laser fire, while green and purple bursts of light barraged the sides of the airflow tube from her unleashed fury.

One of the laser blasts ricocheted off the tube and struck the side of her hoverbike. The bike shifted from the force and wobbled, it sides scrapping against the metal tube with a horrid screech and a shower of sparks, which ignited the gas behind her. Rynah clenched her jaw and her muscles tensed in her efforts to keep control of the bike, ignoring the panic the rose within her as she faced what could have been her end.

Once she straightened out, she accelerated. The heat of the flames behind her seared her skin, despite the security uniform jacket she wore, which was insulated to protect one from burns or moments of extreme cold. The licking flames formed hands that reached for her, but Rynah refused to give in. She punched the accelerator of the hoverbike again, pushing it to its breaking point in her efforts to escape. A speck of light lay just ahead, and she only needed seconds to make it to freedom.

While Rynah raced through the airflow tube, Solaris ran to the intake valves of the ship. She reached one and fired, ducking as it exploded. She raced for another. She reached a second valve and fired upon it. Something crashed into her hand, knocking her down, as the laser pistol fell from her grasp and landed a few feet away.

Looking up, Solaris watched as a hoverbike flew away, arced, and headed straight for her. She ran for the laser pistol, but the hoverbike had reached her first, forcing her to drop downward and flatten herself against the ship. As it flew away again, Solaris scrambled to her feet and raced for the laser pistol, but the ships vibrations caused it to move a few inches closer to the edge where it teetered, threatening to fall over the side.

Just as the hover bike came in for another pass, Solaris grasped the weapon and rolled out of the way of her attacker's laser fire. She found the third air intake valve. While the hovercraft returned for another try at ridding the world of her presence, Solaris destroyed the valve, and a fourth.

The whine of the hoverbike's engines filled her ears. Solaris ran across the top of the city-sized spaceship, away from the hovercraft, and ducked just as it reached her, rolled on her back, and fired at the bottom of the bike. It tilted and spun, careening for the ground below, where it burst into flames. She spotted another intake valve and fired at it.

The ship jolted. As Solaris rose to her feet, the giant vessel leaned to the side, forcing her off balance. She righted herself and smiled, knowing that Rynah must have succeeded. As the ship continued to tilt upward, Solaris ran towards the edge where the airflow tube was, and where Rynah was supposed to come out of. She waited. Still no sign of Rynah.

The ship jerked again, rattling Solaris as she looked behind her at the flames that burst free from the confines of the spacecraft and into the open air. The fires neared. Knowing she had little choice, Solaris looked down at the tube. A soft whine touched her ears. She cocked her head, listening as the whine increased. An explosion erupted behind her, pelting her skin with debris. Solaris jumped.

Just as she did, Rynah burst from the airflow tube and positioned herself underneath Solaris so that she landed on the back of the hoverbike. They sped away from the massive ship as it dropped to the ground, dipping lower and lower until it had turned vertical and crashed into a building, disappearing in a cloud of dust, smoke, and fire.

Solaris clapped Rynah on the back, pleased that they had succeeded.

"I thought my grandfather made you promise to keep me safe," joked Rynah.

"He did," replied Solaris, "and now you are. For the moment."

Achilles sat atop the First National Bank Tower, wrapping wires around battery cells with what looked like shields scattered around him, while hoverbikes flew past, releasing their fury, and giant ships settled over the city. On occasion, he looked up to see if either Tom or Solon had arrived, as they were to meet him there. No sign of them. Annoyed, and a bit worried that something had happened to them, he continued connecting the wires to the battery cells in what would form a triangular shield device, as he called it, remembering how such devices were in constant use in his day, but unsure of how well this one would work, being built from such crude materials. A small spark zapped, singeing his skin, telling him that he had finished.

A hoverbike came straight for him. Achilles rolled across the ground for his laser weapon, reaching it just in time to destroy it. The bike fell to the earth, but another rose from its ashes, catching Achilles off guard. He fired his laser weapon, but it jammed. Left defenseless, he fiddled with his weapon, trying to get it to work.

A high pitched sound told him that the pilot was charging his weapons, savoring this one moment of triumph. Refusing to go down a coward, Achilles placed his laser weapon in its holster and planted both feet on the ground, rising to his full height, and faced his fate. Another whine filled the air, and two laser blasts plowed into the hoverbike before him. In its place appeared Tom and Solon atop their own hovercraft.

"Where have you two been?" demanded Achilles, relieved that they were there.

"Well, you know..." began Tom.

"Get down here, now!" yelled Achilles.

Tom landed the hoverbike and Solon jumped off, while Achilles handed them each a battery cell and shield.

"I need you to take this and fly to the top edge of that ship over there." Achilles pointed at a stadium-sized vessel that had settled near them, over the city. "I am going to take this other one and fly under the ship."

"How?" asked Tom.

"Let me worry about that," replied Achilles. "You"—he turned toward Solon—"take this and direct it to the ship. When this turns green, press it."

Solon took the shield that Achilles had handed him, pointing it at the ship, while waiting for the indicator at the top to turn green.

While Tom sped off, Achilles snatched what look like a backpack, but more solid, and jumped over the side of the roof. Horrified by the man's rash actions, Solon hurried to the ledge and leaned over, thinking he might die, but Achilles clacked the heels of his specially made boots, which he had crafted while traveling with the others, and a board popped out, forming a rocket propelled snow-board. Achilles rose into the air, racing for the ship, following Tom's path, and dodging and swerving to avoid the hoverbikes that filled the skies.

Solon watched as Tom and Achilles took their positions around the ship. The indicator light turned green. Following his instructions, Solon pressed it and was propelled backward as a burst of energy escaped the shield, striking the shields in Tom's and Achilles' hands. Mesmerized, Solon watched as an ion net formed around the egg-shaped spacecraft, enveloping it in its charged atmosphere and disabling the ship's engines. As it dipped downward, Tom and Achilles raced away from it, becoming black specks to Solon's eyes.

A hoverbike crashed onto the roof of the tower, skidding across it before coming to a halt near Solon. Wary, Solon crept closer to inspect. The pilot remained still. Solon moved even closer, spotting a laser rifle on the bike, and wished to get his hands on it. Without warning, the pilot leapt to his feet and slammed into Solon, knocking him down. Stunned, Solon almost failed to move out of the way as the pilot brought his foot down upon him.

Solon scrambled to his feet. The pilot charged. Unable to get out of the way, Solon took the full impact of the pilot's attack, but his feet remained firm on the ground as his body absorbed the punches. Because of Alfric's training sessions, Solon's muscles had toned and strengthened, giving him the endurance to overcome the pilot's charge. He wrenched his attacker's arm away from him and kneed the man in the stomach. Before the pilot had a chance to recover, Solon ripped his helmet from his head and bashed the pilot in the face with it five times, until the man fell to the ground, a maneuver that would have made Alfric proud of his student.

Satisfied that the pilot was no longer a problem, Solon reached for the laser rifle and held it up in a defensive posture, while he waited for Tom and Achilles to return.

Tom landed beside him. "Where is Achilles?" Solon asked.

"He went to find Solaris," replied Tom.

Solon grimaced. That wasn't part of the plan. Achilles was supposed to stay with him and Tom until the next phase began. Solon surveyed the chaos that filled the skies around him, searching for Achilles' form, but lost him among the pandemonium above, before glancing down at the band around his wrist.

A shadow crossed over them. Both Tom and Solon looked up and watched in dismay as another oval ship settled over the city, dwarfing them.

"How many of those things does he have?" asked Tom.

"The number is not important," said Solon, "only the achievement of our goal."

"Let's hope so," said Tom, checking the band he had wrapped around his wrist; it hadn't changed color yet. Solon, Rynah, Solaris, Alfric, and Brie all wore the same band.

"How's yours look?"

"The same." Solon glanced at the ship. "We need a way of distracting them."

The moment Solon said that, Tom's eyes fell upon the very top of the tower they stood up, and a slim ladder, built into the side, that led to its tip. He also noticed the circuit breakers nearby with wires strung between them.

"I think I have an idea."

Solon grinned, having become familiar with Tom's ideas that, though they worked, tended to be less than safe.

"Will I like it?"

"Nope!"

Amidst the chaos, Solaris and Rynah flew over the city while being chased by five hoverbikes. Purple laser fire whizzed past them, scorching the bike they were on, which irked Solaris as she didn't much care for being shot at. Rynah dove downward, before bringing them up in a vertical motion, pushing the engines until they almost stalled and heading for one of the massive ships that hovered over the city. Just before they crashed into it, she swerved and barrel rolled away; one of the hoverbikes behind her was not so lucky.

With four still on her tail, she zigzagged between buildings and poles in an effort to shake them, but their pilots proved as adroit as she was at flying. Solaris snatched Rynah's laser pistol and fired behind them, catching two and forcing them to drop away, but the two that remained closed in, avoiding her shots. In a desperate attempt to be rid of them, Rynah soared above the buildings, almost crashing into another hoverbike, and straightened out. When she was certain the two that pursued her and Solaris were still right behind them, she jerked the controls, veering upward before arcing back down and dropping behind them. Rynah fired. Both hoverbikes burst into flames and crashed on the ground, pelting Stein's ground troops.

She steered the hoverbike back in the direction of Stein's shuttle. As they wormed their way through the tall buildings of the downtown area, a laser cannon fired upon them; its blast detonated below them, sending a shockwave that forced Rynah to tip the bike on its side.

"Solaris, you okay?" Rynah yelled.

No answer.

"Solaris!"

Rynah glanced over her shoulder. There was no Solaris.

Frantic, she stopped midair, scanning the terrain below her until she found a wriggling speck hanging from a flagpole, sticking out of the side of a building 30 stories up. Rynah charged for her, but the moment she moved, another laser cannon detonated beside her, forcing her to veer off in another direction away from Solaris. Her hoverbike lurched as the engine sputtered; the blast had damaged it, causing her to lose altitude.

Another hoverbike settled behind her, choosing her as a target. She dodged the laser fire that shot past her, but her bike jerked again, making her stomach feel nauseous from the sudden movement. She punched the accelerator, but instead of increasing its velocity, the bike slowed, losing speed and altitude.

Something caught Rynah's eye. As she headed for an area covered in trees, walkways, and what looked like a tiny field, doing her best to slow her momentum, an F-15 Eagle fighter aircraft flew over her, heading for one of the massive spaceships. The ground approached. Rynah used flaps to slow down and jumped from the bike just before it smashed into the moist grass. She rolled for several yards before stopping. Dazed, Rynah sat up, shaking her head in her attempts to clear her cloudy mind.

More fighter jets roared as they passed above her, but something else caught her attention, the ominous growl of a lion who viewed her as an invader in his territory. Rynah and the lion locked eyes for a moment. Though she had never seen such an animal before, its behavior told her she need to get away from it. It lunged. Rynah bolted, half running, half stumbling, as she ran for the door that allowed zoo personnel into the pen. Locked. The lion approached. Rynah checked for her laser pistol, but found nothing, remembering that Solaris had it when they were separated. She jumped out of the way just as the lion reached her. It lowered to the ground and glared at her; its venomous growling filled her with fear.

She spotted a hole in the top of the bars where a part of her bike had crashed through it. Rynah eyed the lion, waiting for it to strike. She didn't wait long. The lion leapt for her. She dove out of the way, taking a running leap at the bars, clinging to them, and bracing her feet against the metal as she climbed up. She crawled through the hole, crashing to the ground, just as the lion reached the bars, sticking its paws through, claws out, in its effort to grab her.

Strong hands seized her. Rynah found herself being thrown through the air until she rammed into a cart that held the lion's food. The man that had chased her watched her crash and had landed nearby to be certain she had died. Rynah stared at him as he came for her; his bulky size reminded her of Alfric. She scrambled to her feet and tried to hurry away from his grasp, but her foot caught in the handle of an abandoned plastic bag that had blown across the ground, causing her to slip, lose her balance, and fall straight into the muscular arms of her quarry. He turned her so that she faced away from him, while he placed his meaty fingers around her tender neck. As she struggled to breathe, and the sides of her vision faded to black from lack of oxygen, Rynah remained calm, lifting her right foot to where she could reach the knife in her boot—something she always kept concealed there—and pulled it free. Twisting it so that the blade faced her, she jabbed it backward, ramming it into the one weak spot of the man's armor—it was Lanyran body armor and Rynah knew its properties well from her time in the fleet— and twisting it until warm blood oozed over her fingers. She let go. Breaking free, Rynah whirled around and stabbed him again, before kicking him hard. The man staggered back into the outstretched claws of the lion that had watched, and waited, for an unsuspecting victim to fall in his grasp.

The lion dug its claws into the man, ripping through his body armor and into the delicate flesh beneath. Rynah looked away. She saw the abandoned hoverbike and ran for it, leaving her opponent to his fate.

"Solaris?" she said into her earpiece.

No answer.

As she started the engine and rose into the air, another fighter jet flew overhead. Rynah looked up and watched as a cannon blast plowed into it, ripping the wing apart. Its cockpit opened and a black shape shot out of it, slowing as a white parachute opened.

One of Stein's men flew towards the pilot. Rynah kicked her hoverbike into gear and sped off, rising into the sky at an almost vertical angle and ignoring the craft's threats of stalling. She charged the approaching hovercraft as it lined the pilot in its sights and al-most sideswiped it. Rynah sped ahead, turned around, and raced for the man on the bike, releasing two laser blasts, but not before he had discharged his weapons. The hovercraft exploded. Rynah glanced at the pilot that had jettisoned from his plan. His parachute had been shredded. He dropped to the ground, but his tattered chute caught on the corner of a towering building, swinging him as though he were a puppet.

She pressed the accelerator and careened through the air towards the man before slowing her bike down and hovering next to him.

"Give me your hand!" she yelled at him.

The fighter pilot reached for her and tried to undo his harness, but it stuck. The sounds of laser fire swarmed towards them.

"Come on!" shouted Rynah.

The pilot pointed at his harness. Realizing what he meant, Rynah seized her knife from her boot and handed it to him. He snatched it, cut himself free, and jumped on the back of her hover-bike, just as two of Stein's men appeared. Rynah sped away, weaving in and out among the buildings around her and trying to evade the two bikes behind her. She spotted Joe.

"Joe, I'm heading for you and have two on my tail," she said in her earpiece.

Joe stopped and raised his laser weapon just as Rynah passed over him, and he fired upon the hoverbikes behind her, striking both of them.

"Thanks, Joe," said Rynah and he waved as she flew away.

Once she spotted a place to land, Rynah guided her hovercraft to the ground and let the pilot seated behind her jump off. Before she could leave, the click of a gun stopped her.

"I'm not your enemy," said Rynah as she stared down the barrel of the pilot's weapon.

"Why should I trust you?" demanded the pilot.

Laser fire pelted the ground by their feet as a group of Stein's ground troops approached. Rynah jerked her bike, aiming her weapons at them and pulled the trigger, burying them in smoke and ash. She looked back at the pilot, whose life she had saved, waiting for him to make the next move.

The man handed her back her knife, which she stuck back in her boot. With a curt nod, she gunned the engine of her hoverbike and took off as only one thought filled her mind, Solaris.

Unbeknownst to Rynah, when Solaris fell, she had caught hold of a flagpole—losing her earpiece in the process—that stuck out of the side of a building. Her fingers clung to slippery metal, which still had droplets of water on it from that morning's rain, as her feet swung 30 stories above the cracked street below, while a geyser of water, from an exposed and broken pipe, shot upward, mimicking a waterfall as the sun's rays created a rainbow within it. She looked around, dismayed that Rynah had been forced to fly away.

The pole lurched. Looking up, Solaris noticed that the metal had been weakened over time from being exposed to the elements; it would not support her weight for much longer. It dipped again, bending downward, while she still hung onto it. Three hoverbikes noticed her plight. They left their pursuit of the innocent people below, who ran in their desperate attempts to escape the onslaught, and veered towards her. The pole dropped again. Unwilling to give up, Solaris raised Rynah's laser pistol, which she still had with her, and fired. Her first two shots missed, but the third struck one of the hoverbikes, forcing it to crash into the side of the building and send a plume of smoke in her direction.

The two other bikes fired at her, striking the windows just above her head and sending shards of glass down upon her. Her nano skin rippled as it absorbed the impact and healed itself. Solaris fired again, but the pilots had expected it and dodged her feeble attacks. Again, the pole lurched, and Solaris knew that it would not hold for much longer. She watched, helpless, as the two remaining hover-bikes closed in for the kill. Remembering one of Marlow's last messages to her (*You cannot give up. You must not give up.*), Solaris aimed the laser pistol at one of the pilot's heads, but before she could fire, a green sphere fell from the sky, landing on one of the bikes before reducing it to a pile of ash.

Achilles appeared from above, racing past them on his flying snowboard and distracting the remaining hoverbike. As he did, he tossed another green sphere onto it, and it too burst into flames before turning to ash.

"Achilles!" yelled Solaris.

Achilles spotted her. He raced for her, tugging a small pack off his pack, but just as he reached her and tossed the bundle to her, the pole snapped and Solaris plummeted to the ground, disappearing behind the veil of spraying water with the pack in her arms. Dismayed, Achilles stared at the towering wall of water, certain that she had died and he had failed once again. As the battled raged around him and he remained hovering in the air, a glint of light caught his notice. Achilles looked closer, flying downward. Solaris burst from the spray of water with a pair of wings—indeed they were spectacular, made from a rare metal that always remained flexible and pliable, which Achilles had found during the years he had spent exiled on Earth and fashioned into a pair of wings—strapped to her back. They flapped like a bird's would, and as Solaris hovered before Achilles, the thin band around her forehead, that connected her telepathically to the wings, gleamed red, accentuating her purple skin.

The wings, which looked like a cross between a hawk's and an eagle's, glittered gold in the robust sunlight, as bits of purple and rose wound their way around the edges. They made Solaris look every bit the guiding star that Marlow had named her after.

She scanned the city and its buildings, as well as the men that marched through the streets, firing upon any who crossed their path, and noticed a tiny figure weaving among them, with a group of five right behind her. *Brie.*

Brie raced through the city streets, the bag with the crystal strapped to her back, breathing hard in the moist air as she fled the five that pursued her. Against Stein's orders, they had intended to kill her before bringing him the crystal. Laser fire pelted the ground around her feet, but Brie never faltered, continuing her dash through the streets. Debris crashed around her. Brie stopped, jumped around it, and continued running. One look behind her told her that the five had done the same. Aggravated at not being able to shake them, she picked up her feet and moved as fast as she could.

A wall crashed in front of her, blocking her path. Covering her head to protect herself from the falling chunks of concrete, Brie halted. When she looked up, she realized that she would never be able to climb over it. More laser fire scorched the fallen wall, reminding her that she had to move. Brie spun on her heels, looking for any means out of there. She spotted a small hole. Brie darted for the cramped space, getting on her hands and knees and crawling through pooled, brown water, until she passed through the hole. She had just entered it when her bag snagged on a metal rod. Frightened, she yanked and tugged on it until a rip told her that it had been freed.

Laser fire struck the ground next to her hand, stopping her. Brie looked behind. A masked face greeted her—the five men had caught up to her. She put her hands up in surrender, but the man raised his laser rifle in response. Before he could pull the trigger, a barrage of laser fire struck the masked man and his four companions, allowing Brie to continue her slow crawl through the tight space.

Solaris had arrived.

As Brie wriggled free of her confined space, she watched Solaris fly away, and though amazed that her friend had acquired wings, she waved her and ran off.

* * *

Samuel drove the truck into the desolate streets of Omaha, meandering his way past overturned, and in most cases, the shells, of cars and pickups that littered the area. Small, smoldering fires marked the landscape as a warzone; their flames charring anything that ventured too close. He held Joe's burner phone in his hand, waiting for it to ring. With each passing second, Samuel's eyes widened in horror as he observed the blackened bodies around him, doing his best to not run over them out of respect. A child's toy rolled across the street in front of him. Saddened, but knowing there was little he could do about it, Samuel continued moving forward.

The cell phone rang. "I'm here," he answered, and after a few moments, he said, "Understood."

Samuel turned left, rolling the truck over the pole of a fallen traffic light—it's blinking, red light cast shadows on the revolving doors across from it—and underneath a walkway, whose glass windows were riddled with cracks that zigzagged their way across and holes. A single plant, saved from the devastation, caught his attention. For a brief moment, Samuel remarked at its vibrant green leaves that swayed in the breeze, oblivious to the melee around it.

He stopped the vehicle. Snatching his weapon from its holster, ready to defend himself, Samuel stepped out of the truck, allowing the driver's door to hang open, as his eyes roamed the area. Something cracked beneath his shoes. Lifting up his foot, he nudged the shards of glass that lay scattered around him as a piece of paper, its edges burnt and still glowing, drifted past him. Stunned, he wished he had listened to Joe earlier, but the past can never be undone, only the future can be written. Fighter jets raced by above him, their shockwave pounding his ears as he craned his neck to watch.

A harsh hiss made him turn around. Peeking around the edge of a building was Joe with a laser rifle in his hands. Once he had made certain it was safe, Joe ran to Samuel.

"You bring it?" he asked.

In answer, Samuel pulled back the beige tarp covering the truck bed. Joe smiled when he saw the grenade launcher, assault rifles, and an M-240 Machine Gun, a wingsuit, and more ammunition than Samuel had ever seen anyone acquire in a lifetime.

"You know, some of this stuff is illegal," said Samuel.

"Well," replied Joe, taking the grenade launcher out, "as a friend of mine once told me, always be prepared."

"Look, I'm sorry I didn't believe you earlier."

Just then, a hoverbike appeared, heading straight for them and firing laser blasts that created craters in the asphalt around them. Both Joe and Samuel dove behind the truck for cover. Joe loaded the grenade launcher, aimed, and fired at the hoverbike, destroying it. As he reloaded, Brie appeared from an alley with another hoverbike and four of Stein's men chasing her. She stopped in the intersection, looking around for a means of escape.

"Brie!" Joe called her name, tossing her his laser rifle.

Brie spun around. She ran for the laser riffle, skidding across the oil soaked surface and underneath the hoverbike as it zoomed past, caught it, rose to her knees, and fired at the masked men behind her. She turned and noticed that both Samuel and Joe were locked in battle with more masked men that had arrived from another alleyway. She raised the laser rifle, but gloved hands seized her shoulders, yanking her backwards and off her feet. Brie crashed into the hard ground, her hands burning as pebbles scraped the skin off; the laser rifle flew out of her grasp and landed several feet away. Brie lunged for it as the man pulled out a baton. She snatched the laser rifle, aimed, and pulled the trigger. Nothing happen. Startled by the weapon's refusal to fire, Brie grasped both ends as though it were a staff, just the way Alfric had shown her, and raised it above her head just in time to block the baton that careened for her. They locked with a metallic ring that hurt her ears.

The masked man paused, amazed that Brie had the fortitude to defend herself; he had expected easier prey. Brie pushed against him, throwing him away from her. He staggered back, but he recovered and sprang for her, clipping her in the shoulder with his baton. Brie ignored the sharp pain from his strike. He attacked again. Remembering Al-fric's training, she sidestepped and ducked, using her small size to her advantage, moving around the masked man, and bringing the butt of her laser rifle down hard against his back, knocking him to the ground. Brie aimed the laser rifle again, but its firing mechanism had jammed. As her opponent rose to his feet, she chucked the rifle at him and dart-ed away, running for one of the others that had been chasing her, but now lay dead on the street. She yanked at the laser rifle in his arms, desperate to pull it free as the clomping boots behind her told her the masked man neared. She got it. Brie whirled around and fired, striking the man in the stomach. Even though all she could see were his eyes, their widened expression as he fell told her that she had surprised him.

The hoverbike returned. It charged Brie, determined to capture her. She jumped to her feet and ran as fast as she could to a narrow slit between two buildings, but before she reached it, an explosion knocked her off her feet; she rolled across the ground, losing the la-ser rifle, and landed on her back. Silhouetted by smoke and floating bits of smoldering debris, and holding a grenade launcher, was Joe. He walked over to her and held out his hand, helping her up.

Shouts and yells rose around them as a U.S. fighter jet crashed to the ground three blocks away. They watched as the bright yel-low flames turned orange before dissipating to black swirls that disappeared behind a swarm of hoverbikes and small shuttlecrafts pointed in their direction. Joe and Samuel hurried back to the truck, filling their arms with the firearms that Samuel had brought, while Brie searched for an escape route. She spotted a fire truck next to one of the tall buildings, its occupants dead inside.

"This way," she said as she ran for it.

They reached the fire truck—it's once bright red color had been dulled by the scorch marks left from laser blasts. Joe yanked open the door to the cab, reaching far in until he found what he searched for, the control to the ladder.

"Up! Now!" he yelled.

Samuel climbed up first and held his hand out for Brie, who took it after checking the crystal in her bag and assuring herself that it remained secure, and Joe made up the rear. They hurried up the ladder, its swaying unnerved Brie, but she refused to show her trepidation, while hoverbikes swarmed around them, their high pitched whine filled their ears. Ignoring the chaos, they moved upward to the top of the ladder; the metal rungs stuck to their clammy hands each time they released one for another. A blast from a laser cannon plowed into the side of a nearby building, showering them with bits of concrete and insulation as it fell to the ground. Coughing, they continued, determined not to stop.

Hoverbikes sped past them, so close that all they had to do was reach out to touch them, making the ladder shake. Brie looked down, something she knew you never do when high above the ground, but the temptation to do so always proved too much, and she inhaled, astonished that they had already climbed three quarters of the way up. Another hoverbike banked for them; the pilot tossed a hook at the ladder apparatus, latching onto one of the rungs and ripping it off. The violent jerk forced them all off-balance. As Joe and Samuel clung to the rungs, Brie's sweaty hands slipped and she fell. Her stomach caught in her chest as she felt gravity take hold, but before she dropped too far, a strong hand gripped hers, pulling her to a stop. Her breath was knocked out of her lungs when her body slammed into the metal side of the ladder. She looked up and met Joe's grim face.

The ladder jerked again. Gunshots and tinkling glass prickled her ears as Samuel reached the top rung and fired at the giant window and crawled inside.

"Come on!" he yelled.

A moan filled the air as the ladder tipped to the side; its base had weakened under the assault of the hoverbikes.

Brie looked down and knew that neither of them would make it if Joe didn't release her.

"Let me go."

His grip tightened in response.

"There is no point in both of us dying. Take the bag and let me go!"

Joe refused Brie pleas. He tightened his hold on her and the ladder, using all of his strength to haul her up. Once Brie touched the metal rungs, she latched onto them and scrambled upward to Samuel's outstretched hand.

"Why didn't you let me go?" she asked through heavy breaths.

Joe looked at her as though she should have known the answer, but replied, saying, "I didn't want that crazy Viking coming after me, avenging your death."

Brie grinned in response.

Laser fire pelted the window, forcing them to duck and run. They hurried through the office floor of abandoned blue-gray cubicles, flashing monitors, and overturned chairs with their spinning wheels in the air. Papers flew in the air from enemy fire, sticking to them and making it difficult to see where they went. Joe and Samuel took turns firing their weapons as they ran. A door with a rectangular slit of glass loomed ahead. Brie jerked it open, and slammed it shut once they were all through. They raced down the stairs and stopped. Stein's men filled the stairwell, their stomping feet echoed off the brick walls, and headed straight for them. One fired, striking the side of the wall just above Joe's head.

"Go up!" screamed Joe, shoving both Brie and Samuel up the stairs to the roof. Their feet pounded the linoleum floor as they raced up the steps, dodging laser fire and hoping to reach the top. Samuel stopped at another door that led to more offices, but Joe pushed him away from it, urging him to continue up the steps to the roof. Their legs burned and their lungs begged for air, but still they refused to stop: the hammering of the boots behind them spurred them onward. A laser blast struck the railing near Brie's hand, chipping the wood. Despite the splinters that lodged themselves in the skin, she moved onward, picking up speed and ignoring her legs as her muscles turned to rubber.

A steel door blocked their path to the roof. Joe twisted the knob. Locked. As the marching feet drew closer, he fired at the lock, disabling it, and shoved the door open, with Brie and Samuel right behind. Before Stein's men reached them, both Joe and Samuel blocked the door as best they could. They looked out at the city and the massive oval-shaped ships that hovered above it, with hoverbikes and shuttlecraft forming specks in the distance, resembling a swarm of bees.

A silver and indigo sphere plopped on the ground by Brie's feet. Though it looked unusual, both Joe and Samuel recognized it for what it was, an explosive device. Before Brie had time to react, Samuel slammed into her, shoving her away and shielding her just as it detonated.

"Samuel," Joe ran to his colleague, rolling him onto his back.

"Sorry... I never believed you," whispered Samuel before going limp.

As Joe laid Samuel's head down, the door burst from its hinges and clattered to the rough surface of the roof with masked men pouring through the doorway, surrounding them. They lunged for Joe, punching and kicking him. Brie tried to help, but one man tossed her aside with ease, while another seized her shoulders. She kicked herself backwards, catching the man by surprise, and wriggled free of his grasp, darting away and squirming through the crowd; her small size made her difficult to catch.

A whistle stopped everyone. Brie stood on the ledge, holding the pack out, ready to drop it if they refused her demands.

"Let him go," she demanded, her voice sounding firmer than she had expected.

The men in masks laughed.

"I'll drop this," said Brie, letting the bag slip a bit to prove her point and forcing the men into silence. "Let him go, or I'll drop this. Good luck finding it."

Unwilling to risk Stein's ire should they return without the bag's contents, the masked men released Joe. He rose to his feet and stood near Brie.

"Go," she told him. "Go!" she screamed upon Joe's reluctance to leave, and he noticed that her earpiece was missing.

Joe put on the wingsuit he had brought with him, teetered on the edge of the roof, taking one last glance at Brie, and jumped. The wind rushed his face and jolted his body as it caught the flaps of the suit, allowing him to soar.

Brie watched Joe fly away before—she gasped as a net shot out from a nearby hoverbike, enveloping her, jerking her off her feet, and carrying her into the air and away from the building below. She watched as she was carted away, the speck of yellow and black that vanished behind a tower.

Chapter 27
MYSTERIOUS PYRAMID

The towering rock loomed before Fons and Tre as they walked up—Rynah had managed to transport them within five miles of it—admiring the way it looked, a castle spire alone amongst the rosy sky. Their necks craned upward as they stared at the massive rock before them; their feet carried them closer despite the wonderment that consumed them.

The horizon glowed, warning them of its arrival, and the soft light casted long shadows on the gritty sand beneath their shuffling feet.

"Now what?" asked Tre.

"The poem Rynah mentioned said something about a hunter's belt," said Fons.

"Hunter's belt?" said Tre. "That doesn't make a lot of sense. And what are you doing?" Tre smacked away Fons' hand as he poked him for the third time since they had met.

"Sorry," said Fons. "I've just never really seen an alien before."

"You've been around Rynah," snapped Tre. "And I'm not an alien. I'm a Lanyran."

"Yeah, well, she has this whole 'I'll kill you if you touch me' thing going on. Seriously, that woman is intimidating."

Tre laughed. "At least she didn't blow up your home, forcing you into exile."

Before they knew it, Tre and Fons were comparing stories about how each of them had been ripped away from the security of their home and thrust into a world of extraterrestrials, and how neither of them had had a moment's peace since. They would have continued in their telling of tales if it hadn't been for Fons glancing up at the sky and noticing the constellation of Orion as it faded, having been marred by the top edge of the rising sun.

"That's it!" shouted Fons.

"What's it?"

"Hunter's belt—it refers to Orion. Look!" Fons pointed at the sky and understanding dawned on Tre's face. "Quickly, before it fades, we need to find something that matches up with it."

They scoured the area, wandering among the base of Shiprock, searching for anything that lined up with the constellation of Orion, but as their search continued, and they remained empty-handed, they began to lose hope. Fons was on the verge of giving up until Tre tripped over a black rock that protruded from the ground.

"Are you all right?" asked Fons.

"Fine," said Tre.

Fons didn't listen. He squinted as he studied the rock that Tre had tripped over and noticed two more sitting next to it in a perfect line. With lightening movements, Fons pounced upon the rock, brushing the dirt off them with his hand and revealing their tops and sides, gawking at what he had found. The three rocks lined up with Orion's belt, and even looked like it.

Tre watched in fascination, ignoring the sun's light as it spilled over the horizon and hit him in the eyes.

"We need to uncover these," said Fons, dashing to another rock, dropping to his knees and sweeping the sand off a third weathered stone.

Together, the two of them darted from rock to rock, clearing away the dirt that covered them, revealing the constellation of Orion burrowed within the ground.

"Now what?" asked Fons.

"Rynah said something about the hunter's spear," said Tre, "but I'm not sure..."

He stopped speaking, for at that moment, the robotic firefly left Fons' pocket and settled on the stone that formed the spear, causing it to emit a yellow glow. He reached down and touched it. The rock dropped into the ground and turned clockwise three times before stopping. Before either of them could speak, the sand beneath their feet shifted and lowered into the ground, taking them with it, while the firefly settled back in Fons' pocket.

They turned on the balls of their feet as they looked around in the darkness that swallowed them, the only light coming from the hole in the ceiling above them. The small elevator stopped. Tre and Fons stepped off, unbothered when the lift rose back up, closing the opening above them and sealing it.

Before either of them could say a word, the robotic firefly left Fons' pocket and nestled in the side of a wall, melting into it. Unknown to them, the mechanical firefly carried an energy crystal, and when Rynah had read the bit of the poem about the hunter's spear, it activated the secondary programming to the tiny insect-sized device; as it fused with the wall, its crystal was released.

The shadowy wall lit up as symbols, connected by multicolored lines, burst to life, springing from where the robotic firefly had landed. The ancient writing stretched up in a mishmash pattern, spreading to another connecting structure. Fons and Tre stepped back, enthralled by the illuminating sight before them, realizing the connecting walls formed a pyramid buried deep beneath the ground, and what was referred to as Shiprock was its crown. Once the light stretched to the top, streaks of blue with gold mixed in burst from the pyramid, scattering as it stretched across the ground and beneath their meandering feet. A loud clunking noise filled their ears, and they watched as massive, triangular doors opened, releasing a tiered set of ivory steps for them to climb.

Jaws dropping, the two men stumbled over to the steps and climbed up them, turning in circles as they went and absorbing every detail of the ancient structure. Trembling, Tre and Fons passed through the doors and into the center of the pyramid, while oblong-shaped lamps sprang to life, casting their marigold-colored light upon them. Their feet carried them to the center of the chamber until they stopped. The floor opened and computer consoles sprang from it, rising until they were waist high, followed by holomonitors that enveloped them in a cocoon of pale green light with images of other ancient temples and pyramids staring back at them.

"I recognize that one," said Fons, pointing to one picture of a temple in India.

"These were all built by the Mulyra?" said Tre as he watched the images zip across the monitors.

"Or their descendants," said Fons.

Tre tapped the holomonitor, zooming in on an image of a place in the Ukraine, accompanied by a series of symbols. As he studied it, he realized it was a command code.

The next hour rolled by with each of them fiddling with the holocomputers until they had learned that each symbol represented either a location in the world, or the Earth itself.

"I think I got this figured out," said Tre. "All of these structures are connected, and each one has its own character. This one is for the planet, and this"—he pointed at one that looked very similar to a biohazard sign—"most likely means worldwide destruction."

"So how do we connect them to activate the shield?" asked Fons.

After more fiddling, both of them exclaimed at the same time, "I've got it!"

Fons touched the monitor and up popped a globe of the Earth

with empty circles dotting it. He touched the image of the Sphinx in Egypt and it filled the circle that represented Egypt on the map.

"Rynah," said Tre into the communicator she had given him before they had parted.

"Yes," came Rynah's out-of-breath voice.

"We found it."

"Can you get it to work?" she asked.

"I think so," said Tre.

"Wait for my command," said Rynah.

Once Tre put the communicator away, he and Fons finished filling in the circles on the map of the world, except for the last one. That would have to wait, until Rynah issued her command.

Chapter 28
A Battle and a Reunion

Brie winced as the nylon fibers of the net dug into her skin, leaving burn marks that looked more like charcoal stripes. The hoverbike slowed. She felt the jerk as the flaps were extended to decrease momentum and the ground approached at a steady pace. When they were only a few feet from the road, the pilot released the net. Her stomach jumped as Brie plopped on the asphalt; a stinging sensation caused her knee to throb. As the net fell away around her, Brie looked up, still clutching her bag, into Stein's calloused and hollow eyes—the black pupils drew her in, filling her with dread. Determined not to show her anxiety, she set her mouth in a thin, grim line, doing her best to keep her face impassive.

Stein approached her, a smug grin on his face. One of his men snatched the bag from Brie's arms and handed it to Stein, who took it, pleased that he had won. He reached in and pulled out the crystal, holding it in the sunlight and admiring it, but not the rainbow that poured forth from it.

"I thank you," he said, sticking the crystal back in the bag. "Dispose of her."

Brie plowed into one of the men guarding her, knocking him down, and tried to get away, but strong hands stopped her, forcing her to kneel on the ground.

"What about my mother?" she demanded as laser rifles were aimed at her head. "Would you deny me the chance to see them?"

Stein stopped. He faced Brie, an amused expression on his face, pleased that she had done what he wanted, playing into his plans.

"Deny you? You have been spending too much time with… what was his name? Oh, yes, Alfric."

More fighter jets flew above them, locked in a battle with shuttlecraft from Stein's armada.

"I suppose not. Your mother has been dying to see you. Perhaps I should grant you all a family reunion."

Stein reached out to touch Brie's face, but she smacked his hand away, only to have it wrenched behind her back by one of Stein's men.

"Ah, so the mouse has grown some fangs. How appropriate."

He flicked a strand of her mousy brown hair away from her lips.

"Yes, you should see you mother and sister again. I trust you will find that they have been well taken care of in my charge."

The hands that held Brie heaved to her feet, and she was marched into the waiting shuttle behind her, followed by Stein and Gaden.

"What of the city," asked one of his men.

"Destroy it," replied Stein. "Leave none alive."

The hatch to the shuttle closed as the ramp was drawn in, leaving Brie in the pale, cold light of the craft with a man she detested. She looked at her hands, which had been cuffed, before using her eyes to glance around, all without moving her head, keeping her head bowed low, draped by strands of her hair, adding to her defeated look, while her mind raced with possible scenarios of escape; but there was one question on her mind, something for which she needed an answer, just to make sense of all that had happened.

"Why?" she whispered.

Stein's eyes narrowed in response to her faint voice.

"Why?" asked Brie again, with more force.

"Why?' replied Stein.

"Why are you doing all of this? Why did you betray Klanor? What are the crystals to you?"

"A means to an end."

"What end?" asked Brie.

"Look at them," said Stein, pointing out the window at the people below who scurried around, ants fleeing a boot, trying to escape the carnage that pursued them, all hoping that it would end. Innocent people, desperate people, who just wanted to be left alone to live their lives as they saw fit, now forced to flee from the man seated across from Brie, from a man intent on spreading the depth of his own pain.

"Pathetic, aren't they? All of them consumed by their own want, their own needs, each thinking that their ills are the only ones that matter. Look at them, oblivious to the sufferings of others, not caring about anyone but themselves.

"These crystals will allow me to right all of that. Your world thinks it has experienced pain. I will show them real suffering, and when I deem that they understand, I will annihilate your planet, but not until Rynah has suffered as well. Think of the torture this will put her through. The woman who failed to save her own home, and who has failed to redeem herself by saving this insignificant rock."

"Rynah?"

"Oh, did she not tell you?" said Stein. "Her grandfather is the reason why my wife and son are dead. His foolish pursuit of power—yes, he sought the crystals and the mystical power they are said to possess—resulted in the decimation of an entire region of Lanyr. My wife and child were there that day. Marlow was never caught, never brought up on charges."

"You cannot hold her responsible for what he did," Brie said, unwilling to inform Stein that she had already known about the misdeeds of Rynah's grandfather.

"I can and I will," replied Stein. "They died, and you all act as though it means nothing. And Klanor, he promised me a way to bring them back, saying that these crystals have that power. I thought it preposterous at first, but then I witnessed how the absence of one crystal destroyed an entire planet. And I knew then how powerful one could be with them."

"You can't bring back the dead."

"Perhaps not."

"Why Sunlil?" asked Brie, unable to contain her curiosity. "Klanor helped you, why leave him on Sunlil with us?"

Stein laughed. "Help me? He used me, much like he used everyone else in his life. I realized that he had no intention of keeping the promises he made me, besides the fact that his will faltered. He actually loves Rynah. He was a hindrance, and the time had arrived where I no longer needed him. Those left on the ships think the same way I do."

"Those left?" Brie detested the sound of that statement.

"Why, yes, my dear," said Stein. "Any who challenged me learned what it means to be left in the cold, desolate blackness we call space." Stein pulled the crystals from the bag and its translucent shade turned black in his hands. "Through this, other worlds will know what it means to feel loss, and I will start with yours. You will be reunited with your dear mother and sister. I will give you all a front row seat so that you can watch your planet burn, before you, too, know what it means to be left in the cold of space."

Brie's face hardened as she listened to Stein. She noticed Gaden, who sat away from them, staring at his feet, fidgeting. Brie remembered meeting him for the first time on Lanyr when she and the others went back there to get some data storage disks. He was a weasel, and she still disliked him, but Brie never thought of Gaden as a hard-hearted individual, not like Stein.

"How can you align yourself with him?" she demanded of Gaden. "How can you stand by and watch as he destroys innocent lives in the name of grief?"

"Don't bother with him," laughed Stein. "He is a follower;

he always follows the strongest and boldest, but is too much of a coward to stand on his own."

"I…" began Gaden.

Stein reached over and backhanded Gaden, knocking him on his side. "You will only speak when I tell you to."

"Stop it!" yelled Brie. "You talk about pain, but the only thing you know how to do is cause it. Do you think you are the only one to lose someone you love? People die every day, people who don't deserve it, but those that are left learn to move on because if they don't, then their guilt, their sorrow, will consume them until they are nothing but a shell of their former self. You speak of justice, but you don't know what that means. You have displayed your true colors and the monster that you always were. Your wife would be ashamed of you. At least she isn't here to see what you have become."

Stein lunged for Brie, smacking her with a force that knocked her to the floor of the shuttle. As she lay there, cringing from the burning sensation on her cheek, she glanced through the slit in the door to the cockpit of the shuttle and noticed one of the pilots place a warning hand on the arm of the other. Before she had much time to ponder it, Stein flung her into a sitting position, bearing down upon her and bringing his lips to her ear.

"You will know pain when I am through with you." He sat back in his seat. "I'm just curious, why didn't your little band of heroes kill Klanor? I left him there in your grasp, yet you allowed him to live. What did you see in him, that you do not see in me?"

Brie stared Stein in the eyes, her hardened expression boring into him.

"Remorse."

The shuttle pulled free of Earth's upper atmosphere and glided to the massive space station—which dwarfed the entire state of Rhode Island—that hovered over the round, blue planet, passing through a pair of doors that opened before them and sealing them inside. Once they had landed in the shuttle bay, clamps attached to the landing gear, snapping into place with a bang. Once again, Brie found herself lifted to her feet by rough hands and the barrel end of a laser rifle shoved into the middle of her slender back. She allowed herself to be marched down the gangplank as she took in the familiar sight of the shuttle bay and her brief time within its stark white walls, decorated only by the steel pipes the ran up them and to the ceiling.

"Take her to where she can see her mother and sister," said Stein. "Hope you enjoy your little reunion," he said to Brie, cupping her chin, before stalking off.

Another nudge told Brie to move. She walked through the doorway into the darkened corridor, watching one of the pilots as he followed Stein, and the other disappear around a bend, both with their helmets still secured over their heads. As she moved through the hallway, Brie lifted up the sleeve of her jacket, checking the band around her wrist, before concealing it again, remaining aware of where she was, the exit points, and the position of the two guards who marched behind her, while Gaden remained by her side. They turned away from the main detention area. Confused and concerned, Brie glanced back at the two guards behind her, receiving a harsh shove in response, almost tripping over her feet. An elevator greeted them.

"Where are you taking me?" she demanded.

"Where I was ordered to," replied Gaden in a despondent tone.

The elevator doors shut behind them and Brie realized that they led her to the other detention center, one she had heard some of the members of the crew speak of in hushed whispers when they thought she was unconscious from her interrogation sessions, but she never thought much of it, until now. An ominous feeling filled her.

"You know," she said to Gaden, "you don't have to do this."

Gaden looked at her, his sallow face betrayed the mixture of emotions within him.

"You don't have to do Stein's bidding," Brie continued.

"But, I do," whispered Gaden; sadness filled his voice.

Brie glanced into the metal sides of the elevator and the reflection of the two guards.

"You're not like him," she whispered back. "I saw it in your eyes that day on Lanyr. Despite all of your faults, you can choose to act differently."

"You believe that people can change?"

"Yes," Brie replied.

The elevator doors opened and a poke in her back reminded Brie to step out into the narrow hallway, its black siding filling her with dread at what lay beyond and the circular door that awaited her. A holographic keypad popped out of the door, awaiting a command, which Gaden punched in when he placed his hand on it.

"It's too late for me," he said as the guards shoved Brie inside, and the door closed behind her.

Locked in a dark room with two armed guards, Brie observed her surroundings as best she could, wondering why she had been brought there and where her sister and mother were. Blue lights flickered on, surrounding her, until Brie found herself encircled by holographic images, depicting a room, much like the cell Klanor had kept her in when she was his prisoner, and two people, crumpled on the cold floor.

"Mom?" said Brie as she realized what Stein had in mind for her. Impulse made her run for her mother and Sara and reach out to them, but the harsh reality that all of it was a hologram smashed into her when she met the far wall. "Mom!"

"Brie, honey," her mother cried, clutching Sara, who buried her face into her mother's lap.

"Mom, what's going on?" asked Brie.

"He said…" began her mother, "he said that we were to show you the true meaning of loss."

Brie's face fell. Stein had tricked her, the same way he had fooled Solaris.

"Brie?" whimpered Sara; bits of her tangled hair framed her tiny face as she looked at Brie with red, puffy eyes.

"Sara!" Again, Brie tried to touch her sister and mother, but her fingers passed through the particles of light, reminding her that they were not there.

A hiss filled her ears and Sara screamed when she saw green gas spill from a pipe above them and two oxygen tanks pop out of a panel on the wall. Brie's mother wrapped the mask of one around Sara before securing her own.

"Brie," she said, "these tanks only have about 20 minutes of air. Enough for us to say our goodbyes and for you to…"

Tears streamed from Brie's eyes when her mother's voice trailed off, while she watched in horror as the gas filled the cell her mother and sister were locked in. Those tears soon turned to anger, and a fury that Brie had never known rose within her, filling her, and for the first time in her life, she wanted revenge. One of the guards shifted his weight, alerting Brie to his position. Without warning, she leapt to the side, plowing into him and knocking him to the floor. Stunned, the man never saw Brie's fist when it rammed into his face, breaking his nose. She scurried to her knees, dodged behind the guard she had attacked, and wrapped the band of her handcuffs around his neck, positioning him in front of her just as the second guard fired. She tossed his body aside.

Brie jumped to the side and into the shadows, concealing herself from the second guard. He turned on his feet, searching for her, firing anything that moved, but Brie remained elusive. The guard circled the room, thinking that Brie was in every dark crevice and every shadow; his focus on the shadows kept him unaware of the soft steps that crept across the sides of the room, drawing nearer, until…

Brie jumped out of the shadows, pounding both her clenched fists between the man's shoulder blades. As he staggered forward, Brie gripped the laser rifle, wrenching it free of his grasp and kicking him in the stomach, before striking him on the head with the butt of the weapon.

She seized the guard's hand and placed his thumb on the holopad of her cuff, freeing herself from the wrist restraints. Brie dragged the unconscious guard to the door and placed the palm of his hand on the holopad that appeared, opening it. Laser fire struck the doorway, missing her head by an inch and forcing her to retreat back inside the room. Peeking around the corner, she saw only one guard. Brie glanced around, but found no other exits. She stepped out in the hallway and fired, before dashing back behind the protective barrier of the doorway. More laser fire pelted the wall beside her. Brie checked her watch. She didn't have much time. Summoning her courage, she jumped back into the hallway and prepared to fire, but stopped when a massive shape leapt at the guard from behind, slamming him into the wall and ripping his weapon away from him. Brie watched as the mysterious man removed his helmet.

"Alfric!" she said, relieved. "They're not here. Stein must have them in the main detention area. We haven't much time."

She ran off through a set of doors with Alfric—who had snuck aboard Stein's shuttle with Obiah through a small, and usually forgotten, escape hatch, disposing of the pilots and putting on their armor while Stein remained distracted by Rynah and the others—right behind her. They burst into another corridor, racing to the elevators. The doors opened. Alfric seized the man, who stepped out and tossed him aside with ease, while Brie punched the button that took them to the floor of the detention center. She looked at Alfric, amazed that the alarms had not sounded, but hoped that her luck would last.

The doors opened. Brie and Alfric stepped out into an empty hallway. *Where are the people?* Brie thought to herself. When she had first been aboard the space station, the corridors were crowded with personnel, but now they resembled silent tombs, and Brie guessed that, in his zeal, Stein had murdered most of them, leaving enough alive to maintain the ship. Rechecking where she was, Brie remembered the way to the detention center and motioned for Alfric to follow her, hoping that Obiah succeeded in fulfilling his part of the plan.

Up in the command center of the space station, Stein clutched the crystal he had taken from Brie, reveling in his triumph—thoughts of how he would destroy the earth and make her watch filled his mind—

as he looked out at the mesmerizing scene of dodging and swerving spacecraft before him. The crystal glowed for a second before turning dark, matching Stein's nature. Something caught his attention. Turning around, Stein watched as a baseball-sized swirling mass appeared, creating a vortex that pulled and tugged at everyone within the room, swallowing small bits of metal and people's wristbands before vanishing. Though unsure of what had caused it to appear, Stein refused to worry about it, caring more about his plans for the planet below.

The com unit beeped. "Sir," said the one in charge of communications, "we are receiving a transmission from... pirates."

Intrigued, Stein nodded his approval to relay the message. A holoscreen flashed to life in front of him with Jifdar's face filling it.

"I am Jifdar, captain of the..."

"I know who you are," interrupted Stein.

"Indeed."

"What is it you want?"

"To warn you," said Jifdar.

"About what?"

"You have traitors in your midst."

"Really?"

"I can tell you who they are," said Jifdar.

"And why should I believe you?"

"You shouldn't."

Stein eyed Jifdar.

"But aren't you curious?"

"Name your price." Stein knew that pirates always guarded their own interests, but Jifdar's audacity at negotiating with him raised his curiosity about the veracity of his statement, as well as played into his paranoia of being betrayed by anyone close to him.

"I want Klanor dead," replied Jifdar.

"He is not aboard this ship," Stein said.

"That is not my problem. I've named my terms. Do you agree to them?"

"Done."

While all eyes remained locked on Jifdar's holographic image, and their ears tuned to the exchange between the pirate and Stein, one member of the ship, still wearing his helmet with the visor down, moved closer to Stein. He unclasped his holster, gripping the handle of his laser pistol.

"So where is this traitor of mine?" demanded Stein.

Jifdar smiled, displaying his crooked teeth. "Behind you."

At that moment, Stein whipped around in time to witness the mysterious man shoot the two guards next to him. He aimed at Stein, but Stein was quick; he deflected the kill shot—being struck in the thigh instead—and dropped the crystal. The helmeted man snatched the crystal, fled the command center—by now, you should have guessed he was Obiah—and charged down the corridor, despite the laser fire that followed him. He turned a corner and fired several shots behind him, before jumping over a rail and to the walkway below. Shouts rose up behind him, but he had part of what he had come for. He just needed to find the other eight. He turned a corner and jumped back behind it when armed guards greeted him. More approached from the other end. Finding himself trapped, Obiah fired random shots to steal a few precious moments, enough to think of a way to escape. A shrill hum startled him. Jumping, he studied the metal plate he had backed against, realizing that it was a garbage chute. Laser fire zipped around him, flashing multiple colors as he placed his thumb on the keypad, opening the chute. He looked into the dark, grime-covered chute, not liking his options. Tearing off his helmet and sucking in a deep breath to avoid breathing in the stench, Obiah dove, head first, into the dark hole.

* * *

"Deploy our ships!" yelled Jifdar when the transmission with Stein had ended.

Hangar doors opened, creating black holes along the charred

sides of his vessel, as shuttlecraft burst from them, freed from their prisons. They banked and dived, going in every direction towards Stein's mass of giant ships that orbited the blue planet, firing, while avoiding being struck by return fire.

Holoscreens popped up in front of Jifdar, filling the command center of his vessel alight with red and green dots. He watched, hands clasped behind his back, as the dots converged. Jifdar opened a transmission to his ships. Taking a quick glance at Klanor, who sulked off to the side, irritated at being forced to stay aboard when he preferred being in a shuttle himself, Jifdar spoke.

"Men, we are pirates. It isn't often that we are asked to do something for the sake of others. This one time, I ask of you a selfless act. We've always taken from those who could fight back, but we never plundered from the innocent. This man Stein is worse than us. He doesn't take for the sake of stealing, or to survive; he destroys anything that is good in this world for sheer pleasure. This one time I am asking you to forgo your pirate ways and act as men, men who protect the innocent. So let's give him hell!"

Cheers rang out on the com units, until they were drowned by laser fire and cannon blasts.

"Rousing speech," commented Klanor.

"I have my moments," said Jifdar.

A rumble echoed across the outer hull as a laser cannon blast detonated just beyond it. Jifdar watched as his ships, marked by the green dots on the holoscreens before him, engaged the enemy. He wished that more of his pirates had decided to remain, but could not blame them for choosing to leave with his first mate.

"All vessels converge on a target! Remember, keep them busy."

The ship jerked as a cannon blast plowed into it, but the shields held for the moment. Jifdar just hoped that his vessel would last long enough to do what he needed to.

* * *

General Delmar raced past the massive ships (the size of apartment complexes), dodging their laser canons, unfazed by their blasts that ricocheted off the hull of his single-pilot fighter craft. Laser fire whizzed past him. He banked and swerved as he dodged it. Enemy ships appeared ahead of him. General Delmar accelerated, heading straight for the ships in front of him, while blocking their view from the one that chased him. Just before he reached the two vessel before him, he dove downward and the one that chased him plowed into the other two ships, disappearing in flames.

More laser fire dinged his ship, leaving black marks—not that they stood out among the grime that already covered the hull plating. He jerked the controls. Zipping past other ships that weaved about, each locked in their own battles, Delmar plunged into the center of the armada. His ship circled the giant vessels amidst the colorful display of laser fire, as another locked on his position. Metal shards flew past his vessel, as one exploded near him, struck by one of the cannons on the larger ships.

General Delmar moved closer, almost scrapping the hull as he flew over the massive vessels, his shadow racing across the jagged lines formed by the rivets that held the hull in place. Another blast exploded near him, rocking his ship. Muscles straining, he held the controls rigid as he guided his fighter craft away. He spotted a laser cannon up ahead that fired repeated blasts at the pirate ships that littered the area. An idea struck him.

Delmar banked to the right, heading straight for the laser cannon and ignoring the ship that remained behind him, determined to eradicate him. He focused on the laser cannon, its blasts almost blinding him, drawing closer until he almost crashed, but yanking the controls back at the last second and avoiding certain death. The shockwave pushing his ship forward told him that the craft that had followed him had crashed, but before he had time to relax, the spire of another stadium-sized vessel jumped in front of him, surprising him. General Delmar reared back, swerving to the left before arcing upwards, his ship spinning as he struggled to maintain control, before leveling out.

"Cutting it close, weren't you?' came Hylne's voice in his earpiece.

Another fighter craft dropped in beside him and the pilot waved. General Delmar returned the gesture.

"Do you remember Commander Hofnor's training exercises?"

"I try not to," replied Hylne. He looked ahead and saw two of the massive armada ships creep past one another, and as he realized what General Delmar had in mind, he blurted out, "Hell no!"

A smirk snaked across General Delmar's face. While they had been in basic training, with Commander Hofnor as their instructor, they had been forced to practice mock suicide missions, exercises that almost resulted in the deaths of the cadets who had participated. As punishment for his severe negligence, the Lanyran fleet's tribunal gave the commander a choice between demotion to sergeant and a desk job, or honorable discharge. He chose the latter. Since that time, General Delmar had agreed with the sentence, but now he saw the merit in his commander's exercises. He flew away.

"You're insane!" yelled Hylne in the com unit, but he followed his friend anyway; having vowed to accompany him, he was not going to let General Delmar commit such a foolish act alone.

General Delmar dove behind one of the massive ships, out of sight of Hylne, and fired upon it, welcoming its return fire. He swerved and dodged his small fighter craft, allowing him to zigzag; his quick movements made him a difficult target. Still, the giant ship fired upon him, focusing its attention on what it viewed as a little annoyance. Maintaining his act of foolishness, General Delmar dove closer, skimming the hull of the ship, leaving a black, jagged scratch, as he fired upon it. A blast just off his starboard side told him that he had succeeded in angering the ship's captain. General Delmar fired his thrusters, accelerating his small craft, as he flew towards the ship's stern. He neared the edge. Just as he reached the end, Hylne appeared with the second massive ship behind him. Both of the giant vessels fired at the same time, each aiming for either Hylne or General Delmar, but the tiny fighter crafts hurried away and the spaceships' cannon blasts struck one another, gouging red and orange holes into their sides.

Each of the ships drifted, losing their artificial gravity fields, which helped them maintain control, and banked to the sides, dipping lower into the earth's atmosphere. The fire of re-entry engulfed them, spreading across their hulls as they entered at the wrong angle, before bursting into several pieces and raging fires consumed each chunk.

General Delmar released a triumphant howl.

"I always knew you were nuts," chided Hylne.

One of Stein's ships appeared, clipping Hylne's vessel in the wing and sending him towards the planet below. He gripped the controls of his fighter craft, angling it just right so as not to burn up in the atmosphere, while the ship that had struck him remained in pursuit. General Delmar dove after him. He locked onto the vessel that chased Hylne. Flames arced across his sides and turned to wispy clouds that swirled around him as he charged after his quarry. He watched as Hylne weaved left to right in an effort to shake the enemy ship, but all of his attempts failed. General Delmar's eyes narrowed. He lined the small craft in his sites, ignoring the laser fire that attacked his friend and blocking out all distractions. Releasing a slow breath, he fired. The vessel in front of him exploded.

"Thanks," said Hylne.

"No pro—"

Another ship appeared from above. It fired upon General Delmar's ship, striking the cockpit and destroying the entire vessel before turning its attention to Hylne, but its weapons jammed, so the pilot fled.

Angered, Hylne chased after the small craft, determined to seek justice for the loss of a great general, and his friend. The ship in front of him banked. Hylne mimicked its movements. It swerved in its efforts to break free of his pursuit, but Hylne refused to be defeated, maintaining his focus as he lined up his sights on the ship. Before he could pull the trigger, it arced upward, ramming its way through the high clouds and back into space. Undeterred, Hylne followed. They raced past other small fighter crafts—some of which were pirates, and the others were Stein's—and almost crashed into a few, but each maintained their calm demeanor, dodging the other ships that were locked in battle. The craft in front of him dropped. Hylne followed, but stopped. His target had disappeared.

Infuriated at losing the one who had killed his friend, he pushed ahead, plunging into the thick of the battle and ignoring every ship that passed him as he searched for the one he wanted. He found it. Nestled in the crook of the wing of one of the armada ships, the craft hoped to escape detection, but lost against Hylne's fortitude. Hylne dove for it. He charged through the swerving ships and their hailstorm of laser fire that lit up the skies above Earth. The ship fled. It flew between two passing gigantic vessels with Hylne right behind it, dodging the laser cannons that fired at him. The shadowed surfaces of both ships raced past him as he navigated the maze that the craft in front of him charted in its efforts to escape. It turned left. So did Hylne.

Once again, the blue planet loomed before him as he chased the craft that had killed General Delmar, crossing the line that separated day from night. They entered Earth's southern hemisphere, soaring past dark clouds and going straight down, until they each were forced to yank their controls upward to avoid crashing. They flew over the Australian outback, sand flying up behind them in waves as the force of their engines kicked it up. Hylne inhaled slow, steady breaths, lining the ship in front of him in his sights. Tall cliffs lay just ahead. Knowing that he had little time to fire before both would be forced to fly upward or crash, Hylne pushed harder, determined to finish this fight. His targeting systems beeped. Before he lost his target, Hylne fired and the ship ahead of him exploded, lighting up the night. Before he reached the cliffs, he jerked back the controls, going straight up through the thinning clouds until he entered Earth's orbit once more and delved back into the fray.

* * *

Obiah dropped several feet before crashing into a bend in the chute, but his journey did not end there. Another shrill hum, and a series of clacks, filled him with unease as he lay covered in a pile of slime and moldy scraps of food that had been tossed out by the kitchen. A door fell away beneath him. He dropped, and before he could regain his senses, he crashed into a solid surface, expelling the air from his lungs and staring straight into the barrel of a laser rifle. His eyes darted upward and he recognized the one holding the weapon—Brie.

"Don't shoot! It's me!" Obiah yelled, holding up his hands.

Brie relaxed, lowering the laser rifle and breathing a sigh of relief before giving Obiah a hug. Despite his initial intentions, Obiah had ended up in the main detention center just as Brie and Alfric had entered through the once well-guarded door; the guards lay in a crumpled heap where Alfric had deposited them.

"Where's your family?" asked Obiah.

"They're supposed to be here, but we must hurry. Stein filled their cell with gas," replied Brie.

Worried for her sake, Obiah raced to a computer console and brought up the list of cells on that floor, locating the one with the gas turned on. He pointed it out to Brie, who took off running. When she reached the door, she smashed the keypad, disabling the locks, and the door propped open, smothering her in the toxic cloud that spilled into the corridor. Ignoring the noxious gas, Brie covered her mouth and nose with her jacket sleeve and ran inside.

"Mom! Sara!" she coughed.

No one was within the cell.

Crestfallen, Brie stood statuesque in the center of the room, unable to move as her mind wrestled with the fact that Stein had fooled her again. Obiah and Alfric rushed into the gas filled area, seized Brie, and dragged her away from there, sealing the door behind them.

"They're dead," cried Brie. "They're dead."

"You don't know that," said Obiah.

"But they're not here," Brie replied, a tear streaming down her cheek.

"I know where they are," said a snide voice through the slit in the door, through which food trays were delivered, from the cell next to them.

Following Brie's example, Alfric smashed the keypad to the cell, stepping back when the door opened and revealed Fredyr. He lunged for the man, grabbing him by the collar of his shirt and lifting him off his feet.

"Tell me!"

"You cannot force me to talk, nor do you have the time to torture me into submission."

"Where are they?" demanded Brie.

"I'll tell you," replied Fredyr, "for a price. I even know where those crystals are kept."

They each glared at Fredyr, unsure if they should take the risk in trusting him, but his taunting made the decision for them.

"Tick. Tock," sneered Fredyr.

"What are your terms?" Alfric demanded.

"You take me with you."

"Agreed." Alfric brought Fredyr closer to him so that he could whisper a warning into his ear. "If you betray me, I'll kill you."

Fredyr chuckled in response. "There is another holding center on this level."

Alfric pushed Fredyr ahead of him and they left the detention center. They raced down the corridor, past other hallways and some of Stein's most loyal followers, not bothering to take the time to fire back. The space station lurched. They paused, regaining their balance and wondering, for just a moment, what had happened, but Brie remembered her mother and sister and took off in the direction Fredyr had taken them in. The elevator's gold doors loomed before them, but just as they were about to reach them, they opened, allowing armed men to fill the hallway, firing at them. Dodging behind a corner, Fredyr remained at a loss for how to continue, for he only knew the one path.

"Where are they exactly?" demanded Brie.

"One floor up and on the other end of the ship," said Fredyr.

Remembering the maps she had stumbled upon and studied while a prisoner under Klanor, Brie realized where they were and knew of another way, used only by maintenance personnel, something Fredyr Monsooth would never dare to think about. She found the panel that led to a concealed ladder and kicked it away before climbing upward. Alfric seized Fredyr, shoving him at the ladder, before falling in behind him, with Obiah taking up the rear. A low moan echoed around them as the ship tipped to the side a bit and the artificial gravity field struggled to compensate.

"Sounds like those pirates came through," muttered Obiah; his voice carried through the metallic tube.

Brie stopped. "This part gets a bit tricky," she said, pointing at where the ladder ended. A long, narrow beam, one foot in width, stretched out before them, leading to another ladder which would take them to the next level. Above it stretched towering walls that vanished into darkness, while below remained an endless abyss, and certain death should they fall. Brie shifted the laser rifle around her shoulders before stepping onto the beam, stretching her arms out for balance, and taking slow, careful steps to the other side. A shiver ran through the ship as another cannon blast struck it, ripping into the hull. Brie teetered on the beam, shifting her weight to her left foot as she struggled to maintain her balance, her leg muscles straining to support her weight. Before she fell over, she hopped onto her other foot and hurried to the other side, taking small, quick steps.

Alfric shoved Fredyr to the beam, while Brie aimed her laser rifle at him. Getting the message, Fredyr stepped onto the metal joist, creeping across with little difficulty, while Alfric followed close behind should the man try something. Once they had reached the other side, a rumble emanated around them before bursting into deafening thunder as a chunk of the wall above them fell away, crashing into the plank—not breaking it, but denting it and weakening it. Obiah glanced at the others, summoning his courage. He dashed across the beam, not daring to look down, but keeping his eyes fixed on both Brie and Alfric. The joist lurched beneath him. Knowing that at any moment it could give way, he picked up the pace, taking light steps. Just as he was about to reach the other side, the beam fell away, but he jumped, using all his strength to propel himself to the other end. He felt himself drop. Before he fell too far, a hand gripped his and he looked into the eyes of Alfric, who heaved him to safety, while Brie kept her weapon trained on Fredyr.

The ladder wasn't far. "Come on," said Brie. "We haven't much time."

They reached the next floor. Brie positioned herself just above the metal panel, giving herself the leverage needed to kick it open before dropping onto the linoleum floor of another corridor. Once they had all crawled out of the tube, everyone turned to Fredyr.

"This way," he said.

He led them through another maze of corridors to where a black door blocked their path. Fredyr punched in the code, but nothing happened. Confused—he had used this area before to keep others captive—he turned to Brie and shrugged his shoulder.

"It should work."

Obiah shoved him aside and took the panel away from beneath the holographic keypad. He ripped out the wires, stripping two of them and coiling them together. A beep sounded as the door slid open, allowing them entrance. Brie charged in. The cells that lay within had transparent walls and doors, but one was filled with a green gas. She ran for it and fired at the locking mechanism. Once the door opened, Brie barged inside, holding her breath, and snatched her sister, who was huddled in a corner with an oxygen mask around her mouth, while Obiah grabbed her semiconscious mother, dragging them both outside of the prison area. Both Rebecca Reynolds and Sara coughed, expelling the fumes from their lungs as they sucked in fresher air. Her mother looked up. She jumped, seizing Sara, when she saw Alfric, Obiah, and Fredyr watching her.

"Mom, it's okay," said Brie, kneeling before Rebecca. "They're with me. We're here to get you and Sara out."

Her mother's eyes flickered back and forth between Brie, whom she almost didn't recognize with her dark jacket and laser rifle slung around her shoulders, and Alfric's intimidating size.

"But he's..." she pointed at Obiah.

"He's not with Stein," said Brie.

Her mother looked at her, not believing that she had her oldest daughter with her again, but one look into Brie's brown eyes, full of love and joy at seeing her family again, told her that it was not a dream. She placed a gentle hand on Brie's cheek, stroking it before enveloping her daughter in a giant hug, with Sara nestled between them.

"You've grown."

"Not to break up this touching moment," said Fredyr in a dry tone, "but we have other problems."

"The crystals," exclaimed Brie. "Where are they?"

Upon Fredyr's hesitation, Alfric grasped one of his arms and wrenched it behind his back, pinning the man against the wall.

"Tell her what she wants to know, you filth, or you'll suffer the wrath of the bloody eagle."

"Stein's quarters," said Fredyr. "They're not far. Just a few levels up."

Alfric released Fredyr. He tore off his body armor, freeing his sword, which Obiah had helped him conceal beneath it, and handed it to Brie. "For the girl."

Brie snatched the armor and strapped the chest and back plate to her little sister as best she could, though it gave the girl a penguin-like appearance when she walked, it would protect her from any resistance they would encounter.

They raced down the corridor to another elevator, dodging laser fire—Sara screamed when another laser cannon struck the ship, disabling the gravity centers for just a second before destabilizing—forcing their way through. Alfric was a wild man, barreling into small groups of men that tried to stop them and dispatching them with ease. They ran into the elevator and Fredyr punched the button, taking them to the proper floor.

Thunder rumbled around them, vibrating the walls just before they reached their destination. The elevator stopped. Not wanting to become trapped, Obiah slammed his fist against button after button, but to no avail, the elevator refused to budge.

"We need to pry these doors open," he said.

Alfric wasted no time. He slipped the blade of his sword between the doors and craned it to the side at an angle, wresting it open wide enough to grasp the edges of the door with his hands: Obiah gripped the other. Between the two of them, they managed to slip Alfric's sword in, using it to hold the doors open. Alfric picked up Sara, who shrieked, and heaved her through the door to the floor above them. Next, he lifted Brie and her mother up. Laser fire hounded them. Brie crouched beside her mother and sister and fired back, but more of Stein's men filled the hall. While Obiah and Fredyr crawled through the slim opening of the elevator doors, Brie spotted a dangling piece of the ceiling and fired at it. It crashed on top of their attackers, taking half of the ceiling with it and forming a blockade. As Brie turned to help Obiah lift Alfric through the doors, her mother snatched Obiah's laser pistol and fired at two armed guards who turned a corner, striking both in the neck.

"I am an Army wife," she said when Brie gave her a questioning, and surprised, look.

Freed from the confines of the elevator, they fled down the hallway, following Fredyr's directions to Stein's quarters. Once they found it, they smashed the locks and pried the doors open, stepping into the dim interior. They found the crystals displayed in a glass case. In Stein's arrogance, he had placed them on full display to demonstrate his triumph and power. Behind them was Fredyr's *Kresnyr* sword, something he took note of as his calculating mind formed a plan.

Brie ripped a tablecloth off the table and folded it, tying the ends until it formed a sack, placing the crystals within it with care, including the one that Obiah had stolen from Stein in the command center. After she had secured the crystals, she lifted it onto her shoulder, but before she had gotten to her feet, Fredyr snatched his sword from the case and Sara, holding her up with the blade against her pale neck.

"Give them to me," he demanded.

"You fool," spat Obiah.

"I think you will find that you are the fool," said Fredyr. "Those crystals are worth something and I can make a lot of money by selling them to the right buyer, or perhaps I can use them to control the Twelve Sectors after I pillage every bit of worth I can from this insignificant little planet that you call a home."

Brie tightened her grip on the crystals.

In response, Fredyr pressed the blade against Sara's neck, drawing a few droplets of blood.

"The crystals. Now."

Infuriated, Brie flung the crystals at Fredyr, who released Sara to catch them, before doubling over as both Brie and her mother shot him in the shoulder. Before he had time to react, Alfric plowed into the man, pinning him to the floor, but he knew his grip would never hold.

Brie snatched the crystals.

"Go!" yelled Alfric. Upon her reluctance, Alfric repeated himself. "Take your mother and sister and the crystals and get out of here."

Obiah's hands pulled Brie to the door, who remained torn between saving her family or helping a friend.

"GO!" screamed Alfric.

When they left, Alfric's hold on Fredyr slipped, giving the man enough room to elbow the Viking in the stomach and force him to stagger back. Both raised their swords.

"Are you sure you want to do this again?" taunted Fredyr.

Alfric charged, but Fredyr sidestepped, avoiding the blow, and twisted on his feet, slicing Alfric's side. Ignoring the pain, the Viking charged again. Fredyr blocked and Alfric's sword caught in the crook of his three pronged weapon, locking the two swords. Using the opportunity, Fredyr punched Alfric three times in the stomach; with each strike, the Viking bent over until he rammed the heel of his boot into the man's thigh, forcing him to stumble, and wrenched their weapons free. He swept Fredyr's right foot out from under him and brought his sword upon him, but Fredyr rolled out of the way. Sparks flew as Alfric's sword struck the floor, leaving a dent.

They remained locked in their battle, breaking furniture, overturning a desk, and shattering lights, as they moved around the room. Their fight spilled into the hallway. An unlucky guard stumbled upon them and Fredyr rammed his sword through him, tossing the body at Alfric, who deflected the blow with no remorse. Fredyr charged. Despite the tight space, Alfric dodged, bringing his arm up and catching Fredyr in the chest, but before he could finish him, Fredyr dropped to the floor and somersaulted away, leaping to his feet as he attacked again. The hilt of his sword smashed into Alfric's back, knocking the air out of him. Again, he found himself covering a fresh wound with his hand. He faced Fredyr. The pompous man laughed at Alfric, toying with him.

They stabbed and blocked, their feet moving in time with one another as they moved into the domed area of the ship. Those who passed by ignored them, concerned about their own safety, as the ship continued to take fire from the pirate ships. Their swords locked again. In a desperate move, Alfric let go of his weapon and rammed both of his fists into Fredyr's face, forcing Fredyr's grip to slacken.

Alfric seized his sword again, freeing it from Fredyr's. Alfric lunged. Fredyr positioned his sword so that Alfric's would go through the slit in the center of the blade, but Alfric, remembering that aspect of his opponent's weapon, parried to the right, plunging it into Fredyr's other shoulder.

Infuriated, Fredyr tackled the Viking, flinging him onto his back. Before Alfric could jump up, the ship tilted to the side, causing him to roll to the left until he crashed into the railing; his sword fell from his grasp, clattering several feet away. Leering over him, Fredyr grinned in triumph, assured that he had won, and tightened his grip on the hilt of his blade as he prepared for his final strike. Alfric spotted a fallen pipe nearby; its end had been sheared into a sharp point. Before Fredyr could finish him, a cannon blast detonated near the dome, flinging shrapnel in every direction. Alfric seized the pipe, releasing a terrifying battle cry, and stabbed Fredyr in the stomach with it, picking him up and hoisting him over his shoulders before throwing him over the railing. He watched, maintaining his stolid demeanor, as Fredyr, clutching his bleeding wound, fell into a swirling mass, where a portal through time and space had opened, swallowing him.

As glowing embers floated around him, Alfric sheathed his sword and ran down the corridor he had come from, following the path that Brie and the others had taken. His heavy footfalls pounded the floor beneath him as he raced against the ship's clock. Just as he rounded a corner, an explosion jettisoned him further down the hall, away from his goal, as a bulkhead and debris crashed around him, blocking his path. Shaking his head, Alfric used a fallen support beam to hoist himself to his feet. A hole, just large enough for a child to squeeze through, allowed him to look at the door that led to one of the shuttle bays, and the hurrying feet that charged for him.

* * *

Another cannon blast tore into the ship, forcing Klanor to cling to the slick rail along the side of the command center in an effort to maintain his balance. Sparks streaked across the ceiling as one of the holomonitors fizzled out, leaving only one that displayed the targets outside. Again, the ship lurched as a laser blast ripped through its hull, tearing whole sheets off that floated away into space.

"Where are my ion torpedoes?" demanded Jifdar, hauling himself back to his feet after being thrown across the room.

"They won't deploy," said one of his pirates. "Something is blocking the tubes."

"What? What is blocking the tubes?"

Klanor's mind raced. He studied the ship's stats on the single holomonitor on the wall next to him and knew what was needed to free the ion torpedoes. He bolted from the room. His sudden movements caught Jifdar's attention, who ran after him, but Klanor proved too fast, passing through the door and rounding a corner before another cannon blast struck the ship.

"Klanor!" Jifdar yelled as ceiling panels crashed around him, hindering his movements.

Klanor ignored Jifdar's shouts and curses that followed after him as he ran down the corridors; the sludge on the uninviting walls burned from the fires that had been started by dangling wires, which had been torn from their secure holds and zapped, sending sparks in every direction—little embers lighting up the darkness. The ship jerked. Stumbling, Klanor slumped to his knees before regaining his composure and continuing his mad dash to the shuttle bay.

CRASH!

Pipes and bulkheads pummeled the floor around him as Klanor dove through a small hole before it had been blocked by more metallic debris. The ringing sound of laser fire pierced his ears as he ran past exploding wall panels that gave way from the change in air pressure. The shuttle bay doors lay just ahead. With a burst of speed, Klanor rushed them, breaking through them and refusing to wait for the automatic doors to finish opening. With five hurried steps, he stomped up the ramp of the ancient Lanyran ship that General Delmar and Hylne had arrived in, and raced to the front, slamming into the pilot's seat and started the engines, welcoming the high pitched squeal as they turned on. A tin, metal band dangled before him. Remembering what Rynah had told him about how she connected telepathically with Solaris, Klanor rammed it onto his head.

Awaiting your command.

Depart, replied Klanor, telepathically.

Initiating start up proce—

Ignore them!

Klanor thrust the controls into forward and raced out of the shuttle bay and into the melee beyond that consumed the pirate vessel. He arced over the top of the ship and came up the other side, finding the blocked torpedo tube with ease.

"I see the problem," he said into the radio. *Scan the torpedo tubes,* he told the ship's computer.

It appears that a smaller vessel has become lodged within the conduit, replied the ship.

"Get back in here!" Jifdar screamed at Klanor.

As Klanor studied the blocked tube, he decided that a couple of precision strikes from his ship's laser weapons could break the blockage.

"I think I know how I can fix it."

"That's crazy!" yelled Jifdar, reading his mind.

Klanor lined the tube up in his sights.

Sir, according to my calculations, there is a large margin of error...

Target the blockage and use a low pulse blast, Klanor ordered the ship.

Acknowledged.

Klanor fired. Yellow light filled his visor as the blockage was vaporized, thus freeing the tube.

"You crazy son of a..." began Jifdar.

Klanor switched off the com unit. He scanned the area, his eyes falling upon a series of ships entering the planet's atmosphere. He recognized them. He punched the throttle of his vessel, propelling it towards the mass of ships, and fired upon them. A few smaller ones broke away and chased him. Thrusting his vessel into a spiral, Klanor arced out of the way of the laser fire that pursued him, while making certain to remain a tantalizing target for the ships that had broken away. He jerked the controls, banking to the left and pointing back at the ships that entered the atmosphere. Klanor swooped down upon them, skimming the exterior of the ships, until he spotted one that had a weak point.

Scan that vessel there, he ordered the ship's computer.

Initiating scan. It appears that the ship's air intake valve has been damaged. A single strike to the shaft should disable it.

Laser fire struck the wing of Klanor's ship. Before he could be destroyed, Klanor yanked back on the controls until he was perpendicular to the massive vessel beneath him and fired his thrusters, striking the air shaft and hurrying away.

"Jifdar"—Klanor turned the com back on—"we need to take out these ships before they enter the planet's atmosphere!" He turned his radio back off before the pirate captain could chastise him for his rash actions.

A swarm of pirate shuttles dove at the field-sized ships below him, firing and releasing ion torpedoes, while evading their laser canons. One exploded next to Klanor. He swerved away from it, lining up the command center of the ship in his sights. Once the targeting scanner turned green, he released the ion torpedoes that his vessel carried, mesmerized by the streams of light they left behind as they closed in on their target. They struck—plumes of smoke and flames spurted from the ship before him, forcing it to dip, and it disintegrated as the Earth's atmosphere grabbed it, swallowed by fire before vaporizing.

* * *

"Alfric!"

Overjoyed at hearing a familiar voice, yet angered that she had disobeyed his orders, Alfric peeked through the hole at Brie, who had returned for him, unable to abandon a friend, leaving her mother and sister in Obiah's care.

"I told you…"

"I think I see a way through," interrupted Brie, knowing what Alfric was about to say.

"It is too small for me. You should go. Do not trouble yourself with me."

"Cover your eyes!" Ignoring him, Brie raised her laser rifle and aimed at a bent beam, hoping that she had guessed correctly, and fired. The plank broke in half, swinging away and enlarging the hole just enough for Alfric to squeeze through.

"Come on!" yelled Brie as the debris shifted; it wouldn't hold for long.

Alfric shoved his head through, wriggling his body until his broad shoulders had cleared, before squeezing the rest of the way through. The beams and pipes crashed behind him just as his feet cleared.

"I told you to go," scolded Alfric.

"I wasn't going to leave a friend behind."

A warm smile crossed Alfric's weathered face as he looked upon Brie, who was no longer the pusillanimous girl he had met months before.

They stormed down the hallway, past flying sparks that reached out for them from hanging wires, and hurried down a set of steps until they reached the shuttle bay. A guard barred their path. Refusing to be stopped, Alfric emitted another horrifying battle cry, ripping his sword and knife free as he ran to the guard and used his body as a battering ram, slamming into the poor man and forcing him aside. Stunned, the guard dropped his laser weapon, which Brie seized upon her passage, and put his hands up in surrender.

A whistle drew their attention. Obiah stood in the opening of a shuttle, screaming at them to hurry. Both Brie and Alfric headed for him, climbing into the medium-sized craft, and sealed the hatch behind them. While Obiah jumped into the pilot's seat, Brie hugged her mother and Sara, strapping her sister into a chair.

The shuttlecraft shot out of the shuttle bay, speeding away from the monstrous ship and heading for the blue sphere below them. An explosion ripped into the outer hull. Brie hurried to a tiny, port window, pressing her face against it to see out.

"There's one on our tail!"

Obiah jerked the controls, pushing the craft into a spinning maneuver, but the ship remained in pursuit.

"Where's the weapons array?" demanded Brie.

"This is a transport vessel," replied Obiah, "not a fighter craft. There are no weapons!"

Dismayed, Brie settled in a seat next to Sara, embracing her and trying to comfort her while wrestling with her own emotions about failing to save her family. More laser fire rattled the ship with Pip!—Pip!—Pip!—Pip! sounds until silence fell. The ships that had chased them vanished behind a veil of flames as another plowed into it. Relishing the small miracle, each of them stared straight ahead as the Earth grew larger in the windshield until clouds filtered past them before parting and allowing them to see the ground below.

* * *

Lights whizzed overhead, drawing Klanor's attention. He forced the controls away from him, diving downward to the upper atmosphere of the planet below at a dangerous angle. Sweat dripped down the jawline of his face as fire stretched along the sides of his ship, giving him fiery wings, while laser fire continued to hound him. Just before he burned alive, Klanor yanked back on the controls, ripping himself out of his nose dive and careened upward away from the planet and back into the welcoming shadows of outer space. He arced over the ship behind him until he dropped behind the spacecraft, ceasing to be prey and becoming the predator. Klanor fired.

The ship burst into flames—shards of glowing shrapnel flew past him, streaking the windshield and outer hull of his vessel.

More flashes of light caught his attention. Glancing over, Klanor watched as a lone transport shuttle sped away from two of Stein's fighter crafts, taking massive damage.

Scan that transport vessel over there. How many aboard?

There are five aboard. One Lanyran and the others of unknown origin.

As Klanor watched, he knew that this transport shuttle carried Brie and her family; there was no other explanation for Stein's men to fire upon it. He pulled the trigger on his ion torpedoes. Empty. Klanor switched over to his laser weapons, lining the two ships in his sights, and fired. Nothing. Panicked, he pulled switches and punched buttons, but nothing worked. The burning shrapnel that had struck him had damaged his weapons, rendering them useless and leaving him with only one option, one he intended to make good use of.

"Jifdar," said Klanor, tearing off the metal band that linked him telepathically to the ship and switching on his radio.

"Klanor! I want..."

"Tell Rynah that I'm sorry and I hope... I hope she finds peace."

Klanor moved his vessel, lining it up so that when he reached the ships before him, he would be between the transport vessel and the two that pursued it. One last check of his weapons confirmed that this was his only chance to save those aboard. Lasers filled the darkness around him, flashing upon him and revealing the grim, yet sorrowful, determination upon his face. He was almost there.

"Kla—"

Klanor burst between the transport shuttle and the two fighter crafts behind it, striking one, before the other plowed into them, unable to avoid the collision. Orange tongues of flames stretched out, illuminating the transport vessel as it entered Earth's atmosphere before vanishing.

Back on his ship, Jifdar's face fell, saddened by Klanor's death; all of his loathing, all of his hatred, dissipated, driven away by Klanor's last act.

Chapter 29
HEROES' STANCE

Brie's teeth chattered and ground together as the shuttled bounced about from the tumultuous force of re-entry, her arms wrapped around Sara in a protective squeeze. Smoke filled the shuttle, choking them and forcing them to cough, but Brie remained firm in her hold on her younger sister, glad to have her and her mother back.

"Hang on, everyone!" yelled Obiah from the cockpit.

Brie squeezed tighter and glanced at Alfric, who remained rigid, his usual stoic manner, not allowing the least bit of worry to crease his bushy brow. The shuttle lurched, forcing Brie's stomach into her throat, but she remained calm and shared a look with Rebecca; both gave a reassuring smile to the other. Deafening squeals erupted around them, stabbing their eardrums as the vessel landed and skittered across the ground—the landing gear had failed to deploy— sending chunks of concrete flailing about in a shower of sparks as they were all flung forward. It stopped. Shaking her head, Brie stood up and checked Sara and her mother. Grunts and an incessant pounding filled the area as Alfric rammed himself against the hatch, forcing it open. Hands on the other side seized it as well, and together, they ripped the hatch off its hinges, allowing fresh air to burst in and fill their nostrils.

Brie and Rebecca carried Sara out of the shuttle, while Alfric and Obiah disembarked last. Familiar faces surrounded them. Brie looked up into Rynah's smiling face—a part of her wished that the woman would smile more—and returned the gesture.

"I told you we would get them back," said Rynah.

"Thank you," whispered Brie, eyeing the others—Rynah, Solon, Tom, Joe, Achilles, and Solaris— around her; they had each ran for the transport vessel when they saw it drop from the sky. She glanced at the band around her wrist and frowned—it remained red. She showed it to Rynah, who returned the disappointed feeling.

"Tom," Rynah said, "you did set the autopilot correctly?"

"Yes," replied Tom. "I followed Achilles' precise instructions."

Rynah grimaced. "Something is wrong. It should have been here by now."

"You must learn to have faith," said Solon. "Sometimes what is perceived as a bad omen can prove to be an advantage." He held up his band which had just turned yellow. "It is close."

A thundering roar sounded in the distance, growing stronger and more intense until it reached them, pouring over them as it pounded their ears and sent a blast of wind howling past until… silence.

"Okay," said Tom, "I am going to ask the obvious question: what was that?"

Before anyone had a chance to answer, slow, steady thumps echoed around them, drawing closer. They all looked up as a giant wheel, mirroring a tank's, but the size of a parking garage, crept towards them, the pounding being nothing more than the grinding of its gears. The ships flew in from above, twisting and turning, as they changed shape and melded together, forming a barricade, with a long laser cannon for a snout that dwarfed even the tallest of trees and rolled through the streets, crushing cars and anything unfortunate enough to be in their way. In horror, they watched as the new, fortified vehicles strolled through the city, blasting the buildings, tearing holes in them, and plundered a path towards them.

"Jifdar," said Rynah in her com unit, "get me Klanor."

"Rynah, I..."

"Now, Jifdar!"

"Rynah,"—Jifdar's firm tone stopped her—"Klanor is dead."

Rynah dropped her arm, allowing the com unit to dangle by her side as Jifdar's "I'm sorry" came through. She watched as fires consumed the buildings nearby, while terrified screams fueled the chaos surrounding them. Rynah pulled the page with the watermark on it from her pocket, holding it in the pale sunlight, its rays burning through it, putting it on full display. Lines of the ancient tale flowed through her mind.

> Alone amidst darkened ruin
> stands the woman from whom all is written.
> Fires burn and chaos swarms,
> but none can compare to her scorn.

> Bravery unmatched against metallic monsters,
> our heroes summoned must save the city of towers.
> Six souls, whose will is stronger
> than any; aided by heaven's helper.

All of Marlow's warnings, his reaction to her when he had caught her creating a fancy signature for her name, his insistence that she learn to read ancient Lanyran, and his hours spent in his workshop came back to her. She realized—though in her heart she knew the answer the moment she had first seen that watermark— that the prophecy was never a prophecy, but an account of actual events, an account written by her. She crumpled the torn page and let if fall to the asphalt, carried away by the breeze.

"He knew," Rynah whispered, turning to Solaris who had walked up from behind.

Solaris nodded, a sorrowful and understanding look on her face.

"Look out!" yelled Achilles as the rolling building-sized tank fired a pulse cannon at them.

With quick movements, Alfric snatched a manhole cover—big enough to cover him—from the ground, placed there by a previous explosion, and ran to Sara and Rebecca, covering them and using the manhole cover as a protective shield, while the others dove behind overturned cars. They covered their heads from the debris that swept past them, pelting them, stinging their skin, and leaving red marks.

"Aim for the eyes!" Solaris yelled at Alfric, pointing at a section of the tank and what looked like gleaming, red eyes on a hideous beast that searched for prey.

Alfric obeyed. He stretched up to his full height, intimidating all around him, and swung the manhole cover behind him like a discus, before flinging it with a terrifying battle cry. It soared through the air, a deadly, spinning projectile, and struck the tank, shattering the "red eye" into hundreds of pieces. The tank stopped, its gears seized, spinning in rapid succession, as black smoke rose up, building into a thick fog with bright orange sparks, before—KABOOM! The tank exploded into bits and pieces and shards of metal crashed around them, clattering on the street.

More explosions ripped through the streets, sending searing infernos through the alleys that stretched for them, charring and burning everything in their path, followed by the marching machines, which had once been ships, that fired cannon blasts at civilians fleeing their onslaught, or punched holes into the sides of office buildings, bringing them crumbling down; clouds of ash and dust spewed into the air, swallowing them and coating them in white powder as it dissipated, though some remained, floating in the air, making them cough. They looked up just as another of the stadium-sized ships closed in, hovering above them; a crackling, electrified charge spilled from it.

"Move out!" Rynah yelled.

They all jumped to their feet, racing through the streets and dodging flying shrapnel, falling telephone lines and shards of broken glass that dropped from above. Sara tripped. Brie snatched her sister into her arms, while Joe helped her mother as they ran across the vibrating ground that shook beneath them, causing their sense of balance to become unsteady. They covered their mouths and noses as they ran through the fog of smoke while bits of burning insulation and paper floated around them. A chunk of smoldering concrete smashed into the ground near Solon's feet, forcing him to jump to the side in an effort to avoid it, while another cut off his path. Alfric yanked him away from danger as they continued to flee.

The ground shook, rattling their jaws. Another trembling thump echoed around them. Turning around, their hearts sank as they found one of the newly formed tanks behind them, its laser cannon aimed right for them. Just then, the sonic boom of two Air Force fighter jets deafened them as they dove for an attack, but the tank fired its laser cannon at them, vaporizing both planes; the falling embers being all that remained of them.

It turned its attention to Rynah and the others. They dove out of the way, seeking protection from anything they found, just as the tank fired. Sides of the towering buildings crashed around them, cracking the pavement of the street they were on as bits of rock stabbed their exposed skin, drawing a few spots of blood.

Another explosion ripped into the ground near Rynah, propelling her into the air; her gaze swept over those she had learned to call friends before she slammed into the ground; the air burst from her lungs, leaving her heaving for more. She watched, unable to move, as the tank approached, surrounded by Stein's men, its sights focused on her.

Brie burst from her place of hiding and ran for Rynah, aiming her laser rifle at the tank and releasing repeated fire at it. A man in armor dove for her. Brie dodged out of the way, clipping him in the stomach with the butt of her laser rifle, before firing two more shots at others that approached. She rushed to Rynah, hunkering next to her and checking her for injuries. The steady creak of the gears in the tank filled the eerie silence around them as it drew closer, with Brie and Rynah in its path.

"Brie!" Obiah tossed her a charge.

Brie caught it, detonated it, and chucked it at the tank before hauling Rynah to her feet and dragging her to safety.

They cheered as the charge ripped the tank in half, stopping it, but that joy was short-lived when a grinding noise alerted them to danger. Turning, their faces fell as they watched the damaged tank break in half into two pieces, one that had the ability of flight, and another that transformed into a hover vehicle as Stein's men closed in.

"GET DOWN!" screamed Solaris as she released a stun grenade into the air at shoulder height. It detonated just as they all dropped to the ground, sending a paralyzing, electrical charge in a radius of 300 yards. Stein's men dropped to the ground, quivering from the effects of being stunned, but the two pieces of the tank remained intact.

Before anyone could say anything, Joe bolted for a concrete truck that had been abandoned by a construction crew the moment the attack on the city had begun, while Solaris took off after the one man flying ship. Joe jumped over the jagged edges of the uneven road, avoiding falling debris as he raced the hover vehicle for the rig. He reached the cement truck. Ripping the door open, he jumped inside, finding the keys in the ignition. The hovercraft neared. Unwilling to allow it to escape, Joe turned the ignition; the engine roared to life, rumbling around him as he shifted the truck into first gear, and moved it in front of the oncoming hovercraft. Just before they collided, Joe leapt out of the truck, rolling on the asphalt, and covered his head when the hovercraft plowed into the construction vehicle, sending a mixture of smoke and liquid cement everywhere.

Elsewhere, Solaris chased after the one-man spacecraft, pushing the flying device that Achilles had made to its limits. She swerved and dodged the cannon fire that headed her way, but could not avoid witnessing the destruction that took place below her. The craft dove under a walkway in an effort to shake her. Undeterred, Solaris followed, missing the walkway with ease and startling a few people that had sought refuge there, and weaved in and out of the buildings, keeping her victim in sight. The spacecraft rose into the sky at a 90-degree angle, but that did little to stop Solaris, who matched its movements with ease. She closed in. Focused on it, Solaris fired her booster rockets, propelling herself straight upward. She slammed into the small craft, clutching it with her strong fingers.

The pilot jerked the ship to the left. Solaris held on. The craft banked to the right, and though her feet flailed to the side, Solaris refused to allow herself to let go. She jumped up on the ship and ran to the cockpit. The pilot dropped in altitude, forcing Solaris to fly away, but not for long. She chased after the spacecraft, closing in until she had caught up with it again and clung to the side. Pulling out her laser pistol, she fired at the hinges of the cockpit, forcing the shield to tear away and exposing the pilot. With quick movements, she reached in, unbuckled his harness, and grabbed the man, yanking him out of his seat and releasing him to gravity's clutches. Solaris hurried away from the ship and hovered in the sky, watching as it and the pilot fell to the ground below.

When she returned to her companions, she found them huddled together, watching the spreading fires from the massive machines that roved through the streets, sending out streams of fire and killing any who dared stop them. More Air Force fighter jets dove for the tanks, only to be shot down. Dismay greeted her when she landed beside Brie and Rynah.

"There's too many of them," said Obiah. "We cannot defeat them all."

"We can't give up either," said Brie.

"But we can't win," Obiah said.

"It depends on how you define victory," said Solon.

The others turned towards him.

"Hope is all we have now. Hope will be our victory," Solon continued. "Their numbers are more than ours, but that is not how battles are won; they are won by never giving up. We can leave now and will most assuredly lose, or we can finish what we started. The true measure of victory is about the completion of a task, even if it means ours deaths. Remember what it is we set out to do." He held up his wristband as it glowed yellow.

"It's not that simple," said Obiah.

"Make the choice you can live with," Solon replied.

"It ends now," Rynah said, her face set in grim determination. She checked her wristband; it still remained yellow.

"We can't leave them," said Solaris, referring to the city and its residents.

"Listen up!" yelled Rynah. "We are going to save this city, and then we are finishing this. You were right, Tom, that poem was more than a story, but it never predicted events; it recorded them, like an historical record."

"How do you know?" asked Brie.

"Because I wrote it," said Rynah, refusing to divulge further information upon their puzzled expressions. "Achilles, Obiah, if we can capture a couple of those things and get you inside, do you think you can use it to take out the others, or at least protect this city long enough for us to destroy the crystals?"

Obiah nodded his head, while Achilles added, "Sure, no problem. I was getting bored of all this running around anyway."

"Here"—Joe handed them a bag of explosives with their detonators—"you might need these."

Before Rynah could take them, Tom snatched the bag and looked inside, recognizing them and the fact that the detonators could be remotely controlled once activated. A plan formed in his mind.

"I can rig these."

"What?" demanded Joe.

"These detonators all have a computerized chip in them; that is how you are able to use a remote to set them off, but I can rig them so that one remote sets all of them off at the same time, even if they are in separate locations. I can also make it so that they serve as homing beacons for these tanks' targeting systems. I just need some time."

"How much?" said Rynah.

"Ten minutes."

"The crystals," said Rynah.

"Right here," said Brie, holding up her sack.

"Maybe Solaris should…" began Obiah.

"No," interrupted Rynah, "Brie can protect them. We are going to capture two of those things and then we go to the ships. Obiah, I'm not sure how…"

"I'll find my own ride," interrupted Obiah.

"Right," said Rynah. "Let's go."

Before Brie had a chance to move, Rebecca seized her wrist and pulled her closer, while Sara clung to her waist.

"You have to let me go, mom," said Brie, looking into her mother's worried and tearful eyes. "They need me."

"Brie…"

"Please, I have to finish this."

"I know," said her mother, releasing her. "Just come back."

"I will."—Brie hugged her mother and Sara—"I promise. Joe, take care of them." She pried Sara off her, despite the girl's terrified screams, and handed her to Rebecca. "Sara, I love you. I swear I'll come back! Joe!"

Joe took the girl and Brie's mother. "Go. I'll look after them."

Brie ran to Achilles, while Joe led her family away. After a quick explanation of the plan, Rynah gave Tom a communicator.

"Contact me when you're ready."

Brie jumped on Achilles' flying snowboard, disappearing into the sky with him, while Rynah allowed herself to be carried by Solaris, but before they left, Obiah grabbed her arm and whispered in her ear. "Be careful."

"Well, it's not like things can get any more interesting," Tom said to Solon and Alfric after Rynah and the others had left.

A sharp cry screeched behind him, forcing him to turn around just as a swirling mass of blue and green appeared, growing larger and expelling strong gales that whipped his clothing and forced him off his feet.

"I think they just did," said Solon.

The high pitched screech sounded again. Alfric grabbed Tom and Solon, throwing them to the side and covering them with his massive form just as a pterosaur burst from the swirling mass, flying high into the sky and causing a fighter plane to crash. Its wings stretched out as it streaked across the blue sky, an ominous shape foreshadowing the coming of death and destruction. They watched as the pterosaur banked to the left, coming back to them.

"Seriously!" yelled Tom. "What in the…"

"We need to get up high," interrupted Alfric, looking back at the machines that rolled through the city. A cable caught his attention. He snatched it and coiled it for later use.

"Agreed," said Solon.

"And you want to take on a dinosaur?" said Tom.

"I fear no beast of the sky, nor of the sea," replied Alfric.

"Of course you don't. You know, you're going to need a plan," Tom said.

Both Alfric and Solon stared at him.

"What are you looking at?" Tom demanded.

"Live bait," said Solon.

"Hey, I may look like chocolate, but that doesn't mean I taste like it!"

Both Alfric and Solon gave him quizzical looks, not understanding the reference.

"I'm not doing it. You can't make me." Tom crossed his arms in defiance.

Alfric pulled out his sword and held it before him.

"Nice knowing you," said Tom.

He darted out from behind the fallen concrete wall they had hidden behind, tucking the remote in his pocket with care so as not to press the button. Tom's eye's darted in every direction, every shadow spelled danger, but he refused to show fear. Another cry pierced the silence. He stopped. Looking upward, he thought he saw a dark shape fly overhead, but he could not be certain of the truthfulness of his senses. He continued meandering through the empty street, past fallen lamp posts, his feet crunching the shattered glass beneath him, all the while vowing revenge against Solon—he'd get even with Alfric, but thought it might be too risky to take on a hardened Viking—if he survived.

"Come out little flying dinosaur," Tom mumbled to himself. "Come and get the nice, tasty morsel."

A bone-chilling cry from behind stopped him. With trepidation, Tom turned around, raising his head, until he stared into the yellow eyes of the pterosaur. He wiped his sweaty palms on his pants leg, allowing his nervousness to dictate his movements. The prehistoric beast reared its head back and released an earth shattering cry as it prepared to strike, but before it could, Solon burst from a pile of rubble with a metal trashcan lid in his hands, holding it up so that it reflected the sunlight into the animal's eyes. Blinded, the pterosaur jerked its head to the side just as Alfric dove from above, his sword held before him, and plunged it into the side of the pterosaur, wounding it. The beast flapped its wings and took off, forcing Alfric off it, but the Viking refused to be subdued and jumped to his feet, twirling the cabled over his head before releasing it. It wrapped around the pterosaur's leg. As the line pulled taut, Alfric gripped Solon's arm, who in turn, seized Tom's, and all three left the ground as the ancient beast pulled them into the sky.

"You're seriously insane!" Tom screamed at Alfric, who ignored him.

The ground grew smaller as the pterosaur carried them higher—a national guardsman saw them, almost dropping his weapon, but Tom just waved, for lack of anything else to do—and closer to the building that Alfric kept his eyes fixed upon. They great beast flapped its massive wings, its breaths coming in short gasps as it tired. Alfric spotted the edge of a roof. Timing it as best he could, he released his hold on the cable, and the three of them plummeted to the roof below, landing hard, while the pterosaur disappeared through another swirling mass of fog and vanished.

"You know," said Tom, as he caught his breath, "a little warning would be nice."

One of Stein's ground troops appeared from nowhere, attacking Tom before he had a chance to regain his feet, but before he could finish him, Solon jumped on the man, sweeping his feet out from underneath him and plunging a dagger into the man's chest. Another attacked. Solon whirled around and flung his knife at him, striking him in the neck, while Alfric took out three more.

"I think that Viking has had too much of an effect on you," Tom joked to Solon.

The whine of a hoverbike approached. Before it had reached them, Tom snatched a lone brick from the roof and flung it at the pilot, striking him in the head, and watched as the bike spiraled to the ground below. Tom and the others raced to the ledge of the roof, leaning over the side and watching the spiraling flames that rose upward amidst black smoke that filled the sky, turning it burnt red.

"I hope she knows what she's doing," Tom said, referring to Rynah, as he set to work rigging the charges.

Rynah, Solaris, Brie, and Achilles soared over the city, trying not to think about the devastation below, as they focused on the armed hover vehicles they aimed for. They dove for one of the tanks. Rynah pulled out her laser pistol and nodded at Solaris to go in, taking the lead. As they lowered, Achilles handed Brie two homemade charges—his own design—before depositing her on the top of the rolling tank.

Brie crouched low, steadying herself, as Rynah landed beside her. They looked at each other before Rynah pointed, saying, "Up front!"

Brie ran to the front of the tank, holding her arms out to maintain her balance from its rolling motion. She stopped. A gap between her and the hatch led straight to the ground. If she fell, she would be crushed by the giant wheels. Stepping back a few feet, Brie clutched the charges tighter before breaking into a sprint; she stretched out her legs and leapt over the gap, landing on her knees. She jumped to her feet and looked behind her at Rynah before continuing on. She watched in horror as a hoverbike flew next to Rynah and the pilot jumped on her. Rynah rolled over the side of the tank, reaching out, and grabbed a rail just before she fell to the ground; her feet dangled beneath her, the tips of her boots brushing against the grinding gears.

Brie started for her friend, but Rynah waved her away.

"Go!" she yelled. "Just go!"

Brie obeyed, leaving Rynah to heave herself back up onto the machine. The incessant drumming of the machine's gears hammered Brie's ears as she raced for the hatch in the front. A hoverbike buzzed past her and a man jumped off it, landing next to her. He seized her arms and threw her to the side, but Brie hooked her foot around his leg, using her momentum to knock him over. She clambered back to her feet, the charges still in her hands. With no sign of the man who had attacked her, Brie hurried to the hatch. Unslinging her laser rifle, she fired two blasts at the latch, breaking it off, and forced open the hatch, tossing the two charges inside, and jumped off the tank into Solaris' waiting arms.

As they flew upward, a strong grip seized her foot. Looking down, Brie realized that the man who had attacked her moments before had lunged at her, making one last effort to be rid of her. She kicked him on the top of the head, but his grip remained firm. Brie's stomach jumped into her throat as they dropped a few feet while Solaris struggled to fly away, but she could not support the extra weight. Brie kicked the man on the head again, ramming the heel of her foot down as hard as she could. He let go. With the extra weight gone, Brie and Solaris shot upward, forcing Solaris to spread the flaps on her wings to slow them down as she swerved and headed for the second tank.

Just as they almost neared their target, a laser blast struck one of the wings strapped to Solaris' back. They smashed into the pavement below, rolling across it at an incredible speed before coming to a slow stop. Dizzy, Brie lifted her head, standing on all fours as she cleared the fog in her mind, wondering why her backpack felt warm against her skin.

"Solaris?" whispered Brie.

She looked over at Solaris, who lay sprawled on the ground, shaking her head amidst silt and bits of crumbled marble that danced around her as the ground vibrated. Brie glanced around, but the tank was in front of them, so why did she feel as though something was wrong? The wind picked up, blowing bits of her mousy brown hair into her pale face before drawing it upwards. She looked up. Hovering above Solaris was another swirling mass of ashen fog; the clouds that formed it spun with increasing speed, pulling at everything that lay within its reach. Brie felt her jacket tug at her.

She jumped up to run for Solaris. The moment she had gone four steps, she fell to the ground; her foot had gotten caught in a fallen cable.

"Solaris!" she yelled, but covered her head the moment the fender of a car raced past her, disappearing into the churning fog.

Solaris reached at the ground for something to grab hold of, her hands clawing at it, leaving scraggly lines in the dust, but nothing supported the strain of the force that clung to her. Brie watched, helpless, as Solaris' feet lifted into the air. The warmness of her backpack had increased, until it burned through the material, singeing her skin. She ripped the bag off her back and opened it. The crystals glowed. Curious, Brie reached in and pulled one out, it's black color changed to a pale white as the warmth filled her hand, not a burning feeling that caused pain, but a comforting one. The black color of the others faded to an amber glow. Brie didn't know why—and in the years that passed, she was never able to explain it—but she felt her mind linked to the crystals, different from the telepathic link she had once shared with Solaris.

"Please," whispered Brie, "help her."

The crystal in her hand glowed even brighter. As her eyes met with Solaris', a streak of blue light shot from the crystal to the others in the backpack, connecting them in a jagged web before shooting away from her and striking the swirling mass above Solaris. It disappeared.

Brie untangled the cord around her foot and ran for Solaris, helping her to her feet.

"Are you okay?"

"I should be asking you that," replied Solaris.

"I'll be fine," said Brie. "Come on. We need to get back to the others."

They both ran down the street back to the rolling tanks where Rynah was, hoping to reach her in time.

Rynah watched as Brie ran off to the hatch, the gears gripping the soles of her boots as she tried to brace her feet against the side of the vehicle so as to boost herself up. Straining, Rynah tightened her arm muscles and hauled herself back onto the tank, where she lay for a moment, catching her breath. A flicker of movement raced past her eyes as a steel blade headed for her. Rynah rolled out of the way just as the tip of the knife jabbed the metal surface with a plink, sending sparks out to the sides. She reached for her weapon, but a sudden jolt caused her to drop it, and it clattered to the side, getting stuck between two hooks.

The man with the knife lunged for her again. Rynah shoved her arms out, bracing it against the man's wrist and holding the knife away from her, but with each millisecond, it dipped lower until… Rynah jerked her head to the side just as the blade stabbed the tank; it's edge pricked her cheek, drawing a few droplets of blood.

While the man drew the knife back, Rynah rammed the point of her knee into his back, knocking him off balance before wrenching his arm to the left, forcing him on his side. She jumped to her feet. They faced each other. The tank turned to the right, since, thanks to Brie, no one was operating it, and the man jumped to his feet as the side of the hovertank tore into the outer walls of office buildings, creating a shower of crumbling insulation and marble. The man charged Rynah. She leapt to the side and spun around, elbowing him in the back before swiping his left foot out from under him. He recovered with ease and faced her again, waving the knife before him.

A laser blast stole her attention long enough for Rynah to watch as Solaris was shot out of the sky. With no time to think what had happened, she turned back to the man with the knife. He sprang towards her, knife outstretched. Remembering her basic training from her time in the Lanyran fleet, Rynah ducked to the side, brought her arm up beneath her attacker's wrist, deflecting the blow, and used her other hand to grasp his thumb, breaking it. He dropped the knife.

She dove for it, but her attacker caught her around the middle and slammed her into the surface of the tank. She wriggled free of his grasp and did a backwards somersault away from him. Both on their hands and knees, they glared at one another. Rynah faked an attacked. While the man tried to block, she spun around and kicked him hard in the face twice, knocking him off the hovertank and to the ground below.

The hover vehicle rolled back into the street and weaved from side to side as it attempted to correct its course. Rynah looked up. *Where was Obiah?*

The roar of a motorcycle answered her question. She whirled around and watched as Obiah raced up from behind on an abandoned motorbike he had helped himself to. Rynah welcomed the sound of its engine as he rode up beside the hovertank, matching its speed.

"Obiah," yelled Rynah, "we need to switch places!"

He brought the bike closer.

The wind whipped Rynah's emerald hair to the side as she glanced ahead in time to see the tank close in on a car directly ahead. She dropped to her stomach, clinging to the rails that were there, while Obiah turned the bike, jerking away from her to avoid the car. The tank rolled over it, jumping into the air. Rynah's body bounced in time to its movements, hitting hard against the metal siding; she felt the bruise form on her knees and elbows. When the tank straightened out, she hurried to her feet, and Obiah pulled up alongside her again, near the foot well that was just below her.

Rynah gripped a handhold, eased herself down the side of the speeding tank, and placed her foot on the foothold. With her back against the rumbling tank, she looked into Obiah's eyes, who nodded his head. They both jumped at the same time, before either of them could rethink their actions, with Rynah jumping onto the motorcycle, while Obiah leapt onto the side of the tank and clutched the handholds in a tight grip. He scrambled to the top of the tank, signaling to Rynah that he was fine. Rynah gripped the handlebars of the motorcycle and sped away down a side street to where she remembered seeing Solaris and Brie fall, while Obiah ran across the hovertank to the open hatch, jumped in, and seized control of it.

Tom's hands were a flurry of movement as he took the detonators apart, pulling out the microchips with care, and resetting them so that when activated, they would light up the screens of the tank's computers. With all of the time he had spent with Solaris and her instruction, he knew enough about the Lanyran targeting systems to put their codes into the chips. Once he replaced them, Tom stuck a detonator in a block of C4. He handed them to Solon and Alfric, who placed them back in the bag.

"Careful," Tom reminded them. Though the detonators were rigged to not activate until he pressed the remote, he preferred caution.

"My hands are steady," Alfric said.

"Rynah," Tom said in his communicator, "they're ready. Where's Achilles?"

"On his way," replied Rynah. "You have the remote?"

"Yes," Tom said, holding a black box in his hands.

"With a big red button," mumbled Alfric.

"Don't press it until I tell you to," Rynah instructed.

"You expect me to wait that long?" joked Tom, receiving a reproachful look from Alfric. "Understood," Tom said, clicking off the communicator.

Achilles flew in from above, hands outstretched, and Tom tossed him the bag. As the man left, he settled in for the part he hated most—waiting.

Unaware of Rynah nearing their location, Solaris and Brie ran off to the nearest tank, following the plan. They ducked when laser fire struck the ground near their feet as they hurried toward an overhang where they crouched while two hoverbikes flew overhead. They watched as the hoverbikes came back for them. Brie noticed the edge of a thin, brick wall with posters advertising the state fair on it, with an open manhole before it.

"I have an idea," she said, pointing at the wall.

Before she could step out from under the overhang, Solaris snatched her arm, knowing what the girl had in mind.

"I'll do it."

The hoverbikes approached. Solaris bolted from beneath the overhang, just in time for the pilots of the hoverbikes to see her. She ran, pacing herself, while staying just ahead of them, using her body to block the view of the edge of the brick wall. Laser fire pelted the ground near her feet, singeing them, but her nanotechnology absorbed the damage as she ran. The whine of the bikes pursued her. Just before she reached the wall, Solaris dropped to the ground, sliding on her side as she fell into the uncovered manhole and covered her head while the two hoverbikes crashed into the wall.

She poked her head out of the dark hole. The point of a laser rifle greeted her as Stein's men surrounded her, shoving Brie, who held her hands up, into the middle of the circle they formed. Solaris crawled out of the manhole, raising her hands, while giving Brie a curt nod. Understanding the message, Brie dropped to the ground, while Solaris seized the laser rifle of one of the men, pointing it at another and fired. She bashed the butt of the weapon into the first before firing at him.

A laser blast clipped her shoulder, causing the nanotechnology in her skin to flicker as it attempted to heal her, though a black hole remained in her jacket. In turn, Solaris fired at him. More of Stein's men approached. She crouched low just as they pulled the triggers on their weapons, but Brie lunged at the legs of one of them, forcing him to the ground and giving Solaris a chance to recover. While Brie struggled with the man she had attacked, Solaris moved from person to person in swift, fluid movements, disarming them before killing them.

A shriek stopped her. Solaris turned from the men she had dispatched. The man Brie had attacked held her around the throat and, try as she might, she was unable to break free. Before Solaris could react, the roar of a motorcycle pierced the air, echoing off the buildings around them as Rynah rode up, jumping off the bike and plowing into the man that held Brie. They rolled across the asphalt, but Rynah was quick, jumping to her feet and lunging for the man and forcing him into a pole. He swung at her. She ducked, seized the knife from her boot and jammed it into the man's throat.

Shots rang out as National Guardsmen appeared, killing those of Stein's men that attempted to sneak up from behind. Once done, they pointed their weapons at Solaris, Rynah, and Brie, who clumped together.

"Drop your weapons!"

They obeyed.

"Girl," said the commanding officer to Brie, "come over here."

Brie remained next to Solaris and Rynah, who observed the situation, each looking for a way to overcome it.

"I said come over here," repeated the commanding officer.

"No," Brie replied.

"Get over…"

"I can't do that," said Brie. "They are my friends."

"They are the ones responsible for this attack."

"They are trying to help us."

Solaris moved. In reaction, the soldiers trained their weapons on her, ready to fire, but Brie got between them, unwilling to allow any of her friends to die.

"Get out of the way," said the commanding officer.

"Soldier," said Brie, "if you wish to kill them, you'll have to shoot me as well."

They hesitated, having orders not to harm civilians, but before anyone could make a decision, the pilot Rynah had saved earlier, and who had joined with this unit after landing, burst through the crowd, yelling, "Stop! Stand down, all of you!"

"Sir, they…"

"I gave you a direct order," said the pilot.

"With all due respect, Major…"

"As you have noted, Captain, I am a Major, and despite the fact that I am Air Force, I outrank you. Now, I am telling you one last time, stand down."

The captain gave the go-ahead to his men and they lowered their weapons, allowing Rynah and Solaris to retrieve theirs.

"Sir, permission to speak freely?"

"Granted."

"Why are you trusting them?" asked the captain.

The pilot looked at Rynah before answering. "Because she saved my life."

A cannon blast struck the building the next street over, its resounding boom drowned by the screams that emanated from it, as people had taken refuge there in an effort to escape Stein's attack. Next to it was another of the hovertanks. It's lanky top half swiveled, firing laser blasts at two people who had attempted to flee, before turning back to the cornered survivors.

"Achilles," whispered Rynah into her earpiece, "how are you doing with those charges."

"Give me another minute," came his reply.

"Thirty seconds," replied Rynah.

Four hoverbikes drew near, ignoring them and heading straight for the complex with the cowering survivors. Rynah spotted a fire escape; a plan formulated in her mind as she watched the trajectory of the hoverbikes and the massive ship hovering above, firing streaks of teal electrical light at various points of the city.

"Do you think you can fly one of those?" she asked the pilot.

"Sure," he replied. "What do you have in mind?"

"Those people need our help," said Rynah. "Solaris, we need a distraction."

Solaris smiled and ran off.

"The pilot here…" Rynah began.

"Major Dawson," the pilot interrupted her.

Rynah gave an apologetic look before continuing. "Major Dawson and I are going to commandeer two of those hoverbikes, the rest of you need to get those people out of there."

The captain of the National Guard unit glanced at Major Dawson, who nodded his approval. Before Rynah and the major left, she pulled Brie close to her, whispering in her ear, "No matter what happens, keep those crystals safe, and when its time, get to the ship."

"Understood," said Brie, clutching the bag closer, determined to not fail.

Rynah and Major Dawson hurried over to a fire escape, pulling the ladder down and scrambling up until they had reached the fourth floor. She watched as Solaris strolled into the fray until she stood between the approaching tanks, marching men, and those hunkered in the complex. But Solaris did something that Rynah couldn't believe. She pulled out a handheld laser cannon—and Rynah had no idea how she had managed to get one of those—and fired, striking one of the tanks in the center, before disappearing behind a hailstorm of laser fire.

The whine of the hoverbikes grew louder. Focusing her attention on them, as both she and the major slunk into the shadows, she waited.

"Now!"

Both Rynah and Major Dawson leapt over the railing of the fire escape, each landing on a hoverbike, both of which took up the rear, and threw its pilot to the ground. Rynah locked onto the two in front of her and fired, sending them plummeting downward. She glanced at the major. Though he had never been on a flying motor-bike, he figured out its controls quickly, as the logistics of flight are the same no matter where in the universe you are.

"Just ease into the controls," said Rynah. "They don't take a lot of pressure. Where you look is where you'll go."

He nodded, indicating that he understood.

They veered off to the hovertanks below, splitting apart and at-tacking one hovertank from both sides. They fired. The hovercraft kept moving. The air filled with laser fire as Stein's ground troops fired upon them, sending shockwaves towards them as they tried to converge on the hovertank. They closed in. Just before either of them could pull the trigger, the tank's main laser gun swiveled around and focused on Rynah. It fired. She banked to the right, but the blast damaged the systems on her hoverbike, causing it to sputter and dip.

She managed to keep it in the air, but could not turn. *Pew!—Pew!—Pew!* A hoverbike had settled behind her, firing all of its weapons at her, and with her inability to change course, Rynah was forced to go straight and hope that he missed. Her bike lurched. Her pulse thudded in her ears as she tried to keep her craft level, while avoiding being shot down. The hoverbike behind her lined her up in its sights, the pilot's finger closing on the trigger.

Green laser fire slammed into the hoverbike behind her and

Major Dawson burst from the chaos, firing more shots at the hovercraft behind her, knocking it from the sky. Rynah's bike groaned as it dipped again. She looked up. A triangular office building loomed ahead and she headed straight for it. She fiddled with the controls, doing her best to make a quick repair so that she could fly the craft, but nothing worked. Her cheeks burned from the stinging wind as her hoverbike headed for its doom. Major Dawson appeared beside, maneuvering his bike as close to hers as possible.

"COME ON!" he yelled, holding his hand out to her.

Rynah drew in a breath and jumped. She slipped and dropped to the side of the major's bike, clinging to the seat, and her feet swung to the side from the force of its flight. A strong arm reached down, seized hers, and yanked her upward until she was positioned safely in the hoverbike's seat. They turned, speeding away from the office building as her abandoned bike burst into flames, showering those below with chunks of burning metal.

They headed back to one of the hovertanks, but Rynah paid no attention to it; in a small clearing, where none could miss her, stood Solaris, her arm outstretched with one last remaining explosive charge.

"There!" Rynah pointed at Solaris.

Major Dawson diverted their original trajectory, aiming for Solaris as she fired upon any who tried to take her down, while keeping her arm stretched high above her head with the charge in her fist, glinting in the sunlight. They dove for her, buzzing the heads of those below them, speeding towards Solaris. Rynah leaned out and snatched the explosive device from her hand and Major Dawson flew upward, banking towards the hovercraft and snaking their way through the city streets.

"Get down near one of those," yelled Rynah, indicating one of the hovertanks.

Major Dawson obeyed, hovering low, just above one of the tanks.

"What are you going to do?"

In response, Rynah jumped off the hoverbike, landing on the hovertank below, while Major Dawson flew away to provide cover fire. Amidst the stray bits of laser fire that streamed in every direction, Rynah raced across the top of the hovertank, leaping over the gap in its center, and skidded to a halt when she reached the hatch, forcing it open. She set the charge to stun and dropped it in. Before it detonated, Rynah jumped off the tank, somersaulting to a stop. She looked up. More of Stein's men closed in.

Wasting no time, Rynah ran for the complex where Brie and the National Guardsmen were busy helping the people gathered there get to safety.

"Get these people out of here now!"

In response to her orders, Brie and the guardsmen worked faster, dragging the frightened civilians out of the building and pushing them down a manhole into the sewer and the safety it provided.

"Achilles!" she yelled into her communicator.

"Here!" Achilles flew in on his flying snowboard and Rynah directed him to the hovertank she had just disabled. He saluted her and took off.

"Tom," said Rynah, "press the button."

Within seconds, the charges that Achilles had placed on the ships hovering over the city detonated. All around them fire spewed from the spacecraft above them as the hovertanks spread throughout the city, stopped, turned, and aimed at the nearest ship; their red targeting lights illuminating the underside of each vessel. Thunder rocketed the area around them, shattering the remaining glass in the buildings surrounding them as the hovertanks fired upon their new targets, tearing them to pieces. One by one, each ship burst into flames and plunged into the streets below.

A light drew Rynah's attention. She glanced at the thin band around her wrist, situated next to the bracelet Marlow had given her long ago; it had turned green. A flicker of movement forced her to look up. Solaris walked towards her, ignoring the ashen smoke that swirled around her, and not a mark was on her body. They locked eyes a moment until Solaris touched the band on her wrist and disappeared in an array of yellow and orange light.

"Achilles…" began Rynah.

"Good luck," said Achilles, knowing what she was about to tell him.

"Fons, Tre," Rynah said into her communicator, "it's time."

She touched her wristband, just as Brie, Tom, Solon, and Alfric touched theirs, and vanished.

Chapter 30
THE DRAGON SHIP

Rynah appeared on the transporter pad with Solaris already there. "The others?" she asked.

"They've reported in," replied Solaris.

"Brie," Rynah said into the com unit.

"Here," Brie's voice echoed from the speakers; she had transported to the ship on the moon with Alfric, while Tom and Solon had gone to the one that had just arrived from Mars, having been set on autopilot and timed to arrive after Brie had rescued her family.

"Converge," ordered Rynah, putting a thin, metallic band, no thicker than a finger, around her forehead; the others did the same, including Solaris. Their thoughts linked as one as they each connected with the vessel they were on.

The hanger doors, which had been disguised as the lakebed, completed with underwater plants and pebbled sand, opened, allowing the water to rush inside and consuming what had once been protected. The ship rose through the dark waters of Lake Tahoe; white crests peaked and foamed on the surface, forming fluidic towers that crashed into the glassy surface of the crystal blue water as it ascended, slowly poking through—drops of white liquid sprayed any in its path—until it had cleared the lake. Upward, the massive vessel went—those strolling on the beach watched in awe when the ship blocked the sun—as water poured from it, draining from every crevice where it had collected. Gold spires cast long shadows across the roving waves, stretching up the white sand and overwhelming the vendors that had set up shop, which lay abandoned as their owners joined the gathering crowd that gaped at the spectacle.

The engines rumbled, causing the ground to tremble and the pine trees to shudder—needles fell from their limbs—as the ship rose upward, silhouetted by the dark blue and cloudless sky.

Engines at maximum, Rynah said telepathically to Solaris.

The people below watched as the engines revved up, generating enough power to break free of the Earth's gravitational pull. An orange glow surrounded them, matching the deafening sound that escaped before a—Pop!—and it had gone.

A similar spectacle took place on the moon as Brie piloted the ship. A dark crater opened—causing quite a stir at NASA, taking as many pictures as they could with the Hubble telescope—and yellow light spilled from the gaping hole with a sliver of silver poking through, reflecting the sun's rays. The sliver grew into a slanted oval that stretched to a darkened window, which resembled the pupil of an eye, followed by a spectacle of gold and jade, twisted together; its smoothness reflected the gray surface of the moon. It eased out of the crater, freed from its prison before speeding to the earth and the other vessel, its twin, that lingered near the planet.

Brie's hands shook as she directed the ship, taking a quick glance at Alfric, who also wore a band around his head, linking him to the vessel and her mind, her nerves consuming her.

You'll do fine, Alfric's voice said in her head. *We all have complete faith in you.*

Brie smiled as she concentrated on directing the ship to where the third piece stood alone, amidst speeding fighter ships and blasts of laser fire. She watched as the vessel Rynah and Solaris were on approached the lone ship from behind, blocking her view of the earth for just a moment, before falling in line with it. She raced for the two ships, only slowing down when she had reached them.

Our thoughts are linked, Solaris spoke to all of them through the telepathic link. *We just need to connect the three ships.*

Easier said than done, came Tom's thoughts.

If it can be spoken, chimed Solon, *it can be done.*

Just think it. Solaris' irritation came through.

One by one, they each thought of the three parts being a single ship and the vessels they were on, as though knowing what to do, lined up, extending docking arms that connected to one another and retracted until what had been three distinct ships, morphed into one massive vessel with seamless lines. Metal flaps popped up, clinging to one another with a magnetic seal and forming what looked like spikes stretching down the center of the vessel from end to end. Ridges lined the bow of the ship, curving and twisting in such a way that it gave it the appearance of a head with fanged teeth and a stubby snout with whiskers and honey-colored eyes that burned red as it crept into the sun's light, watching all that moved before them. More ridges curled around the base of the ship, giving it the appearance of folded wings with rainbows that burst from its edges. To anyone with an ounce of an imagination, the massive vessel looked like a dragon.

The small fighter ships stopped mid-battle, awed by the shadow that the newly created spacecraft formed, which engulfed them all. None dared move, transfixed as they watched the ship take shape and steam escape from where its locks sealed, as though the dragon's nostrils flared.

Once the gears stopped grinding and the echoing sound of the snapping of the locks dissipated, Rynah and Solaris, who nodded her head, faced each other before Rynah spoke to the others through the telepathic link. *We need to find the dragon's heart.*

Solaris, where is the center of this ship located? asked Tom.

Why would you need... began Solaris before Brie cut in.

Because the heart of anything is the center of it—it's core: like the phrase, "The heart of the matter."

Precisely, replied Tom.

Solaris brought up the specs of the ship—shapes and dots danced before her as holoscreens materialized—her fingers tapping the specs that floated before her as she studied the schematics. *Here.* Solaris pointed at a small area that formed the center of the ship. She sent the map to the others.

Meet us there, said Rynah though the telepathic link. She ripped the metal band from her head and paused as a low rumble emanated along the outer hull of the ship; the battle outside had started again, except all of Stein's vessels focused on the dragon ship. She gripped the rail just as the vessel shifted from a laser canon blast.

"Solaris..."

Before Rynah could finish, Solaris snapped her fingers and more holoscreens flickered to life and her hands sped across it in rapid succession—white circles forming where she touched it—before disappearing.

"Your orders?" came a male voice.

Rynah cringed when she heard it, but turned around to face the holographic projection that had made itself known when she first boarded the vessel under Lake Tahoe.

"Defend the ship," answered Solaris.

"I meant her orders," said the holographic man, pointing at Rynah.

"We are under attack," said Rynah. "Defend this ship at all costs. If I am unable to issue you a command, you are to follow Solaris' instructions."

"Understood," said the holographic man.

Rynah and Solaris dashed off, charging through an open doorway and into a narrow corridor. Neon lights lined the sides with small specs of different colors—resembling gems more than bulbs—that flared to life as they raced past, leading the way. The hall forked.

"Which way?" asked Rynah.

Solaris pointed to the left. Their stomping feet pounded the metal beneath them as they ran. They slid down the rails of a staircase to a walkway until they entered another corridor. Just when Rynah began to question Solaris' sense of direction, she stopped before a domed entranceway—bronze spirals snaked up the sides, outlining it—with strange writing carved into the double doors. Light spilled from it, scanning her and Solaris. Before she could move, the locks released, emitting loud clangs and bangs as the doors opened, swinging inward, and a purplish-gold light spilled from it, outlining Rynah's astonished face.

"Whoa," whispered Tom as he ran up behind her with Solon.

The same light scanned their faces before allowing them passage. They each stepped through the doors into a room with a spire—jagged pyramid shapes dotted it—in the center that stretched upward, going through a transparent domed ceiling, with gold lines that spread from its center to the outer edges, and allowed the stars to shine through it. In the spire itself rested a hole that lit up the moment they approached.

"Rynah!" Brie ran towards her. She and Alfric had entered the chamber moments before the others.

Tom glanced around at the luminescent walls that displayed the same jagged pyramids on them, which also lined the spire. He reached out to touch one, but Solon jerked his hand back, shaking his head as a warning.

"You're right," said Tom, remembering that they had a more important matter to attend.

The ship tipped to the side a moment as the gravity center shifted from being bombarded by laser fire, missiles, and ion torpedoes. Each of them held out their arms to balance themselves, while hurrying over to the conclave of the spire.

"Now what?" asked Tom.

Solaris recited lines from the poem.

Journey's end you have reached,
but now I must beseech
you to pay careful attention
to you inner intentions.

Remember well that the crystals
feast off your innermost thoughts
and all that dwells within your heart.

Make what is broken whole
Make what is broken one.
And not just the treasured gems,
but the place where your anger stems.

In the blackened space, now empty tomb,
you must now replace, and dispel the gloom.
Put back what has been broken apart.
Give back the dragon's heart.

"The crystals," said Rynah.

Brie handed her the bag with the crystals, still a pale blue from when Brie had asked them to save Solaris. They each took one, clutching the different-shaped pieces in their hands, and placed them in the small hole, but none of the crystals remained. As they tried to get them to stay put, Solon realized why the crystals seemed to jump back out.

"It is a puzzle," he said, "and we must put them together as such."

Scolding herself for being so stupid, Rynah studied each piece as she pictured how it went together. Again, the five companions fit the crystals together, while Solaris watched, knowing that she was not to touch one, and as each piece fused with another they glowed brighter, until they had all eight pieces joined.

"We're missing one," said Solaris.

"No," Alfric countered, "we are missing two." He pointed at the chipped area on the top and the empty space at the base, which seemed to be missing a curved, rectangular hold.

"Curse this!" screamed Rynah, the crystals turned red, matching her anger. "We're missing the ninth and now you tell me there is another!"

Before Rynah had a chance to allow her frustration to control her, Brie placed a gentle hand on her shoulder. "We'll figure this out. All of us."

As Rynah calmed herself, the crystals color changed back to pale blue. "I don't know what to do, or where to look."

"Which is why you have us," said Brie.

"Yeah," smiled Tom, "because six misfits are better than one."

As another ion torpedo struck the outer hull of the ship, and its weapons returned fire, something sparked in Rynah's brain—a thought, and a very delicate one at that, but the more she focused on it, the more she remembered Marlow's message.

"The power of three," she whispered.

Confused looks stared back at her.

"Remember the planet we were transported to and the holographic version of my grandfather and his message: 'Remember the power of three.'"

"How does that help us?" asked Tom.

"Most of Lanyr's legends stem from the notion that three is a powerful number," Solaris answered.

Rynah pulled Marlow's amber ring out from under her shirt and yanked it from the chain around her neck. Though amber was in abundance on Lanyr, there were three regions where it seemed to form the most, but Marlow always insisted that this ring was special, just like her, saying when she was still a child about how Rynah was stronger than the power of three. She flipped the ring over and looked at the inscription 3^3 that was on the back. She had never given it much thought until that moment. The memory of the time she had visited Marlow in the psychiatric institution and his insistence that she protect his ring struck her and she now understood why he was so adamant. It wasn't just a ring, but a vessel for something else.

Two things caught her attention: the metal of the ring, which matched the metal of the wristband she had always worn, and the amber of the ring, which had abandoned its usual honey color for the same pale blue of the crystals. It was the ninth crystal. Rynah twisted and pulled at it, breaking the glue that held it to the metal band, and placed it in the area that appeared to be chipped and watched as it fused together and glowed even more. With the crystals joined, her bracelet sprang to life as lights danced across it, lighting up the symbols that were engraved on it. The flickering light continued, slow at first, but its pace increased until it flashed at such quick intervals that their eyes thought that the bracelet had turned into a single light.

A gust of wind blast their faces, choking them. Coughing, they bent their heads low as Rynah struggled with the fact that she had carried two pieces of the puzzle for so long.

"Rynah now!" yelled Solaris, over the roar of the wind.

Rynah took the bracelet her grandfather had given her and placed it in the empty space of the crystals' base. The wind stopped, but before either of them had a chance to breathe, the newly formed crystal turned white, sending a force that knocked each of them backward. The winds started up again, tearing into them and forcing them to remain on their knees.

"We need to get out of here now!" yelled Solaris. "Achilles warned that they might not be stable after having been separated for so long."

Rynah nodded in agreement. "Computer!" she yelled, but stopped as the air grew still with an eeriness that chilled her. The ship lurched to the side, flinging all of them to one end of the room, before jerking again. Each of them crashed against a wall, except Brie, who lay in the middle of the floor, shaking her head in an effort to regain her senses.

A swirling mass opened next to her and tugged at her.

"Brie, get out of there now!" screamed Solaris, who recognized the anomaly.

Brie turned. Before she could react, Rynah raced across the room and shoved her aside, away from the swirling mass, just as another lurch of the ship flung her towards it, and she disappeared behind the pale fog of the anomaly—the replicated crystal she had made fell from her pocket and was also snatched by the vortex— just as it vanished, plunging them all into darkness with the newly formed crystal as their only source of light.

"Rynah!" screamed Brie, trying to get to where Rynah had been, but Alfric held her back.

"We cannot help her now," he said. "She is gone."

Tears rolled down Brie's cheeks. "Why?" she asked. "Why did she do it?"

"Because you saved her life once," said Solaris.

"All of ours, actually," added Tom.

"Yes, well," continued Solaris with sadness in her voice, "when we found you, Rynah vowed to never let another die, so long as it was within her power to save them."

"It is the greatest sacrifice one can make," said Solon.

"No," Alfric replied, "it is an honor."

"Your command," said a male voice as the same holographic figure from before appeared again, in answer to Rynah's summons, pulling them back to their present predicament.

Fire erupted above them as the ship jerked again.

"What is happening?" demanded Solaris. "These ships systems…"

"Are damaged," interrupted the holographic figure, "due to the energy being emanated from that." He pointed at the newly formed crystal.

"Do you have enough power for one last trip at hyperspeed?" asked Solaris.

"Yes," replied the holographic figure.

"What about the transporters?"

"If I reroute power from the weapons and defense systems, I should be able to summon enough for both."

"Prepare the transporters. I will input the coordinates when I get there. Once we have transported off the ship, you will take this vessel into this solar system's star, using the hyperdrive."

"Acknowledged." The holofigure disappeared.

"We need to get to the transporter room," said Solaris.

They all headed for the door—Alfric, Tom, and Solon ran down the hallway—but Solaris stopped Brie. "Except you."

"What?" said Brie. "But I'm coming with you."

"Not this time," replied Solaris. "We aren't just going back to your planet. I have to send all of you home, back to your time. You are already home, Brie. You must get to the escape pods. You will go to your right and follow the stairs down."

Brie remained still, tears in her eyes.

"I'm sorry, Brie," said Solaris, "but this is good-bye."

Brie gave Solaris a hug and ran off, following her instructions, disappearing around a bend and down a spiral staircase. Solaris paused in the doorway and looked back at the newly formed crystal. She didn't know why she did, but something deep inside told her to, and as she stared at it, a peaceful smile crossed her face.

With time running out, Solaris raced through the hallway, past the falling bulkheads as the ship tore itself apart, until she caught up with the others.

"Where's Brie?" asked Tom.

"I sent her home," replied Solaris.

A cannon blast ricocheted across the ship, reminding them that they had to leave. They turned a corner, ignoring the flickering lights and the thunder that roared outside the ship. The ship lurched, causing them to stumble as they ran. Ahead loomed a hatch. As more fire erupted from the side paneling, they jumped through it and into a room with a lift. They headed for it, but just as they opened the doors, an explosion rocked the ship, and the elevator plummeted to the decks below.

Solaris ripped a panel from the wall, revealing a tube with ladder rungs. She ushered them inside, and none questioned her as they each gripped a rung and climbed upward to the next deck. Sweat streamed down their necks from the sweltering heat inside the tube. Vibrations moved through the ship, shaking their hands as they climbed. They reached the next level. Alfric, who was in the lead, plunged his sword through the slit in the metal panel and forced it open.

"Hurry!" said Solaris as they crawled out.

They dashed through the winding corridor to another hatch, which led into a circular room with an octagonal pad encased in white tiles and black stripes. Solaris ran to a computer console and brought up a holoscreen, her fingers tapping away at it.

"On the transport pad, now," she said.

"Wait," said Tom as Solon and Alfric stepped on the pad, "four of us were brought here."

"And four are going back," Solaris replied, finishing the calculations and using the power generated by the crystal they had put together to open a hole in time.

"I am taking Brie's place," said Solaris.

Tom stepped ono the transporter pad with Solaris, joining Alfric and Solon.

"You will all be going home, back to your time, though it may not be the exact hour that you left," said Solaris.

"So this is good-bye then," said Tom, his voice somber.

"Yes," Solaris replied.

Silence fell as orange and yellow light swirled around them, engulfing them until with a loud—Zap!—they disappeared.

* * *

Stein's face contorted in fury as he watched the dragon ship assemble, knowing that Rynah had to be aboard it with the crystals.

"Where did it come from?" he demanded.

"I don't know, sir," said one frightened member of his ship.

Infuriated, he yanked out his laser pistol and shot the man who had answered his question. "I want to know about that ship!"

"It appears to be on a collision course with the sun. It's powering its engines now."

Stein's howled in rage. He refused to allow Rynah to get away with the crystals, and if she were to die, it would be by his hand.

"Ram it."

"Sir?"

"RAM IT!"

"I will not," said the man at the helm.

Stein charged him, throwing him from his seat, and steered his vessel for the massive ship in front of him, determined to stop Rynah and those who insisted on joining her. Those within the command center left, heading for the escape pods, not wanting anything more to do with him and his madness.

Another ship approached Stein's vessel. He glanced at the holo-screens and screamed when he realized that it was the pirate ship—Jifdar had witnessed Stein maneuver towards the dragon ship and, his weapons empty, had given the order to stop him—and increased his speed. Jifdar's ship did the same, locking onto Stein's position.

The dragon ship loomed before him, its size filling the holo-screens around him as he neared, racing against time and Jifdar's vessel. Before he reached his target, his ship lurched as Jifdar's ship plowed into his and thunderous roars pounded his ears, while fiery explosions ripped through his ship, tearing it apart from the inside out and destroying any aboard, including him.

* * *

Brie's heavy feet stomped down the metal stairs of the spiral staircase as she raced for the escape pods in accordance with Solaris' orders. She had never expected to be leaving the others like this, though, she had never thought much about the time when they would have to part. Chunks of metal and aluminum insulation crashed around her, slamming into the staircase with harsh bangs and showering her in dust. She quickened her pace. A massive jolt rocked the ship, flinging Brie over the railing of the spiral staircase.

She gripped the metal, her sweaty palms slipping, as her feet dangled in the air and fire spewed from the bottom with sparks floating around her. Using all of her strength, Brie pulled herself back up, crawling over the railing and tumbling down the remaining set of steps. When she reached the bottom, she paused, her mind dazed from the spinning. A moan filled her ears. Realizing that it was the slow scraping of metal against metal, Brie jumped to her feet and bolted out of the way just as metallic rods plunged into the floor where she had been.

She focused her mind in an effort to remember where the escape pods were. It hit her. She charged through the open area, ignoring the embers and scalding heat from the fires and plunging down a hallway. Ceiling panels hung low as Brie raced under them just as a bulkhead crashed behind her. Her feet crisscrossed and she stumbled when another lurch propelled her forward, sending her sprawling on the floor; her hands burned from sliding over the copper tiles. A portion of the wall burst outward—brittle pieces of paneling rained upon her—and forced Brie to roll on her side, curling in a ball, with her hands over her face. Covered in white dust, she leapt to her feet and hurried down a set of steps, stopping before a closed door.

Brie touched the holopad that lit up. Nothing happened. Frustrated, she punched the holopad with the same result. She searched for anything she could use to pry the doors open and found an inch thick, rectangular sheet of metal. Brie snatched it and shoved it into the doors, her muscles straining as she pulled, forcing the heavy doors open just enough for her to jump through. They slammed shut behind her.

She found herself in a narrow corridor with small, oval hatches lining both sides, each leading to an individual pod. Brie chose the nearest one. She lunged inside and the door sealed behind her as pale lights flickered on, showing a cramped seat with a harness and a window the size of a cup. Hissing resonated around her as the pod jettisoned from its hold and drifted into space.

"Destination?" asked the computer.

"Earth," said Brie.

"Destination unfamiliar."

"Scan for the nearest habitable planet," ordered Brie.

"Planet found."

"Set a course," Brie said, giving a set of coordinates.

The pod fired its thrusters and Brie strapped herself into the uncomfortable seat, while pressing her face against the window to watch the massive ship she had just left. It vanished. Within moments, the sun flashed, and a gigantic solar flare, the likes of which the solar system had never seen before, headed straight for the Earth.

* * *

Back in the underground pyramid, Fons and Tre waited for Rynah's command. Once they had received it, they filled in the last circle of the holographic globe of the Earth. It turned red before switching to green with yellow sparkles glittering across it. A series of clangs reverberated around them as the panels within the pyramid shifted into place and a low rumble echoed beneath them, its rhythm vibrating through their bodies.

Outside, the ground shifted, moving Shiprock to the side and revealing the crest of the pyramid below. With a crack of thunder, a cylindrical, amber light shot from the ancient structure and disappeared into the sky, where a honey-colored, translucent shield of light spread out, stretching across the sky and sealing them in.

Around the world, similar cylindrical streaks of light formed, emanating from ancient structures which were visited by tourists each year. The semi-transparent escutcheons weaved its way across the sky, melding together into a single entity. People stopped, dropping their wares, entranced by the scene that unfolded before them.

Back in the confines of the underground pyramid, Tre and Fons watched from the holomonitors, hoping that Rynah and the others made it back in time.

* * *

Brie's breaths fogged the window she stared out of as she watched, helpless, while the solar flare headed straight for her and the ships that flew around her, each locked in their own battle. Her tiny pod slipped past them, unnoticed. A zigzagging pattern of light caught her attention. She looked at it, unsure of what it was, but knew it meant disaster if her escape pod struck it.

"Can't you go any faster?" she screamed at the computer when the Earth grabbed her in its gravitational pull.

No answer.

Fire spread across the pod's exterior, turning the inside into a sweltering oven that burned her skin. Gripping her seat so tight that her knuckles turned white, Brie watched through the small portal, holding her breath, as her tiny pod, along with a few pirate ships, slipped past the planetary shield that had encompassed the Earth before it sealed. At that moment, the solar flare reached them. It swarmed over the shield, turning the sky a burnt orange and red for several minutes before dissipating.

The pod shook with violence as it plummeted to the ground below. Brie's stomach lurched when the parachute was released, slowing her to a point where she could land safely in the precise spot she had directed the pod to take her. With a sudden thump, the pod crashed into the ground, leaving a small crater. Brie unfastened her harness and sprang from her seat, opening the hatch, but stopping when she noticed the point of a laser rifle in her face as one of Stein's men, who had spotted her pod in the sky, waited for her.

Before she had time to react, a gunshot rang in the air and the man fell. Brie looked past him and gave a sigh of relief as Joe ran up to her with Sara in his arms and Rebecca by his side. Abandoning any sense of caution, she ran to her mother and sister, giving them each an overjoyed hug, determined to never let them go.

Brie looked up into the sky, which had turned blue once again, and twisted the pendant Alfric had given her when he thought she had died, a lugubrious expression on her face.

"What is it, honey?" asked her mother.

"I never got to say good-bye," said Brie. "I hope they don't forget about me."

Rebecca hugged her daughter. "I don't think they will."

"You better find Rynah and let her know that we need to scoot!" said Achilles, charging up with Obiah.

Brie's face fell.

"What is it?" he asked.

"She's gone," said Brie.

"Gone?" demanded Achilles. "What do you mean gone?"

Brie looked into both Achilles' and Obiah's eyes and her expression said it all—Rynah was not coming back.

"Marlow would have been proud of her," said Obiah.

"Solaris?" asked Achilles.

"Gone as well," replied Brie, "but not before she sent the others back home."

"Then, I guess I better leave as well," said Obiah as he watched National Guardsmen round up what was left of Stein's men.

"Where will you go?" asked Joe.

"Back to the Twelve Sectors. We have a new home to establish."

"What about them?" asked Brie, pointing at the remainder of Stein's followers.

Obiah smiled. "I have a solution for that, as they have a lot to answer for. Brie, Joe, take care of yourselves." Obiah spotted a lone shuttle and headed towards it. "You coming?" he asked Achilles.

"No," said Achilles. "After much deliberation, I've concluded that my place is here."

Obiah waved and left in the shuttle. He later met up with Hylne and the few of Jifdar's pirates that had survived. They made their way back to the Twelve Sectors, where Hylne and Obiah acquired a transportation device, which they used to come back to Earth and track Stein's followers to a secret government facility, transporting them aboard—Obiah left a note, thanking the U.S. government for their help—to take back to the new Lanyran colony for a trial.

"You know," said Joe to Achilles, "technically, you're an illegal alien and I should arrest you."

"Technically," quipped Achilles, "you have broken about a thousand of your own laws since the day you ripped me out of my hotel room."

"Where will you go?" Brie asked Achilles.

"I'll be around," said Achilles, "though I think I will meet up with Fons and Rynah's funny, little friend. He's going to need a lot of help adjusting to life on this dismal planet of yours."

Achilles ran off before any of the federal agents, who had just arrived, could detain him.

"Come on," said Joe to Brie. "Time to face the music."

Chapter 31
SOLON'S RETURN

On the marbled steps of the library, next to the ionic columns, an orange and yellow light appeared, the only light on a moonless night, forming a tangled web until it vanished, leaving Solon in its place. He glanced around at the familiar scenery: the gentle waves of the sea that brushed against the shore, the columns next to him, and the steps that once tired him each time he ran up them. Brushing himself off, Solon rose to his feet and charged down the steps as the chilled air seeped through his exposed skin. He paused by the pomegranate bush. Its deadened leaves and bearish appearance puzzled him. Didn't it have fruit, bursting with flavor, when he left? Yet, now it looked dormant, as though in a deep slumber.

Shaking away his questions, Solon dashed across the courtyard to the road that took him home. He ran the entire two miles, without pausing for a breath, and didn't feel the least bit tired when he reached his home. The soft glow of the lamps formed a circle around his parents' abode, just like it always did when night fell. Solon walked to the front door and opened it, stopping when he heard a crash.

His mother stared back at him, thinking she saw a phantom.

"Mother," said Solon, "it's me, your son, Solon."

His mother took a shaky step towards him, crushing the shards of pottery that lay scattered on the floor and reaching out to him, tears in her eyes.

"Solon?" she whispered. She ran to him, embracing him in a bone-crushing embrace, overjoyed at seeing her son again.

"Amynta, I thought I heard..." Solon's father stopped at the doorway, astonished at seeing his son again, and at the change in his physique, from scrawny and boney to muscular and toned. "Solon?"

"It is me, father," Solon replied. At first, he was puzzled by the reception his parents gave him, before remembering that Solaris had warned him that he may not return to the exact moment that he had left.

"The master scribe at the library said you disappeared in a mass of light. That Zeus himself must have taken you," said Solon's father.

"How long have I been gone?" Solon asked.

"Just over a year," replied his father.

"And my brother?"

"Returned from war," said his father, "and he is now a general in the king's army. We must send him a messenger straight away, alerting him of your return. He prayed daily, making two pilgrimages to the temple, for your safe return."

"No," said Solon, "let's not wake the servants at this late hour. The morning will be soon enough."

"As you wish," said his father.

Solon noticed a strange looking helmet, its tip pointed, but coated in gold and gems with a braided rim.

"What is this?" he asked.

"Oh," said his mother, "your brother brought that back with him as a gift for you."

Solon picked it up, examining the exquisite workmanship. "It's cool," he said, using one of Tom's phrases, before putting it back on the shelf, ignoring the puzzled looks on his parents' faces.

"Where have you been?" asked his mother as she pulled him to a chair near the fire. "You must tell us."

Solon paused as he tried to think of how he could tell his parents about his adventures and the things he had seen. How would he tell them about visiting other planets and being aboard a ship that not only could talk, but had a personality to match? He thought about the technological marvels he had seen, realizing that there was only one way to explain his absence to his parents.

"I found myself in the most marvelous of places and met others who were equally intriguing, all from different worlds. We were summoned by Solaris."

As the years passed, he became known as a great philosopher, and even became an advisor to the king, but he never forgot about his friends, having their memory carved onto pottery, which he kept in his home.

Chapter 32
ALFRIC'S RETURN

Amidst the swirling snow and frigid breeze, an orange and yellow light appeared before vanishing, leaving Alfric in its wake. Someone charged him from behind. Alfric turned, dodging the blow, and brought up his fist, striking his attacker in the nose. He unsheathed his sword, clipping the man in the arm before knocking him to the frozen ground.

As Alfric leered over his attacker, sword raised, he stopped, recognizing the man as the same one who had led the raid against his homeland, and for the first time, noticed the man's weakened nature and the look of starvation in his eyes—desperation had driven him to steal. He glanced around at the powdered snow and ice encrusted trees, realizing that he had been returned to the exact moment when he had left.

"Kill me and be done with it," spat the man on the ground.

Remembering Brie's merciful nature, and how she had forgiven the man who had tortured her, Alfric lowered his sword.

"No."

A look of surprise crossed the man's face.

"I'll not kill you, not today," said Alfric. "Go, but if you ever return, you will not find me in such a merciful mood."

The man stood up with caution, keeping a wary eye upon Alfric's sword, snatched his weapon, and ran off through the frosted trees just as Alfric's men arrived.

"Let them go," ordered Alfric of his men.

"My lord," said one of his men, "we should hunt them down and ensure they can never strike us again."

"I have given my command," said Alfric in a tone that none challenged. He turned and walked back to his home.

Once he arrived, he embraced his wife and children, refusing to let them go, thus startling them because they had seen him that morning, and were unaware that Alfric had left them for a period of several months.

"Alfric, your pendant," said his wife, "it is gone."

Alfric just grinned without a word, giving the same knowing smile that Solaris had given him many times and knowing that his pendant was where it belonged.

Chapter 33
BRIE'S RETURN

Several weeks had passed since the incident in Omaha, Nebraska, and since Brie had been forced to say good-bye to her friends, when she was allowed back into school. Though she had missed most of the school year, the principal, upon the school psychologist's insistence, had agreed to let her finish so that she could have some form of normalcy back in her life. With Joe's testimony, and the many videos springing up on the internet showing her, Rynah, Alfric, Tom, Solon, and Solaris risking their lives to save innocent civilians, the FBI dropped all charges against her, so long as she sought psychological counseling to help her deal with her traumatizing experience. The President of the United States even awarded her a Medal of Honor for her heroic actions.

Brie allowed them to have their way, laughing at their attempt to help her deal with being ripped away from home before being thrust into a war. If they only knew half of the things she had gone through; but she didn't feel traumatized by them—she felt that they had strengthened her.

Only at her mother's insistence did she bother to go back to school.

Brie had no desire to return to her old life—it was too mundane, filled with painful memories. She wished to start fresh, make a new start. Instead, she planned to spend the summer studying for her GED and take the test in September. Her mother agreed to help her, so long as she finished the current school year and made the authorities happy.

She clutched her notebook close to her—it was filled with memories of her time with Rynah and the others as they searched for the crystals—as she strolled through the hallway, pausing by the water fountain with its multicolored coating of chewed gum. *Some things never changed*, she thought to herself. Shaking her head with a chuckle, Brie hurried through the hallway, pushing her way through the meandering swarm of tacky fabric, billboards, and the gaudy fashion sense of her schoolmates on her way to her locker.

"Hey, Army girl!"

Brie stopped, recognizing the arrogant voice. She knew she was going to have to face Jenny at some point, but had hoped to forgo it a while longer.

Jenny leaned against an open locker, putting on glittery-pink lip gloss, surrounded by her friends with a smug look on her face.

"I couldn't believe what I had heard," she said, stepping forward, "that you were back and all."

Brie remained still.

"So where were you?" demanded Jenny.

"I heard she had a mental breakdown and had to be institutionalized," mocked one of Jenny's friends.

Brie remained silent.

"What?" said Jenny. "You're not going to tell us?"

"Just leave me alone," said Brie.

"Oh, she speaks!" Jenny noticed the notebook in Brie's arms and the pendant around her neck. She snatched them both, hurrying back to her friends and waving her prize above her head. "What's all this?" Jenny flipped through the notebook and tossed it aside. It landed on the tile floor with a soft plop, but that wasn't what Brie cared about most.

"Give me back my necklace!"

"Or what?" challenged Jenny. "You gonna cry?"

Brie's eyes narrowed as she glanced at the open locker, spotting a broom and a mop bucket next to it, which the janitor had forgotten to put away, and calculated in her mind what she needed to do to win this fight with Jenny, just like Alfric had taught her in his many training sessions.

"I am going to say this once," said Brie, her tone low and firm, "give me back my necklace."

"Or what?" spat Jenny, waving the pendant before her.

In a flurry of movement, Brie shoved one of Jenny's friends aside, snatched the broom, and jabbed Jenny in the stomach with its handle before shoving her into the open locker. She seized the pendant from Jenny's hand and shut the locker door, turning the dial so that no one, except the janitor, could open it. Brie faced the shocked faces surrounding her, ignoring the banging and screaming coming from the sealed locker, and put the pendant back around her neck before scooping up her notebook and walked off.

"Miss Reynolds!" shouted the school counselor, who had witnessed the entire incident.

Brie stopped, giving a defiant glare to the counselor.

"Such behavior is unacceptable," the school counselor scolded her. "You are supposed to talk to those who hurt you and discuss…"

"I just did." Brie's stern voice carried through the still hallway of the school. Ignoring the eyes that followed her, and a tongue-tied school counselor who couldn't believe that she had been talked to in such a manner, and by a student well-known for her squeamishness nonetheless, Brie left.

School was out and she had plans to meet with Joe, who had transferred to the Phoenix area, as he had a letter to give her from Fons, Achilles, and Tre, all of whom had managed to disappear without a trace.

Chapter 34
TOM'S RETURN

Tom found himself back on the stage in front of the podium with the academy heads staring at him in confusion, trying to figure out how he had managed to vanish and reappear in the space of five minutes right in front of their eyes.

"What a rush!" yelled Tom.

He half-expected to hear Solon give a philosophical remark at his statement, but his face fell when he realized that he would never see his friend again, or the others for that matter.

"Mr. Sanderson…" began one of the academy heads, but Tom cut him off.

"I want to thank you all for your lack of belief and staunch criticism, but I am going to take my ideas elsewhere." Tom walked off the stage and headed for the exit.

"Tom, if you leave here, you will never be allowed back, and you will lose your position here."

"Keep it," said Tom as he closed the door behind him.

With all that had happened to him, he had realized that the

time had come for him to move on. He took his idea for the magnetic engine and turned it into an enterprise, starting his business in his apartment, and as his engine gained in popularity, Tom expanded, becoming the first entrepreneur to create the fuelless engine, thus changing the way people travelled.

As he left the lecture hall, a newspaper article scrolled across the wall, which was really just a giant television screen. "Famous author comes to Atlanta," it read with a picture of Brie—though she was quite a bit older now, but still didn't look to be a day over 50—next to it. Tom smiled, recognizing those gentle, yet determined, eyes, and he took note of where she would be, deciding that he would say hello to an old friend.

Chapter 35
RYNAH'S PEACE

On the raspberry-colored, sloping hills of the Ancient Lanyran countryside—with clusters of violet zinnias and magnolias dotting it—an opaque, swirling mass formed, small at first, before growing to the size of a horse. With a—Pop!—Rynah shot of out the mesmerizing fog, landing hard on the dusty ground and rolling a few yards down the hill until she slowed to a stop. Dizzy, she lifted her head and saw the swirling fog. Not wanting to be stuck in this strange place, and concerned about Solaris and the others, Rynah jumped to her unsteady feet and ran to the vortex, but it disappeared before she reached it. She shoved her hand into her pocket, pulling out only lint as the replica of a crystal she had made while on the dragon ship had fallen out. Dismayed, she stared at the empty space where it had once been, in the faint, purple glow of the sun, unsure of what to do.

"May I help you?"

Rynah spun around, having never heard the soft steps of the man that had approached her from behind; he had been out for his evening stroll and noticed the strange vortex and her and had decided to investigate. Rynah gave him a quizzical look, recognizing the ancient Lanyran language that he spoke, glad that she had taken the time to learn it. Glancing around, she turned in circles, looking at the lavender-colored leaves of the trees and the waist high grass, with its purple tint that waved in the soft, warm breeze that she had loved since she was a child.

"Where am I?" Rynah asked.

"Desmyr," said the man, as though she should have known.

Rynah gasped. She remembered Marlow talking about how Desmyr was one of the oldest cities of Lanyr and realized that she was home, not the Lanyr she knew, but a more mysterious one.

'Where are you from?" asked the man, unconcerned about her security uniform, and how it differed from the elegant robes that those in ancient Lanyran society wore.

Rynah glanced back at where the swirling mass had once been and reached up to twirl her grandfather's ring, having forgotten that it was no longer around her neck, and wished that she could have had the chance to say good-bye to Brie, Tom, Alfric, Solon, and Solaris. Though saddened that she would never see them again, Rynah turned toward that man who stared at her with his keen eyes, remembering something Marlow had once told her.

"All things come to an end," he had said, "but sometimes, from that end comes a new beginning."

"From far away," Rynah said, in answer to the man's question. "What is your name?"

The man shook his hands, appalled at his own lack of manners, saying, "Arnor. And yours?"

"Rynah."

"Come," said Arnor, leading Rynah away, wanting to know more about this strange woman who appeared from nowhere "you must be famished and my sister makes the best onion stew."

Epilogue

Marlow warned this day would come: the day when Lanyr, my home, was destroyed. But he never mentioned the people whom I would call friends, nor the bond that we would form.

And in case you are wondering what happened to Rynah the day she repaid her debt to Brie, I can tell you that she did not perish when she fell through the wormhole—she went home, back to Lanyr, or what we called Ancient Lanyr. The wormhole released her near a small village, where she met a man and found the joy and love that so many seek, and that she desperately wanted. As her life neared its end, she wrote, in poetic verse, about her time on a ship and the adventure she shared with four of the most unlikely heroes from a planet she had once thought was a myth, leaving them a guide.

And as for the replica of a crystal that she had with her at the time, it had fallen from her pocket and turned up in a cave on a planet of desert sand where it was discovered by the most unlikely of heroes, all of whom came from different worlds and bore exile's blood.

And so the story of Rynah, of the crystals, comes to a close. Just as every myth has a beginning; every legend has an end.

And if you hear stories about a woman with skin that matches the sunset sky, do not dismiss them. For every legend has some truth to it as Rynah once learned. Perhaps one day, you will find yourself about to fall off a precipice and a hand reaches out for you. Reach for that hand. It is mine, fulfilling a promise.

Appendices

The Ancient Poem

What follows is the poem that Rynah used in locating the crystals. Most Lanyrans believed it to be a story created in their ancient era and told as a form of entertainment, but some, such as Marlow, believed it to be so much more. And by now, you know that it was.

Gather now and listen well
To this tale that I must tell.
Of magic crystals young and old,
A lost crystal too deadly to behold.

The beginning is always the best.
Do not sneer, laugh, or jest.
Think of where it's been.
Think of where it was last seen.

Six crystals in evil's grasp:
one lone exile with fury's wrath.
Four you need from thirteen:
four heroes of faith and belief.

The warrior of nobility,

descended from the line of kings.
Strength and prowess he commands
from his frozen homeland.

A philosopher whose wisdom all need;
knowledge and learning are his deeds.
A scholar of myth and history
will guide you on this journey.

The inventor with guided skills,
machines and mechanics fulfill
his days; all of which shall prove
most useful in the darkest grooves.

And the one who loves when all is lost;
do not let timidity
blind you and deceive,
for he shall bear the highest cost.

Blood ties that run deep,
Blood shared from conflict reaped.
Traitors they were called.
Heroes they are all.

You will acquire world's ire,
tumultuous, searing fire.
Terrors all must endure
to overcome troubles more.

Time passes as it always does;
second by second, minute by minute,
but the gems you seek exist beyond time,
outside, it's far from its grasp.

While you must tread time's path,'
the slower way, full of wrath,
despair not, tis a good thing,
allowing one to ponder and grow.

The crystals lost for time untold
will not be easily found. So be bold
on this arduous quest
and where to start is your first test.

The beginning is always the best.
Do not sneer, laugh, or jest.
Think of where it's been.
Think of where it was last seen.

There lies your path, twisted, but true.
Cast aside the old to embrace the new.
Sorrow and tears will follow,
but so will joy, if you allow.

But beware! Old friends you will meet;
once trusted, cold will they greet
you, bearing a traitor's mark,
forsaking the light for the dark.

But go you must with the four.
No crystal is there, but infinitely more.
Do not ask what; you will know,
and together he and four shall grow.

Old love you will see,
forcing you to bended knee.
Stay away from vengeance's wrath.

Death lies at the end of that path.

Once small disk you have acquired,
flee before you are all mired
to the ship whose voice guides
you all to time that bides.

But, far from safety are you
as a map you possess anew
and the first crystal is not far,
even though it lies amongst the stars.

When two suns meet so shall the power of the gods.

So, listen now to this one clue
and it shall lead you true.
On a planet you know well
from stories others tell,

of plants dressed in vivid colors,
leaves mirroring lizard's wings,
sharp, dealing deadly sting
to any who dare enter.

A lush land filled with life
and terrors of immense strife,
where monsters dwell in hordes
sowing internal discord.

Tread lightly and be vigilant
lest you fail to supplant
the dangers surrounding you
and your hailed crew.

Treasure the one among you
whose courage seems lacking
as he is the key
to gaining the treasure you seek
and rescuing a depraved people.

But, lo! your journey just begins,
for another awaits at watery end,
deep within roiling seas,
a confined appellee.

A vessel of the past will you find,
an exile lost and confined
before quest he could complete,
Death he did meet.

Words you'll read,
such familiarity,
but beware
of foe's snare.

They, too, know these secrets
and seek the gem in watery locket.
Loss is a common acquaintance
and you'll learn of its prevalence.

But keep thy anger to yourself.
Choose not your first target
for you know who is to blame
and shares in the shame
of your current trials.

If your watery adventures

did not go true,
seek newer ventures;
make straight what is askew.

The next treasure will not wait,
as others have crossed its gate.
They seek it more than you
and have learned the next clue:

A field of rock hovering alone
Jagged as a sharp stone.
Pass beyond to a gold sphere
where treasure looms far and near.

Buried twice deep in darkened hole
Is the stone whose touch is cold.
Be careful about what you seek
For you may well be deceived.

But don't despair.
A gift in disguise you bear.
One whose worthiness
in the end shall bless.

But terror looms in the deepest space
where pirates wander, seeking gold.
Appeal not to their mercy or grace,
but to their code to which they hold.

A captain is only as good as his word.
Should he fail to abide by sworn oath
his authority is squandered
by his betrayal of his crew's troth.

A lesson you'd do well to learn.
before bridges you burn
due to fury and carelessness,
too proud to beg forgiveness,

not from others, but from yourself
for failings you continue to berate
your own soul for, because you loved
and trusted. So you think your head
is better served than your heart.

Icy wilderness shall grant second chances.
Do not cast it aside with poisoned lance.
Embrace the company you are within
and the stranger, merely an old friend,

whose help you'll need to mount rescue
of your trusted vessel.
He is not the man you once thought;
he know aught

about you and your mother's father.
Time has worn and weathered
him, but trust you must
before you yield to anger's lust.

See your companions with new insight.
See their strengths, not their plight.
Notice their stubborn tenacity
and how they conquer adversity.

Be the warrior whose cloak is honor,
strength, integrity, and courage,

the keeper of sworn oaths,
where deep within dwells mercy.

Be the philosopher whose silence
conveys keen study, and observance,
who acts with diligence,
yet with tenderness and humility.

Be the inventor, whose curious nature
propels him forward to learn and discover
the unimaginable and unconquerable,
but clings to friendship's loyalty.

Be the forgiver, whose love is like a mother,
self-giving to those who need it;
compassionate when wrath dominates,
understanding when others posture.

To quell the turmoil within your heart,
you must with them start.
Temper your frustrations;
allow their transformation.

They shall guide your path
and help bear all you hath
borne, because of inward guilt.
Rise, before more innocence is spilt.

And go forth
and seek your guiding star
before vagabonds destroy
what love wrought from afar.

While thieves prance in revelry,
seize the opportunity
to save a companion,
always bold with sound reason.

But joy's reunion is always short-lived;
as darkness dwells overhead.
A man in shadow who covets
your treasures' contents.

Here you face the first trial.
Trapped in danger's swarm,
fire and light burn and rampage,
sealing you in greed's cage.

You will choose your sacrifice,
but be swept aside
by one you thought a vice,
but what fear once kept tied

has broken loose,
freed from its frightened bonds,
as love's bravery he now dons
to save all from betrayal's noose.

How you meet this end
only you can tell.
But you must mend
the void hard to fill.

For another crystal awaits
in its metallic crate.
Claws seek and surround

its copper crown.

On the planet of eternal light
lies an object black as night.
A gift it is from the gods
of stark material bold and odd.

Light cannot thrive without the darkness.
Night cannot thrive without the sun's rays.
A gift this is, with a price. So beware.
What seems far away is actually near.

Keep the gods' gift close to thee
for its blackness is the key
to your salvation
and all of its revelations.

Remember to tread lightly
since to a fortress you must go,
and bear in mind the brevity
of a thief's woe.

And if you escape
with crystal in hand,
never forget
fortress master's inscape:
a most unforgiving man.

Thieves you became by necessity.
As thieves, hunted will you be
by the fortress master for eternity.

Do not fret over such strife,

for to prevent untold rife
you must continue your journey
to reach your destiny.

But though the crystal you now possess,
tumultuous storms await your distress,
to seize you and your meager crew
in its claws where there is no rescue.

Stranded in darkness, seek not despair,
nor dwell on situation's severity,
but listen to the warrior's tale
and seek gentle creatures of luminosity.

Ancient and pure they are
and let them lead you
back to your guiding star.

Horrors you all have yet to witness
of greed and grief's menace
and their vile legacy
as it spreads fiercer than leprosy.

Amidst the smoky veil,
drowned by silence's wail
one among you shall receive
treasured words that allow one to see.

Do not dwell on the woeful destruction,
for you shall gain a friend of fortitude.
Tho' trapped in mind's interrogation,
freed he'll be and break four's solitude.

Search you must,
but beware whom you trust.

In clutches of mercenaries
await heroic measures, so be wary
of forest's calm, serene nature,
which seeks to quell and conquer.

But if this test you all pass,
then forgiving love shall be in your grasp.
Help you it will
to find the elusive crystals.

Most tricky will be the sixth
as it lies deep in fiery mist.
Gods of fire, you will face their wrath
and delve deep within the mountain's cast

The labyrinth traps all in its lair.
None enter who aren't caught in its snare.
So enter, now, the eagle's head
and cast aside all dread.

But more than courage you will need.
Friends' devotion and the girl who heeds
the call of sacrifice and pendant's glare.
Only she will escape the enemy's snare.

Read well and remember this,
Numbers that most will miss.
thirty-five, sixty-eight, nine;
fifty-two, one and twenty's bind.

Mark and trace as you go.
A circle each forms with arcs that flow;
and crossroads that one seeks
the way one climbs the highest peak.

Far from home are you now.
Cross the bridge to the maze's bow.
What eyes have seen do not trust.
Only the wise will find the invisible crust.

The maze you've entered, its path must be tread.
Stray, but a little, you will all be dead.
Let the philosopher's wisdom be your guide;
tempered by love, you'll reach the other side.

Seek with lover's heart, not the warrior's sword,
or lest you forget
the part you played in conflict borne

by men whose grief
molded them like clay,
refusing to release
its puppeteer's hold.

If philosopher's wisdom is true
what is ancient, you'll know as new.
It was once your past, but is now your future,
a narrow road you must venture.

In domed light is the seeker's prize,
but still your mind and anger's lies.

Coveted treasure you now possess.

Thieves upon you, they will transgress.
Lost will your prize be,
yet gain another from the sea.

Fire surrounds you from within,
while enemies trespass your glen.
A friend you'll lose, but one you'll gain;
reborn in body, but spirit same.

Trust him you must and be aware
of the secret that he bears.
A gift from the crystals' hand,
a guide in a foreign land.

Weep not over your lost prize,
as danger awaits all inside
what was once ancient myth
and serves as the zenith
of heroes' noble quest
and the one whose behest
is revered when trouble nears.

Flee fire's vengeful snare,
and poisonous air,
treading molten rivers
and decayed timbers.

Seek salvation from the burnt skies,
not gods or angels, but thieves shall
descend upon you and help you rise,
above the reaper's fray.

An extra number you'll have acquired;

let thy judgement not stem from heart's ire,
but from the one who you thought a burden,
and holds to philosopher's sagacious wisdom.

Broken and mired in deceit,
he was, stained by sorrow's bittersweet
touch, but a new declaration
he will make and bring about fruition
of a crystal and a shield
to save an unknown people.

Six you know of,
but one you do not
Another there is, pale as a dove,
Time and all it's taught.

This one you need to control the others.
Without it, useless they are.
Seek it not, it comes to you like a mother.
Small like a pebble, but greater than a star.

It will lead you to its brothers
that you must also recover.
All a part of three's power;
all will witness in the last hour.

Assembled the puzzle must be,
or risk destroying eternity.
The four and one are the key
to saving all that must be.

But one must make a choice,
and commit ultimate sacrifice,

wearing the key in amber;
to him the past is the future.

And so, on a blue planet of thirteen
rests a civilization separate and whole,
unaware of blackened heart's wrath
as he blazes a solemn and scarred path.

Here is where your search ends.
Here is where the legend begins
as past, present, and future mends
severed bonds that deepen.

In this world both new and strange
you must find what lies hidden.

To begin, seek a guardian of the law
who honors justice and its call,
protecting the great seal
with olive branches, arrows, and an eagle.

Honest and true he is
bearing strange marks: FBI.
Their importance being the same,
Joseph Harkensen is his name.

But be wary of foes around.
Their number will abound
in great quantities,
so numerous, so many.

Hunted will you be by a man so maligned
and steeped in ire that his irascibility

is ever present, ever-growing. His vexation
seek companions and decimation.

Trust your new ally
and let him be your guide.

On this planet beautiful and strange,
let not it's wonders detain
you, or lure you into deceit
for closest enemies you must meet.

In a place both alien and familiar
will you join together.

Tarry not, for there is no time to waste.
Another gem awaits in treasure's cove.
Rest assured that others will make haste
to pluck it from its guarded trove.

Great battle will ensue
and ancestor's secret will be revealed.

Cities shall burn
and mothers will mourn
while leaders scorn
the oath you've been sworn

But not all are enemies
seeking to fulfill another's iniquity.
With friend's help you'll meet a hermit
bound to you by another's intent.

And across great plains of yellowed grass,

you'll witness treasures of the past
until you reach vast lands of desert sand.

Alone you may think you are,
but alone you are not.
All stems from myths and legends
and times past has sent a friend.

Many a millennia has passed since his exile,
but for you it is only a mile.
Seek his wisdom, the knowledge he holds;
trust him, not his anger cold.

One of the ancients brought back
from the distant past.
Only he knows the crystals.
Only he knows what they hold.

But remember this:
all have committed vice;
forgiveness is my advice,
do not dwell on his remiss.

Hidden among strangers will he be,
bearing their distinct mark.
But his knowledge you will need
to learn what the remarques
on cherished jewel that adorns
you from night to morn
mean to unite what has been torn.

But more than precious gems
will you need to find the hidden lair

of one who was condemned
as he tried to spare us from fate's fear.

Seek the ancient people
who dwell in desert sand
where rocks form steeples;
in barren scope as islands.

Great monuments to those seeking refuge,
tall and proud despite arid deluge,
reaching for the stars
and a people that have traveled far.

Seek these cliffs;
seek their gifts.

Find the path that dwells deep within,
fear not the dark, nor the echo,
but go forth companions of ten,
plus one more forced from his den.

Heed well the underground
constellations that surround
you with neon light.

Let starlit words guide you
to dragon's heart.
There the crystals must part,
Only then, will you stop foe's coup.

Listen now to what others have missed.
Heed these words as they're more than myth.

In the beginning was the word
and the word was with the dragon.
Its treasure makes clear what time has blurred
and will brighten what has been blackened.

Seek dragon's secret lair;
act without fear.
One, now three, must be one again.
Only legend's blood can enter its glen.

But be warned, for not all are worthy;
sacrifice must be endured
to prove honor and earn mercy.

Search deep within darkened waters
whose depths remain unknown.
Not sea, nor river,
but on land it was sown.
As tall as the highest peak,
a border most unique,
near fiery ring that mires the meek.

Search night's white orb.
Sun's light it absorbs.
Mysterious cavern you must tread
before its shadow spreads.

Search red star, for a star it's not.
Many men follow what it has taught.
Warfare, is its legacy.
Peace, it considers heresy.

But more than beasts you must find,

for the realm still lies in danger's bind.
A shield must be found, a shield most unique.
It will brighten and protect what has turned bleak.

Do not scoff or turn away
for that is how many have strayed.

Salvation lies beneath arid sand,
below a cliff's lofty tower.
Search for hunter's belt made of rock,
and enter the temple below
by undoing the lock.

Be wary of the hunter's darkened spear.
Touch it not, until you see shimmering sphere.

And beneath dismal ground
is a temple of renown
from civilization's past
and guardian of light's mast.

But despite the discovery of this great place,
trouble brews, planning to lay waste
to all who dwell on thirteen's base.

Alone amidst darkened ruin
stands the woman from whom all is written.
Fires burn and chaos swarms,
but none can compare to her scorn.

Bravery unmatched against metallic monsters,
our heroes summoned must save the city of towers.
Six souls, whose will is stronger

than any; aided by heaven's helper.

Tho' on land is where the war is fought,
the sky is where victory should be sought.

See you now dragon's treasure,
vast and rich beyond measure.

Take thee now to the belly of the beast
where time stills and worries cease.
Study well the dragon's heart
where the end must now take part.

Its gleaming scales reflecting the sun,
and watch as it returns to where it's come
from, back to its noble home,
back to its mighty hoard.

And marvel as it releases it righteous fury
on those who invaded its den.

Journey's end you have reached,
but now I must beseech
you to pay careful attention
to you inner intentions.

Remember well that the crystals
feast off your innermost thoughts
and all that dwells within your heart.

Make what is broken whole.
Make what is broken one.
And not just the treasured gems,

but the place where your anger stems.

In the blackened space, now empty tomb,
you must now replace, and dispel the gloom.
Put back what has been broken apart.
Give back the dragon's heart.

Once done, now you must run
and your number will be reduced by one.

Home is where you must all flee.
Save your farewells.
This is how it must be.

Four torn from their home.
Four torn from their time.
Returned they must be.
Cast away by guiding star.

Do not weep, do not mourn.
For their parting is not forlorn.
Memories they will pass
into legend where they will last.

And as for the one, worry not.
Heart's peace is what she sought,
and heart's peace is what she got.

And so ends this tale I tell.
I hope you have listened well.
If not, just remember this:
not everything is just a myth.

Lanyran Time

Event	Lanyran Year	Earth Year equivalent (estimate)
Base Year	0	4300 B.C.
Prophecy First Written Down	1300	3000 B.C.
Crystal in Geo-Lab Found	4865	565 A.D.
When Our Story Begins	6314	2014 A.D.
When Our Story Ends	6315	2015 A.D.

A Little Bit About Lanyrans

Some of you may be wondering about how General Delmar could know someone for over 40 years and not be old. In truth, he was around 133 years old, but Lanyrans age much slower than we do and have an average lifespan of about 177-200 years. The oldest reported Lanyran was named Florayn and she lived to be 217. Rynah was 34, making her a youngster in Lanyran society.

About the Author

Ms. McNulty began writing short stories at an early age. That passion continued through college until she published her first book: Legends Lost: Amborese under the pen name of Nova Rose. Since then, she has gone on to publish a mystery series, children's books, and even a dystopian series.

Ms. McNulty currently lives in West Virginia, where she enjoys hiking, being outside, crocheting, or simply sitting around and doing nothing. She continues writing and is busy finiahing the final book in her Solaris Series.

The Solaris Saga

Solaris Seethes
Solaris Seeks
Solaris Strays
Solaris Soars

Every myth has a beginning.

After escaping the destruction of her home planet, Lanyr, with the help of the mysterious Solaris, Rynah must put her faith in an ancient legend. Never one to believe in stories and legends, she is forced to follow the ancient tales of her people: tales that also seem to predict her current situation.

Forced to unite with four unlikely heroes from an unknown planet (the philosopher, the warrior, the lover, the inventor) in order to save the Lanyran people, Rynah and Solaris embark on an adventure that will shatter everything Rynah once believed.

More by Janet McNulty

The Enchained Trilogy

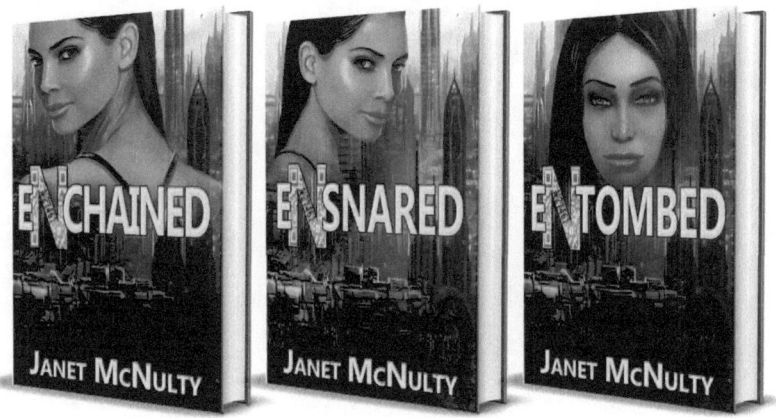

Enchained
Ensnared
Entombed

In Arel, weakness if failure, failure is death.

Dana Ginary lives in a world where every aspect of her life is controlled by the Dystopian Government. Forced to work in Waste Management, her life becomes a nightmare with hunger and survival is her only constant. Before she knows it, she is caught up in a resistance movement and exiled from Dystopia, forced to find her way in the barren wastelands. While there, she must learn to live independently and discover how far she is willing to go to live and achieve freedom.

The Mellow Summers Series

Mellow Summers moves to Vermont to attend college, accompanied by her friend Jackie. They soon find themselves running into ghosts and one mystery after another.

The Dystopia Trilogy

 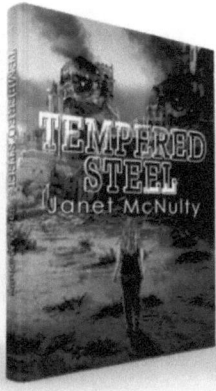 

Dystopia
Tempered Steel
Liberty's Torch

**Imagine living in a world where
everything you do is controlled.**

Dana Ginary lives in a world where every aspect of her life is controlled by the Dystopian Government. Forced to work in Waste Management, her life becomes a nightmare with hunger and survival is her only constant. Before she knows it, she is caught up in a resistance movement and exiled from Dystopia, forced to find her way in the barren wastelands. While there, she must learn to live independently and discover how far she is willing to go to live and achieve freedom.

The Legends Lost Series
Published under Nova Rose

Tesnayr
Amborese
Galdin

Enter the Lands of Tesnayr and join on an epic fantasy adventure that spans over 1,500 years.

Begin with Tesnayr, the first king of the five lands as he unites the against a savage foe bent on their destruction.

Next, Join Amborese as she fights reclaim the throne after her family was forced to flee from it.

Thinking peace has finally entered the land, follow Galdin as he returns to Tesnayr to find it greatly hanged. Barbarians, led by a mysterious sorcerer, burn and destroy as they go. And only Galdin can stop them if he chooses to accept his fate.

A Little Something for the Little Ones.

Mr. Chili Books:

Mr. Chili's Chili
Mr. Chili Goes To School
Mr. Chili's Halloween
Mr. Chili's Christmas

Others:

Mrs. Duck and the Dragon
The Hungry Washing Machine
Rhymes-a-lot
Are You the Monster Under My Bed?
How Do You Catch An Alien

Grandpa's Stories

My grandfather grew up in Arizona during the 1920s and 1930s. One week after the attack on Pearl Harbor he joined the Navy. During the summer of 2012, my mother visited him and recorded his stories about growing up, World War II, and his time as an employee at the Pacific Bell Telephone Company. This is the history of the 20th century as he lived it. These recordings make up this book. These are his words.